HOW NICHOLAS BECAME SANTA CLAUS

SANDRA JO TROUPE
&
DARRELL R. TROUPE

Copyright © 2022 Sandra Jo Troupe & Darrell R. Troupe.

All rights reserved. No part of this book may be reproduced, stored, or transmitted by any means—whether auditory, graphic, mechanical, or electronic—without written permission of both publisher and author, except in the case of brief excerpts used in critical articles and reviews. Unauthorized reproduction of any part of this work is illegal and is punishable by law.

ISBN: 979-8-88640-565-1 (sc)
ISBN: 979-8-88640-566-8 (hc)
ISBN: 979-8-88640-567-5 (e)

Because of the dynamic nature of the Internet, any web addresses or links contained in this book may have changed since publication and may no longer be valid. The views expressed in this work are solely those of the author and do not necessarily reflect the views of the publisher, and the publisher hereby disclaims any responsibility for them.

One Galleria Blvd., Suite 1900, Metairie, LA 70001
1-888-421-2397

With much love and thanks

To my husband, Darrell, my love and foundation.

To my children and grandchildren, my inspiration.

To our sons, Daniel and Darrell II, for the many hours they spent editing, and a special thanks to Daniel for taking the authors' photo.

To my parents, Walter and Dorothy Darwell, my grandparents, and my great-grandparents. Their stories of Saint Nicholas became the foundation for this book.

To Benjamin and Theresa Troupe for sharing their son with me and for teaching me that "words have power."

To our family past, present, and future, keep the magic of innocence and love in your hearts.

The pleasures and blessings of life are found in the simple things, which should never to be taken for granted but always appreciated.

—Sandra Jo Troupe

Thank you to my mother, Theresa; my father, Benjamin; my sister, Stephanie; my children and grandchildren; and especially to my loving wife, Sandra, for her encouragement and support.

—Darrell R. Troupe Sr.

Contents

Prologue:	Destiny	vii
Chapter 1	Home	1
Chapter 2	The Sheriff	30
Chapter 3	The Trip	41
Chapter 4	Trouble with the Aurora	55
Chapter 5	The Visitors	66
Chapter 6	Wallace Listens	85
Chapter 7	Wallace Brings News	93
Chapter 8	Making Plans	110
Chapter 9	The Challenge	134
Chapter 10	The Lizard Men	144
Chapter 11	The Dragons	170
Chapter 12	Reconciliation	188
Chapter 13	Child of Two Worlds Revealed	202
Chapter 14	Hope	211
Chapter 15	Doubt	217
Chapter 16	Something You Should Know	225

Chapter 17 Timing Is of Utmost Importance 230

Chapter 18 The Rescue 236

Chapter 19 The Castle 248

Chapter 20 Sarah Found 262

Chapter 21 Wallace Takes Control 279

Chapter 22 Distractions 300

Chapter 23 The Brothers 309

Chapter 24 Solstice 331

Chapter 25 Council of Elders and Kings of the Auroras 343

Prologue

DESTINY

"I pray your death shall assure my destiny," he said softly, his prayer-clasped fingertips inclined toward the ground. The blustering wind whipped, pluming his long, wild hair as he lifted his dark eyes to the sky. He prayed to be denied no longer. His dark heart raced as the churning black clouds seemed to obey his whim, slowly moving across the blue to block the sun. He grinned as morning appeared as midnight.

Drawing his sword from his scabbard, the young prince dug into the earth at his feet. Lowering his left hand to the earth, he scooped a fistful of gravel, which he sifted through his fingers. Grasping the choice remainder in his palm, he lifted it slowly, mindfully to his chest. There he held it over his beating heart.

Around his right forefinger, he wore a mystical red ruby ring, named the Firestone by the troll clan. The size of a cat's eye, the red stone was faceted and clasped upon an outer ring, which revolved upon an inner ring. Revolving the faceted stone three times, the prince clenched his left fingers on the dirt. With nearly the last of his purchased magic, he concentrated, imbuing the dirt with his deep and abundant avarice and evil. Crushing the dirt within his palm caused a crack of lightning to permeate the darkened sky above his head. Fulgurating white light twisted through the spaces between his fingers and shot into the ground.

"My dark creation. Do my bidding," snarled the prince.

※

Within the castle grounds, a spot of red light the size of a man's fist flashed in the outlying brush beyond the window of the royal doctor. A melting, spinning mixture of sticks, frogs, and insects gathered on the spot and folded into a pulsating mound of mush like a four-foot hill of dirt. It took quasi-human form.

Swooping from the sky, a bird as black as coal landed on the being's newly formed, burlap-clad shoulder. One by one, the bird's feathers painfully loosed from its skin and fluttered away. Plaintively cawing, it began to flap.

Curling his bee-stung lips, sneering delightfully, the diminutive mud creature rolled his black eyes beneath his heavy brow and shouted in a gruff, leaf-rattling voice, "Have you lost your birdbrain, Mr. Krahe? Get off." He dropped the burlap cowl covering his head of black, scant, coarse hair. His eyes darting left to right, he placed his stubby, knurled finger thoughtfully to the side his irregular head.

Flapping, the bird leaped above the creature's shoulder and hovered. "Mind you, Jax. Reserve your treachery for your master's enemies. I have orders to watch you, yet you've tried to kill me," the raven murmured.

"Fool that you are. I absorb life; you know that. All but one who touches me dies slowly. Now, leave me to my work. You need not watch. I am loyal to my master and am no laggard." He growled, pointed to the sky, and stomped his foot three times. "Tomorrow." He grinned. "Storm clouds shall gather within the Orphic Forest to complete the deal." Peering at the horse cart parked along the yard fence, he tilted his head. The diminutive monster quickly slipped beneath the trailer.

The Crash

At the top of the world, within the tiny county of Castleton, within the kingdom of Illuminae, lived Christopher Northland, the physician of King Dobromil of Aurora Illuminae. As was his habit this time of year, he prepared to make a four-day trip to the Village of Waters. Up long before dawn, he headed to the stables to ready his horse Philly for the trip.

The air was crisp but clear. Having experienced several frosts in previous times, he knew the nights might be long and cold. He expected nothing less in late fall, and he could see his breath.

Standing twelve hands high, bred from the Akhal-Teke line, a hardy breed, Philly could stand an even colder climate. A strong horse, she had made this trip before, but that made Christopher's journey no less arduous. To assure Philly was fueled for the trip, Christopher gave her an extra ration of food. He packed sacks of oats, alfalfa, apples, and carrots for the trip. He wanted to ensure she had good strength in her stride. Eager for travel, Christopher decided to start as soon as morning broke.

He and his wife Margaret settled into their warm feather bed, their infant boy beside them in a slatted wooden box fitted with a rocker bottom. To settle his mind, Christopher counted the snowflakes falling on the frosted window at the foot of their bed until he fell asleep.

The sun was barely peeking above the horizon when he rose. Christopher completed his chores for the trip. Margaret remained beneath their comforter, feeding the baby. It was cold. She thought it cute the way the baby tugged at the locket on the lanyard around her neck. The wood-burning oven kept the room warm mainly in a narrow perimeter around the oven.

Through the window at the foot of the bed, Margaret could see frost glistening on the trees. Over a dusting of snow, Christopher traipsed to the barn. The vapor from his breath curled around his face. Clad in a heavy coat and gloves, he held his fingers under his armpits to keep them warm.

He entered the barn. "Good morning, Philly."

The horse whinnied and bobbed her head.

"There, there, girl," Christopher breathed. Rubbing his fingers together, he reached into her stall, lifted the latch, and opened the slatted gate separating them. "I think we will have a pretty long ride ahead of us."

Lifting her slender legs from the bed of hay in her stall, he examined them and each of her feet. Standing, he peered into her eyes. He slid his hand up and over the star between her eyes and down along her neck, raking his fingers through her long blonde mane.

"Eat well, girl," he said, arranging her food into a trough before her. Turning, Christopher saw the outlying forest rising above the castle gate. "I hope our trip will be uneventful and safe."

After brushing Philly's chestnut coat, Chris walked her from her stall and backed her up to the trailer, a red-and-green varda ornately embellished with polished brass leaves and vines. It was parked along the yard fence. He eyed their home for the road. Their lives would depend on the sturdy wagon.

Having hitched her to rigging, Christopher gently led Philly up the path to the house, where he and Margaret would load the baby and their supplies.

He and Margaret quickly packed the varda. They were used to these trips. As a benevolent gesture, King Dobromil encouraged his private physician to make trips at least once a year from Castle Illuminae to lend his services and attend to patients and business in outlying dwellings. Although Christopher spent most of the year getting ready a little at a time, he still left things off his list, so he checked it twice, occasionally three times. He always had much on his mind. Margaret suggested, if left alone, Christopher would make lists of his lists. Securing the house and barn, they started out.

Within moments, they reached the wooden-paved road leading over the main bridge. They were soon at the main gate and drawbridge of the castle. From an overlooking turret, they could hear the gatekeeper's call echoing from the castle to the outlying forest.

"Drop the draw, drop the draw!" armored guards shouted in relay as the varda made passage. They heard the ratcheting of the gigantic drawbridge chains and gaffs as they rolled over the moat and beyond the far side of the bridge. Upon their departure, they heard faintly, in the rear, "Lift the draw!"

Soon they were off castle grounds and journeying into the hinterland. The sun was strong, and the weather turned mild by midmorning. Hours passed. The small family enjoyed an easy journey.

Less than a half day out, they arrived at the outskirts of the legendary and magical Orphic Forest. Their noses filled with the spicy scent of pine. Christopher pulled the varda over to take in the forest's beauty. They would travel across many hills and valleys. Breathing deep, he looked to Margaret. She reached to his knee, upon which rested his hand. She touched the back of it.

"I know it sounds silly, but I never tire of it," she said with a satisfied smile.

The thick pine trees seem to rise to the sky. Among them, there was a dusting of snow. Shivering a bit on the bench seat, Margaret moved closer to Christopher. He held the reins. He gently snapped them, and Philly loped over the uneven ground, mixed with rock and some residuum of snow.

Nodding, Christopher leveled his finger at the road ahead. "Much beauty is spread across this mountainous terrain," he said to Margaret.

"And many trees." She smiled.

"And other ... things. Sadly, it has its dangers." Christopher sighed. "But it is better known for its magical creatures and wonders."

She shook her head.

"I know you know this," he continued, "but it's hard to resist saying."

"And I *do* know of its dangers," said Margaret, her expression flattening. "Then we must remain vigilant."

Christopher nodded. "Most of the road will continue uphill," he said. He glanced at the horse. "I know Philly is tired."

Ahead they could see the forest elevation cresting to a tree-studded summit. They were approaching a more mountainous area. The cold there would be challenging. They hoped to make the passage before nightfall and camp on the down side of the mountain.

Within the hour, they made their most challenging ascent. At times, Christopher and Margaret walked alongside the trailer to lighten the horse's load. The climb taxed Philly nearly to the limits of her extra rations. Christopher still hoped to make camp on the other side of the summit while there was still adequate light. He kept glimpsing the sky. Margaret observed his vigilance.

"Christopher," Margaret pleaded. "What? What do you see?" Squinting, she stared at the horizon.

So as not to worry her, he said nothing. He could, however, see something beyond the mountain summit—a coming storm, maybe. It seemed to be moving fast. It threatened to make crossing impossible. The storm charged across the sky like a pack of angry beasts. The unusually dark sky quickly blanketed them. Soon he and Margaret were certain that crossing was impossible as midafternoon was turned to night.

"I have never seen a storm approach with such narrow focus, so quickly." It seemed to have stopped directly over them. "Have you, dearest Margaret?" Christopher asked.

"Never …" murmured Margaret. "I'm afraid." She trembled. Christopher could see the worry in her eyes.

"Every path we've taken, every turn we've made, the leading end of that storm has pointed our way," Christopher muttered. "It's tracking us. I have never seen a storm react as if it watched us. It's like a stalking animal."

Margaret gazed into Christopher's eyes. "Watched us? But it cannot. Can it?" she entreated, trying to remain calm, not eager to entertain such an outlandish idea.

Off in the distance, the mountain turned from green to white before their eyes, trees suddenly smothered in snow. The sky dumped load after load on tree after tree as it raced toward them. They needed cover now; they needed to get to safety before the storm hit. Reaching the village was impossible. "To The Powers That Be," Christopher thought, "help us. This will be big."

Out loud, he said, "This will be bad."

Suddenly, Margaret shrieked, "The *baby*, Christopher! We have the baby with us!"

The temperature began to drop—fast. They shivered. Easing back on the reins, Christopher stopped the wagon, jumped down, and ran to the back. Through a narrow door, he dashed into the varda to check on the baby, and to get rope and a blanket for Margaret. She insisted on staying outside, on the bench with Christopher. But he knew frigid winds would pound them mercilessly; they needed to protect themselves. They were confident that within the heated varda, the baby would be shielded from the elements. But Christopher needed to drive them to safety.

"The storm comes in too quickly," he muttered. When the heralding wind hit, the cold reached into their bodies and down to their bones like a knife blade.

"Here, take this, Margaret," Christopher said, pushing the blanket up to Margaret. He cut short sections of rope, tying them around Margaret and to the bench. He did the same for himself. The wind whipped and howled. "This will help prevent us being blown from the bench." Checking to make sure the rope around her waist was taut, Christopher took up the reins and snapped them sharply.

She saw his silent glare. He was going to send her inside. She responded, "I know that look. I can't just go inside the varda. I need to help, to be with you."

"I know," Christopher said. "But we've got to get off this road. We need to get to a town, or we could be buried in this snow." He looked to the sky, which grayed more. "We need to go, and we need to go now. And we can't stop."

Shivering, Margaret moved closer to him.

In nearly another hour, they were at the crest of the mountain they had seen from a distance, and they were starting down the other side.

Chris could not stop worrying. The worst place they could be was there, trapped on the crest of the mountain during a snowstorm. They were safe from avalanche, but they could be packed in and freeze to death. He knew, however, things could get much worse if they stayed.

Like a cannon shot, the storm hit. As if the sky had ripped open, the snow fell upon them—a complete whiteout, the twisting mountain trail all but obliterated, choked with ice and snow.

Christopher used force to slow Philly's stride, but the scared horse bucked, sidled, and whinnied. Her footing unsure, she was moving much too fast and going out of control. Christopher forcefully tugged back on the reins. "Whoa. Slow, girl."

At the instant of Christopher's command, Philly's rear legs collapsed. She pitched backward, bounding onto her rump. She glided, whizzing into an ice-coated trench. Whirling onto her side, her body spun, her legs flexing like a scorched spider. Her breeching, fifth-wheel hinge, and rigging barely held.

The trailer flipped and swung around, skidding sidewise. Jamming, and crammed with rock, sticks, and ice, the wagon wheels stopped turning. Rims and axles ground into the ice-laden road. Snow sifted through the spokes. Momentum, acting on the leading edge of the roof, forced the wagon to gouge into the ice. Over a declining length of snow-choked road, it toppled down the mountain, smashing repeatedly against the ground, thundering as it hit. Broken wood and ripped cloth tore away. The varda exploded from the repeated impacts, one-third of the wagon careening farther down the mountain toward a lake, the baby inside. Two-thirds of the wagon whirled across the side of the mountain, personal belongings scattering, pots and pans clanging.

It came to rest in a thicket of trees. Except for the winnowing winds, all was silent, still. The shattered timbers were swiftly covered by the blizzard. Snow filled the mangled road as if nature wanted to hide the evidence, but it was not over.

Compelled by more than just the wind and gravity, the broken varda's slide began again. Slowly at first, then faster and faster it shot down the steep road, the larger parts spinning on their sides.

Independent of wind, the trees moved as if aware. Their energies seemed purposefully focused on the shattered varda. Branches, like rope, spiraled from the treetops. Thinning, twisting, whirling, whipping, the elongating branches shot across and down the road like harpoons. They knitted together to form a flying net. The mass of intertwined branches constantly regenerated a series of barriers across the road. They slammed transversely onto the roadway to catch the hurtling wagon.

Sadly, each net was as mere paper against the momentum of the massive pieces of wagon. They collapsed as fast as they formed, one by one.

Coming to the aid of the branches, loops of ivy sprouted from the ground and tore down the road as if blasted from a nest of snakes. Woody tentacles rocketed over the blanket of snow. Twisting ringlets of branch locked on to any piece they could. The shoots wove baskets and hooks for grappling the varda and its occupants. Alas, the momentum of the heavy wagon shattered basket after basket, loop after loop, net after net.

Careening downward toward the lake, a large piece of wagon dropped into a slick road rut. The wagon lofted. In an arched trajectory, the varda flew over the bank of the icy lake, its contents falling to earth. The wooden debris descended into the water.

Up the road, the front third of the varda, still connected to Philly and her rigging, spun away into a ten-foot snowdrift at the edge of the road, along a row of trees.

Free-falling, the front end crashed toward the lake, Christopher still tied to the bench. Within the blanket, Margaret came down separately. Chattering, startled birds in treetops flushed to the air. Flocking high, they became protesting dots against the blue sky exposed by the waning storm.

Christopher and Margaret hit the frozen surface of the lake at nearly the same time: he at the center, and she at the edge near the bank. Shards of black water and ice recoiled from the lake. Upturned, the varda and bench seat rested upon an underwater cliff, just feet below the surface. Christopher's midsection was pinned beneath the heavy fraction of the wagon. His neck had been broken by the impact of the wagon's massive center beam. Margaret's body, dashed, lay at the water's edge, wedged against small boulders at the lakeside.

All was truly still. Only the silence and the cold were left.

Eyes fluttering open, Margaret whimpered softly, vapor streaming from her nostrils. Her feeble moaning echoed among the surrounding trees.

"C-C- Christopher," she murmured, her teeth bloody. In pain, she could only move her upper torso. Blood streamed from her left side.

"My baby, my baby," she repeated, her voice soft, her energy sapped. Brushing aside tattered flaps of her cape and bodice, she saw a sharp, dagger-size stone broken off in her left rib cage. The sensation of pain was deep and dull. She felt like she had been kicked in the ribs by a bull.

She closed her eyes to rest. She prayed the crash had been a nightmare. Mustering her meager energy, she tried to breathe but found it hard. After several failed tries, she called out again. "Help. Help me. My baby … my husband."

Her voice, however, was small and weak. No one was close, no one near to hear. She saw no Christopher and no baby. Only white: snow, ice, trees covered in snow.

The storm suddenly stopped. She heard nothing but the wind. Where she had been cold, she suddenly began to feel inexplicably warm. The snow packed around her was pink and steaming with her warm blood.

"Help. Help me. Somebody, please. Help me," she feebly cried. "I have a child, my child, a baby, my husband."

Her long, dark-blue shirt and bodice were heavy with water and mud, encrusted with ice and snow. Her lower half still rested in the shallows of the ice-choked lake. She dragged her slight frame higher on the rocks. She tried to lift her gaze over a low line of thick shrubs. Grunting, she prayed with every fiber of her body. She was in very little pain, but she became concerned because she could not feel her legs. She persevered, crawling, dragging her lower body several more inches onto the rock, until she was out of the water and on the snowy bank. On one side, her hair was clogged with mud, sticks, dirt, and ice. Small lacerations bled along her hands and neck.

She groaned, breathless. No longer able to hold her head up, she dropped her right cheek upon the bank. Fresh powdered snow blew onto her eyelashes. Mud mixed with blood was in and around her lips. She huffed it out. Sometimes she mistakenly thought she had called out for help, while other times she realized she was drifting in and out of consciousness.

The cold sapped the feeling from her blanched fingers. She ceased to worry about her lower half. In fact, oddly, she began feeling comfortable. She fought to stay conscious. Taking a deep breath, Margaret rolled from her left to right side and fell over on the snow.

"My baby. Christopher," she breathed. "The Powers That Be, please save my child."

Dazed, she peered into the clearing blue sky. A blurred, rounded shadow descended toward her. A basket woven from forest vines lowered toward her from the pines.

"What is this?" she groaned.

She heard a baby's cry within the basket above her.

"My baby." She smiled feebly, blinking.

The magic of the forest had saved the baby.

She heard her baby cry again. Her weakened heart raced. "Thank you," she said. Reaching up, she bent her fingers over the edge of the basket. She felt the baby move and saw him through the weaving of the basket. The trees limbs flexed down to her. The basket stopped inches from her face. The basket gently rolled the baby to Margaret's bosom.

Margaret heard Philly's distant squeals. The horse's plaintive cries seemed to echo from all directions.

"Poor Philly." She coughed, blood spilling between her lips. She wrapped her arms around the baby. Margaret could do nothing but try to remain conscious through her pain. She could do nothing for Philly. She hoped she would live long enough to get her baby to safety. For now he was pink and warm, but unless someone found them soon, he would not survive.

"Where is your father? Christopher, where are you?" she slurred. But Margaret could not move. She could not see that her beloved Christopher lay only feet from her, his head beneath the water, drowned.

"Christopher. Chris ... topher. Chr ... Uh," she coughed, swallowing when the brackish taste of blood bubbled in her mouth.

In the snowbank, Philly's nostrils rapidly puffed. She snorted and stirred. Steamy vapor swirling around her mouth and tongue. She lay on her flank. Frost crusted her lips and whiskers.

Darkness reached into the heart of the woods, and Margaret grew more frightened—not for herself but for her baby. She weakened with every passing minute. She removed the locket from around her neck and placed it around the baby's, tucking it into his bunting.

She smiled weakly. "This," she coughed, "was a gift from Lady Hydra to my mother, your grandmother. It was gifted to me." Margaret shivered but less than she had before. She was comfortable now, as if she were before her warm oven. "Lady Hydra said I should keep this locket near for all times. Now you must keep it the same." Pausing, she struggled to breathe. "It holds ... the essence of all the love created ... by all things living, and more."

At sixty years old, Tom was stout and strong for his age. Clad in buckskin and fur, he was a comely sight, with his full gray beard falling softly upon his chest. Tom's eyes darted through the treetops to the sky. He saw birds flush up. He heard the great crash and felt its vibration in the ground.

"What do you think it is, boy? I've been in these forests since I was a child, and I have never heard anything like that before," he said to his dog. He peered down, but his dog was gone. At his side, he saw only footprints in the snow, trailing into the distant trees.

"Boy? *Boy?*" He turned in a circle, searching the perimeter for his dog. He crisscrossed his cold arms over his chest.

"Jingles. Here, boy. *Jingles.* Where is that dog?" he muttered. Cupping his hands to the side of his cheeks, he turned and shouted, "JINGLES!"

His voice reverberated through the trees. He heard Jingles barking in the distance, through the trees. In the knee-high snow, Tom tromped in the direction of the barking. Jingles came toward him. Tom could see the dog galloping over a small rise. Jingles stopped, but only for a second. Then he ran straight toward Tom. The snow was up to Jingles' belly. With one flying leap, he was in Tom's arms. Part sheepdog, part St. Bernard, the weighty dog knocked Tom backward in the snow.

"Whoa. Please, boy. I'm not as young as I used to be." Leading Jingles, Tom climbed the small rise. What he saw left him aghast.

He saw the shattered varda.

"Stay here, boy. Be good this time." Turning sidewise, Tom made his way down the small rise. The forest opened up to the clearing through which twisted the road, littered with pieces. He glanced back at the dog. "Be quiet, and watch everything for me," he murmured. "I do not wish to become a dinner side plate for a hungry dragon."

He surveyed the crash. Tom took a deep breath, pondering his next move. He had been caught off guard by the freak snowstorm, and it looked as if someone else had been as well.

He held out his palm and shook his head. "Not a flake. Very unusual. My helpers usually inform me of such things."

On a four-day trip in the Orphic Forest, Tom had gathered exotic woods and stones. Tom had expected nothing unusual during this routine excursion, but it was becoming anything but usual. He ran back to the hill, needed his own varda to bring around to the crash site. Anyone who had survived, whole or injured, he could offer a warm place to rest.

Tom found an intersecting road to the crash site and drove the varda around. As he did, he could see his horse behaving unusually. "The weather, now you? What's wrong with you, Henry?" Henry's ears turned to the breeze. "Do you hear something, boy?" Tom cupped his hand over his own ear but heard nothing. Henry pulled jerkily at Tom's varda, nostrils flaring. "And you can smell something too. Settle down." Tom was concerned, observing Henry's sustained restlessness.

Tom climbed down. He rubbed Henry's broad neck as he passed. He surveyed the littered road. In the distance, he saw the lake. Tom climbed to the bench seat and sat. He snapped the reins. The struts of the varda creaked under Henry's continual tugging. The road declined to a rut and a slight rise. Thick trees rose on either side. It looked to Tom as if there was ice in the rut. The ice was gouged out. He saw nails and screws on the slope.

Tom and his horse had been through much. Tom trusted that Henry's ears were far better than his own. A big stallion, Henry was fifteen hands high. Tar black, he was part Russian mountain horse, part Clydesdale. Tom thought Henry's snow-white mane, tail, and longhaired fetlock boots were particularly fetching. For years he had turned down offers to sell him. Tom did not only worry about his friend but also loved him. Nodding wildly, Henry's ears stood high. He stomped his feet. He loudly neighed, nose flaring. He tugged the varda toward a distant call.

"What is it, boy? What do you hear? You want me to go this way?" Grasping the knob of a thick wooden lever leading down to the brake, Tom pushed it away from the wheel. Loosing the reins, he allowed Henry to lead. "Are you finding what you are looking for? I suppose we would have gone some time ago had I not released this brake, huh, boy."

They went several yards, swaying over the uneven ground. The varda rocked behind as Henry trudged forward. Gradually, his gait increased from a walk to a trot. Tom could see an increasing amount of litter: clothing, food, torn canvas, and broken wood. All led to the lake. Tom needed to get down there quickly.

He arrived at the bottom of the mountain within minutes; there, the road took a bend around the lake. The accident appeared to have ended here. To his left, he saw the bank of the lake, obstructed by a low line of thick shrubs.

Recent, he thought. "Poor souls, whoever they are. That demonic snowstorm did this. That was the noise we heard on the other side of the rise, Jingles," he said, glimpsing the dog. Jingles barked.

Climbing down from the varda, Tom tromped through the battered snow. He heard moaning. Jingles barked and leaped from the bench seat. "What was that?" Alarmed, Tom's heart raced. His eyes scanned the area. "Dear Lord, people are alive. Where are the people? *Where are you?*" he shouted. "Ghastly. *Where are you?*"

He heard more moaning. It was over there, to his left. Holding his breath, Tom cautiously approached the shrubs. He saw a woman, her icy clothing frozen to the snow, a basket in her arms. "Oh, *dear.* Henry!" he shouted.

Henry stood several feet behind, anxiously snorting, vapor whirling from his nostrils. He watched Tom shove through the icy brush. As Tom forged ahead, his feet broke through ice, plashing in the water, which dashed against the rock on which the woman lay. The woman was pale and looked dead.

"Help!" Tom shouted. "Somebody help me! There is a woman hurt!"

His shouting echoed through the forest. In return, all he heard was an echo and the wind. Debris littered the bank. It was laden with slick mud raised from beneath the fresh powdered snow. Slipping as he climbed over shattered pieces of wagon, Tom trod closer to the woman. He fell to his belly on the thick ice, and came face-to-face with the woman. Close up, she appeared white and lifeless.

Then she gasped and stretched her arm to him, her eyes open wide.

Startled, short of breath, Tom scrambled back from his belly to his buttocks. He tried to make sense of what he saw.

"My Lord. I saw you from over there. I thought you were … but you are alive? What can I do? *Help!*" Tom screamed. His voice echoed amid the trees. "Bandages. Do you need …?" He spotted the stone impaling her chest. "How stupid, yes, you need bandages and more. You need a physician." He thumped his head, his hands hovering over her. *This is ridiculous*, he thought. *What can help now? Nothing.* Frantic, Tom could not think.

"I have water," he said finally. "Lord, you must be scared." Seeing she was half in and half out of the water, he rolled his eyes. Water was not what she needed. "How long have you been here?"

Her eyes rolled up to his. He could see her blue lips. Looking deeply into Margaret's beleaguered eyes, Tom heard distant groaning. He gazed over the low bushes toward a mountain of snow in the distance. There he saw the shattered front third of the varda on its side, swaying. He was sure it belonged to the woman before him.

"Were you out here alone?" he asked.

He heard noises and saw a horse tangled and kicking in her rigging, mired in the snow, the cart shaft jabbing around her back legs. Not quite to her feet, Philly groaned deeply as she slumped, her flank against a young pine tree. It bowed under her weight. Her own body mass restricted her from taking adequate breaths. The vapor of her breath shrouded the front part of her body in a cloud.

Blood collected at the corners of Margaret's mouth. "Please, find my husband," she whispered.

"Husband?" Tom asked.

"Help my baby. Help my horse," whimpered Margaret. "Please."

"I will, but I need to help you too."

"There is ... nothing ... that can be done ... for me."

"What a mess," Tom cried desperately, his arms flailing. "I just wish I had more hands."

Tom reached under Margaret's arms and tried pulling her further from water. The water soaking her dress not only made her heavy but froze her to the snow and rock beneath her. The strain on her body made her moan woefully. Tom looked along the shore for something with which he could chop the ice—a stick, a rock, anything of substance. Finding a heavy stone, he hurried back to Margaret.

As he went, he saw part of the frame and roof of the varda wrapped around a tree at some distance from Philly. Another part of the carriage was partially submerged in muddy water. He saw a man below the surface. Her husband? He was pinned several feet under by the center beam of the shattered wagon. Tom approached the water's edge and crossed himself. He said a hurried prayer before returning to Margaret.

"Terrible, terrible, terrible. Dear Creator, Powers That Be, please be merciful." He sighed, dropping to his knees before Margaret.

Gazing up at him, her eyes pleading, Margaret pushed the covered basket toward Tom. "Help me. I—I have a baby."

He looked up from breaking the ice around her lower half. "Baby?" Tom closed his eyes in silent prayer, and felt vines wrapping her waist.

"Take him. Save him!" cried Margaret, "Make him your son."

"A baby? Take him where?" said Tom. "I can't take a baby."

"Oh, please!" she cried.

Tom heard a voice speak softly to his mind: *You will take him. He was meant to be your son.*

"Mother Forest?" Tom whispered. He hesitated. "I will take him now."

But before he could do anything, the air about them began to tingle with static electricity. All around Tom's fingertips swelled a swirling cloud of red and green sparkles. The light traveled from his fingers to Margaret. When the sparkles streamed around her waist, the vines slowly uncoiled, loop by loop. Around the baby, the Listeners formed a blanket of thick leaves, hiding the baby from Tom's sight. Vines caressed the pair to prevent Margaret and the child from slipping back into the water.

In contrast to the frigid air surrounding them, a warm breeze generated by the light gently floated and fanned Margaret's red hair. She appeared angelic.

Gritting his teeth, Tom widened his eyes and nodded. Margaret levitated a few inches from the icy bank. With only a finger, Tom nudged her, effortlessly guiding her from the water's edge to the base of a pine tree several yards up the bank. With a down gesture of his hand, she settled, her weight crunching on the crystallized snow. He propped her against the tree trunk and spread his coat upon her legs.

Tom peered askance, certain he saw movements beneath the leaves in the small basket she caressed at her chest.

Carefully, gently, Margaret peeled the layer of leaves away. Tom heard the gentle cry of the child. Margaret's face brightened, her tired eyes smiling. Not knowing Tom's name, Margaret showed him a quizzical expression. Tom interpreted it correctly and introduced himself. "I am Tom. A toymaker and, uh, master carpenter."

"Tom," Margaret repeated. "This is my son."

Tentative, Tom reached for the baby with his gnarled fingers. Unsure what to do next, his hands shook. It had been a long time since he held a baby. "He's wet, and hungry too, I bet." Tom touched the baby's forehead with his forefinger. "He's chilled to the bone. That's right, chilled to the bone." He peered into Margaret's face. His eyebrows knitting, Tom smiled with ruddy cheeks. "I know I am."

"Listen to me … Tom, the master toymaker," Margaret whispered. "His name is Nicholas … His father is dead. I know that now. If he were alive, he would have come to us by now."

Margaret coughed, straining to lift her hand to her chin. She wiped blood from her lips. "I will be with him soon." She looked into Tom's face. "We have been here so long, I think. You are losing the light."

Tom could see it was still early and bright; there was much sunlight now. In fact, she was losing the light from her eyes. Tom knew her death was near.

"I still feel—ah," she groaned, turning. Her voice weakened. She saw her shoulder where Nicholas had lain, smiling fleetingly. "I still feel his warmth. I ... I ... love him very much." Her hand reached to Tom's face, and her voice quavered. "Please love him. Teach him. I haven't long." Margaret peered into Tom's eyes. "The foretelling was true. It was true."

Befuddled, Tom stared into her face.

"Take—take care of my little boy," said Margaret. "Teach him, teach ... teach. Oh," Margaret said, stopping midsentence. "What is that? My, I never thought— Oh, it is milady ..."

Before she finished her sentence, her hand fell from Tom's face. From her other hand, a baby's glass bottle fell to the ground, tinkling as it rolled across the rocks toward the frozen lake.

Silent, Tom stood. There was nothing he could do. She was dead.

Dragging his coat from her legs, he drew it over Margaret's face and held the infant to his chest. Without his coat, he shivered—not from the cold but from the weight of his newly acquired responsibility. Tom gazed into the infant's tiny face. The wind winnowed through the pine boughs softly. Although the storm had long passed, somehow it was colder despite the brightness of the midday sun.

"May your mother rest in peace. I have you now, little Nicholas." Tom sighed. "I'll take care of you."

Tom made his way back to his varda, where Henry waited. "We'll have to be introduced. In case you didn't hear, my name is Tom, Tom the toymaker. I am a carpenter. This is my horse Henry, and soon I will gather up your poor mama and papa. It will be a big job." He looked around the empty clearing. He was alone. "But I will need help. Let's get you into the varda while I work."

Within the varda, Tom quickly fashioned a pallet of hay and blankets. Tom gently positioned Nicholas squarely upon the hay.

"Ho," Tom chuckled. "It's been a long time since I've done this. Come to think of it, never having had children, I've never done this. Ho." He drew the blanket up to Nicholas's neck. It was fortunate the child was so young, Tom thought. Perhaps he would never feel the full impact of his parents' deaths.

"You look comfortable—nice, warm, and dry. You are dry. You'd let me know, right?" Tom smiled nervously and snickered, "Ho, you sure are wiggly."

Jingles was in a corner, his head on the floor, his brown eyes peering up to Tom.

"Jingles! Jingles, come here, boy. Thatta boy. Good boy." Wiggling, panting, Jingles rolled over on his back so Tom could rub his belly. "Got a job for you, boy," Tom told him. Jingles rolled to his feet and eased toward the baby, nose first. "It's all right. Go on." Tom allowed Jingle to sniff the baby. "Nicholas, meet Jingles. Jingles, meet Nicholas."

Jingles barked.

"He will warm you up," Tom said. The dog lay next to Nicholas. Tom rubbed the dog's head. "You know something about babies, right? All dogs know something about babies, don't they?"

Within the hour, Tom stood at edge of the water, peering into the frozen lake. Just feet beneath the surface, he could make out the figure of a human—the deceased body of Christopher. Minute vortices of blowing snow chased across the frozen surface. The cold wind cut through Tom's clothing. He began to shiver. Margaret's small body lay beneath his coat, which glistened with the blown powder.

The heaviness of Tom's conundrum became acute. He had to retrieve the dead bodies of Nicholas's parents, a task he could not complete alone. It would be laborious, and he wanted to be back home in a timely fashion. If he was late, Mary would worry, and he dreaded putting her through undue fright.

Concentrating, Tom stretched out his arms and his mind. He considered his words and spoke them carefully.

"Mother Forest, dear oddlings, and friends. Please, hear these words. Humans and magical oddlings of all clans have lived and worked in harmony together for centuries. I *need* your help now. May I have your help?"

Tom took a deep breath and sighed. "I have faith you have heard me." He looked back at the varda. "That baby needs care, and fast," he said, "and so I will do my best to gather his parents." Tom thought about the coming years and the effort of raising a child to adulthood. He was not exactly sure how, but he was determined to keep his promise to Margaret. He wanted to be a loving and successful parent. However, where to start?

Tom surveyed his surroundings. Tapping the side of his nose with a finger, he wagged it in the air—an epiphany. "Baby stuff. Got to find baby stuff."

A horse whinnied in pain. He turned in her direction. His stomach dropped. "Saints alive." While pondering Nicholas's plight and the cleanup ahead, Tom had forgotten Philly.

Tom ran to her. He struggled to release the bindings that hobbled her. It took several minutes for him to loose her feet and hindquarters from the confusion of leads, straps, breeching, and smashed pieces of wagon.

Finally, Tom lifted the yoke from her neck. "Sorry, girl," he whispered. "That should make you feel a lot better."

With Tom's help, the horse righted herself. He took her to his varda. Tom could see the injured horse's name Philly burned into its bridle. Hobbling, she trod slowly right up to the nose of Henry. The two horses grunted, lifting their heads and bowing. They touched noses.

"Henry, meet Philly. Philly, meet Henry. She will need a friend tonight. Can you help with that?" Nodding, the horse seemed to understand.

Throwing a hitch line between the two, Tom pulled it taut and tied it securely. He fashioned a secure knot and attached their combined reins to a cross line. "That'll keep you two together where I can find you." Tom rubbed his hands. "That should hold you."

He turned to complete the grisly task ahead: gathering the dead. Just as he began, Jingles barked wildly. He had heard someone coming, approaching from the forest. Tom assumed that, whoever it was, they could help. He finally felt some relief. "Good. Help is coming."

Tom heard crunching on the snow from fifty feet away. An eight-foot giant of a man stepped from behind a tree. He had long black hair and a broad, unsmiling face, and was clad in hunting gear. His arms were at his sides; his hands held a longbow. He gazed into Tom's face, then charged, his giant feet pounding the snow and mud. He leaped chunks of ice and broken wagon fragments, screaming, his sonorous voice rippling through Tom's chest.

From behind, Tom heard the deep roar of an animal. Spinning on one foot, he saw before him an enormous polar bear rearing on its hind legs, its mouth wide, its plate-size claws striking the air.

The man whooshed by Tom and vaulted into the air, right for the bear. Tom staggered backward, falling onto the snow.

His feet barely touching the ground, his fingers spread and arched, the giant raised his hand to the bear's ear. They slammed together, the bear's fore claws coming down and around the giant's back.

Gripping tightly, the bear shouted in human voice, "Beast!"

"Ursa!" the giant shouted back. They embraced, hugging affectionately. "My old friend. You look no older," the giant said. "You old flatterer, you. I'm a polar bear," the bear bellowed, "You can't detect the gray hairs in the natural white of my coat. Enough, my old friend. Save your troll gruel for someone else."

With a beckoning claw, the bear gestured to the woods for his wife to come forward and greet his old friend. "Beast, my wife, Ursara."

Tom strode toward the bear and the Giant.

"Hello, my friends—Ursa, Ursara, Beast." Tom nodded. "Beast, my old friend, you gave me quite a start a moment ago. I thought you had forgotten me."

"How on earth could I forget you, Tom?" said Beast. "You've been to my house a thousand times."

"Well," Tom said, his eyes scanning the forest and the skies. He stared at the crevices in the exposed ground. "With all that has been going on in the last several months, the reports of … Outlanders and all, one can hardly tell." Tom laughed nervously. "I want to thank you for answering my call. But where are the—"

Tom hushed when he heard noises: the cracking of twigs behind a grove of shrubs. Tom turned. "Who strides with such a reckless gait?" he asked Beast.

A plaintive muttering arose from the shadows close to the ground. "There," Beast said, pointing down. "Our short, lyrical friends with the hobbling stride."

Three trolls, four feet tall and thick as tree stumps, limped toward Tom in single file. As was characteristic of their clan, each possessed one leg shorter than the other, convenient for balance when sidewinding from below bridges up steep riverbanks. Marching in lockstep, they stopped a foot from Tom and gazed up.

"Who speaks of troll gruel?" asked the first in a small, tinny voice. "Do not deny. I'm no fool."

"Trying to make us hungry, ay?" asked the second, his voice no different.

"I smell nothing here today," said the third, gnashing his teeth, sniffing the air.

"Do they never tire of speaking in verse?" whispered Beast to Tom. Tom shrugged. "They do not need to, but for them it is easier not to go against their nature."

All the trolls had long noses, the length of a man's hand, and teeth nearly too big for their mouths. Throwing back his shoulders and pulling in his chin, the first troll glanced at the other two, then peered up into Tom's eyes. Rubbing his short chin, he spoke in the characteristic rhyme of the troll clan. "The Whispers sang of the carriage fall, to us your plea, to help the family, all."

He raised his stumpy arm and pointed to the other two. "Tend to the horse; we'll stand upright. Inside we work to make things right." He pointed to the broken varda. Though small, the trolls were powerful. In their tiny bodies, they had the strength of several men. Each of the trio stood at one point of the varda, creating a triangle.

Beast marched to the crash site as two of the three trolls lifted the embedded varda from the mud. They manipulated the massive fragments as if the pieces were as light as butterflies. Beast knelt before the third troll, who was behaving as supervisor, directing the other two.

"Such strength, my small friend. You have many surprises." He laughed, "And I thought you trolls were just ugly."

Rolling his eyes, the troll continued to work and said nothing.

"I kid you." Beast said. Tucking his lips, he glanced away and back. "It is good to see you again."

Never turning his eyes from his fellow trolls, the supervisor mumbled from the side of his mouth, "A bad time to meet, Beast. I want a better time to greet."

"Aye," replied Beast.

With ease, the trolls lowered the varda to the mud. Brushing off their hands and kicking the ice from their large, gnarled feet, they looked proud. The diminutive creatures converged on Beast. They and Beast shook hands.

"The horse in pain you must now tend; she needs your help if she's to mend," said the second troll to the third.

The first troll opened a sack he had dragged from the varda. He sifted through several items of clothing, food, and medicine that he set aside. He studied the horse.

"Blanket, tack, and liniment in the varda must be found. They will help to make her body sound."

The wind blew cold.

Beast made a fire. He took the edible supplies packed for Philly and set them beside the fire to warm. Ambling to where Tom had tied the horses, Beast stood between them. He laid one large hand upon Henry's cheek and the other on Philly's neck. "Good boy, Henry. Good girl, Philly."

Philly pitched her ears forward and gave a loud whinny that reverberated through the forest. The echo from the mountain was ear piercing.

Examining Philly's flank, Beast felt swelling at her ribs. There were several lacerations over her rib cage and others under her belly. When he touched her, she flinched. He looked tenderly into her large brown eyes. "Those ribs of yours must be very sore. Let me try to make you feel better."

Her head bobbed up and down. Beast was unsure whether she knew what he meant, but he hoped to gain her trust. From a pocket within a satchel strapped around his shoulder, he withdrew a handful of dried plants and flowers. He sauntered to the fire and put them into a pot of boiling water. When the fragrant aroma began to rise, he drained the mixture through a cloth. He twisted the cloth until he had expressed most of the water, forming a mushy paste. Beast folded that into another cloth. Twisting, he squeezed the resulting liquid into a small amount of warm water in another pan. He took the warm liquid back to Philly.

"Drink this now," he whispered, holding it beneath her mouth. The horse was hesitant. Combing her mane with his fingers, Beast soothed her trepidation.

Philly drank. She groaned softly.

From the salvaged supplies, Beast withdrew her blanket and warmed it by the fire. He covered her. He closed her eyes. "You'll feel better in the morning. I promise you."

Beast turned to Henry, rubbing down his face. "Henry. Stay close to her, boy. She might need your help." He stroked both animals. "Do a good job, boy, and she might give you a kiss."

Tom searched through the fragmented varda for the baby's belongings. He felt a sense of urgency to resolve the situation with Nicholas. The cleanup took most of the light. Dusk was coming, and it was getting no warmer. He continued searching high and low.

"We can help with that." came a voice from behind him. Startled, Tom quickly stood, smacking the back of his head on a wall cabinet, now on the ceiling. He turned. "Who the …?" he groaned, rubbing his head. He looked through the open rear wall of the varda to see the giant polar bears Ursa and Ursara standing before him in the snow. On one bear sat the elf prince, Chlora, and on the other his sister, Princess Faunett. Tall and thin with long, flowing hair, the prince and princess were dressed in long-sleeved, ankle-length robes apparently woven of spider silk and starlight. Tom had not seen the royal siblings for years.

He'd noticed the bears lumbering off into the forest and had wondered where they had gone.

"I thought you'd gone back to your kingdom," Tom said to the bears. "But you went to get more help. I thank you."

"We not only sent our attendants to help," said the elf prince, gesturing to the polar bears, "but we have come too. We waited on the outskirts of the Orphic Forest until the time was right. We are prepared, but we remain cautious."

"I understand your caution," said Tom. He turned his head when he heard Jingles howling from his wagon parked near the trees. He heard the faint cries of the infant Nicholas as well. Tom's heart bled for the poor child, who sounded uncomfortable and unhappy. But perhaps he projected onto the child what he thought he himself might feel. He was not sure. Tom was sure, however, that the baby wanted his parents.

"Nicholas needed attending." Tom murmured, excusing himself. Several moments later, Tom was with Nicholas. Feeling his way around his varda, Tom tried to identify things in the dark. Beast and the trolls collected belongings fallen from the Northlanders' carriage and placed them into Tom's wagon.

The trolls carried Christopher's remains close to the fire. "We retrieved him from among the reeds just in time. Some of the forest vermin were preparing to feed," said one troll.

The fire roared, casting dancing yellow light. As light and dark striped their faces, they said a prayer. They cleaned the body and wrapped it gently in a blanket. Beast did the same for Margaret.

Tom watched the trolls standing in the flickering firelight, their gnarled faces tinted sepia. In unison, like soldiers, they turned to the roadway. "As troll, along the road we must patrol when the time of light takes flight. For those in peril we do fight against the hidden in the night." With no further words, they marched away from the campfire, dissolving with their shadows into the night.

The elf prince and princess approached the fire. They called for Tom. Tom and Beast met them at the fireside. Beast lifted Faunett from the back of Ursara like a fine porcelain doll. He gently set her down.

"Dressed in our finest robes, we are prepared to give homage to your dead, if you will allow. We desire to help in any way we can," said Prince Chlora. "We have contacted our friends the wolf clan to guard this camp tonight." Tom heard the wolves howl in the moonlight. They usually kept their distance. In the past, Tom had seen their glowing eyes deep in the forest.

"Light sprites will fly beside you and light your camp as we work," said Princess Faunett. "The mother of the flora gnomes will be here to help with the needs of the child. All oddlings shall help you, Tom the Toymaker, and your new charge Nicholas. You will accept our offer, yes?"

Tom removed his hat as he bowed. "It would be my pleasure and my honor to accept your offer."

Tom marched to his varda to attend to Nicholas. He prepared a bath. Within a few moments, Tom heard noises outside. He stepped to the door and opened it. Ursa and Ursara came to stop several yards from the doorsill. The elf prince stood beside them. From a pouch cinched at the polar bear's flank poked the tip of a pink conical hat.

"Please, my dear. Come forth," commanded Prince Chlora. The hat rose, and a small human-like oddling peeked from the pouch. By rope, she climbed down to the snow. From the doorsill, Tom could barely see her. She was backlit by the flickering yellow light of the campfire. She stepped forward toward Tom.

With a flowing gesture, the elf prince presented her. "I bring you Mother Oddling," he said. "She is a friend of the forest, a friend of ours, and soon a friend to you, Tom. She too is here to help."

The small individual stood no higher than Tom's knee. She looked up at him. "I am Mia, a flora gnome," she said. She was clad in pink trousers and a blue blouse under the conical pink hat, which she removed. She reached in and withdrew a crystal vase the size of a peach pit. It contained a liquid.

She smiled. "This is oil of lavender and chamomile."

She gestured, asking permission to enter the wagon. Tom stood aside to let her pass. She approached the basin in which Nicholas lay. She decanted the oil into the water while singing a lullaby. Mia worked the liquid into the water, which began to froth. "This will calm the baby," she said, "and make him sleep well."

Faunett used magic on the salvaged supplies to multiply the food and make dinner for the entire camp. A dozen or more oddling creatures and Tom sat around the campfire. All held hands, paws, or claws, their faces glowing reddish brown in the flickering light.

"We will give thanks to the creator of all things for our blessings, and for the poor souls who no longer walk among us," said Tom somberly. All bowed their heads. Tom and the oddlings joined in a prayer for the safety of the Northlanders' souls and for the transport of their remains back to town.

Kneeling at the shrouded corpses, Tom stretched out his arms above them. "I am sorry to meet you this way, young friends," he said. "I will take care of your remains until we get to town. Rest easily. Your son is well and with me, as you now most certainly know." Tom gestured for the others to work together to place the bodies on biers. They left the fire and strode to the tree where Tom had hitched his varda. They positioned the biers on the drop-down at the rear of the varda, securing them tightly with quarter-inch braided hemp rope. They were ready for the trip.

Tom strode back to address everyone around the campfire again. "Our work here is finished, my friends." He gestured toward the varda. "I want to thank you all for your help." Tom bowed his head humbly. "Enjoy your meal."

Faunett dished from a kettle, and Mia passed a bowl of stew to each person sitting beside the fire.

"I have a day's travel or so ahead of me," Tom said. "I must take this child's family to Father Bernard."

Little Mia came up beside Tom. She covered a bowl with her bonnet. She removed her hat, sparkles of light trailing. The bowl had transformed into a covered quart tin.

"This is for you, Tom the Toymaker." Mia raised her short arms, presenting the tin to Tom. He accepted it.

"Thank you, ladies, for your help tonight with Nicholas. This meal will be quite tasty throughout our journey." Tom took the tin by its wire handle.

Prince Chlora stood before the fire to speak. "The voices of the forest, the Whispers, have told me of Margaret and her family. My dear Tom and all who hear me," he said. "We are all children of the creator, and should live and help our brethren under the creator. We were glad to help with your needs." He waved his hands over the fire. An image of a bird made of smoke and flame briefly flew up. A few flaps of its ethereal wings and it dissolved into the air. "I have sent Talon, my owl, to King Dobromil with word of this tragic day. His flight will be instantaneous. By now the king knows his physician and wife have been killed, and that their child is in your care." The gathering muttered, praising his forethought. "When you arrive in town, Tom, the castle guard will take possession of the Northlanders' bodies."

Tom felt tugging at his trousers. He looked toward his left knee. Faunett looked up.

"When she changed his clothing," said Faunett, "Mia found Nicholas's mother's locket tightly tucked into his bunting. A note said, 'A gift for the baby, Lady Hydra.' And there was an inscription. 'The Essence of Life is Love.' Within the locket is a crystal vial containing a sapphire liquid. Written on the vial are words, *'Uno nim por vitam duobus minims pro mortem,'* which means one drop for life, two drops for death. One drop and death will no longer be one's keeper."

Faunett and Chlora looked at Tom. "Arbor Falls is an hour southwest of this glen. Your journey will be halfway finished there," Faunett said. "The route is mostly downhill. Jack Frost has cleared the road, so your passage should be easy. From a distance, the Wolf clan will escort you until you reach the village."

Beast hitched the leads of Philly's bridle to the tailgate, while Tom set Nicholas in his cradle on the bench beside him for the trip. Tom gazed at those gathered by, and those still at the campfire.

"Good night, my friends," Tom said. "On your own journeys, travel safely."

⁂

Tom, Nicholas, Jingles, and the horses traveled until they reached the high clearing above the village. They passed Arbor Falls. By now, they were only half a day from the home of Tom's brothers in Elfin. They could see the village down in the valley, and the edge of the forest behind them.

"We'll rest here tonight," Tom muttered. "It is farther than it looks, and it's a little too dark to travel. Wouldn't you say, Henry? You agree." Seeming to understand, Henry nodded, and Jingles barked.

Tom commenced making camp. First positioning the wagon as a windbreak, he unhitched the horses. He watered them and gave the hungry horses oats and hay. Gathering rocks, Tom arranged them in a circle at the center of the camp, a circle the diameter of a wagon wheel.

Tom strode to the edge of the clearing, to a line of tall pines. In awe of their magnificence, he sought out the tallest, stoutest tree. Doffing his hat, he leaned forward and laid his hands on its rough bark. He could feel its coldness but he could also sense its strength. The power of life was among all the trees, and it strengthened his soul.

Thick and thin branches often lay around trees, felled naturally by wind and by age. Tom saw none.

"Hello, mother pine. May I use your branches to keep us warm and make food?"

A gentle breeze rustled through the trees. Several feet away, Tom heard snapping. Thick branches fell.

"Thank you, dear mother. My new charge and I are grateful. And if it wouldn't be too much," Tom said, "will you and your children please watch over us while we sleep?" Again the pine needles rustled, "Thank you, dear mother," Tom answered.

Smoke and cinders floated away on the wind. When the fire came to a blaze and was nice and hot, Tom led Henry and Philly to it so they could warm. Tom was confident the fire would add to their protection. Quiet and tired, he climbed into the varda, onto a pallet next to the cradle holding Nicholas.

They slept, and the night wind blew. It snowed heavily over the next several hours. The mother pine and her children *did* watch over Tom. She surrounded his camp with an invisible dome, a bubble of snow-free ground. There they remained warm and dry.

In the morning when they woke, Tom found his encampment surrounded by three feet of snow, but just beyond their encampment, the road to town was clear of snow.

Tom's eyes went to the large tree. He could just make out a comforting face smiling in the bark. "Thank you, mother pine," Tom whispered, "for keeping us safe." He broke camp and set out for town.

Some hours later, Tom rolled into Elfin, his ancestral home, the town of his birth and rearing. He was relieved to get there. On the road, Tom often thought about home, but never, even in his dreams, had he once thought he would come home with an infant.

Nicholas needed a stable home and a loving family. There was so much sadness attached to the start of his young life. Tom hoped Nicholas would know only happiness from now on. With the blessing of the Powers That Be, that happiness would begin now, with Tom coming home with the baby. Funny, Tom thought, what a reversal: he would be the one to tell his wife Mary that he was with child.

Foremost, Tom had to be practical. After taking Philly to the farrier, he prepared to go to the church so Nicholas could receive care and blessings. It was a short walk from the farrier.

Marching to the church, Tom chattered under his breath: "Lord help us, your children, in this time of need." Many of Tom's old friends saw him and spoke as he passed by. They were bewildered when he seemed to look right through them, ignoring them as he continued chattering to himself.

"What do you have there, old Tom?" several passersby shouted. Tom dodged their prying hands as they tried to peek into the bundle in his arms.

Having just finished with a parishioner, the rotund and quite bald Fr. Bernard saw him coming from the front door of the church. Father Bernard loped clumsily to Tom's side. He shooed away the nosiest of his straggling parishioners. Father Bernard walked backward, facing Tom as he marched to the church. The priest peeked into the bundle. His eyes grew wide with both joy and confusion. "Tom, Tom, what is this?"

"A baby. Father, you surprise me," quipped Tom. "I know you've never had children, but surely you recognize a baby."

"Of course, why of course I recognize a baby," Father Bernard said, becoming shrill. "You needn't be in a snit, Tom."

"I beg your pardon, Father." Tom sighed. "I ... I just have a lot on my mind lately. The baby and all."

"Right. *Baby*. What are you doing with it?"

"I'm not so sure I have the baby, so much as the baby has me," Tom said.

"You're too old."

"Too old for what?"

"Too old to have a baby," said Father Bernard.

"Father, Father, dear Father. I have not had a baby. The poor woman in my varda had the baby."

"You brought her here? How could you? What about your wife, Mary?"

"The woman in the varda, she's tied up—"

"*Tied*? This is very much unlike you." Father Bernard wagged his finger.

Peering at him askance, Tom stopped walking. "You don't understand. It's the woman's baby."

"Woman? Tom, you are at least three score years."

"Older," Tom muttered. "But don't tell Mary. She might think herself too young for me." Tom laughed.

"How can you make light of this?"

"Father, this is anything but light, and it's no fun. His name is Nicholas." The baby cried and writhed under the blanket. Fr. Bernard took the bundle into his arms.

Tom continued, "If he sounds a little irritable, I suppose it's because he's either wet, hungry, or both. It's been a long journey and he's tired. *We* are tired. And I have to see Mary."

"Where are his parents, really? Where, Tom?"

"Dead." Tom nodded.

"Dead?"

"Both," Tom said. "As I was saying, you'll find her and her husband tied to a bier on the varda." Tom pulled at his beard. "Father, we need to bury them."

Relieved of his confusion, Fr. Bernard nodded vigorously. "All along, I was certain. I was certain you couldn't have birthed a child. That would, uh, be trouble."

"Tell me of it," Tom said.

"I want to know everything. Tell me everything. Did his parents receive the last rites?" Fr. Bernard thought. "Of course not. They would have needed a priest. They will need a proper burial."

When the baby cried louder, Tom rolled his eyes and took the bundle from Father Bernard's arms. Shoving open the heavy oak church door, Tom marched inside. There, he yelled as loudly as he could for the priest to come. But, clasping his arm, a nosey parishioner kept Father Bernard outside. He whispered quietly to the woman, soothing her as she gestured.

"Father Bernard, Father Bernard, come in quickly. I need your help!" Tom shouted.

Father Bernard dismissed the woman. The icy wind pushed him along. He swung through the creaking door, "What is it, my son?"

Dipping at his knees, tilting his head, Tom hunched his shoulders and widened his eyes, while gesturing at what he needed. A pungent odor arose from the baby's bunting.

"Quickly, Father," Tom said. "We need to find the good sister or another woman. We need help. Something has spoiled in this bunting."

Nicholas began exploring the depth of his lungs.

"One good woman is worth two mediocre men," Tom said. He laid Nicholas on a table and peered into the cloth wrapping the baby's bottom. "Father, I fear what was on the inside of this baby has now come to the outside."

"Sister is in the garden, some distance from here."

"Then, Father, we must be brave and do this ourselves. Bless us, dear Father, for we know not what we do."

After the men changed the baby, Tom held the child tightly against his full gray beard. He told Father Bernard of Nicholas's woeful tale. Leaning forward from his seat in a rocker, he handed Father Bernard the heart-shaped locket that had been found in the bunting. Delayed grief and fatigue finally beset Tom, and he began to sob.

"Don't cry, my son," said Father Bernard. "Your good deed will be rewarded tenfold."

The baby cooed softly.

Placing his arm across Tom's shoulder, Father Bernard helped Tom up and led him through the church into the rectory. A roaring fire in the fireplace warmed the main room. The two men sat at a large oak table surrounded by twelve chairs. Father Bernard called to the housekeeper, "Emily, please bring hot cider for our friend Tom and warm milk for the little one."

Tom stared into the fire. The priest took the child, examined him, and gave him warm milk. Attending to the strain in Tom's eyes, Father Bernard tried engaging him in lighter talk. "You haven't seen Mary in days, have you? I know you miss her. Of course you do."

Cutting his gaze from the fire, Tom suddenly snapped back into consciousness.

"She was well when I saw her several days ago," Father Bernard went on.

Tom chuffed. Sipping cider, he tried to enjoy the fire. "Mary works hard. When her work is done, she even helps me with my projects." Tom sighed. "She's a good wife."

"You have no children," mused Father Bernard.

Tom gave the priest a sidewise glance. " You know ... I always wanted children, but we missed that blessing," he replied. "Your church allows you to marry, yet you never have, Father."

"We are allowed but not required. My devotion is to the church. I could not do that with a family." Father Bernard smiled while gently bouncing the bundled child on his knee. He watched Tom. "Blessings come in many forms," he said. "It is true: God works in mysterious ways. Walk with me to the church, just for a few moments. I want you to witness something."

In the church, a grand stone basin perched on a pedestal stood before a large, ornate crucifix. The two men stood beside it. Tom held Nicholas in his arms. The priest stood before the stone basin of holy water, his hand clasping a vial of blessed oil. While reciting a ritual blessing, the priest inscribed the sign of the cross with his thumb on the child's forehead.

He recited, "I baptize you in the name of the Lord." Father Bernard saw Tom's full eyes. He finished his blessing, "And forever more you shall be known to the world as ... Nicholas Claus."

Swallowing, Tom's eyes widened with both reverence and astonishment. Father Bernard took the pendant of Lady Hydra. Blessing it, he placed it around the child's neck. Father Bernard looked into the baby's bright eyes. "Be obedient to your new parents, Tom and Mary Claus. Love them and make them proud. Do this in the name of the Father, the Son, and the Holy Ghost. Amen."

Father Bernard took Tom by the shoulders. "You'll be good parents. I'm sure of it."

Tom's thoughts turned to his wife.

"With your new child, go home, my son. Take him to Mary," said Father Bernard.

Chapter 1

HOME

Tom and Mary Claus's thirty-three-acre farmstead was northeast of Elfin, still in the county of Castleton, off the main town road, down in a steep but beautiful valley. An arch of intricately carved oak, resembling a braid of variegated holly, marked the main entry of the homestead. Shiny red berries were woven into the holly design, interlaced with mistletoe. Suspended from the arch, another carving depicted a six-prong elk pulling an open sleigh. Marking the homestead borders was a five-foot high, split-log, notch-lock fence, leading away from the arch post along either side. Ditches drained rainwater runoff, the two fosse connected by a conduit under the road. Above the gate, attached to the wooden arch by short lengths of brass chain, swung a wood-burned sign:

MASTER CARPENTER

THOMAS CLAUS

EVERYTHING MADE WITH LOVE AND CARE

Connecting the main gate to the farmhouse was a wagon-furrowed dirt road, half a mile long. The road ended amid a small cluster of buildings. Three hundred yards south of the brook and water wheelhouse stood the farmhouse, made of logs and stone.

Riding atop the varda, Tom could clearly see the house. With pleasure and wistfulness, he imagined the home he had made with Mary over the years, as he often did when far away. Doing so brought Mary closer to him no matter what the distance. Smiling, Tom could clearly see in his mind every interior.

There were three rooms, including the cooking area, large enough that a full-grown man could comfortably stand and maneuver. An iron bar spanned the hearth, from which hung a forty-pound, four-quart, cast-iron kettle. Beneath an iron grate, the firebox cradled orange embers, which warmed a simmering stew. Before the hearth, inlaid cobblestones six rows deep and five columns wide glistened in the floor. From there ran a plank floor of oak. Near the fire was where Jingles would curl to sleep on the stones.

A big table, centered in the big room, was the heart of all family activities. A trap door in the floor, not far from the table, led to the turnip cellar. To the right of the hearth, red and green curtains surrounded a big window overlooking Mary's neatly laid garden. Carefully placed next to the glazed Dutch door leaned a well-worn handmade sorghum broom. Further still to the right was a small room with a big feather bed; it held a dresser with a hand-carved mirror, and a chair standing at its side. In the corner, a blanket stand held a goose down quilt lovingly stitched by Mary's hand. A narrow stone-covered path led from the back door to the barn. In his mind, Tom saw Mary's smiling face.

As Tom came closer to the homestead, Jingles began to bark. Leaving Tom and the wagon lagging far behind, Jingles scampered up the dirt road and into the barn. He immediately chased the cat, which hissed and dashed behind a bale of hay.

Surprised by the commotion, Mary spun on the stool where she sat milking the cow, Patches. She saw Jingles. That meant one thing: Thomas was back.

Mary felt jittery, and her heart raced like that of a little girl. She patted the cow on her broad side and stood, fingers trembling. It took Mary barely an instant to find her thoughts: the days would no longer seem so long. Thomas was home.

A slight woman, she had long salt-and-pepper hair twisted into a braid that fell to her waist. She instinctively began to touch her face and her hair. She pulled her clothing to flatten out the wrinkles. With her tongue, she wet her lips. She could hear her husband's cart clattering up the path. He was only yards away. Somehow milking the cow seemed unimportant.

Mary rushed to put the sloshing pail of milk into the storage tank. Within a few steps, she was standing at the water pump outside the barn. With several pulls of the pump handle, she drew a column of cold water that poured over her hands. She quickly rinsed. Drying her hands on her apron, she dashed up the path to meet Tom, not quite sure if her feet actually touched the ground.

As he stepped from the buckboard, Mary flew into Tom's arms. She clutched him in an embrace so sturdy a grizzly bear would have fought to get loose.

"My my my, Mary," Tom lilted, grunting, inhaling with some effort. "Ha. Maybe I should have stayed away a little longer? Ho." He laughed. "Come." Taking her hands, Tom spun Mary around. From side to side he tugged her, playfully coaxing her from the wagon, up the path, and through their front door.

Mary was somewhat confused as Tom hurried her across the room. "Tom? Tom? What are you doing?" She laughed tentatively, resisting a bit, as he nudged her toward the chair. He seated her into his rocker before the hearth. "Tom, this is *your* chair."

"Never mind that. I have wonderful news." He could see the bewilderment on her face. She reached up to gently touch him on both cheeks as he stared down to her.

"Mary, Mary, Mary, I have a surprise for you." He tittered like a little boy, clapping his hands with childish excitement.

"Are you all right?" She felt his forehead. "You're sick. You have a fever." But she felt no fever.

"No, I do not have a fever, but I am hot with excitement. Cover your eyes. No peeking," Tom playfully said. He chuckled and clapped his hands.

Happy, excited, but confused, she bounced on her seat, her fingers to her eyes. "Thomas Anthony Claus, what are you doing?"

"No peeking between your fingers," he repeated. Quietly, Tom marched from the house.

Mary waited impatiently, wondering what had happened to her husband. In a few moments, Tom tiptoed back into the house. He brought the small bundle containing Nicholas up to Mary. Her eyes were still closed. The baby did not move.

Face bright and rosy, Tom smiled. "Stretch your arms out, Mary. And ... and ..." Shivering with excitement, Tom placed the bundle into Mary's arms. He bent down to her ear. "You're with ... *child*!" he shrieked.

She startled. Her smile faded. Her ebullient expression flattened, replaced with puzzlement.

Mary felt a soft, full bundle in her arms. The bundle had an unfamiliar shape, yet somehow familiar. It squirmed. She had warned Tom not to bring home another stray dog. They had Jingles. They needed no other.

"Oh." Mary cried. Her eyes flew open. "It's smiling. Its mouth is wide open. He has no teeth, Tom." Mary could see that it was certainly no dog, but a baby.

A grin frozen on his face, Tom bobbed his head. "His name is Nicholas, yeah. Nicholas, meet Mary, your new mommy."

Mary looked into the baby's face. Their eyes met. Nicholas kicked and threw his arms upward, blowing bubbles.

"Nicholas is ours, Mary. Ours forever."

Confounded, Mary shook her head, while at the same time she wanted to take charge of the baby. "Tom, what have you done?" she said softly, with concern. "Whose baby is this?"

"Yours."

"No. How can it be mine?"

Tom knelt beside her. Over the next several minutes, he told Mary the sad story of the accident, and his encounter with the magical creatures of the Orphic Forest.

Mary gasped, "Oh Tom, his poor parents, this poor child." Carefully she removed the bunting and began to rock. "But we can't keep him, can we? I mean, what would people think of us? Old folks like us, seriously. Raising a child, Tom?"

"They won't think anything. They will be happy for us," Tom said. He nodded and rubbed his hand across Mary's head, down to her shoulders. Mary quieted.

Casting down her eyes, she looked into little Nicholas's face. "So you're ... Nicholas. What a fine-looking little man you are." Mary's breathing slowed. She swallowed as she inspected Nicholas from head to toe. He had all of them. "Soon you will be a big, strong man. Today, however, you are my little boy."

Tom parked himself into another rocker across from Mary. Pondering their improbable turn of fortune that was now his new, larger family, he lit his pipe.

Nicholas was asleep. Mary glanced up from the baby to see a pensive look on Tom's face. "What are you thinking?" she asked. He breathed deeply but continued to stare. "What, Tom?" she asked again. She knew that face of his—every line, every wrinkle—and when they came, something was worth thinking about. His face was a roadmap for the course of their lives. She has known him all her life, it seemed. His mind was working overtime. He was studying a problem.

Tom rocked back in the chair. Watching the fire, he took a long draw on his pipe and puffed smoke out from the side of his mouth. He looked at Mary, nodding. "There was something unnatural about their deaths."

Mary squinted. "What do you mean, unnatural?"

"It's something I feel here," Tom said, tapping his middle right finger to his heart. "Someone or something had designs on this family. They were the only ones hurt in the storm. It was worse where I found them. It is as if the storm ... came after them. Why? I do not know." He puffed his pipe, gazed at Nicholas, and blew smoke, which curled around his head. "In the morning I'll construct a bed for him. Tonight he'll sleep beside the chimney, where he'll be warm, dry, and within arm's reach."

Standing, Mary slid Nicholas into Tom's arms. "All this has been so overwhelming," she said, "but I have new business that I must attend to tonight." She smiled demurely, flicking her hair.

It took Tom an instant to grasp her meaning. She could see the light in his eyes when he did.

"It is not just *we* anymore," Mary said. "There are three of us now." She showed Tom her most serious face. After all the years she loved him, she had always hoped to give him a child but could not. She loved Tom with a love as deep as the first time they locked eyes. Mary felt sixteen again. She strode to the hearth to check her boiling pot, licked by gentle yellow flames. She removed a bowl from the mantle and filled it with rabbit stew from the pot. She set it on the table before Tom, with a chunk of bread and a tub of fresh butter.

"The baker made this sourdough bread yesterday." Mary snickered. "He guaranteed freshness. He said, even if I ate part of it and didn't like it, I could ask for a refund tomorrow."

Tom's face furrowed. In an instant, Tom understood her earlier smile. "Oh, yes." He thought of holding her in his arms tonight.

Mary continued, "The baker began the starter four weeks ago, he said." She cut another slice from the loaf and set it beside his porcelain plate. "Now eat your dinner. All of it," Mary scolded mockingly. She looked at Nicholas in the basket where Tom had placed him. "You mustn't worry now, Tom. It will work out. We'll set a good example … Father."

Father, a word Tom had always longed to hear. "Yes—Mother," he replied, smiling. "I'll eat every bite."

Nicholas is Growing Up

As the weeks progressed, Mary and Tom got used to being a family of three instead of two. Life seemed to become more interesting as they watched the young infant's eyes brighten while he learned new things. Nicholas worked his way into each of their hearts. Tom and Mary worked even harder, yet they seemed to enjoy their struggle; as a family, they gained a new sense of purpose.

Time seemed to rush as Nicholas grew. Of his many projects with Nicholas in mind, Tom made a special cart so Mary could keep him nearby while she tended to her chores. A harness fit over Jingle's back and shoulders. The leads attached to a small canvas-covered buckboard. Tom made it to hold Nicholas's cradle and chair. On the floor of the buckboard, two slots fit the legs of the cradle; two long, taut leather straps arched over the cradle and cinched it in place. The straps were locked with silver buckles the width of a man's hand. Jingles moved Nicholas from place to place as he followed Mary. The inseparable trio became a common sight throughout the homestead and in town, with Nicholas repeating every sound and movement he encountered. He proved to be a fast learner.

After learning to walk, Nicholas showed himself to be a naturally spirited and curious child. He followed every man, animal, or oddling, mimicking them. An attentive child, Nicholas always watched as Tom and Mary went about their chores. He pretended to do the same chores alongside them. Always busy, always moving, always curious, Nicholas was almost hyperactive, and flitted incessantly. Yet he was able to focus, remember, and recall things easily.

In the barn on a small stool, Mary sat at the cow's flank, poised to milk, when Nicholas sidled up to her. Years had passed since his adoption into the family. Tom's and Mary's hearts burst with pride at the many things Nicholas had accomplished. So many things beyond his six years they had not expected him to know so soon. Nevertheless, he had never milked the cow.

An average-size cow, Patches was dark brown with a white mouth, black snout, and white ankles. She was five feet high at her withers. Nicholas often asked why he wasn't allowed to milk her. Having been circumspect, Mary admitted to herself that perhaps she was a bit overprotective. "Why not?" was a good question. Perhaps it was time.

Again, Nicholas asked, "Mama, why have you never taught me to milk Patches?" He propped his head on his hand, resting his elbow on her shoulder.

"Because cows are very big my son," she said, shaking her head. "This chore is not without danger if you are small. Cows may kick. They can step on you with their heavy hooves."

"Not on purpose. But you're small, and she might not see you."

"You're small too, and will stay small. I will grow bigger," Nicholas said, hugging Mary around her neck. "I'm getting to be big, like Papa." Nicholas poked out his chest and stood high on his toes. He slapped his flat belly and showed her his small bicep. Mary saw determination on his face. He was still small, but he was a good learner.

"Please, Mama."

"You're a fearless young man and pretty fast on the pickup. Okay, Nicholas," Mary said, her confidence in him welling. "You know what? I am going to show you. Most children your age can't do this, but I think you can." She turned on the stool to face him. "Take your left hand," Mary said, "put it on the udder, and gently squeeze and pull down. You try it."

"Like this." He repeated her actions in the air. "Right hand here, left hand there, squeeze, squeeze, pull, and pull." He latched on to Patches' udder. On an impulse, Nicholas aimed a teat at Mary and pulled. A stream of milk shot into Mary's lap "Ha! It worked!"

"Into the bucket, if you please, son," Mary insisted. Nicholas's other attempts were more successful. Mary smiled. "I knew you could. Now, fill that bucket. Then you and Jingles may feed the chickens."

One afternoon while playing in the barn, Nicholas watched Mary transfer milk from the holding tank to the butter churn.

"Mama, may I help you carry that?"

"This might be too heavy for you. I think not."

"Please, Mama."

Never very surprised by his wanting to do things, she turned the handle over to him. He looped both arms around the handle and lifted. He took two steps and slammed the pail to the floor. Milk sloshed and splashed around the rim. Mary could see the determination on his face. Struggling several times with the heavy pail, Nicholas eventually reached the churn. "See, Mama? Told you." He proudly showed her both biceps.

"Yes, I see. You're a big boy now," she said.

As Mary worked, Nicholas wandered the barn, prying and tugging at things. He discovered a four-foot-high slanted wooden door in a rarely visited corner of the barn. With a little pressure, he pushed it open and walked into a hay-filled room. The air was filled with the dust of hay and mold.

"Mama, can you hear me?" he called in his wee voice. "I'm in here. Look, I found something."

"Where are you, Nicholas?" His voice sounded distant and muffled to Mary; she was concerned. She followed the sound and came to the small open door. Ducking down, she entered the small room. The hay was pulled into piles in the corners. It looked as if the cat had nested there.

"What is this?" Nicholas said, the volume of his voice fluctuating, low and muted. He wandered into a corner. Several things appeared tied in a tarp of sailcloth. He glided his hands over the dusty, soiled canvas. The shape was curious and suggestive.

"Mama, what's this?" he asked, but before she could say a word, Nicholas gave the cloth a sharp snap. It flew up, throwing a cloud of dust and hay into the air. Wadding the cloth, Nicholas tossed it aside. "Oh, look," he said softly.

"Oh, my," Mary said from across the small room. Her heart felt light as she inspected his find. Suddenly she was missing the little boy he used to be. "I remember that," she said brightly. "This is the cart we used to take you around in when you were a baby. Papa made that for you. I needed to keep you with me because you were so little."

"It looks old. How old is it?"

"Silly, it's nearly as old as you are," Mary said.

"It doesn't look ten. It looks older. Do I look that old?"

"Certainly not. All things age differently."

"Everything? Well, I never want to look old, Mama. I want to live forever."

"In each person's heart, the people they love live forever in spirit."

"In spirit? Would I be able to play with toys and other people *in spirit*? Does time affect toys and people in different ways? And how can I tell?"

"So full of questions you are," Mary said. "The answers are yes, yes, and yes, especially people. When you look at something aged, you are looking at the toll time and history have taken on it. Now, off to bed. Papa's taking you with him to the castle tomorrow."

Such an inquisitive lad she had the pleasure to bring up. Struck by the profundity of his thinking at only ten years old, Mary smiled with astonishment. But this was only the start. As the years went by, her surprises at his sharpness would only mount.

The King's Request

As a teenage apprentice under Tom, Nicholas's journeys to town became part of his regular routine. As another began, Tom scrubbed down the wagon while Mary cleaned his best clothing, something unusual for their typically mundane trip to Castle Town. Nicholas was wildly curious about what was so special about this trip. Tom finally had to calm Nicholas down. He cautioned the boy that they would be seeing a very important person.

"You are eighteen years old, and as a young man, you will need to stay clean and be on your best behavior," Tom ordered as he scurried to make space in the wagon bed. A little too calmly, Nicholas gave a nonchalant nod and continued to brush down Henry's coat. Feeling guilty about doing too good a job of calming him down, Tom told Nicolas more. He tried to gauge Nicholas's expression. "By royal request, we shall have a private audience with King Alexander Dobromil."

Still apparently, unimpressed, Nicholas finished brushing Henry's coat. Turning his back to the horse, Nicholas flexed Henry's front leg, pulling it up between his own legs to check for stones and the integrity of his shoe. He did that for all four hooves. After filing Henry's steel horseshoes, he brushed them clean.

"Are you not—are you not excited, Nicholas? It's a privilege, don't you think?"

"Sure, Papa. It's a great privilege," Nicholas said flatly.

Now Tom was befuddled. He understood nothing of Nicholas's laissez-faire attitude. "I'll never understand teenagers," he muttered. "But then again, when I was a teen, I hardly understood myself." Scratching his head, Tom continued cleaning out the wagon bed.

By noon, they reached Castle Town, in Castleton County. When they entered the outer castle gate, they gained an escort that stayed with them over the castle bridge, on through the inner castle gate, and into the compound. On foot, Tom and Nicholas followed the gentleman usher assigned by the royal family. They followed him through the great hall to where the royal chamberlain awaited. The chamberlain said nothing he could not gesture. After exchanging a look, Tom and Nicholas followed the chamberlain through an arched passage that led to an anteroom.

"You will wait here until you are summoned," the tall, thin man said.

Startled, Nicholas whispered to Tom that he had thought the man a mute, at first.

Peering down his nose, the thin man scanned them from head to toe. In an instant, he disappeared behind a curtain; in another instant, he was back. Gesturing with his open hand, the thin man showed them their seats. They were covered seats, thinly cushioned, made of hardwood with finely carved frames. Slipping through a narrow door in the anteroom, the thin man vanished again.

As ordered, Tom and Nicholas sat and sat and sat. They entertained themselves by trying to identify sounds echoing through the outside halls.

Tired of sitting, Nicholas stood. Sauntering aimlessly, he inspected the paintings and oil lamps on the walls, empty suits of armor on pedestals, and glassed-in cabinets of religious relics. He reached for a cabinet door.

"Nicholas," Tom whispered, shaking his finger. "Don't ..." Nicholas moved away, shuffling the bottoms of his shoes along the slick floor of shiny marble squares. Impatiently situating his body in the chair, Tom stared at a wall hung with rich Persian tapestries. He also watched Nicholas, who was definitely bored.

"Will I know a king when I see one, Papa? He is His Highness ... right. Will I see that particular ... *Highness*?" Nicholas quipped, sitting back in his chair. He shook his head. "I've never seen a king."

"You will know him because he possesses ... *majesty*," Tom said, having difficulty finding the words, his eyes searching the ceiling. "He's a great man, my son."

"Then he must be a lot like you, Papa," Nicholas said with an arch smile.

"I thank you, but kings are born, not made. Their destinies have been written in the stars long ago."

"Why not made? There are many good men," Nicholas asked. "But there are many bad men too. One cannot just acquire

kingliness—though, in their folly, many have tried. No, my son, I am sure I am unlike Alexander. My hair is white and my muscles are not what they were when I found you. Nor is he much like me. His Majesty is a kingly man, a muscular man, a younger man, his age just short of two score and ten years. And he is about seven feet tall, with auburn hair and steel-blue eyes."

"Seven feet, is he?" asked a voice from across the room. Startled, Tom and Nicholas spun on their seats. A heavy wooden door shut with a click. A six-foot-tall man, in a black tunic trimmed with gold and black trousers, marched forward to stand between their two chairs.

"It was only last week," the man said, "that I heard King Alexander Dobromil was eight feet tall with eyes of light that could see through solid oak." He snickered, leveling his eyes at Tom. Nicholas saw a decorative knife clipped to the man's waist belt of small silver disks. The initials A.D. were set in gemstones.

"I'm sure the king is just a man, like you or ... me." The man pressed his index finger to his chest.

Tom stood and marched to the man. Nicholas remained seated, his back straight in the chair. In the corridor, Nicholas heard a man rushing, loudly denouncing the reputation of another. Through the anteroom door, he saw the man dashing down a dark spiral staircase.

Tom looked the auburn-haired man in the eye. "Sir," Tom snapped, "whoever you are, I don't know whether King Dobromil would appreciate your outrageous critique. Apparently you do not know your own king."

"Oh, but I do, Tom the Toymaker," the man said, his eyes cutting from Tom to Nicholas. "He looks like … me." The man again laid his fingers against the center of his chest. "I am King Alexander Dobromil." He smiled.

Tom immediately genuflected and was humbled. "I am sorry, Your Highness."

Alexander placed his hand beneath Tom's elbow and gently lifted him. "Please, no. We are alone. I have no need to put on airs in my private chambers. Sit," Alexander ordered, pulling Tom to a chair. The King sat backward on another chair, straddling the seat, his arms across the back top edge.

"I have a request," Alexander stated. Their eyes locked on his. "I am arranging a surprise for the queen's birthday. I would like you to make one of those wonderful moving novelties of yours."

"The clockwork automatons?" Tom interjected.

"That, or something equally unique for Queen Isadora's birthday," Alexander said. "If you can do this, I will bestow a gift upon you of rare value. In that vein, your son shall be educated with the children of my court." He smiled. "But first things first. What can you do for my lovely queen?"

Tom and Nicholas began speaking at the same time. Tom held up his finger to Nicholas. "If you know her favorite music, Sire, I shall produce a special music box, with a fenestrated brass disk to reproduce the euphonious tones. It shall be enough to rejuvenate her soul." At the thought of it, Tom could barely sit on the chair. "Oh, it would be something so unique, Sire. She would take it to her heart."

"Along with me, I should hope." Alexander laughed quietly. His eyes smiled. "Walk with me, Tom. I think better on my feet. Your idea is amazing. What a wonderful thought.

"We visited the Castle of Waters a while back. There, my younger brother, Prince Wallace, rules. As I recall, there was a guest there, a young composer and pianist. I do believe he was deaf. He played a piece with which Queen Isadora seemed enthralled. I cannot recall the whole name—piano sonata number ... thirteen, or something. Oh, It was a long name," said the king, rubbing his chin. "I shall have my servant fetch the name and bring it to you."

"*Piano Sonata in C Minor*, Opus 27, Number 13–2. *Allegro molto e vivace*," said Nicholas.

"How did you know that?" asked Alexander. "It was as if you reached into my head and pulled it out."

The boy's eyes darted; he was perplexed himself. "I don't know," Nicholas uttered. "I guessed?" He stared into the king's eyes. Each remained silent a second or two.

"One whale of a *guess*, young man," said the king.

Tom quickly vied for the king's attention. "Yes ... for the music box, Your Highness?" Tom continued. "I shall ask my friend to make the fenestrated disk."

The king and Tom strode from the anteroom several yards down the hall and watched from a window to a far field, where the royal falconer worked his bird. Alexander looked behind Tom. "Where is your boy?" Tom spun from the window. "He was here moments ago." His eyes scanned the hall. "I'm sure he'll turn up."

"I shall expect great work from you," said King Dobromil. Before the courtyard window, the two men shook hands. A bird soared past— not the falcon but a raven. "Then the contract is sealed," the king said.

At that instant, the men heard a curious, soft laughter and boisterous remonstrations beneath the window. Puzzled, they peered down.

The king saw Nicholas. "Tom, is that not your son following my brother, Prince Zili?"

Tom saw Nicholas dodging behind posts, horses, wagons, and other people. "That is he," sighed Tom. "He has snuck away."

Prince Zili was in the throes of dressing down a subordinate general. Nicholas mimicked and mocked Prince Zili's every move. Not only was Tom embarrassed, he was also livid. Tom's orders had been explicit:

Nicholas was to be on his best behavior. Tom had to do something now. He had to put a stop to this.

"Sire, please excuse him. Nicholas is quite impulsive. I must go, Sire, if you please." Tom had to get to the courtyard as quickly as possible, before something bad happened. Rushing down the great hall, Tom heard the king call to him.

"How old is he?" the king shouted.

Tom hesitated in the stairwell. "Eighteen," he said. "But I am unsure whether he will get any older." He ran back to hear the king. So long as the king spoke, Tom could not leave.

"He's bright. Very bright. And he has audacity," said the king, his ear on the muffled laughter in the courtyard. "I would be pleased to have him attend school with my knights. He will become a better man. I have seen Nicholas with the merchants. He is polite, speaks their languages, barters well, knows the cultures, and respects their religions. Much potential he has."

Anxious to leave, Tom nodded and bowed. "Sire, thank you. Thank you most greatly."

Taking pity on him, the king finally waved him away to rescue Nicholas from himself.

Tom galloped down two and three steps at a time. Leaping from the stairwell, he sent up a cloud of dust when his feet hit the courtyard. Tom straightened and tried to look casual. He did not attempt to catch the eye of anyone. He pushed through the ogling crowd while praying the surly Prince Zili had not seen Nicholas; he certainly had not seemed to hear the muted laughter. Quietly coming up behind Nicholas, Tom clasped him hard by the collar and snatched him back into the shadows.

"What are you thinking?" Tom scolded, flicking Nicholas behind the ear with his middle finger. "That is the king's brother, Prince Zili." The prince was chastising his subordinate, loosing a harangue of insults. The general he reproved kept saying, "It was Jax."

"Ouch, Father. What was that for?" Nicholas whimpered, ducking to avoid another flick.

"What do you think you're doing?"

"Nothing. I was just teasing. I did not know you saw me. Who's Jax?"

"None of that is your business. Yes, I saw you. So did King Alexander," Tom chided gruffly. "I always see what you are doing."

Then his voice softened. He loved Nicholas and only wanted the best for him. He could not stay mad. "Please be careful. You do not want to ..." Shaking his head, Tom coaxed Nicholas into the deeper shadows, beneath an awning, out of view of the prince. "You don't want to end up in the king's dungeon," Tom whispered, his eyes cutting to Zili.

"No, Papa," Nicholas whispered, looking puzzled. "But you said Alexander was king."

"It's not the king about whom I worry," Tom said, glancing across the courtyard at Prince Zili, who had just struck the general across the face with a riding crop.

"Get Henry ready," Tom ordered. "It's time to go home. We will stop by the church to see your uncle, Father Bernard, for your next lesson guide."

"Excuse me," murmured a female voice as Tom and Nicholas turned to the stairwell in the great stone wall. A fair maiden with smiling hazel eyes stood before them. She looked to be near Nicholas's age. At first Nicholas could see nothing but her eyes and her auburn hair, braided in a mound atop her head. Tom looked to her open right palm, with her delicate thumb and index finger.

She reached for the empty, open leather tie hung around Nicholas's neck. "It is quaint. Where did you get it?" she asked. Nicholas looked to Tom, who shook his head. She asked no further. "You are the carpenter Tom and son," she said. Tom nudged Nicholas to introduce himself. Tongue-tied, Nicholas merely murmured.

Curious about the befuddled Nicholas, she reached to the necklace.

"Your name?" she asked.

"Nicholas," Tom answered for him. "His name is Nicholas; he is trying to say. I've never seen him behave this way. He is not usually, so ... so ..."

"Trifling?" she softly admonished. Nicholas frowned and squinted. "What?"

She bounced the leather lanyard on Nicholas's neck. "Does this hang on that?" she asked. "He dropped this during his rather ... childish performance out there." She dropped the heart-shaped pendant into Tom's palm. Nicholas reflexively clasped his empty leather necklace, only now appreciating that the maiden had returned an heirloom he hadn't yet realized he'd lost.

"His Highness Prince Zili found it in the dirt. For some reason, young Nicholas, he thought it mine." She smiled coyly. "I would be less careless around the prince. He is not known for his sense of humor."

Stepping away, the lady turned a corner at the great wall of stone and was soon out of sight.

"Papa, who was that?"

"Now you find your tongue," Tom muttered, pointing up the stairwell. "A distraction, Nicholas; a distraction. That's who she is. Now run ahead of me. Rig Henry. It's getting late, and we must get to the church."

When they arrived at the church, Father Bernard was in the vestry, a room sharing the wall behind the altar. He was preparing a sacrament kit. Exiting the room, Father Bernard had turned to climb the stair to the altar when he saw Tom and Nicholas stopping at the first pew. They knelt to make the sign of the cross.

"Oh, there you are," Father Bernard said. "I was wondering ... it is that day, is it not? Yes. Yes. Sorry. I must postpone our lessons for today," he said to Nicholas. "I've been called to the castle."

"How ironic, Uncle," Nicholas said. "We were just there."

"And you didn't know? Did no one tell you?"

"Know what?" Tom asked. "Tell us what?"

"Oh ... Well, obviously they are keeping it hush-hush. I only sent word to your wife, my little sister Mary, to tell you this very afternoon. But of course you were *there*, then on your way *here*, and not *there*—not home, that is." Father Bernard said. He was the only one amused at his wordplay.

Then his expression darkened.

"And you were sending word to tell me what?" Tom asked.

"That Princess Angelica is ill and I was asked to come to the castle. I thought I might see you there." He clasped prayerful hands and quickly crossed himself. "She may be dying. And, of course, I must tend to the needs of her soul."

Beneath his arm, Father Bernard carried a rectangular metal box that he had packed for his trip. Within it, he carried his priestly sash, wine, wafers, frankincense, and myrrh.

Nicholas shook his head, "We were just there. The king said nothing to us."

"Why would he, my son?" Tom said. "He is king. He need not tell us anything. Moreover, what could we do for her? We are not physicians."

"Did you know, Papa? I mean about Princess Angelica."

Tom nodded. "I knew he had a small child. I recall the celebration of her birth a dozen years ago … nothing more. They keep her close to hearth and home."

"Well, we won't keep you," Tom said, turning to Bernard. "Is Father Bruno here? And my sibling, Father Mark?" Fr. Bernard nodded.

"Mary knew we were coming and … and … Pass to me that sack you've been toting, Nicholas. Ah, yes. Mary has sent her famous buttermilk biscuits and apple pie for you to share with Fr. Mark and Fr. Bruno," said Tom, "Where are they?"

Father Bernard lifted his eyes. "You will find them in the rectory. They will be glad to get food cooked with the touch of such a special woman, for a change. When you arrive home, do tell my sister I miss her."

The Princess Is Ill

During the trip home, Nicholas looked from the mountain road southwest across the forest treetops and into the valley below. He marveled at the distant blue-and-yellow shaded mountain at the horizon, the sun setting.

"Papa." His mind was relaxed by the constant, slow rocking of the wagon over the rutted road. "I have an idea. A wonderful thought, I think." Henry was loping before them; the wagon crept along. The rusty springs beneath the bench seat creaked.

Holding the reins lazily in his fingers, Tom eyed Nicholas on the bench beside him. "Tell me your wonderful idea, son."

"The beautiful sunset has inspired me." He listened to the clop of Henry's feet as they descended, "I want to make a special doll."

"You're much too old for a doll."

"Not for me, Papa."

"I know, I know. I was jesting." Tom grinned. "For whom?"

"Princess Angelica." Nicholas stared ahead. "I want to produce a beautiful angel doll to protect and comfort the princess."

Stopping high in the Carpathian Mountains, Tom and Nicholas set camp for the night. Tall cedar trees bounded the campsite. After building a fire, Tom prepared to feed Henry, who paced up to Tom's side. He harnessed the feedbag to Henry's face and inspected Henry's shoes.

"Look what I've found," Nicholas said. Among the loose branches, he had found wood he thought he could use for the princess's doll.

"You'll need more substantial pieces," Tom said. "And you'll need to be granted the magic of the Linkage ... both halves."

"Both?" Nicholas muttered, walking from the perimeter of the campfire light into the edge of the surrounding forest.

Standing next to a cedar tree, Nicholas closed his eyes. He lowered to his knees, placing his hands prayerfully together. "Mother cedar, will you share your wood with me, that I may make an angel doll to guard Princess Angelica, the daughter of King Dobromil?"

He touched the tree. He could feel vibrations—not just from that tree but all the trees. He felt a linking, a pulling, and a tugging of his soul as if someone had reached into his chest to connect with him. They understood him. The name of the doll came to his mind.

"I will name her Angelis, to honor your magic." Nicholas repeated his request for each of the materials he needed to create the doll. Responding to his request, the treetops aggressively rustled, and the branches knocked with one another. Mystic whispers shook the leaves.

Several feet from him, a branch fell that perfectly suited his purpose. Nicholas stacked the wood into the wagon bed for the trip back to Elfin.

⁂

"Is Nicholas still in the barn?" asked Mary. "He spends many hours out there, all his time. I hardly ever see him. Yesterday, he worked until his food got cold. I had to give it to Jingles."

"I'm sure Jingles didn't mind." Tom looked at Mary. "He's working very hard on the doll for the princess. He will not give up until it is right. You know how he feels about the happiness of a child. It's all-important."

For three long days, Nicholas worked around the clock to make the princess's angel from the enchanted wood. The finest porcelain formed her face. Her hair was made of the finest yellow silk found in the village, her wings of handmade lace woven lovingly by Mary. The doll was clad in a gown of royal purple velvet, accented with beads of silver and pearl, her shoes the finest silver. Into its face, Nicholas set two of the bluest stones ever seen; they would be her eyes. With pigments created by the flora gnomes, Nicholas painted its face and nails. As the last touch, Nicholas threaded a dried twig of buttercups through her hair. He examined her. Satisfied, he knew only one thing was left to do.

From his father's workshop, he took the two-foot-tall doll into the light of the full moon. Nicholas looked into the heavens. Polaris sparkled to his left. He faced the moon in the northeastern sky. He raised the doll high above his head.

"Her name is Angelis. Will you please share your magic with her to heal Princess Angelica?"

The scant clouds parted. Glittering rays of the aurora braided into a beam that shot from the sky through the eyes of the doll. Energized, her eyes flashed in response. The first half of Nicolas's prayer had been granted.

"Now the princess needs your protection as well," Nicholas prayed. Spiraling down from the heavens, starlight encircled Angelis's angel wings. The light permanently bound itself to her. The Linkage had granted its approval. Her wings fluttered. The ethereal figure of a living cherub hovered above and then sank into the doll. The second half was granted. Nicholas watched with amazement and satisfaction as the dried buttercups quickened, becoming alive and fresh.

Nicholas nodded; he had done well.

The Gift

Tom and Nicholas returned to the castle of King Alexander Dobromil to deliver Queen Isadora's birthday present. Always staying the required five steps ahead, the tall, thin chamberlain escorted Tom and Nicholas down the great hall to the throne room.

They walked and walked and walked, listening to their footfalls reverberating throughout the long stone corridor. Both had much time to pray the king would enjoy the gift to his daughter. Over their shoulders, they carried their sacks like sheep shearers carrying bags of wool, but these weighty bags seemed to grow in mass with every stride.

After what seemed an eternity, they came to a large, slatted, dark oak door. Iron hinges supported it, while at its edge a large iron lock secured it. Two soldiers in helmets, chest armor, and swords, held point up toward their shoulders, guarded the door. At the sight of the chamberlain, they stood at ease. They stared flatly at Tom and Nicholas.

As before, the chamberlain did not go through the main door. Instead, he stepped around an abutment and entered through a hidden door in the wall, a panel no wider than he. Nicholas had heard rumors that the castle walls were laced with inner passages, spy passages, passing through or behind very private and secure areas.

They waited. After several moments, footsteps approached from behind the door. The door creaked open just enough for a small man to step through. Tom and Nicholas smelled the aroma of cedar and rose water. The man, no more than five feet high, glanced up to the guards and gestured for them to stand aside. He was clad in a black-and-blue tunic with wide shoulders, and a coif of shoulder-length black hair. The small man's eyes darted from Nicholas to Tom to the sacks over their shoulders.

"I am the royal durward, keeper of his majesty's doors," he growled, his voice disproportionately low. "I shall take you to see His Majesty. He will meet with you in the throne room."

Nicholas and Tom entered the grand room. The durward stood in the rear, watching them stride toward the king. King Dobromil sat crosswise on the throne, his legs draped carelessly over the arm as if he were prepared for the arms to carry him.

"Come closer." Alexander beckoned, waving his arms. "Come. Do not be alarmed." As they strode the narrow red carpet ending at the throne, they could see the king was dressed in hunting gear. His longbow lay on the floor beside his throne.

"Perhaps, today, His Majesty does not look as you might expect," said King Dobromil. "I have been on a boar hunt." He smiled. "Not expecting company, the swine had not cleaned up for me. To fix that, he made sure I became as filthy as he." The king rubbed his hands along his outer thighs, soiling his trousers more. "He was more than pleased to share his stench with me."

Alexander positioned himself properly on the throne, his feet flat on the floor. He leaned forward, gazing at the sacks Tom and Nicholas towed behind. "I fear the king could use a royal shower. Don't you think?"

"Yes, Your Highness," Nicholas retorted impulsively, quickly regretful of his thoughtless answer.

"That was rhetorical, young Nicholas," the king said flatly. The room became silent. Dobromil laughed and rubbed beneath his nose. "He's right, Old Tom. Your boy has brass. One day, everyone everywhere shall know his name."

Tom was lost for words.

Embarrassed, Nicholas was about to drop his head, when Tom nudged him with an elbow in the flank. King Dobromil dipped his fingers into a water bowl brought him by his butler.

"Tom the Toymaster and son, proper greetings from a slightly cleaner king. I understand you have something for me?" the king said, pointing to the sacks behind Nicholas and Tom.

"Your Highness, this is the gift you requested for the queen."

"Show me what you have."

Close to the throne, the butler lit a platter of cedar and rosewood. He marched away furtively, holding his nose as the aromatic smoke wafted through the room.

Tom stepped closer. "We spoke of a music box, Your Highness. It is combined with this."

Several young men, friends of Nicholas, came through the throne-room door, led by the royal durward. They carried thick sheets of stained glass, mirrors, soil, and wood. Tom withdrew thorny plants and flowers from his sack. He situated them into the three boxes, six feet by three feet by two feet, that the men quickly locked together.

"Terrariums?" asked King Dobromil.

"Yes, Your Highness. But they are no ordinary terrariums. I constructed them from wood, soil, and plants from the Orphic Forest. Here, Your Highness, see? Allow me to turn them to the side. They have mirrored backs so Queen Isadora will be able to see all sides of the foliage at once. At the center is a gilded cage with a mated pair of mynah birds to keep her company."

A curious expression passed over the king's face.

"They speak, Your Highness," Tom said. "Turn this key six times—it will play her favorite song. Oh, Your Highness, it will bring her great joy, I assure you." Tom bowed. "I hope it is what you had in mind."

The king smiled widely. "It is much more than I expected. She will be quite happy."

"Sire, you remember the great creativity of my son, whom you lauded. He has something for your family."

"How could I forget the creativity of a young man with the stones to deride my overly intense brother, Prince Zili?" The king laughed. "You must be more cautious, Nicholas. Unlike me, my brother takes himself much too seriously on a good day, and lately he has had many bad days. How shall I say? He lacks ... a developed sense of humor.

But allow me to change subjects." The king stared into the face of each man and pointed to Nicholas. "Tom, he must look like his mother, for he does not resemble you."

"Nor does he resemble my wife, Sire. He is the child of your father's late physician, who was killed in the forest eighteen years ago."

"I remember now," said Alexander. "The message from the bird of smoke."

"I thank you for receiving us and accepting the gift I bear, Sire. But as I mentioned, Nicholas has a gift to give."

"Indeed," said the king.

"After our previous visit, I learned your daughter was ill," Tom said. Nicholas began searching his sack. "I took— Pardon. *My son* took the liberty of making her a special doll." Tom whispered, "Nicholas, do you have— Ah." Nicholas withdrew the doll from his sack. "Excellent," said Tom. "Show His Highness. Go on."

Nicholas withdrew passed the wrapped parcel to the king. "If you please, Your Highness."

Alexander began unwrapping the parcel.

"I made her with all the love in my heart," said Nicholas, "with materials from the Orphic Forest."

"Again, the Orphic Forest." The king smiled. He turned the doll over in his hands. He held it to the light. He sighted it as he would an arrow. "Fine work for such a young man. It has a ... feel to it I can't describe," said the king. "Is he a worthy apprentice, Tom?"

Tom nodded.

Nicholas trod closer. "Will you ..." He hesitated.

"Ask, Nicholas," ordered the king.

"Will you allow Princess Angelica to have this humble gift?" Nicholas looked for Tom's approval.

The king clapped his hands sharply. The durward hastened to the king's side.

"Summon the guards," the king commanded. "Escort Queen Isadora and her lady-in-waiting to the throne room at once."

Within several moments, the guards returned with Queen Isadora and her young lady-in-waiting. The chamberlain stepped inside the throne room door. His hands behind him, he stood erect, his nose lifted. "Her Highness, Queen Isadora, and her courtier."

"Good morning, my queen. Do you know Tom Claus, my carpenter as of late?" the king asked. Queen Isadora nodded, stepping toward her throne beside King Dobromil. "Tom has brought the present I asked him to build for your birthday."

"Thank you, my husband," said the queen, bowing her head to the king. She circled the gift and examined it. "Terrariums. How wonderful. So rustic. To have a bit of the Orphic Forest for my own." She slid her hands along the wood of the tall glass boxes. She glanced in the mirrors. "Tom, this is beautiful. A touch of summer all the year for my bower. It will be lovely in my chambers."

Tom and Nicholas bowed to the king and queen. Her lady-in-waiting came around the terrarium. Stepping up to the throne, she stopped at the queen's right. As their heads lifted, Tom and Nicholas saw Princess Sarah beside the queen.

Nicholas's mouth fell agape. Tom's eyes widened.

The king's eyes shifted from theirs to the one at whom they stared. "I think there is something I do not know," muttered the king. "I take it that you three have met?"

"Something like that, Sire," Tom said.

"I–I–I am ..." Nicholas stuttered.

"Still tongue-tied I see." Sarah smirked, moving closer to Nicholas. "You really should have that checked."

"Ladies," said the king, "this is Nicholas—"

"The mute." Sarah snickered. "I can t-t-talk, Your Highness."

"Can't or can?" Sarah quipped. Her expression was bland until she could not hold in another snicker.

"Nicholas made a doll for Princess Angelica," said the king. "He made it with materials from the Orphic Forest. He believes it will heal the princess."

"I shall not trifle with my daughter's health," said the queen. "She is in dire need of a physician."

"Nicholas is the son of *my* father's doctor," said King Alexander.

"Is he a doctor?" Isadora snapped.

"No, but—"

"So what can he do?"

"If he can do nothing, he can no harm," said the king "Only make her happy. Talk to him. Hear what he has to say."

Isadora yielded to the king.

"Now, since you two seem to be on speaking terms—Princess Sarah, will you kindly take Nicholas to my daughter's chamber, please?" said the king. He beckoned a guard to come closer, a faithful knight. The knight marched from a door in the wall behind the throne, where he watched. The door closed with a click. Nicholas was puzzled; he had not seen where the knight entered the room. *Those secret passages*, he thought. "My trusted guard, Andrew, will escort them," declared the king.

"My pleasure, Sire," Andrew said, bowing.

The trio entered the chamber of Princess Angelica who was lying in a four-poster canopy bed, covered in a quilt made of goose down. Tom and Nicholas could clearly see the princess was pale and frail. She lay so still that she herself appeared as a doll. Nicholas removed the doll he had made from the rest of its binding. The princess's eyes were sunken. She tried to smile but coughed instead.

"It is the bleeding disease. Her skin is bruised; her bowel movements have been as black as coal," the king whispered, leaning near Nicholas's ear. His voice broke "It … it is a scourge among my family. It is what eventually killed my father, King Richard."

Nicholas tucked the doll beside her thin, pale arms. "Her name is Angelis," Nicholas told her. Her eyes barely open, the princess attempted to lift her head. Nicholas held his hand out, cautioning her not to try. "No, don't." He pressed the doll to her side. "She is yours to keep. I believe she will help you soon to feel better."

Princess Sarah situated the doll, placing her young niece's arms around it so that it now rested on her chest.

Already on one knee, Nicholas slipped closer to the bed. He said, his eyes brightening, "Hug her as tightly as you can and make a wish." Nicholas glanced over his shoulder to the king and Isadora. Kneeling on the opposite side of the bed, Princess Sarah appeared tentative, but she held her tongue.

Nicholas continued, "If her eyes sparkle, your wish will come true." Sarah stood and stepped back, her eyes moist and her nose and cheeks red. Tom stepped behind her. Nicholas looked down at the child princess. Princess Sarah blew her a kiss. "Sleep tight, dear Princess," Sarah said. "I will return after seeing Nicholas to the door."

Princess Sarah, Nicholas, and Tom walked to the door of the princess's chamber. "It was very kind of you to do this for the princess," Sarah said. "I had not seen a smile on her face in a fortnight. I do not know what you can do. Sorcery has not worked."

"It is not sorcery, Your Highness," said Nicholas. "What?" he asked, seeing her flushed face.

"Nothing," Sarah said somberly.

"I would do the same for any child," Nicholas softly said. Sarah looked up. "I mean that all good children are special," said Nicholas. "And all children are good. Children should be happy and playing, not sad or ill. I just want her to feel better. Why are you crying, Your Highness, if I may ask?"

Tom placed his hand on Nicholas's shoulder.

"It's fine, Tom." She looked wonderingly at Nicholas. "There is some magic in you," Sarah said, smiling somewhat. "You chose an angel, one of her favorite things. How did you know?"

"I guessed," muttered Nicholas.

That night as the castle slept, Sir Andrew, Alexander's young knight errant, stood guard outside. He marched before the princess's door. No light shone beneath her door to the hall. Lit only by torchlight, the musty halls appeared ominously barren. The clatter from Sir Andrew's sword echoed through the castle. Closely guarding her room, he marched five feet in a straight line and turned on his heel, every bootfall reverberating. On every other turn, the tip of his scabbard scratched the wall.

Suddenly from beneath the door of Princess Angelica's chambers burst the most brilliant blue light Andrew had ever seen. A high-pitched squeal shattered the night silence. Rays poured through every seam of the door. For an instant, the corridor shone bright as day. Andrew shielded his eyes while clanging an alarm bell on the wall. From nearly all areas of the castle, the corridors came alive with soldiers streaming to the princess's room.

At first, the door was jammed and did not open. Kicking, Andrew loosed the lock and flung it open. In he dashed, a throng of soldiers behind. They stopped abruptly in their tracks. They formed a perimeter around her bed. None could believe the sight before their eyes.

On the floor in front of her bed sat Princess Angelica. Pallor gone from her face, roses in her cheeks, she giggled, scooting closer to her dolls, no longer upon the shelves. Her dolls moved and talked on their own. Princess Angelica pretended to serve them tea. She seemed oblivious to the amazed guards.

Angelis hovered high in the air above the princess, her wings fluttering in the blue light, a soft breeze billowing. A marionette jester doll, out of his chair in the corner, juggled four teddy bears blowing bubbles. The ballerina dolls twirled on their toes. Teddy bears and plush puppies tussled as they chased a ball. Two dozen toy soldiers marched in formation, lining up before Andrew and the castle guard.

Slack-jawed, the human soldiers lowered their swords and guns. They smiled. Someone among the crowd whispered, "A miracle."

The princess was in no need of protection.

At her ceiling, a rain of shimmering starlight hovered in the air. Princess Angelica stood and giggled to the soldiers. She curtsied. In awe, they dropped to their knees.

"Hello, Sir Andrew," Princess Angelica said. "Would you join our tea party?"

He barely found the words to speak. "N-no thank you, Your Highness. But I should like to call your parents, if that pleases you."

"Yes, Sir Andrew," Princess Angelica said. "Please do."

Andrew sent the guards to call her father, King Alexander, her mother, Queen Isadora, and her aunt, Princess Sarah Morning-Light.

The guards rushed to the door, bottlenecking at the doorjamb. Andrew's eyes never turned from the princess. He pushed through with ease.

In less than seconds, it seemed, they made way for the royals. The soldiers' ranks parted to reveal the princess standing in the middle of the room. Rushing forward, the king scooped her into his arms.

"Are you all right, Father?" Princess Angelica asked. "You're crying. Is there something wrong? Kings should not cry. Should they?"

"This king does, my child. And nothing is wrong. Nothing. Everything is just fine." He, Queen Isadora, and Princess Sarah gathered close for a hug. The doll Angelis was tightly snuggled beneath Angelica's arm.

Chapter 2

THE SHERIFF

Responding to Zili's tug on the reins, the black stallion slowed from a hard gallop. From a canter to a trot to a pace, Zili swayed upon the horse, finally bringing it to a stop. Foam collected at its lips. It danced in place from side to side. Zili tugged gently on the reins to guide it to a right-angle stance relative to his target, a deer among the trees. The horse snorted as it turned. With one hand, Zili gently stroked the stallion's mane. With the other, he slipped an arrow from his saddle quiver.

"Boy!" Zili shouted. A squire charged to the flank of Zili's horse with a small leather bag. From it he removed a black ceramic jar the size of a plum.

Zili plunged the tip of the arrow into the jar and rubbed it upon the back of a small yellow frog within. Bowing, the squire backed away, carefully pressing the lid flush on the jar. Zili examined the glistening tip of the arrow and smiled.

Still swaying on the horse, Zili steadied the animal and nocked the arrow on the bowstring. Swiftly swiping his dark, oily hair from before his right eye, he estimated the deer's distance at less than ten yards. He sighted down the arrow shaft while watching delightedly as his dinner grazed the forest duff, oblivious to Zili's gastronomic intentions.

His right arm remaining straight, Zili elevated his bow. With a pinch draw, Zili tugged the bowstring taut. The string strained against the leather wrap around his index finger and thumb. He took careful aim.

"You walking tin of soup," Zili murmured. The six-point buck lifted its head. It turned its large black eyes downfield to Zili.

"That's right. Don't move." Zili grinned.

The arrows fledge aside his chin, Zili prepared to release. The horse took a step. Hearing the horse's hooves crunch, the startled buck moved deep into the brush. Perturbed, Zili yanked the reins, causing the horse to whinny and spin. Zili had no clear shot. Dropping its guard, the deer wandered from the brush back into Zili's line of sight.

Zili nodded. "Because I am sheriff," he muttered, "I could actually arrest myself for poaching the king's game." He took a slow, deep breath. "But not today," he sneered, his lips wet. The deer presented its tan, broad flank. Zili twisted in his saddle toward the deer.

The youthful squire placed his finger to his lips for the other five equestrians to hush.

Zili loosed the arrow.

Snap. A twig broke at the rear just as Zili loosed the arrow, and another and another. Hooves pounded the forest litter. The deer dashed away. *Whoosh—thud.* The arrows struck the trunk of the tree behind which the deer had once stood.

Zili flung his bow to the ground and whirled on his saddle. "*What idiot*—"

A youthful rider came up to Zili, one not in the hunting party. Settling his breathless steed, the youth met Zili's furious eyes. "I beg your pardon. I'm sorry, Prince Zili."

"Sorry *nothing*. You've chased away my dinner!" Zili shouted, his eyes large, the corners of his mouth pulled down, tacky with saliva.

"I've ridden miles, Your Highness," the young man breathed. Head bobbing, the rider's horse sidled, spun, and whinnied. "For I have urgent news."

"Young scamp, this had better be important." Zili snorted.

"Cristobel, your beloved horse, Sire. You left word that someone should inform you."

"Spit it *out*, child!" Zili shouted.

"He is ... he is dying. You must come quickly, Sire."

Swaying his stallion in the direction of the castle, Zili reared his horse. Pitching forward, he stood in his stirrups and slapped his horse on the rump. He dashed through the forest, his men in close pursuit, hooves pounding the dirt, clods of soil hoisted in the air.

Over the countryside, their horses' hooves thundered. As they exited the forest, they were spotted by the gatekeeper from the castle steeple. The drawbridge fell. Beneath the underpass and over the wooden timbers, the horses' footfalls were like a storm. Through the bailey they streaked, passing the castle markets and tannery.

Amid a cloud of dust, Zili raised his hand, stopping before the royal stables. Zili leaped from his panting horse and sprinted past the junior blacksmith standing at the open stable door. Seeing him, young and old men snapped to attention, while making sure they were out of Zili's way. They whispered, "Prince Zili," his name reverberating through the stable.

He entered a guarded stall, the largest at the rear of the stable, his feet brushing across the hay-littered floor. There, he saw the senior royal farrier on his knees, rubbing a white horse's broad neck. The horse lay on its left side, its eyes sunken, its breathing labored. Its right forelimb was wrapped with white bandages stained with yellow-green pus and blood. Some of the skin above the bandage had become black.

The farrier's eyes turned up to Zili. "Cristobel's time is short," the farrier softly cautioned. "He is an old horse, Sire. You have owned him since—"

"I was in my twenties," Zili said, dropping to his knees. He studied the horse's broken foreleg. "Has he no chance?" Zili entreated.

"No chance of healing, Sire. The break in his forelimb is fatal. It has become gangrenous. I should relieve him of his suffering, Sire."

Zili's eyes snapped up. "I said no."

"But Sire—"

"Are you deaf, old man? Or stupid?" Zili scolded. "I just said no!"

"But ... he will suffer, die in pain. I must end his suffering, Sire."

"Suffering is a part of life. End it, aye, I should, but I cannot do it," Zili said, tears in his eyes. The farrier looked away. "This horse is my old and only friend. He never wanted anything from me. He never stole from me that which should have been mine." Zili clenched his fist. "I should have had that general shot in the courtyard for this. That weak-minded codpiece would listen to the tricks of a troll. He should never have ridden him. If he had not been Princess Marinna's brother …"

"Prince Wallace's brother–in–law, Sire?"

"Aye. I would have had him beheaded on the spot, the fool.

"I remember when I received the horse," Zili lamented. "In the week of my father's death, I was awarded this great horse. The physician summoned me to the bedchamber of my father, King Richard Dobromil of the Aurora Kingdoms. My mother, Queen Frances, was at his side, holding vigil over his death. My little brother, Prince Wallace, and his betrothed, Lady Marinna of Waters, were there. My twin brother, Prince Alexander, was also there, as was the royal scribe and four members of the royal guard. The royal physician Christopher Northland attended the king."

"Why were you not in attendance, Your Highness?" asked the farrier, wiping down Cristobel's neck with cool water. "And what of Isadora?"

"She searched for me to tell me of my father's impending death. But she said she had no need of me when she found me in the bed of another." Zili huffed. "She said I should return to the whore with whom she found me."

"What did you do, Sire?"

"I did as I was told," Zili said smugly. "I *came* as quickly as I could with the coquette attending me. I then came as quickly as I could to my father's vigil. Aye, Farrier, I was there in poor time." Zili rubbed around the eye of Cristobel. "When King Richard squeezed my mother's hand, she leaned in. Her head to my father's face, her ear to his lips, she listened to his last words. 'Come, place your ear near me,' he said, 'that you shall hear who will be king.' My mother looked at the scribe. 'The king has ordered you to draw near and record his words exactly as I relay them,' she said. With pen and parchment, the scribe did as he was ordered. Mother placed her ear next to the mouth of my father."

Emerging from his reflection, Zili turned his own ear down to Cristobel's chest to listen to the horse's breathing. Its heart was slow, beating with reduced vigor.

Zili continued, "My mother relayed his words. She said, 'Alexander has proven himself fluent in the cultures of the peoples of the Aurora Kingdoms. He listens before he acts. Therefore,' she said to me ..." Zili paused his story. His eyes fixed on nothing. "Then my mother hesitated. Everyone looked at her. She looked at me and said, '*Alexander* shall be the next to sit on the throne of Illuminae.' I should have been happy, but her words were a knife in my heart. 'Wise in commerce, Zili,' she said, 'you shall be sheriff of the Aurora Kingdoms. Wallace will take Lady Marinna of the kingdom of Waters as his bride.'" Zili smirked. "So Wallace rules. He is now known as Crown Prince Wallace of Waters." Zili laughed. "So were my king's last words about me."

Zili muttered, repeating "Zili shall be sheriff" in undertones. He looked at the farrier and at a long pike leaning in the corner of the stall. Zili stood.

"A curse on me," Zili snapped. "He might as well have hurled this through my heart." Grasping the pike, point down, he plunged it through Cristobel's heart. The horse squealed, shivered, and closed its eyes.

As he watched his horse die, Zili remembered storming from his father's death vigil, checking Alexander in the shoulder as he passed. Confused by Zili's ire, the people attending the king's death whispered among themselves. Not long after declaring Alexander his successor, the king passed away in his sleep. That night the northern lights did not appear above the Carpathian Mountains. The kingdoms of Illuminae and Waters were dark as sadness reached to all their borders.

Prince Zili became sheriff of the Aurora Kingdoms but remained filled with envy and fury because he was not crowned king.

He grew to hate his brother Alexander but learned to dissemble his personal animosity in the presence of the new king. Nightly and for years, Zili paced his chambers, cursing his brother, calling him an obsequious, boot licking fool. He vowed Alexander should not complete his reign.

The farrier covered the horse's face with a towel. He was unnerved by Zili's treasonous rant and tried to hear none of it. He turned away.

"I should be king," Zili muttered, as he had for twenty years. "I am the *rightful* king." Zili strode away. "I will set this right. By the time I'm finished with these foolish peasants, the name Alexander Dobromil will be so rotten to the mouth that no one will *dare* whisper it in the dark!"

Zili's Anger

Two days ride from the castle of King Alexander, Prince Zili, with two dozen tired and dusty soldiers on horseback, arrived in the village of Elfin. The large horses and their riders meandered the small village square, crowding out the usual loiterers, shoppers, and passersby. Making themselves more unwelcome, some of his dismounted men wandered in and out of the market and drinking halls. Many caused trouble by harassing young maidens or bullying the men attempting to protect their women's virtue. Unruly troublemakers pulled at baskets looped around shoppers' arms, or snatched loaves of bread from old women. Others tormented or scolded old men for being old. Other of Zili's men merely satisfied themselves by getting drunk, paying naros to young boys to find them ale.

"Shall we stop them, Your Highness?" asked Zili's captain, astride the horse next to him.

"Why?"

"I stopped two of the men determined to reproduce the crucifixion by nailing a priest to a cross."

"I should like to have seen that," smirked Zili. "You are much too serious, captain."

"Me, Sire?" intoned the captain, shaking his head.

Zili gave him a dismissive glance. "Let them have their fun," he said. "Soon they shall have much to do."

Zili's captain watched with detached empathy for the people his men persecuted. With one hand gesture, Zili ordered him to sound a trumpet.

Timorously coming out of their houses and businesses, curious onlookers began to gather.

From his horse, the captain scanned over the heads of the crowd. "Hear ye, hear ye. By order of King Alexander Dobromil of Illuminae, *new* taxes shall be collected on this day by Prince Zili, Sheriff of Illuminae."

Quiet timid chatter and the word *new* hastened on the lips of the crowd.

"Anyone not meeting the assigned taxes shall immediately receive ten lashes of the royal whip." The towns people glanced a large, bald, muscular man as tall as Zili's horse, clad in tan buckskin. He stood by the captain, cracking a whip in the air.

"By decree," the captain shouted, "everyone present in the village must be present to witness said floggings." The large man snapped the tip of the whip near a donkey's ear. The animal brayed and kicked wildly. Impertinent laughter percolated through the band of soldiers.

"Anyone, or any ass, found not in attendance will be immediately executed," the man said flatly. The soldiers still mounted presented their arms.

From his high horse, the captain pointed to a merchant, silently directing his men to sweep clean the merchant's selling table. They did so with their arms. Zili's men overturned his table and his barrels, dumping fish, bread, and fruit to the dirt. Having emptied the table of its wares, the soldiers carted it to the middle of the square. His heels nudging, Zili urged his horse to the table.

"Let us be friends," Zili said, sardonically. "So we may have a productive afternoon on such a bright and sunny day." He breathed deeply. "There isn't a cloud on the horizon."

"Until now," whispered someone in the crowd.

From his pommel bag, Zili withdrew a leather book, thick with sheets of parchment eight inches deep. His eyes coolly sought for and spotted the brazen dissenter in the crowd. From atop his horse, Zili leaned down and dropped the book to the table—*thud*. He carefully removed two bottles of ink from his pocket, one black and one red. A soldier took them from his fingers and set them upon the table, next to a quill pen.

Zili scanned over the heads of the crowd, his expression determined and unsmiling—even regretful, he hoped. He wanted the people of Elfin to know he felt their anguish. Certainly, if he could get them to believe, he might believe also.

"This book—" the captain's voice reverberated, "—contains the names of every man, woman, and child in the Aurora Kingdoms, along with the amount of taxes assessed. Step lively and step forward. Pay your due to the king; make your mark as proof of payment."

Dismounting, his nose high, Zili took a seat at the table.

The villagers stood in a long line leading up to the table where Sheriff Zili sat with a soldier at his left. Flanking the table stood six soldiers: two on each end of the table and two others bracketing the person paying the tax. As the tax was paid, a soldier collected the money, counted it, and placed it into a burlap sack.

One villager, a young family man, approached the table with a look of question on his face.

The soldier read the book and looked up at the peasant. "You owe fifteen naros."

"Sire," he said, turning to Zili, "I have only five naros." His voice was strong but apologetic. "I did not know the taxes came due today, nor did I know they were raised."

Zili glared up. "You're the one."

"The one? What do you mean, Sire?" the villager said.

"The one who thought I was the cloud on the horizon," Zili said, "Sire, I—I—" The man stuttered and quaked.

"You will not address the prince," the captain snapped.

"Yes, but—"

"But nothing. That you did not know taxes were due is of no consequence to me," the soldier stated. "King Dobromil demands his due. You have livestock, I presume."

"I have a pig, Sire," the man said, his eyes darting to the silent Zili.

Zili turned to the soldier sitting beside him and whispered.

"We will take the swine as payment for your debt," said the soldier. The captain ordered another soldier to stand by to obtain the pig. The man held his hands prayerfully. "But Sire—but Sire, how will

I feed my family?"

"That is your problem," the soldier said. "So that you do not cheat the king again, you will pay *thirty* naros on the next full moon."

The readied soldier grabbed the man by the arm and pushed him to his home. There, the soldier forcibly took the pig. He tied it with rope to keep it still, and towed the squealing animal to the man's wagon. There he tied it on the flat bed of the wagon.

Flanked by his wife and child, the man fell to his knees and sobbed. Snapping the reins, the soldier drove away with not only the pig but also the wagon.

"I shall establish the king's will as he directs!" Zili shouted. "Any man who dissents shall follow the same fate."

Zili and his men took as much money, grain, and livestock from the village as any stolen wagon or saddlebag could hold.

Over the next days and weeks, Zili sent his men to every village in the Aurora Kingdom. In the name of the king, they took everything they wanted. Villagers began to suffer widespread starvation, and many died. Others became homeless or fell victim to maladies. Zili sowed the seeds of disgruntlement and misery. He made sure humans and oddlings held King Dobromil responsible for their misery. The people in all lands of the kingdom spoke of revolt.

Since his early twenties, Zili had known of the Linkage, the magic created by the energy connecting all things living. Zili believed he could become all-powerful if he could possess the objects used by oddlings to control things around them. He did have the trolls' ruby ring. He wore the stone on his right forefinger. His magic, however, was incomplete. He had a third of his potential power. Before he could realize full power, he needed to possess three other oddling artifacts. His acquisition of these articles would be his greatest achievement. The task was an arduous one that often left him brooding and short-tempered.

Alongside Zili on his black stallion, the captain saw a gloomy expression on Zili's face. His horse sidling next to Zili's, the captain extended his hand. He offered Zili a drink of ale from a small silver flask. Zili waved the captain away. Brooding, Zili chanced to see a hawk swooping into a nearby thicket. Screeching, the hawk shot up from the brush, a rat in its talons.

"That is what we must strive to do," Zili muttered. "Take what we want and leave."

Along his other flank, Zili saw his general approach. "Begging your pardon, Your Highness," said the general, "would we be hawk or rat?" His men snickered nervously.

Gazing at the general, Zili's eyes burned. "Your tongue has an alacrity for wit, General," he snapped. "Still, do be less hasty with your humor, lest you lose that tongue."

Discomfited, the general glanced at his men, now silent.

"We have more work to do," Zili said, pulling back on the reins. Whinnying, his horse stopped. The two dozen equestrians trailing him slowed and stopped. The horses groaned, spun, and sidled. Zili's second lieutenant pulled the reins of his horse to come alongside Zili and the captain.

Zili gazed at them all, pulling at his beard. He decided what he needed to do. His men gathered around.

"I don't care what you do or how you do it. I want someone to bring to me the following artifacts. I care not the order. Bring me the Crystal Chronaria from the outer lands of Elfin, the Elixir Illuminae from the land of Waters, and the Dragon Stone that resides in the realm of the stone and lizard peoples."

His men were perplexed as to what these things were, but they feared asking.

Zili knew that when he attained these necessities, he could bring about a coup de grâce, crushing his brother Alexander like a beetle. "He will see me take back my right to be king," he thought.

"Generals," Zili said, "take your men and bring me what I ask." He observed through the treetops a sliver of a moon in the bright blue eastern sky. "I want them by the first full moon before the winter solstice. I shall reward the man or oddling who does this for me. Fail me, and you and your men will die. Is that understood?"

"But Sire," entreated one general, "those things exist not. They cannot. We have found them nowhere in our homeland where they were reported held, nor in any other place. One cannot find what exists not." Zili swayed his stallion to his right, his eyes locking on to the general's. His horse clopping closer. Swiftly slipping his sword from his scabbard, he turned it to glimmer in the sun. He twisted on his horse, his face contorted with rage. One thrust, and Zili drove the sword through the chest of his top general. Lifting his foot, Zili carefully placed his boot on the general's chest and shoved him off the blade. Dead, the general tumbled from his horse. His limp body sent up a cloud of dust as he hit the roadside.

Silence.

Zili held his hand out for the flask of drink the captain had previously offered. He caught the eye of each of his twenty-three remaining men. "By the way, as a bonus," said Zili, sneering down at the dead general, "consider your debt repaid for making it necessary for me to kill my horse Cristobel. He was a better horse than you were a man." Zili tilted the flask to his mouth and drank. He exhaled, wiping his lips. "Is there anyone else who desires to call me a liar? Is there? Does anyone else think these objects do not exist? Say so, anyone. Remarks?"

In unison, the three remaining generals responded by shaking, their heads and saluting. "No, Sire."

"Today's lesson is over. We have miles to make," Zili said, checking the position of the sun. "You are dismissed. Remove that garbage from your king's road."

Chapter 3

THE TRIP

Two nights out on their four-day trip to Castle Town, Tom contemplated a hundred things he needed to do in the shop.

"What's wrong, Papa? You have not said much in the last several hours. Did I do something wrong?"

"No, my son," Tom answered, staring straight ahead. Yet he saw neither trees nor outlying, sparse farmhouses nor the farrier farms. He rarely spoke to passing fellow travelers, nodding politely as they strolled by. "It is the holidays. They are coming. We're short on supplies for our annual gift giving."

"How is that possible?" Nicholas asked.

"Church charities," Tom said, "lack naros to buy necessary clothing and materials to make toys. We lack other general supplies. Many sources previously available to us are strapped for resources due to heavy taxes collected by Zili." Tom tugged the reins for old Philly and Henry to turn a gentle corner. "Many productive members of the community have been taxed so heavily, they are unable or unwilling to hire workers. Production has fallen. We just need more supplies than usual if we're to meet our demand."

Nicholas patted his father on the knee. "These problems weigh heavily on your mind." Listening to the clip-clop of Philly's and Henry's hooves, Nicholas lamented his options. To clear his mind, he tried diverting his attention by making out the patterns the stars created in the sky. "Father, the night sky is so beautiful. What do you think is out there?"

"The moon and stars are there. Should there be anything else?"

"I mean out there in the dark parts beyond the stars."

"It sounds as if you've been thinking about it."

"I have. I wish I could … I wish I could …" Nicholas said. "Go on, son. Tell me. What is it you wish?"

"No. It's silly." Nicholas looked at Tom, and again to the night sky. He took a deep breath. "I wish I could fly."

"Fly? How?"

"In my mind I do. I can go anywhere in the world where people need me. I can visit every child in the world if I please. But that's not what you mean, is it? You are asking how I would fly, if I would flap my arms like the wings of a bird. No. Not that way. I want to fly in a way that would allow me to take others along. I would see above all the villages and farms of the world. Then I would know every man, woman, and child's heart." Nicholas tucked his lips and pointed to the sky. "On one special day, I would drive a wagon through the sky." He laughed. "But now I sound like a little child, or just mad."

Nicholas watched Henry and Philly lazily stride forward. Sparkles hovered above Philly's back. The light swirled and darted, streaming along a small circle in the air. Nicholas's eyes whirled as he followed the sparks. They dashed and began dancing over Henry's head. The light came together and concentrated into a humanoid shape. Another point of light danced between Tom and Nicholas. The light faded as it became a second humanoid shape, barely discernible from the brilliance in which it bathed.

"I recognize them," Nicholas said. "They are the—"

"The color sprites, the light sprites," Tom interjected.

"And the flora gnomes," Nicholas added, peering to the floorboard where, in a flash, a gnome materialized at his feet.

In one voice the sprites ad gnome spoke. "For a time, we shall accompany you on your journey."

Nodding, Tom and Nicholas approved.

"But," said the sprite settling over Henry's head. It leaned on Henry's upturned ear. Henry's large eye rolled timorously back toward Tom.

"A news alert comes to us over the airways," said the gnome with tinny intonation. "Listen ..."

Tom and Nicholas did listen. The wind gently blew, stirring vortices of leaves from the forest floor. A warm breeze swirled around their ears like the breath of angels. First sounding like musical notes, the hum compressed into high-pitched words. Tom's and Nicholas's eyes snapped to the dense, dark forest when wildcats whined. Recognizing the winds, Tom placed his finger to the side of his nose and poked the air up with his forefinger.

"Whisperers," Tom murmured, "in the wind. Listen."

"Zili-i-i-i is burning-g-g-g the villagessssss," the choral voices quietly breathed. "He is taking food from the mouthsssss of those in want. He has taken young stock, leaving the old animals to die in the cold. He has even inexplicably hurt formerly indomitable oddlings."

More light sprites formed and danced above the horses' heads and along their spines. Streaming ethereal radiance, they continued channeling the voices of the whisperers.

"The soldiers," they lyrically sang, "say this scourge upon the people was ordered by King Dobromil."

"Dobromil? No, Papa." Nicholas was incredulous. He clutched Tom's forearm. Tom vigorously shook his head, disavowing the suggestion of such deceit and cruelty.

The wind whispered, "Youuu know him, Tom. Dooo you think thissss is truuue?" Nicholas's mind whirled as the vortices stirred the waving grass.

The color sprites shot into the air. Trails of sparkles faded to their rear. Looping and twisting, the streamers shot into the trees. There, they imbued the foliage with fleeting autumn tones.

The wind winnowed. "Zili issss looking for the Crystal Chronariaaaa, Dragon Stone, and Elixir Illuminae."

Deep voices welled from below the sideboards of the wagon.

Nicholas and Tom looked to either side.

Trolls loped alongside the wagon's running boards and wheels. "With these relics he seeks," said the lead troll, "Zili will make another mind weak." Hearing the voices from below, Nicholas startled.

Nicholas was certain someone somewhere had given life to a lie. He had begun developing the rudimentary power to sense when people were truthful, lying, good, or bad. His mind reeled with possibilities, but he was still unsteady about his new sense. Maybe due to his experiences, maybe due to wishful thinking or blessing, Nicholas was becoming more like his adopted father than any seed from Tom's loins would have been. If his powers emanated from anywhere else, he would be dumbfounded. Nicholas refused to believe his senses could lead him so far astray. Could his grasp of the Linkage be that wrong?

"Papa, is this even accurate? Does the Linkage work flawlessly?"

"No. The Linkage is energy. It connects all things in our world. It is neither good nor evil. What matters is the way humans and oddlings choose to use it. You could say it is the magic created by either love or hate. It can be affected by the moral nature of the living soul. It is not flawless."

Lulled by the sway and creak of the wagon springs, and by the horses clopping, Nicholas peered into the darkness at the trees coming toward them and vanishing to the rear, out of the wagon lamplight. Nicholas saw his father. "Is that why we should always ask before we use something of the forest?"

Gently holding the reins looped around his fingers. Tom turned to Nicholas, still peering into the darkness.

"Yes," Tom said, knitting his bushy white eyebrows. "Why did you think we did that?"

Nicholas shrugged. "Because you told me to?"

Nicholas looked down at the oddling on the floorboard. The pointy-hatted, pointy-eared gnome turned his blue, sparkling eyes up to Nicholas. "Mama always said, when you learn better, you do better," said Nicholas. "Please forgive my ignorance, sir? I promise to offer more respect to a power greater than man's."

Before Nicholas's and Tom's eyes, the oddlings gently poofed into spangles of light and vapor. The blending vapor assumed the form of one larger being. Hovering above the horses, it bowed slightly at the waist. From its mouth, choral voices spoke. "We are thankful you have learned better. We will accept your apology, Nicholas. A gift we offer you for another lesson learned. May we be of service?"

"Papa," Nicholas said eagerly, "we are short volunteers. We could use help at the farm and workshop. What do you think about allowing those hurt by the sheriff to stay with us? We can offer aid in exchange for help. There are enough chores." Beaming, Nicholas gazed into Tom's face. "They can stay in the bunkhouse."

"Well now," Tom said. "That is a most charitable proposal." He slipped a chip of hardtack from his pocket into his mouth. "Mama and I could rejuvenate our weary old bones. Yes." He chuckled, jiggling the reins to coax Henry and Philly across a narrow creek. The wagon jostled gently as it climbed from the water on the other side. The trolls had climbed aboard the wagon running boards.

"Helped one another for many years," said Speckles, the lead troll, "much in common, through love and tears. Together we can work through fears." Up he looked to Nicholas, flashing an abrupt, toothy smile.

Cracking another piece of hardtack with his fingers, Tom offered it to Nicholas. "You have supporters, I see. Sounds as if everyone agrees with your idea."

Glimpsing all the oddlings, Nicholas grinned. "We shall meet you back at our home upon our return." Many flashed and vanished like smoke on the breeze. Like cliff divers into water, the trolls leaped headfirst into the soil, vanishing in a puff of sparkles.

"Safe journeys to you all, my friends," Tom said. "Nicholas and I must continue on our way."

Sarah

In Castle Town, Illuminae, Tom and Nicholas collected supplies, filled orders, and did repairs. In the course of his work, Nicholas went to the street market to buy a several bolts of cloth, yards of leather, and candy to surprise his mother upon his return home.

Along the bricked lane of merchants, Nicholas stopped before the cart of a victualler to watch a spider monkey stoke his owner's ivory pipe. The seller's cart was filled with small wooden toys, included a six-inch-long paddle, the ends at cross angles and set upon a center dowel rod, the rod twice as long as the cross-paddle. Nicholas sifted through the wooden toys as the seller's monkey shoved the lit pipe into its owner's mouth.

"Sir," Nicholas said, "what is the animal's name?"

"Silly Sally is her name, boy."

"Does she *bite*?"

"No, boy. She *eats*." The seller roared. "That is how I got this." Into the air, the man shoved a healed nub—formerly his right small finger.

"Oh," Nicholas said, startled. "I see. And what are these?" He lifted one of the small paddles.

"Something special, boy. Watch this," The merchant replied. He took up another paddle and placed the dowel between his palms. Sliding one palm against the other caused the paddle blades to whirl, pushing down air. When he released his grip, the paddle shot into the air, lifted by its whirling blades.

"It is a miracle," Nicholas whispered, wishing there was one large enough for him to ride.

"I see in your eyes a child's dream. I say it has no practical purpose. Dear lad, I calls 'em a trifle; others call them play-pretties. Would you be buying one or ten?" the man said. The monkey stood on the man's neck. "Take one or as many as you like."

"No, sir. I'm here to buy supplies for my father."

"Sure you are, lad, but these are good quality lollygags for children." The man stared at Nicholas with shifty eyes, his mouth agape. The monkey leaped from the man's back across the cart to Nicholas's shoulder. Startled, Nicholas spun and slapped at the beast. But the monkey shimmied down his side and latched on to his flank. It plunged its tiny hand into Nicholas's pocket and withdrew Nicholas's leather pouch of coins.

Nicholas lunged for the monkey but missed.

"Give it back," Nicholas commanded, but the monkey leaped back to the shoulder of its master.

"Thief! That creature stole my money!" Nicholas shouted, his eyes meeting those of other shoppers and sellers.

"He's a liar! My Sally done nothing to 'em. He's a bloody liar! He tried stealing toys!"

"I did *nothing* of the sort!" shouted Nicholas.

The sellers gathered, taking up for the man with the monkey. Afraid, Nicholas backed away. He turned to dash off but ran into someone behind.

"Oh. I'm sorry." He had collided with a young woman. She fell into the arms of a man beside her. She was clad in fine clothing. Nicholas could immediately see she was well-bred.

"You careless fool!" shouted the man strolling with the woman. Clasping Nicholas's upper arm, he shook the boy. "I should thrash your reckless hide."

"Dudley, please. I will survive," she said. Unsteady on her feet, she turned. Her wandering eyes recognized Nicholas. "You," she intoned.

"You. I mean, Princess Sarah," Nicholas whispered.

"Your Highness, Princess Sarah," the paddle-seller shouted, rushing up alongside Nicholas. Nicholas backed away. His eyes enlarging, the merchant dropped to his knees, painfully striking the roadway near her feet. Her stern gaze bored into the merchant's eyes.

"Return what is his," she commanded, pointing from the merchant to Nicholas. The merchant returned to his cart, where he had hidden the pouch.

"Leave us." Princess Sarah said, glancing to her guard. She waved him away with a lift of her delicate chin. "Give me room to breathe."

Stepping up to the seller's cart, she leaned in, gesturing the seller to do the same. "Cheat no one else," she whispered. "As you know, I am the queen's sister. Forget not that I am also Sheriff Zili's sister in-law." She winked to Nicholas, then stared into the eyes of the merchant, who was turning white at the mention of Zili's name. "Next time, I shall not be so lenient," Sarah admonished. Clinging to its master's neck with one paw, the monkey crouched, covering its face with the other paw.

"Yes, Your Highness. I promise, Your Highness. Please do not tell the sheriff," the man whimpered. He rolled the pouch into Nicholas's waiting palm. Princess Sarah and Nicholas strolled away.

"Sarah—I mean, Princess Sarah—I am glad to see you again. I-I've thought about you these many weeks," Nicholas shyly whispered.

Lifting his chin, she said, gazing into his face, "Look at me." Nicholas flashed a brief smile. "My, uh, papa," he said, "sent me to do a task for him."

"And what was your task, gentle Nicholas?" She touched his cheek.

Restraining herself from familiarity, she quickly adjusted her posture.

Clearing her throat, blinking, she ambled back a step or two.

Nicholas withdrew a parchment from his pocket. He held it up. "I-I have this list."

Stepping around, she peered over his shoulder to appraise his inventory. Nodding, she pointed to other merchants' carts. "I trust we can find these effects there—without the drama, I should think."

She sauntered before Nicholas, gesturing for Dudley to follow several steps behind. The gold trim along the hem of her black skirt glittered as her heel kicked out her gown with every stride.

"I had no idea you were so good at making dolls," she said as they walked. "You must be somewhat of … a wizard."

Nicholas glanced up. "Wizard? No. I'm no wizard, Princess S—"

"Stop," she said, pausing halfway across the street. Tugging the fluted sleeve of her white blouse, she exposed her wrist and hand. Gently lifting his chin with her delicate white fingers, she looked into his face. As Nicholas's eyes rose, he saw the colored ribbons adorning the front of her white blouse. "I'm Sarah to you—in private, at least." She gently shook her head. "Of all the boys I've met in my eighteen years, you are the most peculiar."

He gazed into her face. Delicately framed by a ribbon sunbonnet, her underlit face smiled with the aura. Her straight auburn hair hung to her waist.

Nicholas thought it might appear disrespectful to call her by her first name, but it would be decidedly disrespectful not to honor her wishes. "What would your ..." He paused, thinking of her brother-in-law, King Alexander. Nicholas noted the guard was turning his ears to him. He cleared his throat. "I should find these things ... Sarah. I am surprised to have—literally run into you, I suppose. If I might ask, why are you in the market?"

Examining the sellers' wares, she glanced askance at Nicholas. "I sometimes come here to see what new items our merchants have brought from foreign lands. Today I search for saffron," she said, her fingers raking through a cart of books and writing implements.

They continued, Nicholas strolling near, Dudley and the other bodyguards several feet behind. She stopped before a cart stacked with bolts of cloth. "Are these what you seek, Nicholas?" she asked.

Tending the cart, a middle-aged woman in a bonnet and apron approached from the other side. "Princess Sarah," the woman said, curtsying. "It is a privilege to serve you."

"It is not I who shop today but my ... friend, Nicholas."

"May I help you, Nicholas?" the woman asked.

Nicholas shuffled through several thick stacks of cloth. "These, and these, and I am interested in these too," he said. He set the bolts apart from the others. His fingers plowed deeper into the stack. "And these too."

"Lad, these materials can be very expensive." She glanced at Princess Sarah. Princess Sarah gave a nod. "But for you, lad, I shall make them a gift."

"Really, no. I can't."

"You must, for I give. I shall not sell them to you," said the woman. Enthused by the woman's apparent generosity, Nicholas bowed quickly. He searched for other treasures, finding the leather he needed and the candy.

"My niece loves that doll you made for her," said Sarah.

"What?" Nicholas murmured, half listening as he rolled his purchased and gifted effects into a cloth. He tied it with a rope. "I was only too glad to—"

"It healed her," Sarah said. "Did you know it would?"

"Yes. I knew it would."

"It was a miracle, Nicholas," said Sarah, intrigued by his modesty. "I can't stop thinking of it." Sarah turned his face to hers. "I want to thank you." Leaning in, hesitating, she kissed his right cheek.

He rubbed his cheek. "What was that for?"

"For what you did for Angelica. Did you not like the kiss?"

"Yes, but I didn't— I mean, I did l-l-l-like …" Nicholas backed a step or two and blushed.

Sarah glanced away and back. Her guards pretended not to see.

"Should not I be the one to blush, gentle Nicholas?" she asked.

Touching his kissed cheek, Nicholas said, "I need to get these, uh, things back to Papa before he wonders what happened to me."

"Don't rush," said Sarah. "Walk with me." Reaching forward, she looped her thin arm around his. "Come. I command you."

Nicholas nodded. They strode the brick-lined lane. "I shall share more with you." Sarah said. She assured her guards by a look that she was in charge, and for her safety they needn't fear. "My young niece," she said, rolling her eyes coyly, "will go nowhere without the doll you made. Not even to bathe."

Shoppers crossing her in the market curtsied and bowed. Others whispered "the princess" as she passed. She smiled and waved regally, rarely taking her eyes from Nicholas as they walked.

"They love you here," he said.

"I have heard rumors." She glowered. "You stay far outside the castle village. Do you not, Nicholas?"

Nicholas nodded.

The princess held her breath. "Is it true?"

"Is what true, Your Highness—I mean, Sarah?"

"What merchants are saying about Prince Zili? I wonder, for people seem to fear him. Why should one fear the sheriff?" She looked into Nicholas's face. "They say he is stealing from the villagers and oddlings." Nicholas cast his eyes down and away. "I'm afraid so … Sarah. Even some of the people here are under Prince Zili's thumb. You saw the way that man with the monkey reacted to the mention of Zili's name."

"Truly. I know Prince Zili has forced several of the peasant girls to work in the kitchens and laundry when their parents did not have full payment for the taxes. He said the girls' parents were criminals—flouting the tax law."

"That is not the vilest, I fear." Nicholas stopped. She unloosed her arm from his. "The soldiers mistreated the youth. They have melted the children's toys to make weapons for mercenary armies," he said, his voice becoming low. The thought of children mistreated stirred Nicholas's ire.

"They are so defenseless," Sarah said sadly. "They have harmed no one."

"Do you truly know your king?" Nicholas asked.

Sarah stepped back, confused by his question. Wetting her lips with her tongue, she stared at him. "Not only do I truly know my brother-in-law the king, but also I know his heart of hearts as I do my own," she snapped, traces of anger and protectiveness in her tone.

The guards started toward her. Sarah held out one finger for them to stop, and stop they did. Glimpsing their serious faces, Nicholas quickly stepped back, stumbling as his hand slipped from the rim of a barrel upon which he leaned. He fell to his buttocks but quickly rose.

"There are people in the kingdom, Your Highness," he said, "who think your brother-in-law, King Dobromil, is to blame for their misery."

"Do you believe that, Nicholas?" she asked, pacing to Nicholas's side. He could hear the offense in her voice.

"I do not. No," Nicholas strongly said, straightening his posture. "I am glad." Sarah lifted her chin and breathed more easily. "I am glad," she repeated. She gently placed her hand on his shoulder, but Nicholas could still see questions in her expression.

Nicholas softly said, "I believe that Zili ..." He hesitated. "Zili has plotted to sully the reputation of the king."

"Do you have proof of this intrigue?"

"No, I do not, but I believe it is true."

"It has always been my feeling that Zili has retained great envy of his brother the king," said Sarah. "I would talk to you more but ... there are many ears. There are always ears."

There was silence.

She took his arm and strolled the merchants' lane, stopping to smell a bowl of potpourri. Nicholas watched as she swept her long hair behind her shoulder. She closed her eyes and brought the bowl to her delicate nose. "Yum! It reminds me of the forest."

Nicholas felt his heart patter. He wanted to know her better, show her the forest as he knew it, but he worried her station would not permit such familiarity. But he decided he would ask nonetheless.

"I know you're the queen's sister?" Nicholas said.

"You know that I am, gentle Nicholas," she said lyrically, smiling, bemused by Nicholas's curious assertion.

"This is likely a rash query," Nicholas mumbled, his breath taken by her radiance. "Would you—I mean could you? That is, with permission of His Royal Highness, of course …ride with me?"

"Me, ride?" she asked, becoming intrigued by his line of questioning.

"No."

"No? You don't want me to ride?" she asked.

"I do."

"Then we shall go, right away." She grinned.

"I don't want you to go now." His expression was now worried.

"First you want me to go, and then you don't," Sarah teased. "Which is it, Nicholas?"

"I do want you to ride with me."

"Do not worry," Sarah said. Laughing, she playfully skipped, circling him. She seemed to take some amusement in Nicholas's verbal timidity and confusion.

"I'm so sorry." She laughed. "I'm being mean."

"It is okay." He smiled weakly. "So I may do it again?"

"No. I mean, I don't know. I think I don't know what I mean anymore," said Nicholas. He looked away and into her eyes. "I want to ask—"

"You may," she said.

He saw the twinkle in her eye. Both of them were blushing. "I want—I want to show you the forest and all its wonders."

"Well, now, I must accept."

"I'm sorry, you don't want to—" Nicholas began to say, before realizing she had said yes. "Oh. Wonderful. Sarah—"

"Your father is coming," she said.

Nicholas saw Tom marching up the street toward him.

"He doesn't look happy. Does he often scowl like that?" Sarah asked. She nudged Nicholas toward his approaching father. "You go. We shall talk later. Go, now."

Nicholas saw his father shake his finger, scolding. He rushed to meet Tom, intercepting him under the awning of a napping merchant. Tom looked Nicholas up and down, his arms akimbo. "You know we have many things to do. How long does it take to get supplies? To buy a bag of coffee and four pounds of penny nails?" he asked, "You know we have to finish the potion cabinet for the apothecary today. We have a contract, Nicholas!"

"But Papa—"

"Was that the princess I saw you with?" Tom scanned up and down the street among the throng of shoppers. He saw the princess with her entourage slipping into a shop. "You must be cautious talking with the royals. She is the sister-in-law of Prince Zili."

"But Father, she is in accord with our suspicions of him."

"That may be, but you still must be cautious," Tom said. He looked at the position of the sun, and at a nearby water clock. "You should have been back twenty minutes ago."

"I'm sorry. I became distracted, Papa."

"Distracted, I can certainly see." Tom doffed his hat to familiar faces passing by. He turned back to Nicholas. Sternly stomping his foot, Tom started at Nicholas, shouting, "Go!"

Startled, Nicholas quickstepped from beneath the awning and turned the corner. He plowed through a crowd of onlookers and straight into Prince Zili's chest. The prince was unmoved by the impact.

Taciturn, a foot and a half taller, Zili stared down into Nicholas's steel-blue eyes. With a swipe of his hand, Zili brushed off his tunic. Smirking, he glanced at his men and stared back at Nicholas. They quietly snickered.

"I know you," Zili slowly growled, grinding the words over his teeth like grist. "You are the … *charity case* … my brother the king allowed to spar with his knight errant, Sir Andrew." Zili's breath was soured by the odor of black beer and tobacco. "What is your name again, boy?" he sputtered, saliva spraying.

Nicholas stood back. "Nicholas. Nicholas Claus, Sire."

"The carpenter's son?" Zili saw Tom standing on the timber sidewalk at the turn of the corner.

Two of Zili's large men stepped to their master's side. They peered at Nicholas as if he were an insect that needed squashing. They snickered. "Do you need us, Sire?" one asked.

Zili laughed. "This one is not yet ripe. I think I can defend myself from this pup." He spoke deliberately, his eyes sizing up Nicholas as no threat. "It would be wise of you, boy, to watch where you tread. I tolerate carelessness … poorly."

"I shall … I shall … make sure that Nicholas does better, Sire," Tom said, ambling from the corner toward his son and Zili.

"Make sure you do, old man," Zili ordered as he turned to go.

Tom and Nicholas respectfully bowed to the prince.

Chapter 4

TROUBLE WITH THE AURORA

The marble floor of their palatial bedroom led to the entrance of their balcony. Radiating from their quarters, the amber glow of candlelight diffused through the billowing crinoline curtains dividing the balcony from the bedroom. As they sat on the balcony, they could see the near pastures and outlying forested mountains, backlit by the Milky Way. Prince Wallace wrapped his wife Princess Marinna's delicate upper body in his strong arms, his cape across her legs. Under the black canopy of the night sky, they watched the flashing aurora borealis. Carrying the aroma of buttercups, a warm breeze comforted them like a blanket. They reclined on a cushioned lounge.

Enjoying each other, the royals gazed at the sky, but Princess Marinna sensed a change in the Linkage. The sky was turning polluted with a dark wind. The princess grew ill at ease. Tuned to her, Wallace could detect her discomfort.

She shivered.

"You're cold, darling," Prince Wallace whispered. His eyes showed worry. He held her closer.

"Not the cold, no, dearest. I fear more than that." She shivered again. "Can you not feel it?" Princess Marinna asked, pointing to the sky. "The aurora has never been less enthralling, more menacing, its dance less enchanting. Wally, I fear a pall has crept over the land."

She cuddled back into his chest. "Wally" was her pet name for him in private.

He stroked her temple, raking his fingers through her thick, soft hair.

"I feel a heaviness in my heart," she said.

Wallace pulled her head to his chest. She listened to the beating of his heart. "You *were* always more sensitive than I, my princess," said Wallace, his chin gently resting atop her head.

"There is an interference," she said. "And I know not from where it comes."

He kissed her gently on the top of her head. "I see nothing but you, my love."

She wriggled closer to his warm body. "Take me seriously, Wally. Look, up there." She pointed to an area of the night sky through which flew a distant black bird. "Over there, by the bird. Do you see now?" She placed her delicate fingertips upon either of his cheeks, gently positioning Wally's head. He loved the touch of her soft fingertips, and snuggled into her fingers.

But Princess Marinna insisted, her eyes searching the sky. "Please see, my dear prince. For there is an ailing breeze howling through our land. What do you think causes the aurora to act so strangely?"

His eyebrows slightly drawn down, he peered over her left shoulder to that part of the sky to which she looked.

"The colors are dark, gray," she said. "Angry. The familiar colorful tracings are missing. Can you see?"

Wallace nodded to humor her. He knew they would retire to bed soon if he agreed. "Yes, dear," he muttered.

Slightly miffed, she sulked. "Patronize me not, Wallace Dobromil." She twisted her knuckle into his breastbone. "Lest this night you find yourself sleeping with your horse."

"Careful, my love," he teased. "My horse may try to run away with me, and you would be sad."

"I would be sad," she said somberly. "I would die without you." She kissed his cheek. "But do not change the topic, my prince. What say you is the meaning of this change in the aurora? The stars twinkle rarely."

Breathing deeply, Wallace hugged her snugly. The faint smell of hickory smoke wafting in from the countryside mixed with that of the buttercups.

"When I was a child," Wallace said, "my parents used to tell us that the aurora reflected the balance of the Linkage When the balance was as it should be, the aurora was pleasing to the eye, calming to the soul. If the balance listed, it was a reflection of a decline in moral nature. The aurora would be disquieting in appearance and chilling to the soul." Both Wallace and Marinna felt the chill. "Upon my father's soul, I do see," he added.

"What could set the balance so off-kilter as to affect the aurora?" she asked. "We must discover the cause." Turning on the lounge, she slid her bare feet to the cool stone floor. Pulling her upper body away from Wallace, she sat straight. She lowered her eyes from the sky to the distant, forested mountains. "Have you heard certain distressing things about … about your brother?" she asked. Her eyes diverted from his.

"There are rumors," Wallace muttered, reaching for her to lean back on his chest. Hesitating, she finally did. "Rumors which I've refused to believe. Until now."

"What rumors are those, dear husband?" Marinna asked. "I should not wish to make a treasonous remark myself. It is not my place to disparage your blood, or give second life to accusations that should have no first." She tucked her underlip.

"I, too, am reluctant to say," Wallace said.

Marinna stroked his caressing forearm with her fingers. "When we vowed to become one with each other, any barriers lifted. We must express our feelings with no trepidation."

He nodded. Closing his eyes, he drew her nearer. Her nearness fulfilled him.

She looked askance at his arms encircling her. "What say you, husband?"

"My brother Zili," Wallace said, "is trying to ... is trying to dethrone Alexander. There have been reports of raids on villages, both human and oddling. There. I've said it."

"Do you believe this to be true?" she asked, peering into streaks of darkness that had once been streams of color in the sky.

"Until now," he said, "I refused to believe he could be so cruel. After all, we share the same blood."

"You may indeed share the same blood, but you do not share the same heart. I know you. You are a good man. Your brother is not you. He can be impulsive, intolerant, and cruel. People fear him, Wallace."

"And not me, or Alexander for that matter?"

"Our subjects love you and Alexander," Marinna said.

Just then they heard approaching footsteps from behind, along the stone floor in their chamber. Through the crinoline curtain came a figure: the chamberlain, his eyes cast down. In his hand he held a silver platter, upon which lay a giant leather and chainmail glove with a long cuff. Dipping at the knees, the chamberlain presented the platter to Prince Wallace, who stood.

Wallace glanced at the platter. He turned to Marinna, who had also stood.

"No man I know has a gauntlet like that," said Wallace.

"I think he is more than man," said the princess, touching the glove with her forefinger. "Is this his message?"

"Your Highness. Your Highness," said the chamberlain. "A dispatch carrier arrived in full gallop. He brought this ... message. He said he had orders to deliver to your eyes only. Shall I ..."

Wallace turned to the chamberlain. "Yes. You will bring the courier to me. I know this glove."

"At this hour? But we are in chambers," Princess Marinna said plaintively, stepping around Wallace. "Not here."

Wallace noted his wife's sparse clothing. The chamberlain's eyes remained averted from the princess. The prince placed a hand on his wife's shoulder. "Very well. My faithful chamberlain, show this man to the throne room. I shall meet with him there."

The chamberlain bowed, turned, and carried out Wallace's command.

⁂

Escorted by three guards, Prince Wallace briskly strode into the throne room. Six more guardsmen, milling about, snapped to attention as the prince breezed in. They watched. Breaking none of his stride, he marched to and quickly sat upon his throne, his cape billowing as he turned to face the room.

Genuflecting, the courier dropped to one knee and bowed at the neck, his long loops of hair flung over his brow, his brown eyes down. "Forgive me, Sire, for disturbing you at this hour. I have force-ridden six days and five nights to reach you. My orders were specific. To your eyes and hands only; no exception."

Although Wallace suspected, he asked, "Courier, who sends thee?"

"Shibboleth, King of the Golam, Your Highness."

"I did recognize his glove," said Prince Wallace.

In his hand, the courier fisted a rolled parchment closed by a gobbet of melted red wax.

Prince Wallace reached out. The courier pressed the parchment into Wallace's palm. Wallace broke the wax seal, unrolled the parchment, and read the document to himself:

> I have witnessed with my own eyes Prince Zili perform with his own hand the torture and murder of Hessereth, King of the Lizard People, and the kidnapping of their royal prince. Prince Zili then forcibly took possession of key information that, if deciphered, could lead him to the Dragon Stone, life source of my people. I respectfully request your assistance in preventing this theft and avenging the murder.
>
> Shibboleth, King of Golam

Snapping his fingers, the prince called for his scribe. The robed man came quickly with an ink-stained wooden box and fresh tubes of parchments under his arm.

"Your Highness," the scribe, Oather, said. "How may I serve thee?"

Wallace whispered into his ear, and turned to the courier as the scribe wrote.

"Go and rest yourself," Wallace ordered the messenger. The courier rose to his full seven-foot height. "In the morning, you will receive a fresh mount."

Oather presented his inscription to Wallace. He checked the written response. "It is as I have dictated," Wallace said. "In the morning you shall return to your master with this reply." Wallace passed his response to the courier. "Place this in his hand only, with no exception. Guard it with your life. You are dismissed."

Backing down the carpet runner before the throne, the courier hurried from the throne room.

"Captain," Wallace said to one of the three guardsmen standing beside the throne. "Summon General Raptozk to my side immediately."

The captain saluted, running to his mission.

Within the hour, the captain and General Raptozk stood before the prince. Wallace paced with anger and irritation, tapping his forefinger against his thumb. "General Raptozk, I have urgent business in the kingdom of my brother Alexander. Make arrangements. I want you and fifty warriors at my side, clothed as commoners. Make sure our mounts are strong, as our travel will be swift and with little rest. We will depart at first light." Wallace stepped from the throne. About to go, he turned. "Oh yes. And bring the wizard. His services are required."

Assimilating this information, General Raptozk saluted. "General, where is your favorite? And will he be with us?" asked Wallace.

"Ah, Lexi, Sire. Yes, Your Highness."

"Well, General, what are you waiting for? You are dismissed."

Taking Sides

Before the first cockcrow, Prince Wallace and General Raptozk stood on the tourney ground at the rear of the castle grounds. Wallace's massive garrison of commonly clad soldiers watched the two men quietly confer, scraping maps in the dusty soil with sword tips.

The wizard Zorna paced, tightly circling the two men. He appeared as a wizened old man with a long white beard. Zorna's hair fell to his chest and shoulders from the hood of his dark blue robe. The tall, thin master of magic said little as he paced, pondering the problems he anticipated solving. As was his habit when he thought on serious magic, he drew his hood well forward over his head until it dipped deeply over his face. In his right hand, he tapped a seven-foot walking staff to the ground, rehearsing his incantations. The gnarled staff had passed to him from a great ancestry of wizards and was a treasured heirloom. He listened as Wallace planned their ride.

"I should have had my men disguised before they arrived at Castle Waters this morn, my cryptic friend, Zorna," Prince Wallace stated. "Nonetheless, per your instructions, I have delayed. I am intrigued." He looked sideways into Zorna's face. "What deception have you planned for our undisclosed arrival? Certainly you must have a foolproof plan in mind."

"Your Highness, it is not fools we shall deceive. That would be too easy," Zorna said smiling.

"Walk with me," Wallace commanded, heading for his garrison of men and horses in formation along the perimeter of the tourney field. Zorna kept in step, the hem of his dark blue robe kicking out with each swift step, his hood shielding his bearded face. In his gnarled right hand, Zorna clasped his staff, using it as a walking stick, while in his left he held a leather sack the size of a melon, which he occasionally stirred.

"You make me as curious as a child sometimes, old friend," Wallace muttered as Zorna stopped to attend to the sack.

"I beg Your Highness' indulgence," said Zorna. A puff of blue smoke issued through the pursed neck of the sack. "You shall see, and very soon." He shook his head. "You remind me of when you were an impatient lad, Your Highness."

Within moments, both men stood before Wallace's garrison. "Your Highness', as you ordered," said General Raptozk. "We have more than fifty riders. When the people heard you were going to look into Zili's activities, enthusiastic volunteers fell like manna from heaven."

"Continue with your accounting, General," said Wallace.

"We have eighty strong mounts, and thirty horses capable of pulling fifteen open and covered wagons stocked with supplies and munitions." Wallace scanned the tourney field to count.

"Also present," General Raptozk continued, "we have the alchemist—"

"Joseph, Your Highness," Zorna said, pointing to a young man falling from the loading end of a varda. Zorna rolled his eyes.

"I trust his talents extend somewhat beyond falling," Wallace quipped.

The general cleared his throat. "Your Highness, of the elves, we have collected a dozen of the best female archers skilled in battle. Many are in the guise of traveling merchants and circus performers."

"As should we all be—correct, my friend?" Wallace commented to Zorna, who was shaking his staff and staring off while mumbling in Latin.

"Do not worry, Sire," said Zorna, quickly shifting his attention to Wallace. He had heard Wallace's insinuation. "Patience, Your Highness. Have I ever failed you?"

Glancing to his men, the general turned to Wallace. "Everyone here, male or female, is bound to your service by his or her own will and oath. Fifty of our eighty are warriors clothed as commoners. But I fear we may look unconvincing with our fresh-cut clothing, pale skins, and washed bodies."

"Fear not," Wallace said. "I have brought Zorna, the wizard." Zorna bowed. "I am ready, Sire." The wizard withdrew vegetables from his small leather sack. "I have enough for everyone."

The general fanned beneath his nose. "What is that odor? It is like dirty feet wrapped with a skunk's hide."

"They must take it," Zorna said, pushing the food into the fingers of the first several warriors. "I shall give pieces to each member of the garrison. Your soldiers shall pass it down the line until everyone has some."

"Broccoli?" muttered a deep, gruff voice at the front. Taking on life, his grievance hastened through the crowd of large men and rugged women. Several snickered.

The wizard held out a single green floret. "Now who shall be first?" Zorna asked. "Only the bravest and most virtuous shall indulge … and the most beautiful." Suddenly a sea of hands extended from the throng of warriors.

"That is more like it. My army of big, strong men, you sounded like complaining old women." Wallace smirked. "You would die for a cause such as this, yet you feared a handful of *broccoli*."

Mounting a stallion of midnight black, Prince Wallace paced before his garrison, the clop of his horse's hooves loud and forceful. "Who among you will be brave? Step forward and step lively. Who shall be first to demonstrate Zorna's magic? All others shall follow his or her example."

Except for the whinnying of horses and clanking of armor, there was silence.

"Your Highness, I shall be first," came the high voice of a boy.

Eyes darting, Wallace listened, searching the crowd for the voice. A youthful warrior stepped forward. Wallace saw what appeared to be a barely pubescent boy.

"How old are you, child?" Wallace asked, leaning over the mane of his horse.

"Begging Your Highness's pardon," the boy said, "I am no child. I am thirteen years old, Your Highness." The boy looked up to Wallace. Wallace steadied his horse as it stepped back and forth. "My father was to be part of your contingent. Because he is ill with the grippe, confined to his bed, Mother would not let him leave. But, Sire," said the child, his eyes dropping, "even so, I fear he could not have gone if he had wanted. He has become mad with fever. Mother washes him in cold water every night. So, Sire, I am the man. I shall take my father's place."

"This is a brave lad!" Wallace shouted. "Although I fear this 'man' is too young."

The boy plucked the broccoli from the wizard's fingers. Within moments he grew to massive proportions. His face immediately and painlessly melted into that of a brute. His clothing became tattered and small on his gigantic frame. The beast that the boy had become threw his ham-like hands into the air and grinned, showing the eyeteeth of a tiger. He hoisted a wagon with the strength of an elephant and roared like a lion.

Seeing the magic, a hush fell over the throng. Hands shot forward again to take pieces of magical broccoli. One by one, they began to transform. The general took his piece, and Zorna took his. The prince waited until last to take his.

"Each of you may respond differently," said Zorna, gnawing on the broccoli. "This magic will last as long as we need. And another bite will cause you to revert to your former selves."

Wallace nudged his horse forward. Rider and horse loped to the center of the field. Wallace stopped to survey his garrison. He raised his arms to garner their attention.

"My brother Prince Zili, by taxation, subterfuge and violence, is attempting to discredit and dethrone our older brother, King Dobromil, the First of Illuminae. Prince Zili has murdered Hessereth, King of the Lizard People, and he has taken possession of the information that, if deciphered, will lead him to the Dragon Stone and power beyond any he possesses now. The peoples of Aurora, human and oddling, seek our help to return balance to the Linkage," Wallace said.

Plaintive grumbling came from his garrison. He heard a muffled cry: "Prince Zili wears the Fire Ring of Hades, property of the troll people."

"He is convinced its magic will bring him to reign," Wallace shouted. Nudging his horse's flank, he coaxed his mount to slowly stride to the end of the front line. His horse sidled next to the general.

"General Raptozk and I have agreed that we will shall set out on our quest in several smaller groups to arouse little suspicion," said Wallace. "Our bodies and faces changed, our clothing ill-defined, we shall present to the subjects of my brother Alexander's kingdom as troubadours and minstrels. We shall live off the land, travel quietly, blend in, and gather information." Wallace looked over his garrison. "I want you to know our mission. Doubt me not. I neither seek nor want war with my brother. But make no mistake: if it comes to war, he shall have it." Wallace adjusted his posture in the saddle. "You have your orders, maps, and strategies," he said. He made the sign of the cross. "The blessings of all that be, protect us all. Let us be gone."

Amid the clatter of armor, creaking of wagon wheels, and clopping of hooves, the garrison began to rumble forward to their splitting-off point.

Chapter 5

THE VISITORS

Having found no game in the forest after a prolonged hunt, Wallace and his men came upon a clearing. They dismounted and walked their horses out of the forest. Following several feet behind the others, Joseph stopped and bent to the ground when the glint of a shiny object caught his eye. Down on one knee, he reached into the grass.

Lexi rubbed his stomach. "It has been some time since I have been on a *still* hunt and captured absolutely nothing." He unnocked the arrow he'd been keeping taut in the hemp string of his longbow. "It is as if someone or something has other plans for us and—"

"—scared the game away," said General Raptozk. "I understand your meaning. What, pray, is your appraisal, Zorna?"

"It is a mystery," said Zorna flatly, paying more attention to an outlying cabin more than twenty yards away. The perimeter of the cabin was covered in splotchy, burned, and dead vegetation. The cabin was untidy and disturbed. It appeared lifeless and deserted.

"What is this place?" Wallace muttered. Each man wondered into what they had wandered.

"And, Sire," Joseph asked, turning the glittering object over in his hand, "what is this? There seems to be something attached to it."

"A mystery," said Zorna to Wallace, ignoring Joseph. He took not even an instant to look at the object Joseph held up.

"It's a mystery? Is that all the great wizard has to say? It is a *mystery*," Joseph jabbed.

The men continued on their approach to the cabin, now within thirty feet. Lexi swept his feet through the grass as he stepped. "He is without his crystal ball." Lexi snickered.

"Don't bother him," said the general. "He's thinking. Something that might profit you well, if you were to try." The other men shook their heads.

Wallace pointed to dead livestock scattered about the homestead. "Check your maps for landmarks," he said. "Perhaps we may confirm our directions and get a little water. See, the house was vandalized. It is obvious there was a battle here."

They trudged closer. They could smell the scorched wood. The thatch roof, impaled with scores of fire-arrows, was mostly burned away and had collapsed into the standing cabin walls. The wooden fence that had once surrounded the small homestead was shattered. Hoof marks in the mud indicated horses had trampled it.

"It is as dead here," Lexi muttered, "as the forest was there."

"We should announce ourselves, Sire," the general said. Mud and splotchy grass squished beneath his horse's feet.

"Hello!" Wallace shouted.

No response.

"Deserted," he murmured. "During our mission, you must get used to addressing me as Walter," Wallace said to the general. "The same for the rest of you. We are incognito."

The men encircled the homestead, stayed close to the walls. They peered through the windows and the large cracks in the walls.

"Is anyone there?" Wallace called again.

"We are weary travelers who wish refreshment from your well," shouted General Raptozk.

As they converged, they listened but heard no response. Puzzled, the general looked to Wallace, who nodded that they should proceed. They combed the bedraggled grass of the cluttered yard. The general discovered spots of red.

"Blood?" Joseph said, crouching by one spot.

"What is it?" Lexi asked. Joseph pointed.

Tugging his horse along by the reins, Lexi peered at the ground. His eyes tracked a blood trail. "My eyes are not what they used to be," he said, "but I do know blood." He stopped at a slight depression in the ground. There the blood, black and old, was greatest. He eased to one knee. Lexi ran his fingers through scattered white pebbles near the blood.

"Someone has lain here. They dragged themselves out." He pointed to a broad trail of black blood leading from the depression. The whitish-brown, sand-like pebbles were not only dry but also jagged.

The general got down on one knee beside Lexi. He scooped up a palmful of the jagged white rocks. He pressed them to his nose. Their dust burned. He pressed his left index finger into the rocks. Bringing the finger to his lips, he carefully extended the tip of his tongue and tasted.

"Sire, this is salt," General Raptozk muttered, glowering. "I think—"

"Your Highness, over here! At the well!" Joseph shouted. He had followed a separate trail of salt to the rock wall surrounding a thigh-high enclosure. Down the deep well Joseph peered.

Joseph hurled a wooden bucket tied to a long, thick rope. Within a second, he heard the splash below. Reeling up the bucket, Joseph held it under his left arm. He cupped some water just as Prince Wallace stopped at the well. Wallace and Joseph tasted and quickly spat.

"Sorry, Your Highness," Joseph said. "As I thought, this well is salted."

"Poisoned," affirmed Wallace.

Seeing movement in his peripheral vision, General Raptozk broke from the group. He and Zorna led their horses back toward the cabin. Zorna stopped at the front door. Pointing, the general gestured to Zorna that he would check a side yard not far from the front door. Zorna found the cabin door ajar.

"Hello? Anyone home?" asked Zorna, knocking on the door. Hearing no answer, he advanced the door inches and poked in his head. The room was dark. It smelled of death. Exhaling into his cupped palms, Zorna ignited a brilliant, cold flame that grew. Zorna slipped into the cabin, the flame lighting his way.

Pacing the grounds, Joseph stepped among scores of small animal carcasses. He looked at Lexi. "Many of these poor creatures have been shot with arrows, as if for—"

"—target practice!" Lexi shouted. The farmyard was littered with dead chickens, geese, and hogs. Some animals were hacked, others beheaded.

Having made his way to the front of the house, the general stopped in the center of the yard, a blood trail leading away from his feet. "Sire!" he shouted. "Look at this. I've found something, or someone." Loosing the reins of his horse, the general strode several steps before dropping to both knees.

"No one has told me what they thought this was," Joseph said, holding the glimmering, flat object in his hand. He turned it over and saw a soft, desiccated tissue attached.

In front of General Raptozk lay the body of a young man, facedown. Long wavy black hair was tangled around the thin body, which was clad in what appeared to be a uniform of buffed, black, form-fitting leather. A tattered white cape was torn partially from his neck; a gold-handled sword lay at his hand. As the general rolled the body over, he revealed the handsome face of a teenage boy. A pendant mirror on a gold chain fell to his side. General Raptozk saw the boy's hand. "Joseph, let me have that object you found." The general held the glimmering object and fitted it to the boy's hand. "It's his ring and finger. He must have lost it defending himself."

Joseph's cheeks blew out. He turned to throw up. General Raptozk looked up at Wallace, now also standing over him.

"Who is he?" Wallace asked.

"He used to be someone of substance, it seems. Young. Too bad," the general murmured.

Hurrying from the house, Zorna joined Lexi and Joseph by Prince Wallace's side.

"The boy's face is framed by beautiful tresses. His clothing and dead eyes betray his race," said Zorna.

"Look, Your Highness. His pupils are slit like those of a snake," said the general.

"Aye, General," said Wallace.

"I have heard of them," said the general, "but have never seen these creatures."

"What manner of vain devil is this, Your Highness?" Lexi muttered with disgust on his lips.

The general studied the small mirror about the teenager's neck. He slowly turned to Wallace.

"He is no devil," Zorna said. "Do you see the crest he wears on his chest? He is royalty, a prince. I know the lad. His name is Hezia. He is the young son of the lizard people's king. If he is dead, then …"

"If there was ever doubt, it is all removed now. The letter of King Shibboleth of Golam is sadly true," said Wallace, his eyes far away. "The Lizard King is dead indeed. And here lies his kidnapped son. There is treachery afoot in the kingdoms." He pointed to Joseph. "Find something with which we may dig. We must bury him."

"But who does this treachery?" Lexi asked.

Joseph marched to a cauldron still warm over smoldering ashen logs. "Sire, I have something else!" shouted Joseph. "There is residuum of an iridescent substance dried at the bottom of this iron pot. When touched, it flashed over and vanished, and I thought I heard hundreds of tiny voices screaming in pain."

The body buried, Wallace said a prayer over the grave.

"The day is getting late. There is nothing more we can do here," said Prince Wallace. "No doubt we have evidence of great wrongs, which confirms the letter I received from the courier. I trust we shall find who is directly responsible for these atrocities." Wallace turned his back to the grave. "Gather your horses. Let us ride. We have hours to go, and we will eventually lose the light. We must get to the toymaker's farm by sunup."

❦

"Jingles? Jingles? Oh, where is that dog … *Jingles?* What are you doing?" Mary demanded. He ran in wide circles. He ran in tight circles.

He jumped and spun, barking continuously and vigorously. Stopping, he became as still as a statue, his nose pushing into the wind off the horizon. A cryptic odor energized him, an odor too faint for his mistress to appreciate. Mary peered at the mountainous eastern horizon. She expected the sun to rise but not so soon; she dismissed the glow on the horizon. She'd been so busy, perhaps her timing was off, she thought.

Lexi trudged through the mountain pass by torchlight, the forest duff crunching beneath the feet of his horse. He held a burning torch high above his head as he trotted back from scouting ahead.

He slowed his horse as he came upon Wallace and General Raptozk. Sidling his horse beside Wallace's, the general studied a wrinkled parchment map. The map was difficult to read by dawn's blush alone. Lexi held the torch down to the map.

"Sire, according to my map, we have come to the outer perimeter of King Alexander's kingdom. By my estimation, this should be the region of Elfin." The general pointed down the mountain. "In the valley below lies the path to the farm of Tom."

"The toymaker?" Wallace said. "His son is becoming familiar with my family. He saved my niece's life with a miracle." He steadied his impatient horse, which heard the faint echo of a dog far away in the valley. "Our contingent of four shall make the half day's ride to the homestead."

Promptly saluting, the general snapped the reins of his horse to begin.

"Jingles. Stop barking, boy." Jingles stopped and turned to Mary, his tail wagging. His mouth open, his tongue hung from the corner.

Mary shook her head. "Keep me company while I put feed together for the horses and goats."

They entered the yard. She balanced a full bowl of feed in her right hand. Jingles shot off into the yard, barking even more robustly. He returned to Mary, looking back over his shoulder as he came.

"Nothing out there, boy."

Mary saw feet before her. She saw three apples whirling in a vertical orbit, to as low as a foot above the ground, as if someone was juggling. Mary saw no juggler.

Jingles sat. Still barking, he peered to their left.

She looked to her left and was amazed. Three carrots circled a foot above the ground.

Grasping Jingle's collar, Mary slowly stepped backward toward the house, trying to take in what she saw. Her front yard was a circus of invisible actors causing odd things to happen. She thought it was about time she went inside and rested. Perhaps she had gotten up too early. She had begun not to feel so well.

"Mama's tired, Jingles," Mary said. "I should go lie down for a moment. Yes, that's right. Lie down." Jingles barked at the circling, dipping, and flying objects. "So you see it too. There are ... vegetables floating in my garden," she murmured.

"Miss Mary," uttered a disembodied voice, clearly emanating from the empty space before her. The orange glare of the sun had begun poking above the horizon. Shading her eyes, Mary scanned the ground before her.

"Miss Mary," came a squeaky voice from behind. She spun to see there was no one.

"Miss Mary," called a voice closer to her. She felt a tug at the hem of her dress. She slapped at her thigh as she might to shoo an insect. With her left hand, she searched for the owner of the voice. With her right, she felt for the dog. There was another pull at her left hem.

"Jingles, no," she admonished, looking to her left. Jingles, however, was not at her side.

"Who's there?" Mary became confused and nervous, not knowing which way to turn.

"We are, Miss Mary," called the high-pitched voice.

Suddenly, like soap bubbles behind tufts of grass, from puddles, and among scattered twigs, tiny people no taller than tulips popped into existence with puffs of colored sparkles. Lightheaded, Mary rubbed her eyes while trying to keep count: one, two … seven … eleven. Her mind reeled at the fountain of color spewing from every minute pop. Now able to connect the bodies with speakers, she exhaled.

"Greetings, wife of Tom Claus, Mary. We are here so tired, so weary. During our travels, your husband offered us shelter if we would come. Exchange for help with all your chores, he would for us open up his doors," said a troll, visible behind his compatriots.

Intrigued by her visitors, Mary listened, her arms relaxed along the pleats of her skirt, her fingers interlocked.

"We came invisible, we came here quick to mop and sweep your floors, no trick."

Mary gathered her thoughts. She sank to one knee. Jingles sidled to her thigh. Mary rubbed his flank to soothe his breathless barking.

"And it shall be done. Will you not come in?" Mary said, rising to her feet. "Unlike you, Tom must travel overland, and it shall take time. I expect Tom's return this evening."

The oddlings worked for several hours. Then one small creature stood at Mary's kitchen door. "We sense someone coming. The dog does too. We know not who it is. That dog has a clue."

Mary peered from the kitchen window to the horizon. She saw Jingles dashing through the yard, over the fence, and into the pasture. Within seconds, he vanished in the distance, only a trail of dust left in his wake.

"They must be back," Mary said, her heart racing. She saw her face in a small mirror nailed to the kitchen doorjamb.

Up the road, Jingles ran to intercept distant, approaching figures. A familiar scent filled his nose. Jingles ran three-quarters of a mile to the farm entry gate in seconds. He sensed Tom and Nicholas were close to the homestead. Jingles could hear the clanking and jangling of pots, pans, and other supplies swinging from hooks nailed to wagon beams.

The wagon rolled on for several minutes. Jingles came alongside. As proud as if he had captured prey, Jingles followed them back to the house. Tom pulled back on the reins, and Henry and Philly stopped before the house. From his high perch on the wagon bench, Tom surveyed his property. He smelled the air, as was his habit whenever he arrived home.

When the varda stopped rolling, Nicholas jumped, a cloud of dust discharging from his clothing on impact. Bucking and running, Jingles nearly hurled himself into Nicholas's arms.

Sinking to his knees Nicholas threw his arms around Jingles' neck. "Hey, boy," he said. "I missed you sooooo much." Nicholas looked up at Tom. "Papa, he looks smaller."

Tom climbed down. Arching, he stretched his back and legs, rising to his toes and down again, briefly massaging his backside. "That's the hardest bench."

"But even harder the longer we travel," quipped Nicholas.

"And he looks smaller," Tom said. Nicholas nodded. "Definitely smaller." Jingles panted, his tongue slinging saliva.

"Where's Mama, boy?" Nicholas asked, rubbing the dog's belly. Nicholas rose, and Jingles scrambled to his feet. His legs and spine like springs, he bounced and spun, galloping to the stable entrance. Towing Henry and Philly on the long line, Nicholas followed.

Several yards away, Tom saw Mary enter the barn. She pretended she had not seen him, to allow him to surprise her. Mary wanted Tom to believe she was milking the cow and too busy to notice. But when she went to Patches' stall, she saw a female troll already milking the cow. Her arms akimbo, Mary gawked. She had no Plan B.

Jingle shot into the barn, Nicholas and Tom following mere seconds later.

"Please, Miss Mary, do not stare," said the female troll. "For the animals, I help you to care. For shelter, Tom said, 'twas payment fair."

Mary simpered.

"Hello, darling," said Tom.

"Tom," she cooed, trying to show surprise. "You're home." She was overjoyed, although she was determined not to show it. She did not want him to regret ever leaving her with loneliness. "I suppose that explains things?"

"I see you have found my surprise to you, my darling," said Tom with a giggle.

She wrapped her arms around his waist, kissed him, and whispered in his ear, "I haven't collected the eggs." Tom shook his head and drew her near for another kiss.

Turning away, Nicholas peered through the barn door. He saw streams of dust in the distant air. He knew that usually meant riders had come on the property and were on their way.

Pleased to find that his oddling friends and neighbors had accepted the offer of shelter in exchange for help with the chores, Tom watched cheerfully as the female troll carried the milk to the storage can. Having set aside any minor differences, the oddling peoples worked peacefully side by side on the fields and in the workshop. Some built furniture, others toys. Acting as mentors, some taught measurements, cut wood, and climbed ladders. Others stacked finished items to shelves scaling as high as fourteen feet. Some elders taught the youth specific skills for farm or workshop chores. Others worked the fields and cared for the animals. With a blow of breath, the frost elves filled the icehouse to the roof. Everybody helped one another understand. Mary, with several oddling women and girls, cooked, cleaned, and sewed; some using the Linkage, without touching needle or thread.

As the dust subsided, Nicholas could make out five distant riders. Gathering his tools, coat, and scarf from a hook, Nicholas called to his father. "Papa!" Nicholas tucked his scarf around his neck.

Both Tom and Mary turned to him.

He tossed a sack of tools over his shoulder and walked toward the door. A diminutive oddling, Percy, was at his side. "I need to check the bearings on the waterwheel in the back field," Nicholas said. "Percy said it is faulty. That is why the mill is unable to grind the wheat with its usual vigor." He stepped over the doorsill. "I will return shortly."

He looked to the hills and could no longer see the riders. Perhaps he had been mistaken. Perhaps there would be no company after all.

Mouths frothing from the hard ride, the horses of Prince Wallace's men paused below the high mountain ridge directly above the valley of Tom's farm. Dismounting, General Raptozk surveyed the activity below.

"We don't want to run into any of Sheriff Zili's men. We are unprepared for a confrontation," Prince Wallace said. "General, can you identify the farm below us?"

"Aye, Your Highness," said General Raptozk. Withdrawing a parchment map from a leather tube attached to his saddle, he unrolled it across a boulder. He checked the sun and their position against the map. He marked an *X* at their location.

"Your Highness, I am certain this is the homestead and workshop of the master carpenter Thomas Claus. He knows nothing of our arrival. I think we should remind our men of the importance of—"

"We shall spare the briefing, General. Everyone is aware of the gravity of our mission and the part each must play. We are in disguise and shall remain so. As our wizard has said, the spell shall break when it is no longer needed."

Prince Wallace nodded. "They are good men, General. Their memories are as good as mine."

The prince sipped water from a leather pouch slung at his side. Wiping his lips, he gently turned his horse. He pointed behind, up and over a cliff. "While we still have light, we will ascend and wait on higher ground until dusk. We shall descend tonight. I want our arrival unseen." Wallace looked to the sky. "It is much too light. We have some time. I have business with the toymaker; I want a clear and rested mind. In the meanwhile, we shall take note of the comings and goings at the carpenter's farm."

At dusk, the four men carefully made their way down the forest mountain slope to the green trail. The trail led to the main road: a rutted, well-worn, stone-strewn wagon path leading to the archway gate, the main entrance to Tom's homestead.

At midnight, the five riders stopped at Tom's gate. They saw the light pouring from the distant windows of the carpenter's cabin.

Wallace gestured. General Raptozk leaned from his horse to unlatch the gate. The horse's ears lay back and he whinnied when a diminutive, smoky shadow in the form of an inverted vortex twisted in a moonbeam. Spiraling, the smoke became a crooked, crumpled little man. His large nose sniffing, his large eyes flicked from Wallace to the general. Through his oversize teeth, he spoke with a lisp. "You weary travelers in need of rest, you made the trip; now pass the test. Pay the toll before you go, or trouble on you I will bestow."

"Trouble," said General Raptozk, "he threatens Your Royal Highness. I shall kill him where he stands." He slowly reached for his sword.

"Wait, General," said Wallace. "He means us no trouble." Wallace held out his hand and one finger, gesturing for the general to stop.

"Who are you? Whatever you are?" the general snapped. "I am a troll. I collect toll."

The general watched the grotesque creature lift its bony arm to Wallace. "I thought they just lived in the muck under bridges," he murmured.

Beneath the archway threshold, a pipe conducted a trickle of water from one side of the road to the other. Prince Wallace recognized it for what it was. "A bridge, my dear General Raptozk. Small, but a bridge," Wallace said.

The troll smiled a toothy grin.

"Now," continued Prince Wallace, "what do I get for payment to you, troll?" He carefully watched the movements of his pugnacious general, fingering the hilt of his sword.

The troll swayed uncertainly in place, his eyes darting from horseman to horseman. "Grant unharmed you do pass, for your horse the sweetest grass."

"Your name, troll?" the general demanded.

Prince Wallace raised his hand to calm the general's growing ire. His horse whinnied and stomped. "Your name, kind sir, please?" Wallace asked, winking at his general as he folded his forearms across his saddle.

"Musker," said the troll.

"What is the price of your toll, Mr. Musker?" asked the prince.

"A naros for each horse, of course."

Prince Wallace withdrew a leather pouch from his saddlebag. Giving notice with his eyes to his general that he would personally pay the toll, Wallace removed five naros. "Mr. Musker, your payment."

With a nod of thanks and expectation, the troll extended his hand, palm up.

Leaning from his horse, the prince handed the money to the troll. "Will you guide me to the Master of this abode?"

With no further conversation, Musker took the reins of the prince's horse. He turned and marched forward. He led the five riders up the road, to the homestead and to Tom, working late in the barn.

Tom turned as he heard the clop of the horses' hooves. He strode to the open door of the barn, grasping the brass loop of a candelabrum. He held the candle to the side of his head as the men approached.

"Kind sir, could you spare a little room and some hay for weary travelers?" asked Wallace. "If we may impose, we will be fine in the barn, as we are ripe with travel."

Tom gestured the men forward. He backed into the barn, allowing the men to enter. "My home is always open to a kind soul. I'll have my wife bring you dinner and water with which to wash."

"Thank you, Mr. Claus," said Wallace. "Your hospitality will be rewarded."

"Do I know you?" Tom asked. "How do you know my name?" Wallace nodded to the general. General Raptozk announced, "You are in the presence of Prince Wallace of Waters." Dismounting, he stood at attention. "We would appreciate your keeping this in confidence."

Tom bowed. "Of course, of course. You look nothing as I expected."

"Our wizard has cloaked us in a spell so we might travel peacefully," said General Raptozk. He glanced at Zorna, dismounting from his horse. Lexi and Joseph did the same.

"But now you must rest, my friends," Tom said. "I will see to your horses."

Rumor or Not

In the bunkhouse, Mary turned back the beds. She checked some of the younger sleeping oddlings, then returned to the main house.

Tom led General Raptozk in. "I have taken care of your horses, Gen—"

"Shhhhhh," shushed the general, raising his finger to his lips. Leaning into Tom, he whispered, "As you see by our modest garb—" his eyes cut to the sleeping oddlings, "—we have concealed our identity for reconnaissance purposes. Please, call me Leopold. Refer to me as such while we are here."

Tom nodded. "How should I ... How should I address the others?" He pointed, rolling his hands.

Arm over his shoulder, Raptozk walked Tom to a far corner of the room. "You may address the prince as Walter, and the others by their given names: the wizard, Zorna; the apothecary, Joseph; and Captain Lexi."

His hand to his chin, Tom peered at the general. "Leopold? Mary, my wife, told me you arrived after dinner. I apologize. We have finished providing dinner for the help. Nevertheless, my family and I would be honored if the five of you would join us at the main house for venison stew." Tom humbly cast down his eyes. "It—it isn't lavish, but there is enough for all."

Overhearing, the prince came close. "We gratefully accept your invitation, Tom," he said, nodding. "I and my men thank you for your hospitality."

"Come," Tom said. "Just follow the footpath. The main house is over there, not far."

The men strode thirty yards to the house. Climbing two stairs to the porch, Tom unfastened the front door. Hearing the latch click, Mary looked up from the hearth. She poked and stirred the fire beneath her cast-iron pot.

"With whom do we dine, Tom?" Mary asked. Tom crossed the room to her. He drew her ears to his lips. Tom whispered. "They are in disguise."

Raising her eyebrows slightly, Mary nodded. "Not terribly deceptive disguises." She saw the surprise on their faces as they neared. "I know who you are," she said flatly. The four men looked at one another. Their faces had morphed back to their natural forms.

"Zorna?" Prince Wallace muttered, astonished.

"As I predicted," Zorna said. "The protective cloak would last so long as we needed. The disguise has become unnecessary here, Your Highness."

Breathing deeply, Prince Wallace felt his face. "I am at peace here," he said.

Mary nodded and smiled, "Welcome to our humble home."

Tom stretched out his open hand to shake with each man. Mary stood by.

"I am Lexi, Captain of His Highness's guard." He bowed.

Mary nodded.

"Joseph, the royal apothecary." He bowed.

Tom shook his hand.

"I am Zorna, the royal consul and His Highness's wizard." He bowed.

"And I am Prince Wallace of the Kingdom of Waters." Mary averted her eyes and curtsied.

"If you please, Mary. Now we have our faces," the prince glanced at Zorna, "but we should like to keep our true names secret. We want to get used to them, so as not to answer and give ourselves away with our true names. For when we head into the countryside, we must revert to our secret identities."

"I will set the table presently," Mary said. "Venison stew, sourdough bread, and ice-cold buttermilk for dinner. There is no pie tonight, Tom, but for anyone craving sweets, I've made some peppermint and cinnamon rock candy."

Like a child, Tom smiled broadly.

The men took their places at the table. An oil lamp sat at its center. The flame danced and hissed, projecting titanic shadows of the diners upon the slatted walls of gray timber.

Trudging from the back field after having checked the waterwheel, Nicholas stepped through the front door, his eyes down, counting eggs in a basket. Unaware of the newest houseguests, he shouted across the house: "Mama! Forgot these six eggs in the coop!" Still examining the eggs, he hung his hat, coat, and scarf on the coatrack. He dropped a sling of tools on the floor at the base of the rack, his back to the dining room table. "I also have this sack of turnips I intend to put into the cellar below the dining room floor. And—"

Amused, the guests exchanged glances.

"—Papa, Percy got down into the water. The bearings on the waterwheel needed changing and the slough—well, sorry, it took longer than I expected. A few of the bearings rolled downstream. I—"

Looking up, Nicholas finally observed the strange men sitting around the table with his parents.

"Oh. Pardon me." Nicholas squinted. "I didn't realize— Hello."

"This is my son, Nicholas," Tom said. "I am Walter. These are my men."

"I am ... Nicholas. I also have a bad habit of speaking before looking. My parents have taught me better. I'm sorry."

"Nicholas, our new friends have important business at the castle of King Alexander," Tom said. "We shall call them Walter, Lexi, Zorna, Joseph, and Leopold. They are travelers stopping to refresh themselves." Nicholas started for the table but remembered another duty as his father spoke. He headed for the basin.

"Yes. Wash your hands," Mary said.

Afterward, Nicholas served his plate and took a seat at the table. Stirring and ladling his own stew, Wallace brought a spoonful to his lips and blew.

"Tom," Wallace said, beginning dinner chat, "I have heard there's been trouble in the villages. Have you heard the same?"

Tom glanced around the table. "Sadly, true." He sighed, stirring his stew. "Neighbors, friends, and many others here have lost homes or livelihoods as a direct result of Sheriff Zili's plunder."

There was silence.

Looking up to Mary, a diminutive oddling girl whispered, "This stew is quite delicious, Miss Mary." Her finger to her lips, her mother shushed her while gently rubbing her hair.

"Yes, it is," said Lexi.

"Even oddling have fared poorly under Zili's thumb," Tom noted.

"Even oddlings?" Zorna remarked. "With their resources?"

"Afraid so," said Tom, lowering his spoon. "Likely *because* of their resources, some have said. Zili desires to harvest their power in any way possible. He has killed to do so." Nearly every eye cut to Tom. "Sadly, their special abilities and qualities have not insulated them from Zili's evil intent."

"It's dreadful, just dreadful we can't live in harmony," Mary wearily said. "After so many years of peace."

"The talk is of the sheriff. Prince Zili has tortured and murdered Hessereth, King of the Lizard People," Nicholas said.

Joseph looked up from his bowl. "Why, pray tell? Why would he do that?" Wallace could see the grief on Joseph's face. "Oddlings of all clans are King Dobromil's most faithful allies. What's happened is nothing less than insanity."

About to speak, Tom hesitated. He shook his head instead.

"What is it, my friend? Speak, Tom," said Wallace.

Tom inhaled. "The trolls say Zili searches for the Dragon Stone. He searches for a key to decipher the code."

"A code? Your Highness!" Zorna angrily repeated. He pounded his fist against the table. The platters and chalices rang. "He will not stop until the Dragon Stone is in his grasp. This is not only outrage, but is also dangerous."

Sipping his buttermilk, Walter peeked over the rim of the glass, made uneasy by his wizard's disposition.

"What is this—Dragon Stone?" Nicholas asked. Mary shook her head.

"Pray tell," Wallace said to Zorna.

Zorna dusted the crumbs from his hands. "Your Highness, Nicholas. The Dragon Stone is a repository of great magic."

"And, my dear wizard," Wallace asked, "where exactly was such a stone created?"

Gathering his long white beard into his hand, Zorna peered somberly across the table, one by one into the eyes of each, especially Wallace's. "It is said that it was born in the heart of the Cossack Volcano." The room stilled, every eye on Zorna. He continued, "It is a mountain protected by fires stoked and maintained by a diminishing clan of so-called dragons. Many men have gone to those mountains and have not returned."

"We once owned such a stone, Sire," said a troll. His voice was muffled, coming from beneath the table. "It may give life or destroy all life."

Wallace could see the fear in everyone's eyes. Sitting back on his chair, he folded his arms. "Is the one Zili has the same as the one belonging to the troll clan?" he asked.

Having already finished his meal, Lexi sat in a corner, his sword between his knees, point down. He spun the point into the floor. At a glare from Mary, he folded his palms across the hilt. "Could such a thing be the cause of His Majesty's brother's ... malice?" he asked.

"Could it spoil Zili's soul?" added Joseph.

Zorna nodded. "Yes." He turned to Joseph. "Sadly, it is said to concentrate a man's greed, his need for power. The stone absorbs and concentrates the deadly power used against the dragon by those determined to acquire the stone."

A pall fell over the room, broken only by a soft utterance from Tom.

"Please." From his seat, Tom rose and bowed. "Walter, can you and your friends stay a while? We shall not solve this problem tonight." Leveling his gaze at the small creatures spread among the diners—at the table, near the hearth, on shelving, on windowsills, and shooting sparkles of light through the house—Tom nodded. "There are oddlings and others here who may give you better answers than either Nicholas or I. You may talk with more of them in the morning."

Walter somberly looked to Lexi, Joseph, and Zorna. Each man nodded. Their chairs rumbling as they scraped them back, the four men stood. "We shall accept your hospitality and suggestion." Wallace stretched and patted his belly. "We are eager to do anything you will have us do to repay your hospitality, if it is not beyond our competence. You'll find us quite handy and ready after a night's rest, Tom."

Mary smiled doubtfully. Having company meant more work for her. "The privileged speak with great aplomb of their abilities," she grumbled into Tom's ear. Mary wearily looked Walter up and down, and flashed a brief smile. "With great aplomb, I say." She sauntered away. "I've set fresh linens on your bunks. Your travel clothes are on the barrel by the pump. I'll put them into the boil pot. Good night, gentlemen."

Chapter 6

WALLACE LISTENS

A rooster crowed stridently. Sunrise broke on the horizon over the Cossack Mountains. Tom walked the dirt path to the bunkhouse, still lazily swinging the ax with which he had just chopped wood. The whiff of fish blowing from the surface of the waterwheel brook mixed with the sweet, spicy smell of pine from the outlying trees.

Briefly pausing, Tom looked at the gray, slatted bunkhouse door. He pondered the proper etiquette of waking a privileged royal so early in the morning. Raising his hand to knock, Tom startled when the door was flung open.

"Good morning, Thomas," said Joseph, "What's taken you so long? Still asleep?" Joseph laughed. Fully clothed, he stood with his hand on the hilt of his sword, point down to the floor. Behind the door, Tom heard muted snickering. Peering into the bunkhouse, Tom saw Wallace sitting at a small writing desk, a quill pen in hand, a bottle of ink before him.

"Lexi," Wallace said, pointing to Joseph and his sword, "put your pet away. Our only enemy is the untilled soil. We're more likely to dig rows than impale them.

"Good morning, Tom," he continued, his eyes drawn back to the paper upon which he wrote. He dipped his quill. "As is my custom," he murmured, "I write in my journal every morning as soon as the sun rises." He wrote several lines. "I have solitude enough to concentrate on my past travails, rather than the ones coming." Wallace slid the page from the small desk, folded it into thirds, and slipped it into a pouch beneath his inner shirt.

"The day is young, gentlemen and Your Highness." Tom stepped over the doorsill into the bunkhouse. "Yesterday, Your Highness, you requested to meet with humans and oddlings harmed by your brother, Prince Zili."

Waving his fingertips, Wallace gestured for Tom to come closer. "If you desire to keep your identity a secret, you should help with the chores," Tom added.

Zorna nodded. "It is wise, Sire. They will be more likely to talk in confidence with a commoner."

"It is truth," Wallace agreed. "Consider it done." Pushing up his sleeves, he stood and looked into the eyes of each of his men. "There is a certain amount of virtue provided by the rigors of a day's work. We should remain open to that common philosophy."

Rolling his eyes, the general looked away.

"Roll your eyes gently, General," Wallace said. "Life is not all war." His heels knocked the floor timbers as Wallace strode over to his general. He looked down upon him, seated on a small stool. "You should know as well as I that hard work is good for a men's virility.

"He is a great general," he said confidentially to Tom, "but I fear there are battles my general has yet to fight. He has no children. At least none he has told to me."

"Sire, it has been your unofficial policy that sons should not fight alongside fathers," the general said softly, "as it leaves mothers with irreparably broken hearts."

"Fathers with only sons, General, *only* sons. Not my policy. It is the legacy of my father, King Richard, and one we should seek to change." Mildly irritated, General Raptozk smirked. "Sire, about the work—what will menial work do for a man's back at the end of the day that a good beating won't?" Wallace laughed, lifting his eyebrows. "Please forgive my general, our gracious host Tom. I've been told he is somewhat prickly at this hour of the morning. Now, what work have you for us?"

"There are many chores, Sire. We have an active workshop here. Begging your pardon, what would you like to try?"

Rubbing his hands together, Wallace paced in a tight circle. "We could talk with many," he muttered. "Where are the majority of your help working?"

Tom stepped out of his path. "We are bringing in the harvest, so many are in the field. I also have four projects in the workshop. Do you know woodworking?"

"I have many skills," said Wallace. "I know woodworking, metalworking, and swordsmanship. Yes, I can even shovel manure." Wallace smirked, lifting one eyebrow, peering askance at the general and Tom. "As a lad my—His Highness made certain I knew the work of the common man. He asserted I could neither be a proper prince nor king if I neither appreciated nor knew the work of the people I led."

"The king was very wise to teach you that," said Tom. "Aye, no man will ever respect a ruler who assesses his subjects as valueless."

"I admit as a teenager I thought him at best an ogre, and at worse an ignoramus for sullying my princely hands. As we grew older, Alexander and I understood his wisdom. Zili never did." The room seemed to darken at the mention of the sheriff's name. The sun went behind a cloud.

Wallace's face brightened. "As we discussed, call me by my pseudonym. That goes for all. Let us begin there and we shall move to the fields. I will sweep floors and stock shelves. Yes?"

"A good place to begin, Your Highness. I mean ... Walter. I shall make the proper introduction. Tell me ... Walter. What about your men? Where would you like them to work?"

Wallace looked at Joseph, Zorna, Lexi, and Leopold. Stepping forward, Zorna nodded. Leaning against the wall, Joseph straightened and bowed. Standing up from the footstool, the general breathed deeply, rolling his eyes. He bowed.

"Send them to the harvest," Wallace said. "Report to me what you overhear."

Ducking their heads beneath the low door lintel, the four men trailed Tom from the bunkhouse. "Very well, let the day begin," Tom said. Hearing the rattle of a saber in its scabbard, Tom looked over his shoulder. "Lexi, I fear there are no dragons to slay."

"Yet," Wallace added, standing at the door. Jinking back, Lexi flung his sword through the doorway, then turned to catch up with Tom, Zorna, Leopold, and Joseph. Clanging, the sword and scabbard slid up against a wall.

"I shall have them choose work clothing, and we will go to the main house for breakfast. You will meet us there, Walter?" Tom shouted. The prince nodded. Tom walked several yards to a small wooden toolshed with a pitched roof. The four men followed.

"You will need boots and gloves. Search through the inventory. You should find something on the shelves that fits," Tom said. He spotted tall, thin Joseph rubbing his stomach. "Mary makes a more than ample breakfast. You will work hard, but you cannot work without having full stomachs. We shall eat together at the main house table. First, we pray. Then we eat. Then we work hard. Come. Prince— Walter shall meet us there."

The men marched toward the main house.

With single-minded glee, Jingles dashed through the mud to join his master. In the early morning hours before everyone had risen, it had rained. Having been outside chasing rabbits, the dog dripped with rain. He shook, spraying them with muddy water from his fur. Bounding backward, Lexi, wiped his eyes clear. "Indeed, if we pretend to be the great unwashed, your dog has provided ample cover."

Zorna had protected himself untouched within a bubble of air. He closed the bag from which the air had blown. About to slip it back into his pocket, he glimpsed Tom. "Oh. I bet you're wondering," Zorna said. "I call it—a wind bag. Some say I named it after myself."

"For it is not unlike yourself, Zorna," quipped General Raptozk as the men stopped at the front door of the main house.

"Let us not walk into her kitchen with mud. Mama will throw a skillet at us. And she's pretty accurate." Tom laughed.

The men laughed too while wiping as much of the mud away as they could. The smell of bacon, ham, bread, and eggs preceded their entry through the kitchen door. A cacophony of chattering voices and laughter grew as they entered the open refectory: a long, prepared dining table set at its center. Nicholas met them at the door.

"My, my, Nicholas. You surprise me," Wallace said, coming from behind. His men stood aside.

Wallace and his men circled the cedar dining table. From one end of the room to the other, the long table could easily seat fifty men comfortably. On either side, a bench ran parallel the length of the table. Taking in all he saw, Wallace strode to the end of the table. He peered down the table to the other end of the room. Two great armchairs, ornately carved by Tom's own hand, sat at either end. Wallace's fingers brushed the fine wood of the one before him, the artisanship flawless.

Joseph wandered to the east wall, where he noticed a stained-glass window overlooking the garden. Below, abutting the right edge of a sink, was a water pump, its handle autonomously swinging vertically. Situated below the pump were three conjoined bins filled with water for washing dishes and vegetables.

Joseph gazed at the pump handle with amazement. "See! It pumps. Without the touch of a hand," he said. A quizzical expression was on Joseph's brow; his hands hovered above the handle.

Approaching, the master wizard Zorna examined the self-moving handle. "Exactly how is this working?" he asked, trying to determine the spell. He watched as water flowed from the spigot.

Sidling next to Zorna, his face just as quizzical, the general's eyes cut to a tiny pink-and-green light well above the handle. Not sunlight, not reflected light, the flyspeck danced up and down.

Lexi moved closer to see the little dancing light. The closer he got, the more he stared. Inside the glare, he distinguished the tiniest woman he had ever seen. "Can you see that?" Lexi said, "Has anyone seen that?" The woman had long blonde hair. She was clad in a dress made of gold and green, reflecting the pattern of the forest.

"She has four wings. Four little wings on her back," Lexi murmured. Amused, he leaned and tittered, smiling faintly, his eyes nearly crossing as they converged on the tiny creature. His bearded face was so close that his mild breathing made her hovering wobble.

"She is a color sprite, you ninny," the general arrogantly snapped, speaking with feigned authority. "What's wrong with you? Have you never seen a woman doing dishes?" His back straight, he stepped backward from the pump, staring. "Why, if that is the case, you're a sorry excuse of a man. Close your mouth, captain; it's rude to stare." The general admonished Lexi is if he himself had ever seen a color sprite. He had not.

Turning nervously, Lexi realized that Wallace, the general, Zorna, and several others had their eyes upon him. Grinning, he sheepishly bowed and stepped away from the sink. "I, uh— Do forgive me. My, uh, eyesight isn't as good as it used to be." Fist up, thumb pointing over his shoulder, he paced backward. "It is just that I have never seen a person as small as that before." He laughed awkwardly. "I see she is quite capable of doing things for herself, ma'am," he muttered to Mary.

Interpreting her nod as approving, Lexi quickly turned back to the color sprite. He pushed his face within inches of her light. "Hello. My name is Lexi. Yours?"

"I am Glitter," she said in a wee, high-pitched intonation.

Lexi nodded, smiling childishly. "How nice to meet you, Glitter." Three loud bangs on the table reverberated throughout the refectory.

Startled, Lexi turned, joining the call to attention. Tom stood at the center of the table, looking up and down.

"Good morning, my friends," he said. "We have more neighbors joining us today. Please say hello to Walter, Joseph, Zorna, Leopold, and Lexi. They will be helping us with our work for a while."

Voices of varying pitches and accents joined a chorus of greetings that rang throughout the room. They gave the newcomers a grand welcome, as if they were friends of many years just returned. A sea of hands met theirs along the way to their seats at the long table.

"You can find the cups and plates by the window," Mary said. "Utensils are there as well. There is plenty of food on the side tables. Please help yourself. When breakfast is done, Tom and Nicholas will show you where you shall work." She poured coffee for those seated around the table.

A man, slightly balding and grizzled, raised his head from his meal to look down the table at Wallace. He was clad in woolen slacks and a long-sleeved, elk-skin shirt. He stiffly stood, struggling with a slight hump in his back.

"I am Lawrence," he quavered in his elderly voice. A cautious smile plodded to his wizened face. "This is my wife, Carrie." She bowed her head as he peered down at her sitting beside him. "We were bakers in the town of Elfin. We work with the flora gnomes to help Mary with the gardens and the cooking. I am sure I speak for all when I welcome you to this table, but ... would you kindly tell us who you are?" Lawrence asked, his eyes shifting to Zorna, Lexi, Leopold, and Walter with an entreating look. Others seated at the table muttered in low voices. Tom stepped forward, but Mary gestured him back.

The room hushed; the moment lingered.

Lexi spoke. "We, uh, are merchants from the land of Wa-Waters," he stuttered. "Yes. We are on our way to trade at—at Castle Illuminae." His voice rasping, Lexi coughed nervously and cleared his throat. He felt a level of guilt about their necessary deception.

"Pleased, to meet you, gentlemen," the old man said, relieved. "Buttermilk?" Mary interjected, standing at the side. She held a pitcher high in her hand.

"I would," intoned a sonorous voice coming from the roof.

Walter and his men turned in the direction of the voice. It vibrated, penetrating deeply into their chests. The face of a giant peered down at them from a man-size hatch in the ceiling. His massive hand caused the stein of buttermilk look as if it were a child's glass. "My name is Beast, of the Ogre clan. I work with the animals and do much of the heavy lifting for Tom and Mary."

Dissembling his surprise, Zorna lifted his plate. "Mary, you and your lady friends have outdone yourselves. The food is delicious. Yours is the penultimate of sorcery—kitchen magic, madam, kitchen magic," Zorna lauded loudly. "You make me miss my wife."

"How did you, Lawrence the Baker, come to partake of Tom and Mary's hospitality?" Wallace asked.

"Woefully, my dear Walter, because of Sheriff Zili."

"Zili?"

The old man sat. Carrie laid her head upon Lawrence's shoulder. She began to snivel. Angered by the anguish his wife endured from Zili's actions, Lawrence jutted his jaw. "Our sheriff has destroyed our homes," he said, and a chorus of many others repeated his words.

Lowering his spoon, Nicholas turned to Wallace, several seats away. "My parents," he said, "have offered shelter to those in need, in exchange for help with the chores." He looked into the sad eyes of the humans and oddlings seated near him. "Winter is coming quickly. They need help. We need help. So …"

Chapter 7

WALLACE BRINGS NEWS

After leaving Tom's farm, Wallace and his men spent several days spread out over the countryside. They gathered much information. Now at Castle Illuminae, he and his men waited for his brother, King Alexander, in an anteroom. Prince Wallace stood face-to-face with the chamberlain. As Wallace was still in disguise, the chamberlain did not recognize him.

"You will wait here. The king will be with you shortly," the chamberlain said, his voice cracking and curt, his nose slightly high.

"I'm so very glad to see you, dear Chamberlain," Prince Wallace said, but the chamberlain turned. He was about to leave Wallace in the anteroom when Wallace asked him to wait. He did not understand why his old friend was not excited to see him. In fact, the chamberlain looked at him as if he were a three-headed ogre—not unheard of but a rarity. When Prince Wallace lived at the castle as a child, he had known the chamberlain well. The chamberlain's father had served King Richard. Wallace considered them not only servants but also family friends.

Wallace decided to try a new approach. "Over the years, you are unchanged, my dear friend. I see you've gained no weight since I left."

"Left?" asked the chamberlain. Wallace had gotten his attention.

"I'm certain my brother the king is feeding you," Wallace quipped.

Zorna, Joseph, Lexi, and the general stood closer. The general held a squirming burlap sack that caught the chamberlain's eye.

Wallace could see confusion on the chamberlain's face. He stared, locking his eyes with the chamberlain's and turning his face left and right. "Do you remember me now?" asked Wallace excitedly.

But the chamberlain reacted with indifference and took a step away. "No. Look," said Wallace, touching the chamberlain's shoulder. "Unhand me or I shall summon the king's guard," the chamberlain stated quietly.

"But, why would you …" Wallace remembered the magic. They were in disguise again, and his face was unrecognizable. "Ah, yes," Wallace sighed, glimpsing Zorna, who seemed to be amused by the situation.

Closing his eyes, Zorna meditated. Reaching out, Zorna sprinkled sparkling dust of crushed, charmed mother-of-pearl over each man's head and his own. A bright light flashed around each. Within seconds, not only did the visages of all five men reform to their familiar faces, but their clothing also transformed. They became clean, bright, and appropriate, reflecting their noble station.

Smiling, his arms outstretched. Wallace looked into the chamberlain's eyes once more. "How do you like me now?"

The chamberlain stepped forward to embrace him. "Prince Wallace.

It is you. Oh, it is you," said the chamberlain, vibrating with excitement.

He struggled but eventually restrained himself.

"These are my associates from my kingdom. Now, dear Chamberlain, where is *brother* Alexander?" asked Prince Wallace, chuckling.

Holding Wallace's upper arms with both hands, the chamberlain nodded. "I shall tell the king you are here." He scampered to the door. "So wonderful to see you again, Prince Wallace." Closing the anteroom door behind him, he was gone.

Within the instant, the door creaked open. The small durward peeped in, his eyes alight, and met Wallace's smiling face. The durward quietly withdrew and shut the door.

Wallace laughed, pointing. "I've known those two since I was a lad. They were like a second family to me," Wallace said. "Oh, what mischief I would get into! They showed me secrets of this castle I was certain not even my father knew."

Another, more ornate door opened on the other side of the room. Isadora entered. Wallace turned from his four friends. His eyes followed her. She was as beautiful as ever. His eyes met hers. She curtsied.

"Sister-in-law, my beautiful sister-in-law, Queen Isadora," Wallace greeted her. "You are as beautiful as a spring flower. The sun rises in your smile."

"And compliments roll off your tongue like honey. I am afraid bees shall sting me. Stop your foolishness or your brother will be jealous," quipped Queen Isadora. She smiled. "It's been a while since we've seen you. I heard you and Princess Marinna took a trip around the world, and that she is with child."

"I did, dear sister-in-law, and she is. You should try it. Spread your sunny disposition around."

The queen smiled. She was known for being prim, polite, and stately. She, in fact, often restrained her disposition. "Have a baby or travel around the world, dear brother-in-law?" said the queen. "In either case, your brother is a busy man. Besides, if I traveled around the world, where would I go on my next trip?"

The door pushed open and King Alexander Dobromil entered the anteroom. He saw Wallace leaning back from kissing the queen on the cheek. "I was certain you already had a wife, dear brother. I should like to keep mine, if you please. Save your kisses for her hands, thank you." Alexander smiled at his brother.

"Brother," said Wallace, rushing to the arms of Alexander. They embraced.

"It's been too long," said Alexander. "I heard you traveled around the world. I would go myself, but if I did, well, where would I go the next time?" The king laughed.

They looked at one another and the room became silent. Wallace knitted his brow. "I wish I were here under better circumstances. I fear I have dishearteningnews about our brother Zili."

"What of him?" asked Alexander.

"His black handiwork is spread over several kingdoms. He involves himself in nefarious endeavors." Lifting a finger, he turned his eyes from Alexander. "Just a moment, brother," he whispered. He gestured with his other hand. General Raptozk stepped closer. He handed Wallace the squirming burlap sack.

Peering at the sack, Alexander sighed. "I'm unsure what you have in the bag, brother, but I hope it hasn't to do with our brother's black handiwork."

Wallace laughed quietly. "Hardly," he said. He laid the sack at Isadora's feet.

Looking at him sideways, she stepped back.

Lexi knelt to open the sack. Out climbed a rust-toned fur ball with a long, bushy tail and wet, black nose.

"Oh. What is it?" Isadora exclaimed, slightly lifting the hem of her long gown.

"A puppy, dear sister-in-law. A gift for your sister." Prince Wallace smiled. "Its name is Bowes."

The queen summoned her manservant, who came quickly by her side. She whispered in his ear. He stoically gazed upon the dog. "We shall take the dog to the kitchen and … feed it," he said.

"I thought the Princesses Sarah and Angelica would enjoy him," Wallace said.

Slowly closing her eyes, the queen nodded. "I am sure they will like that. But, if you'll excuse me, I must retire so that you and my husband may chat."

General Raptozk gestured; he and his three men left for the corridor. Wallace and King Dobromil went through the door into the throne room.

"So, brother, what is the sum of this 'disheartening news' you traveled so far to bring?" said the king.

Wallace exhaled. "Alex, have you heard from the peoples of the villages and what they're saying about Zili?"

"I've heard the outrageous rumors, unsubstantiated rumors," said Alexander.

"We must invest some credence in these rumors. His behavior has become a reflection on you."

"How?" Alexander asked.

"Before each act of cruelty, Zili, or sycophants acting on his behalf, read a proclamation stating that you, King Dobromil, ordered actions against citizens of the Aurora Kingdoms."

"Surely, you recognize the gravity of what you are accusing our brother of?" asked Alexander.

"Sadly, I do. But I have more than words. I have scoured the countryside, and I've seen the result of his treachery and deceit. I have not only heard stories, I have seen evidence."

"These are acts of sedition, punishable by death," Alexander said stridently. "Why? Why would he ... why would he do this? I have always treated him with love and respect."

His hand to his brother's shoulder, his eyes cast down, Wallace shook his head. "I know. It is a sad day. Sometimes lust for power is stronger than love."

Alexander held back his tears and held up a fist. He paced the room, his face visibly furrowed from the pain he felt in his heart. His hands shook and he became angry. "This is an outrage." Alexander breathed deeply, his fingers writhing. "Of this cruelty, I have ordered none, ever. Zili is our brother. It pains me to think him capable of such treachery. Truly, it is just a rumor!" He turned to Wallace, his face beaming with hope. "We have no hard proof."

"My hopes exactly upon first hearing this; then proof came to me. You are a good king, Alexander. There are others who would require no proof. King Caczmarek, our father's father, would have put the instigator of such crimes to sleep with the iron maiden. But aside from firsthand reports, I discovered a home whose drinking well was poisoned and the occupants burned out. On the property, we discovered the body of the young son of the lizard king, Hezia."

"How did he come to be there?" asked Alexander.

"I would like to think he was attempting to avenge his father's death. Alas, I believe him kidnapped, a victim of our brother's search for the cipher to the map leading to the Dragon Stone."

"The son of our most tenacious ally taken hostage, dead," Alexander intoned. "In your opinion, what are Zili's ultimate intentions?"

"He intends to combine our kingdoms into one and take them as his own, and more."

"It's madness." Alexander took Wallace's shoulders in his hands. His face was desperate. "Has he gone mad? How does he plan to accomplish this feat? Compared to my army and yours combined, his is nothing. He commands only a constabulary force. He is only a sheriff, for goodness' sake."

"And being the sheriff is what he intends to change. Zili works with mercenaries to advance against us. Be not conflicted, brother," said Wallace. "We shall work together to thwart his plans." Wallace pushed a parchment into Alexander's hand. "To bolster my contention, take this and read. A dispatch rider brought this to me not seven nights ago."

Alexander took the parchment, unrolled it, and read. "This missive was from ... I see. I see," Alexander muttered. "From Shibboleth, King of Golem." Alexander looked up, his eyes distant. "The lizard king, murdered? The cipher taken." Anger rose in his eyes. His jaw jutting, he waved the parchment. "Tell me more of what you found, Wallace."

"Yes," Wallace said. Turning, he gazed into the fireplace. "Zorna, my wizard, spoke to the oddlings. Zili wears the Firestone ring—"

"Ring? What ring?"

"A powerful jewel, stolen from the trolls."

"Did Zili steal it?"

"No. But indeed it was stolen. Found in the marketplace, it made its way to Zili's hands."

"And this ring, who created it and what will it do?"

"The ring was created by a wizard from an ancient Dragon Stone. It absorbs and magnifies power. It will concentrate the wearer's greed and satisfy his need for power. But the ring is old and its power low. Zili needs its adjunctive parts."

"It is a great evil," Alexander said. Pacing to his throne, he slouched low on the chair, his palms up. "But why?"

Wallace continued, "Zili believes that with the Dragon Stone, the Crystal Chronaria, and the Elixir Illuminae, he will control not only your mind but also mine, the forces of nature, and the oddlings."

"It is not enough that our enemies spring from strange lands, but now they spring from our families," Alexander lamented. "And you have spoken with those hurt by Zili, you say."

"Yes. Many oddling creatures hurt by Zili were welcomed by the master carpenter, Tom Claus, to stay with him."

"Yes. I know him," Alexander said. "His son Nicholas constructed a toy, no, a miracle that saved my Angelica. I shall forever be in his debt ... But tell me of your travels."

"In disguise we elicited information from those affected by Zili's activities. In exchange for work, Tom and his family offered refuge to those hurt by Zili. General Raptozk, Joseph the Apothecary, Captain Lexi, the wizard Zorna, and I stayed with them so we could hear firsthand what had happened from those injured. Among other things, Joseph discovered Zili's men had salted wells used by the villagers of Elfin to feed their cattle."

"Wanton cruelty," Alexander shouted.

"There is more," said Wallace. "Zorna has since learned that Jax, an evil troll, persuaded Zili that, to possess more power, Zili would need to concoct a potion from the essence of color and light sprites. He revealed to Zili the cruel secrets of extracting such power from these living beings. Brother, I am ashamed to state his methods, for it is a blight on the good name of Dobromil."

"Tell me, Wallace," Alexander commanded.

Wallace paused. "With great callousness, he created his malicious potion by boiling the children of the color and light sprites—their children, my dear brother, believing their essence held the strongest magic. He boiled them alive."

"Atrocious. I can barely stand to hear more." Alexander turned away, pacing to a shelf of neatly stacked scrolls beside the throne. "Do you remember these? This is the repository of the collective wisdom of the crown. Our father used to read these to us as if they were nursery rhymes. They teach goodness and fairness but punishment when it is deemed proper. They say a good king is a fair king. A good king knows the hearts of his people. Has our brother tossed aside all we've learned?" Sighing, Wallace stood beside his brother. "My scribe has recorded and sealed all that I have witnessed, so we may confront our brother."

"Good. You have done the right thing. Sadly, we must take action against Zili. Our father would truly be angry if he could see what Zili has done. He is no longer the brother we knew as children. He has become someone else."

"Tom has offered his home that we might meet oddlings and humans together, and you hear firsthand. Together we may decide what action we should take."

"Excellent," Alexander said thoughtfully.

"As an aside," Wallace said, "his son Nicholas has affection for your sister-in-law."

"Princess Sarah? Another good reason to meet the toymakers? When we have decided the fate of Zili, I shall have to think on this unorthodox relationship. First things first." Alexander reached for and shook his brother's hand. He went to the tube chimes hung from a wall hook near the throne. With one sweeping motion, he brushed the chimes with his hand. Through a thin panel door that opened from a plain wall, the chamberlain entered the throne room.

"Your Highness?" he said humbly, bowing.

"It is decided?" Wallace asked.

Alexander nodded.

"You will send a courier to Tom the Carpenter," Alexander ordered the chamberlain. "Tell him we shall meet in ten days."

Alexander turned to Wallace. "We can put Zili in his place if we all work together. He dares live under my roof. Did he not think things done in darkness should eventually come to light? I will confront him. I shall have my final proof," Alexander said. "Chamberlain, if my brother has returned to the castle, send the palace guards to his chambers at once. I am ordering his arrest."

"As we are usually of the same mind, I have prepared for his capture or war. In case he has fled," Wallace said, "I have taken the liberty ordering fifty warriors clothed as commoners to be on the watch for him. You have met my wizard and the apothecary alchemist. I have humans and oddlings in the countryside, headed this way, using several different routes. They, as well as I, have vowed to defend you to the death. It is nightfall, but they will arrive in a timely fashion."

As he spoke, the chamberlain followed Alexander's orders. Six royal guards began their long march to the farthest reaches of the castle, where Zili's chambers lay.

Far from where King Dobromil and Prince Wallace were meeting, the shadows of scintillating torch flames fell upon the walls. Walking their post, guards' shadows also fell upon the walls. But as two guards passed the chamber of Prince Zili, their shadows failed to follow. The detached shadows slipped beneath the door of Prince Zili's chambers.

Beside Zili's bed, the shadows halted. Darkening, they peeled from the wall and floor, twisting into inverted tornados. They congealed into crumpled, wrinkled, leathery, manlike forms.

They danced playfully at the edge of Zili's bed. Zili lay there fully clothed, his eyes shut. Suddenly his hand shot out and grasp one of them by the neck. Zili lifted the being an inch from the floor.

"*Blackhearts*. You disgust me. Why are you in my chamber?"

"Please, good and kind master," the being's voice rasped. "Don't hurt us. We've come here to warn you."

"Warn me. Of what?" Zili snarled.

"Your brother has dispatched guards to arrest you."

"Yes," said the other. "Your brothers speak in a chamber near to end your terror far and near. In ten days meeting of all kinds, to find a way to bring about your end."

Zili sprang from his bed and spun toward the troll. "Well done, Mr. Jax," he said, reaching for and pulling on his black knee-boots. "Where will this meeting be held?"

"At the farm of Thomas Claus, in a valley two miles from the western edge of Orphic Falls."

"Claus, hum. I'm familiar with the old fool and his brat son," Zili muttered. From a table, he tossed a leather pouch containing seven gold coins toward the troll, who sank into the shadow. The shadows receded beneath the door.

Slipping from the castle through a window, Zili fractured into pieces and mixed into a cloud of smoke the trolls conjured. The smoke twisted and billowed as it gusted to the ground. Rising beneath Zili, it hoisted him up from the ground. An instant later it became a dark horse upon which Zili dashed away in a flash of fire and thunder.

What Can We Do?

Bowes scampered around the slate floor in Queen Isadora's chamber. The queen lay on the bed atop the cover, needlepoint in her hands, a candle flickering on the stand beside her. With a flying leap, Bowes landed in Sarah's lap. Sitting on the floor near the terrarium, Sarah and Princess Angelica rubbed Bowes's belly.

On the broad granite sill of the open stained-glass window above them landed an inky-black bird, a crow. Dark eyes peering askance, it opened and shut its broad yellow beak as if yawning. Next to the window, perched upon a trapeze within a spacious golden cage, the queen's two mynah birds grew agitated, uneasy with the black bird's ominous gaze.

Starlight and a cool breeze poured through the open window. Behind the large black bird, Sarah could see the North Star glittering through rustling trees. Slowly emerging from behind a mysterious dissipating smoke, the black bird curled its black talons as it lifted each foot. It flapped its wings, cawing before it finally settled and preened its feathers.

"Aunt Sarah," Angelica said, gazing up at the windowsill, "Uncle Zili's ugly bird has come to visit with Mama's birds again." Princess Angelica frowned. "It is a scary bird, with his dark feathers and broad, sharp beak."

"It is merely a bird, child, no more," said Princess Sarah.

"But Aunt Sarah, it is the size of a wildcat. There is something behind its eyes. It knows things." Angelica glowered at the bird with a jaundiced eye. "It comes much too often."

"I suppose. It is here nearly every day," Sarah said. "I don't know why. I don't understand why it doesn't stay with its master." She kissed the dog between its eyes. "It is an enigma."

"And enig— An enig— Well, whatever!" Angelica said, scratching Bowes's back. "It sounds very much to me that you don't like it either."

"My sister," Queen Isadora murmured, looking at Sarah from across the room, "did you not tell me the bird talks?"

Rolling her eyes, Sarah hesitated. "Yes. To your birds, dear sister, sometimes."

"Does it speak wisely or nonsense?" asked Angelica.

"It speaks in riddles." Sarah sighed. "Your mynah birds do interpret, however. They tell me what the crow has said but not if I ask. They merely repeat. By my assessment, I find that black bird avaricious and vile.

"Now, young Princess Angelica," Sarah said, noting that the queen's candle had burned down several notches, "it is time for bed. I shall escort you to your chamber. Say good night, Angelica."

"Good night, Mama," the girls said. Sarah nudged her. Standing prim, Angelica lowered her eyes and politely curtsied. "Good evening, mother," she said again. Hesitating, Angelica lifted her chin and smiled broadly. Breaking formality, she ran to her mother. They embraced, her lips falling against her mother's ear. "I love you," she whispered.

The crow flew from the window into the night. Sarah followed its retreat with her eyes.

"May I take your mynah birds to my room? They are so funny at times. I will have both Bowes and the birds. May I, Mother?" Angelica entreated. The queen nodded.

Strolling beside her niece, Sarah lay her open hand upon Angelica's upper back. She escorted Angelica past the heavy oak door from the queen's chambers. Sniffing along the marble floor, Bowes followed. Their shadows grew and danced past each mounted wall torch. Out of their cages, the birds circled, swooped, soared, and banked, following Sarah and Angelica through the corridor.

Princess Angelica climbed into her canopy bed. Bouncing quickly behind her, Bowes leaped through the curtains, beneath the canopy, and into bed alongside the princess. Up to the ceiling the birds shot, perching low in the wooden rafters. Reaching in, Sarah tucked both Bowes and the princess beneath the covers. Sarah held the candelabrum in her right hand, while tenderly stroking Angelica across her forehead with the other. She spoke softly. "Off to sleep now."

As she was about to pinch out the flame, Angelica gently blocked her hand. "May I keep the light? Aunt Sarah, can you sit with me until I'm asleep?"

Sarah used the lit candle to light another, and walked to the other side of the room. Reclining on a daybed, Sarah opened a book and began reading. "I will remain here until your father returns."

"Good night, Sarah. I love you." Bowes jumped up, spun three times, sat, and wagged his tail.

"I love you too, Angelica." Bowes jumped up, spun three times, sat, and wagged his tail again.

"What a peculiar thing to do," said Sarah, watching the dog spin. Sarah read to Princess Angelica, who quickly fell asleep. The candlelight burned low, eventually fading. Sarah found it hard to stay awake. When she dozed, the birds swooped down from the rafters and perched on the arm of the daybed. Through the window above the princess's bed, the moon cast long, gentle rays upon the mynah birds. But for Angelica's subtle breathing, the room was silent. Sarah slept soundly.

The birds' sharp squawks reverberated in the room. "Hear us and be forewarned." The squawks echoed as whispered words in Sarah's ear.

"My word," gasped Sarah, startled awake. Her book slid from her bosom to her stomach. Through her bleary eyes, she saw the birds near her shoulder.

"The physician's baby—" squawked one bird.

"—keeps Zili from the crown," answered the other.

When her muddled head cleared, Sarah peered through the shadows to the other half of the room. She could discern Angelica as a lump beneath the covers, asleep behind the screen of her canopy. Mindlessly, Sarah whispered *Zili*.

"Wizard said. Wizard said. Wizard said," repeated the first bird.

Intrigued, Sarah leaned in carefully to hear clearly. Then she sat up, her naked feet slapping the floor.

"Awk, the physician's baby—" squawked one bird.

"—will keep Zili from crown," answered the other bird.

"Wizard said," repeated the first bird.

Sarah leveled her gaze on the birds' beaks, awaiting their next words.

"I will kill the physician's family before the baby comes," uttered one bird, issuing the words in the tone of Zili's voice. Stomach dropping, Sarah's heart pattered.

Through the shadowy room, Sarah caught sight of the canopy flying out. In a twinkling, she discerned a shadow darting across the floor and heard the eager scraping of nails against the slate—Bowes. The dog leaped. His front paws fell upon Sarah's thigh. Then, with all four paws back on the floor, he spun three times. Bouncing on his rump as if it was made of a spring, he sat before the birds, wagging his tail.

The birds lifted from the arm of the daybed and flew high into the rafters. There, they became quiet and slept. Bowes fell asleep at the foot of the daybed.

Hours on, Sarah slept fitfully, with disturbing dreams waking her. She tossed incessantly, the words of the birds resonating in her ears. Her mind put the meaning of the birds' words together: *kill the physician's baby before it is born, or Zili will not be king*. The hours passed slowly for Sarah as the bird's revelations opened her mind.

Returning to his chamber for the night, King Dobromil, stopped at Angelica's door. Softly knocking, he carefully prodded open the door. Hearing the thump of a boot and the creak of the door, Sarah roused.

"Sarah, I apologize for waking you. We've completed our business for tonight, and I wanted to check on Angelica."

Sarah sat on the edge of the daybed, looking across the room into the darkness where Angelica slept. She peered up at Alexander, squinting against the light behind him.

"Is there anything wrong?" he asked.

"No. Yes. I-I've not slept, Your Highness," Sarah said reflectively, her eyes distant.

Blowing out his cheeks, Alexander tucked his underlip. "Did Angelica behave tonight?"

"Yes, Your Highness," Sarah said with a sigh. "She was an angel, of course."

"Sarah, what is wrong? You look worried."

Sarah looked away. Her fingers entwined, her thumbs danced with each other. "I just have a lot of my mind," she said. Her eyes drifted to the rafters where the birds slept. "No, Sire. I think I am just a little tired. That is all." She wanted to sort things through and understand before she spoke out.

"Well, I think you should go to bed," said Alexander. He sensed she was hiding something.

"To bed. Yes, to bed," she said. Dragging herself from the daybed, she shuffled toward the door and into the sliver of light coming into the dark room from the corridor.

The door pushed open further. Backlit behind the king stood Isadora. "I have waited for you, my king," said the queen. Adjusting the wrap about her shoulders, she shivered slightly in the cool stone corridor. "Is there a problem with Angelica?"

"No, my queen," said Alexander. "It is your sister. She is pensive and weary."

"Just tired. I must go," said Sarah. Slipping past Alexander, she looked into her sister's face but not her eyes.

Throwing her arms around Sarah, Isadora gave her a hug. "You know I love you very much," said the queen. "And if you are worried, you may tell me anything."

Sarah nodded. "I know. I need to think."

Bowes ran before the queen, spun three times, sat down, and wagged his tail,

"You're a funny little dog," said the queen. "He seems to behave this way every time someone does or says something nice."

"Or speaks truth," murmured Sarah, her eyes locking with the queen's.

The queen's guard stepped up behind. King Alexander noticed him. "Guard," he ordered, "escort Princess Sarah and her dog to her room."

He kissed Sarah on her hand. She nodded politely. She and the guard passed through the shadowy corridor, turning down the next.

Sarah eyed the young blond guard marching beside her. She smiled coyly. After several moments of silence, she spoke. "It is late, young guard. Surely your wife awaits you."

"I am not married, Your Highness," he said.

"Surely your consort awaits."

His eyes forward, he continued to lead. "I have no consort, Your Highness."

"Perhaps it would be wise to find one," she quipped. "I can find my room myself. You're dismissed."

"Your Highness," the guard said. Turning, he marched away. "Good night, young guard. Do not worry. I wish to stroll the garden with my dog."

After a few moments of walking and watching Bowes chase fireflies, Sarah stopped at the center of a small, arched footbridge. Gazing into the water, she counted the lilies floating by. Then she heard a familiar voice call her name. A face began to form on the rippling dark water.

"Zili!" she gasped. She saw his reflected face over her reflected shoulder. She lifted her head. Turning, she saw no one over her shoulder. But in the water, there he was. He called her name again. "What sorcery is this?" she asked.

"Have you not learned the etiquette of addressing your betters, girl? 'Good evening Your Highness' should be your response," sneered Zili.

Sarah felt the pressure of his hand taking hers, but on looking, she saw no corporeal hand touching hers. "Where are you, Your Highness? Dispense with your trickery. Please, release my hand."

"Come now. Do not spurn me as did your tightly bound sister."

"Do not speak her name. Hers is far too good to fall from your lips," Sarah snapped.

"Well, it is thrilling to see you," Zili said. "You are out late this evening. You should be inside. It is far too dangerous for you to be out this night. Have you not heard? There is a fugitive afoot." He felt her shudder.

"It is you they seek, sheriff."

"*Don't call me that!*"

Sarah began to back away from the bridge railing.

"*No.* No, dear Sarah, worry not. I would never allow anything to … happen to you," Zili said. Sarah could feel the invisible pressure of his hand looping around her elbow. "I have always wanted you."

"Most certainly we have nothing in common," she retorted.

The reflected face of Zili smiled.

"I have always loathed you," she said, watching his smile quickly turn to a sneer.

"My dear, have you given thought to becoming my bride? On my arm, as an ingénue, you would be the talk of the realm."

"No doubt I would. But I am no ingénue," Sarah murmured. Zili strained to hear.

"You know I have great affection for you. Give consideration, for it would be a grave miscalculation on your part to dismiss my offer."

Suddenly Bowes began barking and snapping at the reflection. From the bridge, Bowes lifted his leg and relieved himself in the water. The image of Zili's face began to break up into ripples.

"This dog is yours? Zili shouted. "There is something wrong with the beast. It is disrespectful. When I speak, it growls."

"Good. He just knows you."

"Knows me? This animal is a stranger to me," Zili snapped.

"He is sensitive to truth. He knows you are an evil liar, a deranged madman."

"This is how you explain his act of disrespect?"

"His is no act. I know not from what level of hell you send this message, but it is craven and wasted on me. I infer that you love me. But your love for me is your misfortune. There is no way I shall ever become your bride. My heart looks elsewhere. Leave me, Sheriff. I and my beast, as you call him, wish to retire."

With a slight bow, Zili nodded. "Princess, it does not matter to me if you care. I will have you. I *will* come for you."

"Try at your own folly."

Storming from the garden, Sarah marched to her room, seeing Zili's face reflected in every mirror she passed. Closing her door, she leaned against it and slid to the floor, her stomach tied in a knot.

Before she went to bed, she tossed a cloak over her mirror. Sarah climbed into bed and pulled the covers over her head. She planned to have the mirror removed in the morning. Zili's appearance and the words spoken by the birds echoed in her head, causing her to have a fitful sleep.

The next day, Sarah had breakfast with Queen Isadora.

"Issey, do you know when the carpenter and his son Nicholas shall return to town?"

"Not for several months, I believe," replied Isadora

"Do you think it would be proper for me to visit their workshop?" asked Sarah.

"Why, sister?"

Sarah thought quickly. "I need a little house and a bed for Bowes. I do not think Bowes can wait several months."

"With a proper escort, it may be agreeable. I shall consult Alexander with hopes of making the arrangements. And Sarah?"

"Yes, Issey?"

"Why are the royal carpenters removing the mirror from your room?"

Chapter 8

MAKING PLANS

Sarah loved the castle, its people, and oddlings. Although the castle had been her home since Isadora married King Alexander when Sarah was young, she always maintained a love for the countryside. She hoped her trip to the country to see Nicholas would be, restful, insightful, and productive. As she approached the hills of Claus' farm, she longed to feel the promise of that.

Princess Sarah and her entourage, including Wallace, traveled many miles and for many days. Well protected, four men of the royal equestrian guard escorted Wallace's coach.

From his high vantage, the coachman saw they were approaching a barricade. He gave the signal to stop. The large wheels of the carriage slowed as the brakeman pulled back on the stick. The coachman tugged back on the reins. The two horses slowed their stride as the carriage drew closer to the hill leading down to the farm.

The carriage stopped. Whinnying, the horses settled their restless gait into a stance as they paused on the muddy path. Napping, the royal occupants felt the coach gently lurch to a stop. Curled at Sarah's feet, Bowes lifted his head. Princess Sarah, facing forward in the carriage, quickly gained her wits. She heard muted conversation outside the carriage between someone and her driver. Curious and unsettled, she tilted her book into her lap. "What is it?" she murmured. From a small, square window, her view was limited.

Bowes barked. Wallace rubbed the back of the dog's neck to soothe Bowes's fretfulness.

"There seems to be some sort of construction, Your Highness," said the coachman.

Lifting the window glass, she observed as best she could. Prince Wallace sat facing her. He noted her curious eyes. "I cannot see what is happening," she said, frowning. She could only hear soft conversations.

From his bench atop the coach, the driver watched a party of workers continue erecting a log barrier across the access road leading to the farm. A tanned, scruffy, shirtless man toddled up to the coach window and peered in at Princess Sarah. Somewhat disquieted, she nodded with a faint, uncomfortable smile. Upon the rotund man's chin, he wore a grizzled beard down to his chest. His head was melon round. Sarah surreptitiously glanced down, then up again into his brown eyes and furrowed face. Presenting a toothsome smile, he would not turn his eyes away. Wallace was about to lean forward to shoo him on, when he heard the man speak.

"Your Highness. It's you," the man said excitedly. "I am the roadman. Pardon me, Your Highness; I've never seen a royal before." He quickly clasped and snatched the creased hat from his round, bald head. "We heard rumors of your coming here. We did not believe it." His eyes darted to his team setting the roadblock. "There was a rock slide and we're closing the road, Your Highness."

Princess Sarah nodded. "When shall we pass—"

"I'm afraid not soon enough, Your Highness."

"Who are you?"

"My name's Fletcher, Your Highness. You may call me Fletch."

"When will you open the road, Fletch?"

"Not until morning." Fletch shrugged.

"Are there other roads?"

"Yes, Your Highness. But all roads to the farm lead downhill. The rain has been heavy in spots, Your Highness. More so here."

The eyes of her coachman searched the sky for rain. He saw the road ahead was blocked.

Shaking his head, Fletch continually shifted his weight from one foot to the other.

"It is the true, Your Highness," the driver said. "I have searched; I have seen the rain on the horizon and in the valley."

"The road will be hazardous. Perhaps Your Highness will return another time," said Fletch.

"No. I will descend to the farm." Glancing outside, Sarah saw a fork in the road before which her coach stood. "I've come too far," she said. The road she saw led to a wooded downhill grade. "And I so want to get to the farm another way—over that way, perhaps," Sarah said, glimpsing Wallace slouched back on his seat. He nonchalantly, lifted his fingers from his lap and raised his eyebrows. He was inclined to accede to her wishes.

Wallace leaned toward her. "Perhaps it would be wise to turn back and—"

"If you are afraid, brother-in-law," she cut in, "I shall hold your hand and tell you a nursery rhyme."

Wallace's eyes widened and he hastily sat back on the seat, muttering. "If only my men were as brave as you, Princess Sarah. My kingdom might be in less jeopardy and twice the size."

"Is there another way, roadman? There, perhaps." She pointed to the fork.

"That way, Your Highness," Fletch said, pointing to a path turning off the main road. "The smaller path will take you through a grove of trees, the deep forest, and downhill to the farm valley." His face was worried. His hat he held rolled into a tube close to his chest. Stepping away from the window, he reached up to the coachman. "Here, take this." Fletch handed the coachman a small piece of parchment. "Read. This is a blessing. It will protect you if need be." He stepped back from the coach. Fletch pointed to the side road. "Downhill most of the way. As yet, the rain has not eroded the earth. Should you decide to take that road, be safe. May peace be upon you."

The driver and coachman, both hopeful with the blessing, felt a modicum of relief. But their relief was short-lived, and their delight quickly faded to dismay and concern when again the rain began to fall, first light, then hard. The road was rough. The tree-lined walls of the canyon rose beside them as they coursed downhill. They often heard small rockslides. The driver maintained the horses' deliberate pace. Both Wallace and Sarah found it difficult to remain calm. Sometimes both felt the wheels slip. The coach lurched and slid sidewise on the drenched downhill. Wallace had seen roads like this flood in a flash. He worried more about Sarah than himself.

Through the front wall of the coach, Wallace could hear the voice of the coachman reading the lines from the parchment: "Mother Forest, please protect us on our path."

Sarah could hear the horses' slow clopping. She sporadically peeked through the window to see their four guards, two before and two after the carriage, proceed cautiously. Their vigilance provided her a modicum of comfort.

"We'll be fine," Wallace assured her, leaning forward. He showed Sarah a strong face, but in his heart he was concerned as well.

With a flick of the reins, the driver guided the carriage through several tricky mountain turns. Then the wheels unexpectedly began to slip. The front wheels hit a pothole, and the rear of the coach pitched up, sliding sidewise. The forward tugging motion of the horses, along with gravity, caused the coach to suddenly whip. Wallace and Sarah pitched from their seats. Bowes rolled beneath Wallace's bench. Screeching, Sarah fell to the floor. She struggled to her seat. Wallace peered from the window while steadying himself, his arms outstretched against the perpendicular walls of the coach. Wallace could see that the wheels remained on the edge of the downhill road by just a hair.

Sarah saw the road's edge break away and slide into the ravine. "Wallace!" Sarah shouted, "The *road* ..."

About to scream, Sarah saw the road come alive. By some force of magic, some power unknown to them, the road bore them up— growing, expanding beneath the wheels whenever they slid or slipped from the friable roadway.

She and Wallace watched with amazement as new road materialize beneath the wheels of the teetering coach. Traction became more steady and sure. The carriage remained on the hillside and out of the ravine. Vines fell from above, intertwined, and metamorphosed, becoming wooden suspension bridges over washed-out gaps in the road. Their ride became smooth and nonthreatening.

With an unusual blast of cold, the outdoor temperature fell quickly but just around the coach. To occupy the royals' minds, frost fairies drew iridescent patterns of ice upon the closed carriage windows. The royals relaxed when they heard distance howling. From the carriage window, Wallace searched out the highest peak showing through passing trees

"Sarah," Wallace muttered, "do you hear that? The songs of wolves. The closer we get to the workshop, the clearer the calls become."

Below, at the homestead, his ears delighted, Jingle's eyes gazed to the hills from which Sarah's coach descended. Jingles answered the wolves, barking and spinning. He ran back and forth before the house, his sensitive nose sensing their arrival.

Soon the distant coach appeared. Sounds of wheels and horse gear jangled in the air. Tarrying in the barn with Patches, Ogre roared at the distant sound. He anticipated resting the cow after her long day of grazing.

"Tom! Tom!" bellowed Ogre. "We have company." Tom ambled to the barn door, his pitchfork in hand.

Ogre scanned the dark horizon, his long right arm out; he stretched his lengthy index finger to the outlying road.

"Four riders flanking a carriage," said Ogre in his sonorous voice.

He saw a quarter moon in the dusky sky.

Tom came alongside Ogre. "Show me what you see," Tom said. He held a torch over his head. It did little more than circumscribe the mount of grass on which they stood. "I see nothing, my gargantuan friend," Tom said, scanning the road vanishing into the darkness and tall brush. They waited in a disk of flickering torchlight, a cloud of peripatetic fireflies filling the air.

"I see nothing either." Ogre snuffled. He peered down to Tom. "My friend," Ogre said, "There are senses other than eyes." Ogre rubbed his nose with his thick fingers and continued sniffing the air, Jingles at his feet doing the same.

"The human nose is little better than decoration." Tom sighed. "There are several travelers, Tom." Ogre laughed. "They smell like … cedar and rosewater."

Within a quarter hour, the carriage rolled out of the dark to a stop before the barn door. The clop of horses' hooves alerted Tom. He and Nicholas stepped out of the barn to greet the carriage. The driver stood by the carriage door, a footman approaching from the rear.

The coachman climbed down, laying his eyes on no one but his footman and driver. He barked orders as Tom and Nicholas stood back, watching.

The coachman ogled Tom and Nicholas from head to toe. "I will need immediate accommodations for His Highness, Prince Wallace of Waters, and Princess Sarah of Illuminae," he commanded in a lilting, nasal tone. He lifted his nose into the air. He wondered why no one moved. "I shall need a place for the royal equestrian guard. The horses shall be groomed and fed. I—"

"*Silence*, Coachman!" Wallace shouted. Capitulating, the coachman stopped midsentence and turned about to face Prince Wallace. With torches held high, Tom and Nicholas silently genuflected.

Peering through the window of the main house, Mary observed the carriage and the flanking royal equestrians.

Wallace continued, "Coachman, these gentlemen are my friends. You will treat them with the respect they deserve."

"Sire," murmured the coachman. Bowing, the driver stepped back against the carriage, lowering his gaze. The footman positioned a footstool at the door left open by Wallace. A delicate foot emerged from the carriage into the yellow, flickering light of the torches.

"Princess Sarah," Nicholas whispered. He wanted to rush to her. Instead, he stood behind Tom and maintained his composure. He dreamed of sweeping her into his arms; instead, he swept aside his eagerness for prudence's sake. His eyes locked to hers; his heart buzzed with excitement.

"Princess Sarah," Nicholas whispered again, up-toned.

She stepped from the footstool, extending her hand. Sidling to her, Nicholas coyly but politely kissed her fingers. Mary remained by the main door, watching. Jingles pressed his way past everyone. The royal guards rushed forward. With the mere gesture of Princess Sarah's upturned finger, they stood down.

Tom stepped forward. "This is an honor and surprise, Princess Sarah, Prince Wallace. Welcome to our home." Standing aside, Nicholas bowed. Sarah reached for Nicholas's elbow. Reserved, and polite, Nicholas slowly extended it, while controlling his joy.

"May I show you to our humble home?" Nicholas said. He saw Mary at the front door. "Mother will be very pleased to meet you."

"Welcome back, Your Highness," Tom said, advancing to Wallace. "An honor to have you."

"You stare, Tom," Wallace lilted, gesturing orders to his entourage. "You have dressed to your station. It feels a bit strange to me."

"Quite a different appearance, yes?" Wallace smiled. "But I am the Crown Prince."

Tom cast his eyes down. "How should I address you?"

"I will tell you, but first, eyes up," said Wallace. Tom did as he was told.

"Now everyone must know who I am. Address me formally when in the company of others." The two men shook hands and patted each other on the shoulders. When Wallace's lips came within inches of Tom's ears, he whispered, "In private, I am Wally." He pointed. "Now, let us proceed into your house," he said aloud. "I miss those wonderful smells. I need to see Mary."

Across the damp grass, the prince, Sarah, and Nicholas strode to the front door of the main house. Romping around, Jingles and Bowes sniffed each other's fur. Barking playfully, they shot into the house and sat behind Mary, where she waited at the door.

"Welcome to my home, Your Highness. I'm honored to have you and your, ah …" Mary saw Sarah. Mary had never met this young woman and had scarcely an inkling of whom she might be. Because she was accompanying Wallace, Mary was sure that she had to be a woman of high station.

"My dear Sarah, this is Mary, Tom's wife and Nicholas's mother," Wallace said. Sarah extended the back of her hand as was customary.

Gently clutching her downturned fingertips, Mary curtsied. "I trust Your Highnesses' journey was ... uneventful."

Sarah and Wallace glanced at each other. "The hills of your forest are truly ... breathtaking," murmured Princess Sarah, turning away to pet Bowes, who came to sit at her feet.

Wallace shifted and cleared his throat. "Indeed, madam, you have a magical country. It is good to see you again. I am thankful for your hospitality. I do realize this visit is ... unexpected."

"You are here on official business, Your Highness?" asked Mary, her eyes exploring Sarah's intricately embroidered blue gown trimmed in gold. Feeling frumpy, Mary unconsciously straightened her bonnet. Twisting a loose whorl of her hair with her right forefinger and thumb, she slid it beneath her top.

Wallace paused. "Yes. Both I and my sister-in-law, Princess Sarah, have business. I have sensitive business to which I must attend." Wallace observed the two women and their questioning eyes.

"Ohhhh, sister-in-law, Your Highness." Mary smiled. "Of course. What else?" Mary exhaled with relief, dipping her chin politely, having thought this youthful lady was a bit young for Wallace. "I am delighted."

"Alas, my dear sister-in-law will allow me to disclose nothing of her intentions. I should suppose," Wallace smiled brightly, "that her business is more, how shall I say ... familial."

Fingertips to her face, Sarah brushed her tresses from her right eye, and catching sight of Nicholas in a near corner, she produced a coy half smile. "I'm glad to meet you and your lovely family," she smoothly uttered. She saw the two dogs playing, and gestured to them. "They seem to be getting along swimmingly."

Nicholas nodded, gazing at her before turning his eyes to the window. He listened to the howl of distant timber wolves. Their songs pacified his timorous heart. Barking, Bowes and Jingles chased figure eights around Nicholas, Tom, Mary, Sarah, and Wallace. Suddenly stopping, the dogs joined in the wolves' chorus, their heads thrown back.

"The wolves …" said Sarah, her spread fingers above her beating heart.

"Their song is as beautiful as it is frightening," muttered Nicholas, lamenting his travels through the magical Orphic Forest.

Faint howls reverberated in the hills outside. Through the window, Nicholas could see their new acting farrier, Ogre, working with the driver and coachman to disengage the horses from the coach.

In confidence, Wallace told Tom that the purpose of his trip was dual. He intended to meet with several village elders along his route during his return to Castle Illuminae. Leaving Sarah in Mary's care, Wallace left later that day and began his circuitous route back to castle of Alexander.

Several days later at Castle Illuminae, the farrier settled a restless horse after prying a shoe away. Sweating over the forge, the blacksmith sized and hammered red-hot horseshoes upon the anvil for final fitting. In the apothecary shop next door, Zorna, shaking his head, worked through the distraction of the sharp pounding as he tried his incantation a third time.

"Blast," Zorna muttered, frowning with frustration. "Another one gone awry." He dumped spoiled ingredients into a rectangular tin box. A red flame flashed just as he slammed the tin lid. Zorna paced to a heavy oak table, cluttered with leather pouches, glass tubing, and small scraps of paper filled with written notes. He pondered the tabletop, stained and burned from years of experiments, his mind preoccupied with the incantation. To one side of the table stood many beakers and test tubes mounted in wire stands. Racks supported twisted glass and metal piping joined by tar and animal sinew. On an opposing table, beakers of ceramic and glass stood on metal stands under which burned small oil lamps.

Closing his eyes, Zorna carefully lifted a beaker of boiling liquid under his nose and snuffled. The acrid vapor stung his nostrils.

"Ooooh, great Caczmarek's ghost!" he hooted, whipping his head back and the beaker away. He shook his head violently. Snorting, he cleared his sinuses. He took a drink of the substance. "Ah, that's good," he sighed. "But enough refreshments. I must get back to work."

Just to his left towered a stand upon which rested a book whose pages looked as though they had been written at the beginning of time. There he took a seat on a tall stool. Slapping the front cover raised a cloud of dust. He coughed. "Let us see," Zorna muttered, his fingers writhing over the book.

Hunched over the book, he read. He repeatedly whispered yes, and nodded as he did. Within moments, his face furrowed. He nodded deeply. Having found what he needed, he marked his place with his finger, and reached for a wooden stick to better mark his place.

Swiveling around on the stool to a chest of drawers, the wizard raked his fingers through his long beard and peered. Sliding one drawer open, he began rummaging through. Moving around odds, ends, sticks, leaves, and dried amphibian skins, he removed a tiny glass vial, from which he poured a measure into a white porcelain crucible.

Carting the crucible across the room, Zorna plunked its contents in an iron kettle resting in the middle of the table. With a wooden muddler, rounded and discolored from many years of use, Zorna crushed the ingredients. He placed them in a cauldron upon a metal platform. Beneath, he lit an oil lamp.

"How about this?" he said. The corners of his lips pulled down. He held a flask of dark red liquid up to the light. With one hand, he decanted the slimy fluid into the cauldron, and with the other, a black liquid as thick as molasses.

Zorna cooked and stirred the mixture until it was thicker and tackier. Sniffing, he fanned the vapors from beneath his nose. "Oh yes," he murmured, nodding. The pungent odor filled the room. The odor resembled the scents of horse manure and wet dog fur.

"Good gracious." He coughed. Retching, he searched for a towel while fanning the vapor away from his face. Drenching the towel in rosewater, he wrung it out and tied it over his nose. "There we go, "he muttered. He dipped pieces of hardtack into the mixture, repeating the procedure until he had one hundred pieces. Satisfied, he stacked them neatly, arranging the portions on a sham of leather cloth to allow for air-drying. Each dried piece released a puff of greenish-gray smoke.

"Yes. Very good," Zorna said, examining several portions. "They are ready." He briefly smiled. He gathered the leather cloth and tied it with a string. He set it aside. Into a small white ceramic vial with a flip-top cork, he poured a blue liquid. Into a small black ceramic vial with a flip-top cork, he poured a yellow liquid. He slipped both into a long leather pouch that he tightened with a leather purse string.

With the pouch in his right hand, Zorna made his way through his cluttered laboratory. Only wide enough for one foot at a time, a path cut through the clutter he had hoarded over the years. Among the piles of books, stools, tables piled high with old papers and notes, and chest and trunks so filled with papers and old experiments that their lids could not be closed, he could find anything he needed. He was pleased to know his laboratory in the Kingdom of Waters was exactly the same as this one. He went to the hearth at the rear of the room.

"Well, my friends," he whispered to the spirits, "it is done. It is time to see the king. That it is safe; we can do this sight unseen. Open, now." With his last word, the scraping of stone on stone reverberated. The floor vibrated and rattled. Brilliant as the sun, the hearth flared. Rays shot through cracks as the flagstones loosened and parted. Sliding on one another, they spiraled open like an iris. The opening revealed a brilliant man-size gate, like a flat, vertical pool of roiling water. Zorna stepped through the rippling element and was immediately transported. As quickly, it closed behind. The stones realigned as a solid wall, and again formed a burning hearth.

Zorna's foot, last to come through, left the liquid wall like a rippling pond. He stood in King Alexander's private chamber. Turning, laying his hand upon the wall, Zorna hardened it back to stone.

Backing, Zorna turned to see King Alexander Dobromil stooped over a long oak table in the middle of his situation room. Studying a relief map spread across the top, Wallace and Alexander whispered as Wallace slid small figurines, knights on horseback, across the map. The map depicted several rulers' dominions: Dobromil, Wallace, Stanislaus, and Lady Hydra.

Striding to the table, Zorna bowed to each king. "Good evening, Sires. You are ready?"

"Zorna," muttered King Dobromil, his eyes only briefly rising from the table. He sighed. "I thought you done long ago. Have you made the necessary preparations?"

"I have, Your Highnesses," Zorna said, bowing his head and lifting the leather pouch of bottles and the sack of hardtack. Stepping back, half sitting, half leaning on a tall stool near the door, Wallace watched with amusement.

"You smile," King Alexander said, glimpsing his brother's expression. "What is it? Do you know something I do not?"

"I muse on our childhood rivalry." Wallace smirked. "I vex myself over whether to fret or rejoice about this trickery our fine wizard is about to perpetrate. Growing up, I thought *one* oldest brother was enough." Shaking his head, King Alexander turned to Zorna. "My little brother worries he might be flanked by more of me than he can handle," said King Alexander. "Wizard, what must I to do first?"

"First, Sire," Zorna asked, "have you have chosen your lookalike-to-be?"

King Alexander nodded. "I have. I have chosen Andrew." King Alexander saw the worry on Wallace's face. "Andrew knows my routine, my mannerisms. I trust him with the life of my family. He has pledged his loyalty to me upon pain of death."

Zorna surveyed the king from head to foot. "As soon as Andrew arrives, we shall begin."

Loose and playfully wide with his gestures, Wallace opened the door to the outer chamber for his brother. His head through the door, King Alexander addressed the guard. "You." The guard snapped to attention. "Summon Sir Andrew Petrove to my chambers at once."

When the chamber guard returned with Sir Andrew, King Alexander gestured that the guard should leave.

"Zorna," said Alexander, his hand presenting. "This is Andrew." Zorna nodded.

"Andrew, you are familiar with my brother Wallace, of course," said Alexander. Filling his chest proudly, Andrew stood tall and nodded.

"We shall now see of what your wizard is made," said Alexander to Wallace, and hurried to remove his sword and crown. Alexander was not so much eager to get started as he was eager to finish before he changed his mind. "We are wasting time, wizard," he said. "Let us begin. Do what you must."

Zorna removed the white vial from the leather pouch. Using his thumb, he triggered the flip-top cork, popping the vial open. Zorna presented the vial. "You must each take five drops of this blue liquid and swallow. Once you do, Sir Andrew shall look identical to King Alexander."

Smirking, Wallace looked away as his brother stared bravely into Zorna's face.

"The effects of the potion," Zorna said, "will last so long as one moon cycle, if need be. Then you will return to your original forms."

"If it is the king's wish," Andrew asked, "can we reverse the potion?"

"Yes, Sir Andrew. I have the reversing potion with me. You need only ask," said Zorna.

"So be it," said Alexander. Wallace's face grew serious as he strode closer. Although the fire blazed in the room, the air grew chilled, and the breath from each man became vaporous and visible.

His arm upon Andrew's shoulder, Zorna drew him near. He lifted Andrew's head back and pulled his chin down, opening his mouth. "Andrew, you will be first."

Zorna trickled the liquid into Andrew's mouth. "One, two, three, four, and five," Zorna counted. "Now you, Your Highness." Zorna likewise trickled the liquid into the king's mouth.

Each man grimaced. Each face reddened. Each began to sweat. Simultaneously, each fell to his knees, vibrating, scratching. Each man lay on his side, his arms reaching up to Zorna.

The conformation of their faces cycled from misshaped to normal. Their skins knotted, flattened, rippled, and boiled. Hair color changed, lengthening and shortening. Wallace covered his eyes. "I cannot watch."

He turned away. He crossed himself and closed his eyes. He whispered a prayer.

All gyrations suddenly ceased. Each man rapidly melted into the floor, like candles in a kiln. Mere feet apart, they formed puddles. The puddles sought each other. They joined into one. As if invisible hands molded a pat of warm wax, the mingled pool rose into two columns. They commenced solidifying into the shapes of individuals. Becoming human, the masses appeared identical.

Hearing groans, Wallace turned. He opened his eyes as the two mounds completed their metamorphosis.

Before Zorna stood two men identical in every way to King Alexander Dobromil. Wallace swallowed and startled when both men toppled back to the floor—thud. They lay on their sides, still, for several seconds. So still, Wallace thought them dead.

"Zorna? Do they live?" Wallace whispered. Dropping to one knee, his hands hovered over the men. He scooped beneath the back of one man while Zorna, also on one knee, scooped beneath the other.

"This is your brother, the king," said Zorna, sitting him up. Wallace sat up the other. Zorna pointed. "That is Andrew."

Both men were dazed but coming around.

"Brother, are you all right?" Wallace took his brother beneath the elbow and lifted him from the floor and from Zorna's grasp. The king stood, extending his arm to Andrew.

"Are you well, Sire?" Andrew asked. "Perfectly well. You, Andrew?" asked the king. "I too am well."

Amazed by the transformation, Wallace gazed at the twins. "Two of you. It is astounding. Well done, Zorna. But how shall we tell them apart? It is impossible."

At that instant, Andrew raised his fingers to his lower lip and pulled it down. In the inner aspect of Andrew's lower lip, where the tissue met the gum, he bore a tattoo, a small *X*.

"I was once captured in war, the Outland conflict," Andrew explained. "I spent time in an enemy prison. My Greedish captors were a resourceful but suspicious clan. I bear the mark of an enemy combatant." He released his lip. "In the event of my escape, it was the

Greedishes' way of identifying a former captive. Capture a man only once, they would say. The next time, kill him."

Silent, the men gazed at one another.

"Now, let's begin," said Alexander, staring at Andrew as he would into a mirror.

Outcry

Filled to capacity, Tom and Mary's refectory hall teemed with representatives from every corner of the kingdom.

A large, bearded man in a white blouse and black trousers gritted his teeth. Reaching behind to a table, he lifted and upturned a large hourglass. Yellow sand sprinkled, collecting in a small hill at the bottom of the glass.

"We have much to do, and we have little time," the bearded man said, shaking his fist with determination. His eyes met with all who shared his concern. His face furrowed, he nodded to the foreign kings, and they sat at the table before him, nodding in accord with many others in the assembly. The sitting kings whispered among themselves. Hesitant to speak loudly, all were humbled by the presence of King Stanislaus the elder brother of Father Time. Acknowledging their repect, King Stanislaus nodded. One weary guest slept, his head down upon the kings' table, a cowl covering his head, his right arm arched along the table, pinning the cowling around his face.

The room was abuzz with tension. Concerned beings had traveled days to get to the meeting. They needed to formulate a strategy to overthrow Zili and rid the kingdoms of his cruelty.

The man in the white blouse pounded the table with a boot lent him by a dwarf sitting just feet away. "We must decide!" he shouted. "Our people can suffer no longer. We need viable ideas to fight this evil magic."

Few eager hands flew into the air. Initially, politely, only a few wanted to speak.

"Have you no fire, no passion? Do you not want your lives back?" cried the man. "Think about the way it was before the Great Peace. Remember. Do you want a return to those fretful times? Well, do you?"

The silence did not last. A crescendo of voices filled the tight room, voices ringing out with anger and frustration from every corner. Every dominion of the countryside was represented.

"This is an outrage!" shouted a man from the rear. His wife, turning to him, pushed her tearful face into his shoulder.

Against the back wall, a pair of ten-year-old troll brothers, barefoot, clad in threadbare clothing, began to fight. Diving for the floor, both troll children tried to catch a clothed brown rat zipping across their feet. Several beings leaped from their chairs. Chairs popped into the air one after another as the rat scurried along the wall. The troll children pursued the rat toward the front. Adults shoved one another out of the way, while some punched others.

"ORDER! ORDER! Stop this! We cannot turn on one another!" bellowed the bearded man in the white blouse. "Save your energy for the real enemy—Zili and his band of thieves and cutthroats. For now, we must bide our time."

Toward the front of the room, the legs of a wooden chair sharply scraped across the dry wooden floor. "Why? How much more of this cruelty must we endure?" said the man who rose from it. "I've been a religious man all my life. I've seen a lot of things change as of late—sadly, not for the better. This used to be a place where people cared for another. Our homes and people are mere shadows of what they were. If nothing can be done, I will leave."

"John is right. I've known him all of my life. He is a good man. If all good people leave, will this kingdom survive? You can't leave." Swiveling on his seat John turned his back to the large man and stared toward the back of the room.

"Our fields have been destroyed," shouted a barefoot teenage boy. The hems of his ragged trousers above his ankles, he raised his fist above his head. "Our seed corn taken, how can we live? My younger brothers and sisters will go hungry. I want to fight."

His mother, clad in a scarf and threadbare peasant dress, sobbed.

She reached for her son.

"This boy makes sense," an old man grumbled. He stood. "Something has to be done. Zili is out of control."

"An old man and a boy; is this what this has come to? A fight between people of the earth and … and a tyrant. I think you must—"

"Must what? He and his men came into our village," said a dwarf, climbing onto the table. The two-foot-tall man strolled the tabletop as if it were a lane. Gently nudging elbows and arms aside, he looked each man, woman, or being in the face. "Zili took our money, he did; our animals too—food gone, and our homes burned. He left the oldest and the weak to die of starvation or cold. We must do something."

Along the gray plank wall behind the man in the white blouse, a gaunt man in tatters stepped from the shadows into the light. Shielded beneath his left arm paced a young boy, no older than ten.

"Look at this child," said the thin man. The old man's gaunt, sunken cheeks and fallow skin fit him like a loose suit. "I am this boy's uncle." Pausing, his eyes searched the room. "Zili has mercy for no one. He chopped off my nephew's arm just below the elbow. *Look*." The old man hoisted the boy's stump for all to see.

A quiet gasp shot through the room, after which one could hear only the wind outside.

The uncle pulled the bandaged nub of his nephew's right arm to his chest. "And why? Because he killed for dinner a rabbit in the Orphic Forest!" The man gazed at every being in the room, but his soul seem dried out, his spirit nearly dead. "Zili said the boy was 'poaching' on the land of King Alexander Dobromil—*poaching*. Why? Why?" The man sobbed. "I could just—I could …" Staggering backward to his chair in the shadows, the man cried. Quietly comforting him, his nephew stroked his graying hair back from his lowered head.

From the ceiling swooped a minuscule light. Like a comet, she shot through the room, a long trail sparkling behind. All eyes followed. She was impatient. Whirling over and around an old woman, the light banked, hovering above the old woman's head.

"And here—this old woman," uttered a wee feminine voice, her winged body ensconced in brilliance. The light flashed yellow and green with each of her words. "She was flogged because her broken husband, hurt in a mining accident, could work not. She bears these reminders of Zili's cruelty." The back of the old woman's blouse, raised by sparkles of light, revealed healing scars. A gasp and whispers hastened through the gathering. The blouse fell to cover her wounds. "Her husband was executed for not witnessing the flogging she took for him." The light sprite's hues deepened, darkened to bloody red. Undulating, she flashed slowly, angrily. "With his men, Zili now tries to find magic objects of all kinds to strengthen his cruelty and power."

"Horrors have affected us all, humans and oddlings alike. I am King Shibboleth of Golem. My own brother, Hesserth, king of the lizard people, was tortured and murdered, and Hezia his son kidnapped and killed by Zili. For centuries, we have been the guardians of the night creatures and the cave dwellers," said King Shibboleth. "We care for the dragons, who in turn protect the forest. From my brother, the Dragon Stone was taken. It is the life source of our people. If it is not returned, those we guard will die."

"I am Beast," another voice boomed. He was over eight feet tall. His thick, straight, grizzled hair completely covered his body and poked from the seams of his leather-and-brass armor. Encircling his wide chest was a gold sash, upon which were pinned medals of valor.

"As you have seen," Beast said, glancing at the green-and-yellow flashing sprite, "the light sprites are beings fully capable of ... expressing their passions. I am a large being. By most human standards, I am a giant. My size commands respect and authority." Beast peered around the room. "In advance of this meeting I was asked to speak for the sprites. The smallest of those here will come to me; the words they speak into my ear, I shall repeat exactly."

Up welled a cloud of multicolored light from a table at the left, and another from a workbench near the rear. Still other specks of light descended from the ceiling, as had the first sprite. From behind the chairs of the kings, more light sprites rose. Their glow brightened.

The three clouds of light, red, green, and blue, combined into a ghostly white humanoid figure six inches high. Up it floated, six feet into the air. Alighting upon Beast's shoulder, it brought its ethereal lips into line with Beast's ears. In a wee voice, the cooperative whispered. Nodding, Beast looked out at the gathering.

"Zili wishes to possess our ability to become invisible," Beast said, interpreting the cooperative's words. Beast listened. "Zili wishes to travel instantly from place to place. To accomplish this end, he stole our children prior to their age of challenge."

The room went quiet again.

"Not far from a homestead whose well he salted, he boiled them in the waters of Hydra and drank their essence." His voice quaked and softened. His head lowered. "Zili rendered and bottled their remains." Listening, Beast shook his head. "But he does not know."

Astonished, the gathering looked at one another. Beast heard many whispers begging—"What does he not know?"

"Our magic will work only for those with clean hearts." Disintegrating, the cloud of light comprising the tiny human form separated into primary colors. Beast turned his head. The wind of their tiny wings gently wafted his hair. The streams of light reintegrated upon his other shoulder into a mournful theater mask. Through its woeful countenance, they whispered, "In part, our sorrow has disrupted the aurora, breaking the balance of the land."

His back to the speaker, the sleeping guest raised his head and sat up in his chair. He dropped the cowl to his shoulders. Only having pretended to sleep, the foreigner had heard enough. Pushing back from his chair, he stood, turned, and took a few steps forward. In a complete circle he revolved, allowing all to see his face.

"I am King Alexander Dobromil of the Kingdom of Illuminae." A hush blanketed the gathering. Whispers of his name quietly whizzed through the room. The room was electric. "My brother has done the things you have said. I did not send him to commit these atrocities, I assure you. I am uncertain of his ultimate motivation, but I suspect his intention is to take my crown, deposing me and our brother Wallace."

"Your Highness."

Heads turned to see Princess Sarah standing from a table in the middle of the room. She removed her cloak and mask so all could clearly see her face. "I may know Zili's motivation. I received a revelation the night you checked on Princess Angelica. 'Twas also the night, I later discovered, that Zili made his escape from the castle. Queen Isadora's mynah birds chatter with Zili's repulsive crow nearly every night. That bird, which, on a lark or two, I'd fed, revealed to her birds and in turn to me Zili's sedition."

"The bird I have also fed?" Alexander asked.

"The same, brother-in-law," Princess Sarah said, turning from the eyes of the gathering to face him. "I watched the queen's birds speak with the voice of Zili. In my journal, I inscribed their words so as not to forget. Twice they repeated. 'It was foretold—The physician's baby shall keep Zili from the crown. Kill the physician's family before the baby is born, the wizard said.' They spoke no truer words regarding Zili's intentions. My dog Bowes, a seer of truth, ran to the birds. He spun three times and sat wagging his tail. I have seen him do this only when people have spoken truth."

A young man rose from his chair, his black, beaded hair dangling to the chest plate of his steel and brass chest armor. "You know me not in my present form," he said in clear, strong voice. Having drunk from a shallow wooden cup, he licked his lips. He placed the cup on the table. They watched as his youthful skin blemished, softened, and wriggled. Beneath his eyes became puffy, his nose heavy, his eyebrows bushy. A long white beard and moustache replaced a clean-shaven face. As his face took form, the armor turned to a cloth robe and cowl, tied at the waist by a rope, a cape at his back. Hurried utterances of his name suffused the gathering—"Zorna."

"I am Zorna, a wizard of the first order." Raking his fingers through his beard, he paused and turned to the king. "Of this prophecy, I am aware," he said. His gnarled fingers slid the wooden cup into a pouch within his cape. "It was foretold in other prophecies since the time of your father's father, King Caczmarek, that his grandson Alexander would be king. Everyone thought the prophecy false because they knew the young King Richard had no wife yet. In his youth, of course, he had no need of a doctor," Zorna said, glancing at Nicholas, who was standing near the hearth beside Mary. "When King Richard married your mother, Sire, it was foretold she would bear two children at the same time, one born a minute before the other, and then a third more than a year later. The twins would be as unalike as two brothers could be. One was destined to sit the throne, the other destined to cry out with envy. The birds spoke truth."

Sarah nodded.

Zorna continued. "It was foretold the firstborn child of a healer, the physician of the king, would deny the second child, the envious usurper to the throne. Without question, Your Highness, the usurper was your twin brother, Sheriff Zili."

Camouflaged against a wall behind the panel of kings and elders, a griffin strode forward and flexed its wings. Feathers upon its lion's body, it preened its wings and brightly flashed its eagle eyes. It had been hiding in plain sight. Dissipating the deceptive pattern of the wall imprinted upon its body, it became clearly discernible to the assembly. Tall from its front talons, its proud lion's chest out and high, its shoulders gave rise to a thin, graceful, serpentine neck that arched back and forward to support its eagle head. Pointed, feathered ears rose on either side of its head. Its true pattern visible, its eagle eyes glared around the room. It could see all from its eight-foot vantage.

"King Richard," it hissed, "accepted the service of a new physician. The physician's wife was a daughter of the forest. She gave up her magic and immortality for the love of this mortal." The griffin's snake tail slithered on the floor around its rear talons. "During the third year of their union, the physician Christopher had a son, whom they named Nicholas. Still a favored daughter of the forest, his wife Margaret received a blessing from the king and queen of nature, Father Time and Lady Hydra. They gave to the child the beginning of many gifts: he would develop the ability to tell whether someone spoke truth or deceit, and more."

King Stanislaus leaned forward from his chair, the knob of his scepter angled. He said, "Indeed, Margaret, princess of frost fairies, fell in love with the mortal, physician Christopher Northland. So in love was Margaret that she chose to relinquish her immortality to wed the human. By order of Lady Hydra, the fairy clan controlling the seasons gave Margaret a locket created from the light of stars; one of the greatest honors of the Cringle clan." With the end of his scepter, King Stanislaus traced the shape of the locket in the air. Trailing the end of the scepter, three sprites of red, green, and blue created a quickly fading, ethereal color image of the locket in the air. "In the center of the locket," King Stanislaus continued, "They placed a crystal vial containing the essence of her former immortality, the Elixir Illuminae. Years ago, Lady Hydra hung the locket around Margaret's neck with sinew donated from the polar bear clan. Their support granted her strength in the mortal world. That was the day when Margaret saw the fate, the future held for her child of *two worlds*; that was the day Lady Hydra rose from the water. So listen to my story and understand …"

The ripples in the lake of Lady Hydra settled and the surface smoothed. As if in tune to the same cryptic instructions, fish undulated to the edge of the lake. Turning to witness, they waited, watching as a mountain of water rose from the center of the lake. The mound of clear water swelled, becoming as big around as several trees. Taller than the tallest tree, the mound of water drew in and took the form of a woman, a towering goddess of water. Her beautiful angular face rested upon a subtle neck of water. Thick, transparent tresses hung from her head and washed like curling waves over her transparent back. A crystalline cloak clad her whole body apart from her right arm. She looked like glass. She leveled her gaze on the black birds settling in the nearby trees.

Swaying, her head down, she looked at the young maid, Margaret, at the edge of the bank. She extended her open hand. "My great-grandchild," said Lady Hydra. "You have chosen the path of dedicated human love. At a given time known only to me, you will bear a child, a gift to the world. In his life he shall do many things, right many wrongs, bestow much kindness upon others. Behold the vision …"

Lifting both hands above her head, Lady Hydra blew warm mist from her mouth. The swirling mist became a gentle white vortex surrounding Margaret.

"I shall grant you three visions," Lady Hydra said in an echoing voice. She directed the end of the swirling white cloud toward the bank. It enveloped Margaret.

Peering up the graceful vortex, Margaret heard Lady Hydra whisper, "This is the future as it is written into time."

As the light focused upon her eyes, Margaret witnessed the first vision. She saw the birth of two children—not hers but the children of King Richard Dobromil and his queen. Later came a third. Whipping back, the vortex shot across the countryside. Margaret peered further into the future. She saw the two boys become teenagers, young royals. Margaret saw the princes become men of two-score years and more, one crowned king, the other becoming not only sheriff but also bitter and vengeful. Margaret saw the second prince plot with conspirators to take his brother's life and his place as king. Margaret saw herself give birth to a boy. She and her husband Christopher named him Nicholas.

In a second vision, she discerned a bearded man—her grown son clad in priestly vestments. He charged through a frenzied, chanting crowd, his eyes fixed on a distant platform, upon which an executioner stood. Broadsword high, the executioner readied to behead the first of three blindfolded men, wrongly condemned to die. Nicholas stopped their deaths. In another vista she saw him, over three nights, toss sacks of money through the open window of a poor man whose daughters would not now be sold into prostitution.

A third vision formed from the swirling mist. Margaret saw a younger Nicholas upon a ceremonial stage within a castle. He stood before a crowd of onlookers, and near him she recognized, from the first vision, the second royal brother. She saw the blurred image of a woman at Nicholas's side. Bound by guards, held by their hands, Nicholas was forced back from the prince. A whipped-up crowd surged forward.

"There is more, but this vision *has* been written. He may save the kingdom," Lady Hydra whispered, "and he may stop the rise of Prince Zili. But he may not. He may still fail." With a thunderclap, Lady Hydra ended the vision. The vortex dissipated. Black birds flushed from the trees.

"Heed me, grandchild Margaret. You shall be mortal, and to mortality you shall succumb," Lady Hydra warned. Fish swam into the body of the towering goddess of water. "Sadly, your life will end before your son has grown. These visions will be the sum of your experiences with your son as a grown man."

Nonplussed, shaking her head, Margaret paced back from the bank. Her face flushed; her hands flew to her heart.

King Stanislaus looked out across the assembly. "Margaret begged to see more, but Lady Hydra would show no more." Finishing his story, King Stanislaus drew his scepter upright. The room fell into an uneasy silence. Beings turned toward one another. The king eyed Nicholas standing uncomfortably in the back, trying to avoid the eyes of everyone in the room. He was unable to believe the words that had hit him as a sledgehammer might a stone. Quiet, plaintive chatter suffused the room.

"This, the prophecy, shall come to completion as foretold," said King Stanislaus in a taut voice.

His heart racing, Nicholas found a chair and sat dumbstruck. He was able to neither speak nor move. His mind reeled. "Why has no one told me before this day? And what do they expect me to do now?" His face full of question, he felt empty and filled with grief for people he had never known.

Weaving through the crowded room, Sarah made her way to Nicholas. Reaching down to comfort him, looking into his eyes, she clasped his fingers. Tom placed a hand upon Nicholas's shoulder. To Nicholas's left, Mary cried into her apron. "I am so sorry, Nicholas," Mary whimpered.

Reaching over Nicholas, Tom pulled Mary close to his chest and squeezed her tightly, Nicholas sandwiched between them. "I'm not sure I know what I would do if I lost you, too," said Nicholas. "The notion of that is too much." Nicholas sighed, shaking his head.

Chapter 9

THE CHALLENGE

Again from beneath the table scurried the clothed brown rat, squealing loudly, its naked tail whipping. It shot across the floor, bearing for a hole in the base of the slatted wall. A commotion ensued. Several beings in the front row jumped or fell from their seats.

"There it goes between the rows," said one of the troll boys, determined this time to get the rat. It would make a fine dinner if cooked correctly.

Chairs crashed to the floor as the pair of troll boys dived, tumbling, rolling, and missing the rodent. They leaped to their feet. In tandem, they dashed toward the front wall, this time the rat within their grasp.

Falling before it, they barely missed the rodent as it shot away at a sharp angle just as the troll boys hit the floor. They careened into the wall, crashing into another table, rocking it. The two-foot hourglass, sand nearly emptied, tilted with the table and shattered on the floor. Shards and sand spread, and a thick cloud of brown dust lofted to the ceiling. Coughing, beings, humans, and kings rushed from the front tables to the side walls. Before the roiling cloud settled, a robed figure stepped from the blinding, whirling dust, his face masked by the shadow of his hood.

A hush washed over the gathering. There was only silence. The troll boys rolled from their backs, ignoring the rat just within their reach. It shot into a hole. On their knees, the rambunctious boys slowly backed into the clutches of their father, who whisked them from the front of the room. The bearded man in the white shirt and black trousers stepped back.

Sauntering out of the hourglass dust, the tall, thin figure dropped the cowl from his skeletal head to his shoulders. He looked around the room. Dipping their chins, the kings nodded with respect.

Silence continued.

"All know me, but more important, I know you all. I am Father Time," the newcomer said.

The silence remained.

"I have counted the seconds of your lives. I have been with you since the beginning and I shall be there at the ending." He paused as he searched the room. "You are all here as creatures of being, and as such your time is short. Some will be new to this life this year. Others will see their last." He extended his hand. His skeletal fingers and skull became flesh as he pointed to everyone in the room. "The choices we make, any action we take, affect every person and everything in the universe. All in this room have a common cause. We must live together with respect and have empathy for one another. This we have done for hundreds of years. Peace in this realm has been disrupted by the action of one, Zili. Thus, action we must take to bring balance back. It is *time* to set things right."

From the table of the kings, Wallace rose quickly to his feet. He looked at his brother Alexander and turned to face Father Time. Wallace steadied his jitteriness while fisting his right hand with resolve. "I have … I approach to ask your assistance to stand against our brother, Zili," Wallace entreated, his voice quavering. He swallowed. "The harm that has befallen Alexander cannot be undone, except with your assistance. We may bring peace back to this land." He stepped closer to Father Time. "We seek any possible options, I assure you. Anyone who is willing to speak, here, now—your words will have weight."

"Pardon my tremor, Your Highness," an elderly man said from his chair. His neck stiff, he turned just his eyes to King Alexander. "With the shaking disease, I have been ill for many years." The old man strained to stand. "Forgive me, Your Highness, as it is most difficult at times." His rounded back bending him forward, he held the knob of a crooked, three-foot walking stick. "I mean no disrespect with my question," he said, "but why could you not stop your brother? He dwelled within the walls of your castle. Was he not within your grasp?"

Snapping his heels, General Raptozk stood, glanced at the kings, and lowered his eyes. "Sires, if I may answer?"

Granting permission, King Alexander waved his hand, and Prince Wallace nodded.

"When at first we heard the scurrilous reports of Prince Zili's actions, we sent men to the countryside to verify the accusations. We waited. Alas, few ever returned. Prince Wallace himself used magic to obscure his identity. He traveled in the guise of a commoner through the Orphic Forest to Castle Illuminae. I was with him. He was determined either to disprove or verify the rumors. Prince Wallace sent fifty of my men throughout the kingdom. Only this morning we received word by courier that Zili was burning a village. My soldiers engaged Prince Zili's men but, sadly, none of our weapons found their mark. My surviving men were lucky to escape with their lives. Many were injured and many died. Zili has shielded himself with powers stronger than any we possess, but he is not yet omnipotent." Bowing, General Raptozk backed away.

A hiss and slurp issued from the periphery of the room. A clothed, torpedo-shaped body uncoiling from a stool. Creeping on all fours just above the floor, the being came up to where General Raptozk had been standing. Yielding more of the floor, the general backed up. The being's slit eyes peered around the room. Some facial features resembled a komodo dragon, but the creature had many features tempered by pleasing humanoid traits.

Rising to stand on two legs, the creature was less than five feet tall. It had dark, smooth skin like a salamander. Its wavy, raven hair fell from its rounded head to its sternum, over the lapels of its robes of white.

"I am Crota, the representative from the lizard clan," he said, his forked tongue flicking between syllables. He slowly blinked his lids over his gold irises. "Lord Zili is protected by the Firestone, once an extremely powerful magic, but the stone has aged. He seeks to rejuvenate the ring, bolstering its power. It was carved from a larger, more powerful crystal." Glinting from a lanyard dangling from Crota's neck, General Raptozk recognized a small, round mirror on a gold chain, like the one he had found on Hezia's neck.

"And to defeat him," said King Alexander, "it will take …"

"Magic, Your Highness," said Crota. "Magic equal to the strength combined of the Dragon Stone and, shall I say, other powerful relics," replied Crota. "Dragons have protected our peoples for many centuries, but their magic reflects the hearts of the beings they encounter."

The window sash was open only a hand's width, enough for a puff of wind to quietly fan the white cotton curtains. The sweet smell of fresh-cut hay wafted upon the air. A flourish of autumn leaves whirled into the room. Upon an eddy, they scattered before the seated kings but to their surprise, not randomly across the floor. The leaves subtly arranged themselves into the outline of a human face. The eyes of the face blinked, and the room hushed at the sight. The lips spoke softly, tempered by the crackling undertones of rustling leaves.

"It takes both worlds," the face of leaves uttered, "that of magic and that of man, to solve this problem. It takes a champion of strong belief and clean heart to lead. We must find one with a unique approach, one with pure intentions. We must find he who will think first before he reacts."

Frigid air blasted through the window. The room chilled rapidly. Glacial winds caused crystals of frost to thicken at the corners of the glazing bars and sash. Frost condensed, racing across the window light. A log of mist rolled beneath the sash and to the floor, billowing and tumbling to a corner workbench. There it eddied up from the floor at a right angle. The mist stacked and layered, climbing in height. The layers stratified into blues, greens, and purples. They took on the solidity and appearance of flesh: a three-foot humanoid being. The head was topped with a soft cloth hat of red-and-green tartan. He cleared his throat, and the room filled with the sound of icicles cracking against a rock.

"Oh, much better," he said, shaking out the wrinkles in his green justaucorps, purple waistcoat, and green breeches. He peered around the room. "Excuse my entrance, Your Highness. I usually enjoy being a bit more dramatic," He bowed to the kings. "I am Jack Frost," he said, an icy mist forming from his breath. "I say that Nicholas should lead us in this task." Nicholas listened as his name was whispered around the room. "This was foretold in the prophecy of Lady Hydra. It is the purpose for which he was born."

A thunderous upsurge of passionate voices and accents shook the room. Men and oddlings stomping feet, and waving fisted arms, calling, "Nicholas! Nicholas!"

The raucous demonstration grew. Men and oddlings came to their feet. "Nicholas. Nicholas. Nicholas." With each repetition, the voices grew louder and stronger.

Confused and overwhelmed, Nicholas's parents scanned the room. King Stanislaus lifted his staff and slammed the point to the floor, the tip hitting with a sharp crack. A brilliant blue light flashed from the crystal mounted at its top. Everyone in the room instantly hushed.

"Nicholas Claus, come forth," ordered King Stanislaus.

From the back of the room, his face uncertain and bewildered, Nicholas wound his way through the excited crowd, his eyes fixed on King Stanislaus. He wanted nothing to do with leading. The thought that so many might pin their hopes and fortunes on him was daunting.

As he passed, hands patted him on the back. Women kissed his cheeks and pulled him into hugs. Men and oddlings shook his hands. Children clutched his waist.

He was no hero. He was a farm boy who made toys. He knew nothing of his so-called inheritance or any special abilities.

Emerging at the front of the room Nicholas stopped before King Stanislaus, who looked into Nicholas's eyes. Nicholas could feel the weight of the people's eyes on his back.

King Stanislaus, his face unsmiling and stoic, said, "You have a kind and noble heart, Nicholas." The king laid his fingers upon Nicholas's shoulder. He turned Nicholas toward the excited crowd. He held Nicholas's right arm above his head amid an upsurge of cheering. "You have made a proper choice," he announced to the crowd. To Nicholas, he said, "When you offered to help both man and oddling, you showed indifference to kind or clan. You demonstrated the compassion of a being, and you have matured to manhood."

Pausing, King Stanislaus looked at King Alexander and Prince Wallace. "I have but one question, which is yours alone to answer," he said. He placed his large hands upon Nicholas's shoulders. "Will you accept the challenge to champion the reestablishment of peace in the Aurora Kingdoms?"

Nicholas's eyes darted to his mother. This was his chance to back out, but he could see the hopeful eyes of his friends and neighbors.

"If you accept this challenge," King Stanislaus said, "you shall have the support of all that forms the Linkage. Should you, however, choose not to accept this challenge, no one will think ill of you, for this task is indeed overwhelming."

Nicholas slowly took a long, deep breath. Thoughtfully turning in a half circle, he again observed the faces of everyone in the room. His parents were embracing with concern. Tom and Mary gazed back at Nicholas with loving eyes, each nodding approval. He recalled his mother's softly spoken words, said to him during his times of doubt: "You are a man now, son. You must make the hard decisions." She would place her hand over her heart. "Listen to your heart," she would say. "Your head will follow if it is right. Remember always that, no matter what you choose, your father and I will stand with you."

Turning back to King Stanislaus, Nicholas looked into the royal's eyes. Genuflecting with bowed head, Nicholas spoke strongly and confidently. "I would be honored, Your Highness, to serve our peoples in whatever way I can."

The room erupted in cheers. Men and oddlings stomped feet and waved fisted hands. The shouts became deafening. "Nich-o-las, Nich-o-las, Nich-o-las."

King Stanislaus stood. Raising his scepter, he slammed it to the floor.

Crack.

"It is done. Nicholas, kneel before me," the king ordered. Onto both knees Nicholas fell. Lifting his head, he gazed into King Stanislaus's face.

The crystal at the top of the king's staff glowed, projecting the light pattern of the aurora borealis. He touched the crystal to Nicholas's shoulders and forehead. Nicholas felt a tingling surge through his body.

"To help you with your challenge, I bestow upon you a gift. From this time forward, you shall know the truth with certainty when someone speaks it. You will also know in your heart the state of well-being of anyone for whom your heart has fondness. This will hold true for all time." Again, the king slammed his scepter, which registered a crack on the floor. The room instantaneously burgeoned with the radiance of the aurora borealis. King Stanislaus took two steps back.

"Rise, Nicholas. Face your neighbors." King Stanislaus faced the crowd of beings. "Behold your champion—Nicholas."

Nicholas stood to a roar of approval.

The Journey Begins

Within hours of adjournment, humans, oddlings, and royals prepared to leave for their respective kingdoms. Nicholas took two horses from the barn and saddled them. Prince Wallace spoke several moments with Crota, the lizard clan representative.

Tom and Mary led King Alexander, Prince Wallace, Zorna, and General Raptozk along the narrow flagstone path to the barn. The captain of the guard waited at the foot of the path.

"Your Highnesses," he said, snapping to attention.

"They have been properly groomed, and fed?"

"Yes, Sire," he said to King Alexander. "The horses are hitched to the royal carriages. We are ready."

"Good," Prince Wallace said.

Also prepared, the royal equestrian guards stood aligned to escort their respective royals and entourages back to their realms. Beside each carriage, a footman stood at attention, holding the door as he waited to help his charges board.

"Mary, Tom," said Prince Wallace, "it has been a pleasure seeing you again, although I wish the circumstances were better." Pivoting on his right foot, Wallace looked at the barn, the house, and the fields. "Curious. Did Princess Sarah find her stay with you satisfying, Mary?"

"Yes, Your Highness," Mary said.

"She should return to Castle Illuminae today. Why, she was here a second ago," Wallace said.

Mary's eyes now searched. Tom began to look too.

Prince Wallace saw Alexander within his carriage, talking to his coachman standing at the window. Wallace gestured for the captain of his guard to come. The captain rushed up, bowing. Wallace whispered into his ear.

"I shall look for her, Your Highness," the captain said, bowing. "Tell her ladyship she will travel home now. Her journey will be

long, and we should get started. Nightfall will come soon. I think it wise to start before sunset." He rubbed his dark beard. "Her journey will be much longer than mine," Wallace muttered, "if she perturbs Alexander."

"We have seen her not within the last quarter hour," Mary said. "Yet an hour ago I saw her coachman packing her things."

Their heads turned when they heard the clop of horses' hooves, and a woman's laughter. Nicholas and Sarah rode up to the barn, Jingles and Bowes running alongside.

Having ridden only a few feet, the captain of the guard spotted them, shouted, and swayed on his horse to face Wallace. Alexander emerged from his coach, glowering.

"She is here, Your Highness." The guard pointed with his sword. "I can see her, you ninny," Wallace chided, himself irritated. "Bring her horse around." Wallace took several steps toward the horses upon which they rode. The guard held the reins of Sarah's horse.

"What is this frivolity, Princess Sarah?" Wallace admonished, reproving the reckless behavior of a young maiden riding alone with an impulsive youth. Wallace's eyes searched high and low beyond the horses and up the path. No one followed.

"I do not see her," Wallace said.

Sarah and Nicholas were perplexed. "Her? Who is it you do not see, Prince Wallace?" Sarah asked, looking back in the direction from which she and Nicholas had just ridden.

"Your chaperone. Where is she, sister-in-law?" Wallace asked.

The smile left Princess Sarah's face. She averted her eyes, for she had no chaperone. Nicholas climbed from his horse and helped her down.

"What has happened?" Wallace asked. "Shall I have my brother order the nuns to instruct you on royal etiquette and protocol?"

"Please don't be angry with her, Your Highness," pleaded Nicholas. Wallace's gaze veered to Nicholas.

"It is not her fault," said Nicholas. "Sire, it's mine. It's mine." Lifting his chin, Wallace softened his stern gaze. "Have we made a mistake from the start with you? You, Nicholas, are uninitiated in proper royal protocol. Whereas you, Sarah, have been here some time and—"

"I beg your pardon." Sarah lowered her eyes. Her voice entreated. "It was the first break of protocol, I swear, Prince Wallace."

"I reprove this behavior," Wallace chided, "but I shall forgive you this one infraction this time, young Nicholas. Learn from your mistakes. You are the chosen one. You saved my niece, the Princess Angelica. You shall learn." Wallace glared at Sarah. "But Princess Sarah should know better."

Nicholas and Sarah felt like bad children as they wandered apart from each other. Tom followed Nicholas from the flagstone path to the edge of the barn, whispering, "You should be more thoughtful. These are not the actions of the *man* we have chosen as champion."

"I am sorry, Father," Nicholas said. "The evening was so, so beautiful. I wanted to take Sarah for a ride through the forest once more, before she left for home. I am merely unsophisticated in the ways of the royals."

"Without an escort, Nicholas? You should know how inappropriate that was." Tom placed his hand on Nicholas's shoulder. "We have a covenant. *You* have a covenant you must honor. We shall not sully the lady's name in the process. You have made His Highness worry, and you have made him late. This shall not happen again."

"But Father …"

"No. There is nothing more to say."

King Alexander strode up behind Prince Wallace. He saw Tom and Nicholas several yards away. "What is going on here?" he asked.

"Nothing, brother," said Wallace, one foot in his carriage. "I have taken care of things."

"So we shall depart," said Alexander.

Nicholas peered over his father's shoulder at Sarah. King Alexander winked as he entered his carriage. Sarah entered behind. The footman closed and latched the door.

"Travel safely, Your Highness's," said Mary and Tom. Nicholas stood back, nodding. His eyes smiled shyly only at Sarah, who was peeking through the square window of the carriage.

"We will meet again soon," said King Alexander.

Chapter 10

THE LIZARD MEN

His head through the carriage window, Wallace was confused. He threw his arm out, gesturing to his coachman high on the carriage bench to stop. Not only had Prince Wallace's surroundings become unfamiliar, but also the path upon which they traveled had narrowed substantially, so much so that he doubted the coach could proceed without becoming wedged among the trees.

Tugging back on the reins, the coachman brought the coach from a steady pace to a stop. The restless draft team snorted, sidled, and stepped backward, their heads bobbing. The large wheels of the carriage rocked back and forth. The restless horses of the royal guard paced within the small clearing as Wallace gazed into the dense forest.

"General!" Prince Wallace shouted.

Startled, the preoccupied general swung his horse around to face the carriage. Not used to being lost, he worried less about himself than he did his horses. The general's mount circled the carriage. "Sire?"

"How far are we from the lizard people's homeland?" Wallace asked. Atop his steed, Zorna raked his fingers through his horse's mane to calm it as it reared away from the carriage. "Whoa," he said, patting his steed's broad neck, scanning the dark forest.

Loosing a leather tie at the top of a leather tube attached to his saddle, General Raptozk withdrew a tightly rolled parchment. He hastily unfurled it across his saddle. He peered at the map. "I, uh, am not sure, Your Highness." Wrinkling his brow, he removed his gauntlet and searched the map with his bare index finger.

Joseph peered over the general's shoulder. "Is it not marked?"

"Let me see," demanded Lexi, steering his horse close. He too peered at the map. Mystified, he shook his head.

"No. I am afraid it isn't here," said General Raptozk. He gazed into the dense forest and to the sky. Puffing out his cheeks, he rolled the map up and slipped it back into the leather holster.

"I thought it was midafternoon," Joseph said with trepidation. Gripping the reins, his knuckles whitened. He brushed sweat from his lip. "It looks like sunset in this secluded place."

Gazing at a glint piercing the distant forest, Wallace pointed hastily to the light. "Hydra Falls is on your map, yes?"

"Yes, Your Highness." The general cautiously leveled his finger. "That direction."

"At least this parchment is useful for something other than kindling," Wallace quipped.

"Your Highness," acknowledged the general, dipping his chin. Wallace said, "When shall we arrive, General?"

"Sire, if we continue our current speed and bearing, about four hours."

"Four?" Wallace glowered. "The lizard people live within the caves beneath the falls, I heard. The entrance is where the water washes the yellow stones. This is correct, Zorna?"

Zorna lowered his head. "Yes, Your Highness."

Satisfied, Prince Wallace nodded, pointing his chin in the direction of the light. Lexi and Joseph rode before the carriage, hacking at small branches with their swords to clear the way. They proceeded slowly as the remaining brush scraped the side of the carriage, encroaching upon every yard they traversed.

Hours passed. Plodding through the woods on their tired horses, the prince and his men remained ever vigilant amid the clop of hooves, the jangling of the harness, and the squeak of the wheels. They heard occasional hoots of owls and howls of wolves.

"Your Highness," muttered the general, "we have been on this path for the better part of a day, yet it has revealed none of it secrets as to the whereabouts of the lizard people."

"The trees," murmured Joseph, "are naturally thick. It is as night, Sire."

And it was not until they reached a break in the tree line and emerged into an abrupt radiance of light that they felt hope.

"The air is cold," Joseph said. He could see his breath. "Crisp."

"I feel the same," said Wallace.

Leaves gently ticked and tapped their way to the ground. The men could hear crunching leaves beneath the carriage wheels.

"Sire," said Joseph, "all semblance of the road has vanished. Old wagon ruts and hoofprints—all gone."

"There is no road to follow, Your Highness," reiterated the general. "The ground is uneven."

"We should leave the carriage and go on foot," suggested Joseph.

"Sire?" asked the general, questioning the wisdom of Joseph's suggestion.

From the window, Wallace turned to Zorna to take his cue. Zorna nodded.

"I agree," Wallace said. "It is done. We will proceed on foot. Unhitch and take the horses. We shall lead them, conserving their strength until we need them."

Wallace stepped from the carriage to the forest duff. Twigs snapped beneath his boots. With a gesture from Wallace, Joseph collected the horses of the royal guard, while taking note of their protest and their desire to protect the Prince. Wallace ordered them to stay with the carriage.

To the captain of the guard, Prince Wallace shouted back as he and his contingent marched into the woods, "We will return." Wallace waved.

Single file, Prince Wallace, General Raptozk, Zorna, Lexi, and Joseph strode over the uneven ground. The ground at various intervals was set like steps, which alternately descended or ascended, yard after yard. In addition, everywhere they stepped, the grass withdrew into the ground like worms to avoid crushing by their boots.

"Sire, the grass is, well, lively," Lexi exclaimed, tittering.

Zorna shook his head. The grass was familiar to him. Indeed, it was lively, for that was what it was: *lively grass*.

Amazed by its animal responsiveness, Joseph trod carefully. Giddy, he nudged Zorna in the arm while lifting his feet high and laying them soft. "Look," Joseph whispered with widening eyes. His arms out from his sides, Joseph teetered to maintain his balance. "With each step, it grows backward into the earth instead of out," he said.

"I see that too," Lexi said, trying to lower his boots to patches of ground already devoid of grass. "And as I lift my boot, it returns."

"What do you call it?" Prince Wallace asked. "Lively grass, Sire," said Zorna, "or spring grass."

"What is its purpose?"

"To live, Sire. Only to live, like us all." Zorna bent his knee and pulled up a blade. Wallace stooped beside him. "Watch," said Zorna. He touched the tip of the blade. It attached to the end of his fingertip. "If you were an insect, it would wrap you up within the tongue of its blade and pull you into its tube to your death."

"I'm glad I am not an insect!"

"In the Outland, they have giant, tubeless relatives that in every way resemble snakes. They see us as insects, Sire." Zorna swept his arm before him. "They travel through the ground the way a fish would through water."

Towing his horse behind, Zorna set the pace: weaving between the trees, tramping through the brush just ahead of Prince Wallace. Following came Joseph, Lexi, and General Raptozk.

Halfway to Hydra Falls, it began to rain, gently at first, then heavily. The path became slippery under the horses' hooves. Though drenched, all pushed on, the men pulling hats or hood low over their eyes. Sometimes the distance between them would widen, but they made it their duty to stay together.

Lightning flashed. Thunder rumbled and cracked, startling the horses.

Stopping in knee-high brush, Zorna leveled his gaze through the forest before him. Cupping his hand to his ear, he tilted his head. His other arm behind his back, finger up, he cautioned Wallace and his men who followed. "Shhhh. Listen and hear."

"What is it? Joseph whispered loudly.

"Young Joseph," Zorna scolded, "one hears not with one's mouth but with one's ears. Quiet, and listen. It is—"

"Silence. I hear silence," muttered the general. Weary, displeased, he was sopping wet. He peeled his flattened hair from the skin of his forehead.

"We are beyond a zone of silence. Now listen," Zorna murmured, one hand wringing the rainwater from his beard. They heard the gurgling and tumbling of fast-moving water, a distant river. They trod slowly. The ground was soft. Suction pulled at the horses' feet and the men's boots.

"Beyond the line of trees," Zorna said. "We approach the river."

"Approach a river?" remarked Joseph, yanking his foot from the suction of a chuckhole. Prince Wallace gestured to him to prevent his horse's feet from getting into such ankle-breaking holes.

"Why couldn't we approach food?" murmured Lexi, pulling his belt tight around his thin waist. Snapping twigs in the distance drew his attention to the surrounding forest. They felt as if they were being watched.

"Here." From a pouch slung around his shoulder, Joseph withdrew a long, yellow fruit. He tossed it to Lexi. "The sailors from the mystic seas call it a banana."

"And what do I do with this?" Lexi muttered. He turned the odd, elongated fruit over in his hand. "You'll pardon me if I don't eat it right away. I'll save this ... banana."

"What was that?" Joseph asked, changing the conversation. At the snap of a twig, his hand slapped the hilt of his sword. Flinging his hood back, he spun around.

"What is what?" Lexi asked, clasping the hilt of his own sword. "It is not the river I hear," said General Raptozk. He slid his sword from its scabbard. "Something is out there."

The contingent tramped several feet farther, entering chest-high brush, their eyes searching. Joseph stood fast. Lexi spun from left to right.

"Something bumped my leg. Hey!" Joseph shouted, drawing his sword.

Roaring, the horses reared. Something had zipped beneath their bellies. They strained against the reins clamped taut in Joseph's fingers. The force of their rearing towed Joseph forward through the grass and mud. Leaping to his aid, Lexi grabbed the reins too. The horses stomped about on restless feet, groaning, pulling, and snorting.

"*There*, there!" shouted General Raptozk, running to help. There was a hole in the brush as if someone had dashed through it. Dropping to one knee, he could see the dark, two-foot-high hole that had not been there a second ago. Someone or something had tunneled through.

"I can see nothing here," the general muttered. "This tunnel may lead to another."

"Maybe it is rats, Sire," Lexi said.

"Rats as big as sows?" the skeptical Zorna inquired, an eyebrow lifted in disbelief.

General Raptozk sat up on his heels. He sighed. "There is another somewhere, I wager. It is a poor rat that has but one hole."

"But, dear General," Zorna said, "I fear these are no rats."

"*Wait!*" shouted Lexi. "Look." He leveled his fingers toward the horses. He saw something darting beneath them. Their bodies crooked, gnarled, they were no more than four feet tall, dressed in burlap, vines, and leaves. They pounded the ground with broken tree branches and rocks before shooting away in a blur through the grass.

Lexi said, "They seem to delight in upsetting the horses."

"And princes!" shrieked Wallace, shoved backward from his feet to his buttocks. *Whoosh.* A creature whizzed past Wallace's head.

"Sire!" shouted the general, running to help Prince Wallace to his feet. But before he could get to Wallace—*whoosh*. Again, something whizzed past.

"Take cover!" shouted General Raptozk, placing himself nearly atop Prince Wallace, who was still in the mud. Rolling the general off, Prince Wallace jumped onto one of the mounts Joseph held. Hoisting a shield and sword from the horse, Wallace turned the neighing animal in all directions.

"Show yourselves!" Wallace shouted. "Off the ground, off the ground," Wallace called to his men. "Onto your mounts."

His men mounted to present a more formidable force. They saw the brush wag like ocean waves as the creatures shot through it. Unsteady and unsure, the horses advanced slowly to a clearing and the start of another thick growth of trees.

Last into the thicket, Joseph jumped from his horse and ducked behind a tree. Hitting his horse on the rump, he sent it galloping into the woods. Farther on, Lexi, Wallace, the general, and Zorna maneuvered their horses to circle and touch nose to tail, their flanks an outward wall of protection, albeit minimal.

"We may somewhat defend ourselves in all directions, Sire," said the general.

"Somewhat?" murmured Lexi.

"We shall keep our eyes vigilant to protect our respective positions," said the general.

"Somewhat," muttered Lexi. A sword in one hand, a knife in the other, Lexi was acutely uncomfortable with his less than perfect vision. "Somewhat?" he continued murmuring, his eyes and ears remaining vigilant.

Having established a somewhat dubious perimeter, the men huddled back-to-back, facing outward in all directions, presenting their shields and swords. They could see blurred shadows darting beyond the perimeter.

"What are those—those things?" shouted Joseph, running to join them within the huddle. "They could've killed us."

Joseph and Lexi, crouching, skulked close to the horses. "If you consider troll children annoying and deadly," said Lexi.

"Trolls?" the general whispered.

"I think so. And they are not the good ones," whispered Joseph. "But they are everywhere."

"I don't— Shhhh, wait." Lexi heard noises deep in the forest. He hesitated.

"What?" Joseph asked, his eyes wide, darting about.

"You didn't hear that. Over there." Lexi pointed into the forest. He hurried to the general's side. A muted cacophony of sounds came from within the forest. "Voices? What do you think it—"

"Quiet," whispered the general, his finger to his lips. "If you like living. Use your ears more than your mouth. If their voices carry, so do ours. I am certain they know we are here. They are just inside those trees. They lie in wait for us."

"Can you see them, Father?" asked Lexi.

"Shhhh!" hissed the general. He shot a look at Wallace to see whether he had heard Lexi.

Several feet away, Wallace readied himself for the coming fight. Leopold loved his son, but in the field, he was the general. If anyone found out they were father and son, one or both of them would be discharged from their beloved service. And there were other, more dire consequences.

General Raptozk growled, "I've warned you not to call me that. If any enemy should learn of our relationship, it would be fatal—for both of us. Even His Highness knows nothing." The general glared into the forest and to the ever-brightening sky. The rain had gone and the sun was showing through. Shafts of light pierced the forest canopy, some hitting the armor of those hidden behind the trees.

"See," whispered General Raptozk. "If you look carefully—see the way the meager glints of light bounce from their armor? The fools. They should have smeared mud on all that shiny metal. They are inexperienced."

"So we may defeat them, yes, General?"

"Not necessarily, boy. Who are they? What are their number and strengths?"

"You said they were inexperienced. Their numbers may be few."

"Or they could kill us all with only blind luck," retorted General Raptozk. He slid closer to the ground. "We will consider their inexperience but we should not be overconfident. Let us try not to die today."

Hearing clanking metal from the forest, Lexi nodded.

Suddenly the pounding of horses' hooves erupted upon the earth and echoed from the forest. Instantly the tiny beings who had harassed them earlier were of no concern.

"They are on the attack," said General Raptozk. "Watch the shadows. See them emerge."

Joseph shouted, "They come from the trees!"

"Prepare!" shouted Prince Wallace. Several equestrians emerged from the forest into the light. "I think those trolls were the gnats sent to harass us and break our concentration before the larger fight."

As the riders closed in, Joseph shouted, his blade above his head. *"Horsemen coming now!"*

"STAND YOUR GROUND!" Wallace shouted.

Backing into Zorna, Joseph whirled. His sword was in his right hand, over his left shoulder, poised to swing. Quietly, Zorna held up one finger, which instantly immobilized Joseph's body.

Zorna admonished him, "The fight is arriving from *that* direction." Finger down, Zorna released Joseph's now-relaxed body.

Whispering an apology with quiet lips, Joseph hurriedly backed away. He repositioned himself for the attack, but everyone else had mounted their horses. Joseph leaped to his saddle.

The attackers comprised a vanguard of six to eight human and nonhuman creatures astride horses. Wallace and his men waited with dread as the attackers charged across the open field: thin, muscular, bear-like beasts on horseback, nets whirling above their heads; massive ape-like creatures in full armor, lances in their hands and hand-like feet.

Whooping, hooting, and howling, they charged, their horses galloping at full stride.

Lexi focused on a being with green scales like a crocodile.

"A croc-man!" Zorna shouted.

Lexi watched. The scaly beast rode at the flank of the attackers, a long battle-ax in its claws, a thick tail whipping the air. "I've always wanted to try crocodile soup," Lexi muttered. Eyes widening, muscles tensing, Lexi drew a third weapon—a large skinning knife. "At least I will not have to eat alone."

The corners of his mouth down, Joseph shot a glance at Lexi, "Yes, but what sorcery have they brought to engineer our destruction?"

"They may have their sorcery, but they look pretty stupid," Lexi said. "I am not worried. We have him."

Zorna hurriedly poured liquid from two small vials into a third containing a thick but clear fluid. He added acid. Sealing the vial with wax, Zorna placed it in his hat with many others previously mixed.

Bounding wildly over the uneven ground, the attackers' horses were nearly upon them. Downwind, Zorna could smell them closing in.

"S-Sire," Joseph stuttered, dashing to the rear of their small front. He found Wallace upon his horse, quiet in prayer. Kissing the crucifix embossed on the hilt of his sword, Wallace ended his prayer before acknowledging Joseph. "Sire. They are not entirely human."

Wallace sighed. "What raider is human when he is about to kill you?"

That was no sooner said than they were surrounded. They found themselves furiously fighting. They swung their swords for their lives.

Up—*clang*—General Raptozk flung his sword to deflect a blade coming for his neck. With his left hand, he punched the brutish human attacker in the throat. Lexi swiped the same attacker diagonally across the back. Bringing his elbow back, Joseph haplessly knocked another attacker from its horse. Lunging forward, Joseph impaled a piglike being as it rose to its feet. When an ape leaped from his horse, Joseph shouted, "Sire!" Wallace darted a look over his head to see an armored shape about to land on him. From his hat, Zorna fisted and hurled a vial that smashed against the ape's body. The ape burst into the fiery streamers of a colorful firework.

Wallace spun on his horse and saw Zorna nodding. Wallace saw a hulking human coming from behind, poised to swing its battle-ax at Zorna's midsection.

Zorna's midsection vanished. Following through, the attacker's blade swung, cutting into nothing.

Suddenly popping behind his attacker, Zorna immobilized the brute with a touch of his finger.

Sword met sword, clang after clang, hit after hit, the ring of metal on metal. When Lexi parried the battle-ax of the croc-man, he spun on his horse. Leaping up, his feet landing atop his saddle, Lexi stood erect. He plunged the first quarter of his broadsword into the top of the green beast's head and withdrew. Sprayed with green blood, Lexi swabbed his face with his sleeve. "What kind of headache would you call that?" Lexi muttered as he swiftly fell back into the saddle to avoid another charging rider's broadsword. With a roundhouse sweep, he beheaded the ape creature.

Screams, shouts, wailing, and crying echoed. Sword meeting shield rang through the forest and reverberated back from the mountains. Their horses roared, reared, and sidled against more attacking warriors.

Falling from his horse, Lexi slammed into the ground. "Oooo," he hooted, the pain shooting through his spine. He looked up to the sky. Over Lexi loomed another ape. The massive beast, throwing his head back, roared. He brought his face down mere inches from Lexi's face, showing his yellowed, three-inch fangs. Rearing, the armored ape hoisted its heavy sword vertically, point end down. He thrust it toward Lexi's chest. Left, right, left, Lexi parried the strikes. The tip impaled the ground. Each time the beast missed. Each time Lexi rolled away.

Lexi latched on to the beast's wrist. It hoisted Lexi, throwing him back and forth. It tried to fling Lexi from its forearm. Turning, Lexi flipped like an acrobat. He charged the men who flanked Prince Wallace. Lexi thrust his sword into the side of the beast closest to him. It dropped to its knees. Instantly Wallace beheaded it, the head falling beside Lexi on the grass. Another crocodile-headed beast turned and stabbed Lexi in the right thigh with a short dagger.

Lexi dropped his sword to his right and collapsed on his right knee. He watched the croc-man as he grabbed his fallen sword. "You scum-sucking reptile!" Lexi screamed, arming himself with a second sword he found at his left. Wielding both swords, he slit the beast on its side. The beast pitched forward. Lexi plunged the point of the other blade in its back. "Try that on for size, you future ... walking waist belt."

Zorna's and Wallace's horses reared together. Both men jerked their reins laterally, causing the animals to spin on their hind limbs. Their outstretched front legs slammed into two attackers' horses, plunging their riders to the ground. Both beastly attackers writhed. Down Zorna's and Wallace's horses came, their front hoofs stomping the attackers to death. Ribs caved; blood ran from their mouths.

A human galloped toward Zorna. He shot an arrow. Hearing the arrow whiz, Zorna whirled. Just an inch from his neck, he snatched the arrow out of the air. When the attacker was within arm's reach, Zorna turned the arrow into a sword and beheaded his attacker. The head bounced away, while the decapitated body slumped from the horse. Before it hit the dirt, it burst into a puff of black smoke and dust.

"Sire!" shouted General Raptozk, galloping alongside Wallace. "I think I have killed the same being more than once."

"Aye, General. I am in accord," said Wallace.

"We are up against powerful magic."

"I too have killed two apes who turned out to be one and the same," Wallace said. "I recognized upon its body the cuts I previously inflicted." Just feet away, atop his mount in a low hiding place, Joseph waited in ambush for the next foolish enemy to gallop by. But it was Lexi who galloped by.

Joseph yelled, "Look up!" inadvertently alerting an enemy crossing his path. Before the words had fully left his mouth, dozens of vines dropped from branches above. Looping about Lexi's and Joseph's bodies, the vines bound down their arms. The taut vines forcefully hoisted them into the trees. The enemy, a hoggish man, snorted and squealed with glee, watching the two fly up into the trees.

Thinking Lexi and Joseph followed behind, Zorna, Raptozk, and Wallace pushed on, racing their horses up a small hill. Hearing no hooves behind, they pulled back on the reins. At that instant, a stone smashed into the general's back, knocking him from his horse. A troll with a slingshot, smug and pleased with his aim, climbed from a nearby rise.

Wallace and Zorna reeled with pain as more stones pelted their bodies. Scores of the small trolls who had tormented their horses in the tall grass lowered their slingshots. Arms and legs flying, both men tumbled from their horses—*thud*.

Groaning, dazed, Zorna and Wallace, momentarily stunned, helplessly weltered like upturned tortoises on the rock-strewn earth. Regaining their wits, they struggled to their feet. Dusting themselves, they raised their heads. Both leveled their gazes on a figure standing before them—Prince Zili.

"Nice of you to … drop in, brother." Zili smirked, stepping back from Wallace. "Both you and your … warlock."

"He's not *my warlock*."

"Semantics, dear brother," Zili sneered, pacing. "Why have you come here?"

Circling behind his master, Zili's minion, Jax the troll, strolled a long arc around Wallace and Zorna. Jax's eyes locked with Zorna's.

Not wanting Zili to know their true destination, Wallace thought fast. "To appeal to you," he muttered.

"Appeal? Appeal for what? Did our brother, King Alexander, send you as his messenger or as a sacrifice?"

"I am neither."

"Really? You're no messenger or sacrifice? And this one," Zili pointed, "you say is not your warlock. Why is it that I do not believe you?" Zili sighed. "You are pathetic, brother. Putting yourself in harm's way, for what? Have you no ambition?" Zili scratched the edge of his nose, signaling the troll. Jax slowly released the clasp locking the knob of his small sword in his scabbard.

Zili shook his head. "It hurts my heart to see you such a fool, Wallace."

"First, brother, you must have a heart for it to hurt."

"For what will I need that?" Zili huffed. "I will be king, and if I have the time, I will hear your appeal. See out there, beyond this hill, in that field and those trees behind me? I have a loyal following of both humans and oddlings. I will be king, brother, and nothing—not you or your warlock, will prevent that."

Zorna's jaws tightened at the slight.

"Then everything is true," Wallace said, his eyes dropping.

"*Everything is true*," Zili mocked in a shrill voice. "Of course it's true. Understand me: this *will* happen."

Circumambulating the two men, Jax sneered. The tips of his filthy fingers grasped and poked at Zorna's clothing. He reached to clasp the floating sleeves of Zorna's robe and cackled maniacally. Recoiling, Zorna sharply slapped away the creature's gnarled fingers.

Seeing his curious pugnacious minion, Zili snickered. "My second is a curious being for a troll. Ordinarily their concern is money: how to get it and how to keep it. This fellow, however, is a curious ... beast. He has an insatiable bloodlust, nearly as potent as his want for naros. Treason costs money. You don't have any, do you, Warlock?"

Leveling his gaze, Zorna sneered. "His Highness has already told you I am not a warlock. And no, I have nothing to give him."

"Nothing?" Zili smirked again. "In lieu of money, he will take ... oh ... your life." Those words said, Jax rang his sword from his scabbard.

Whoosh. Jax swung, his sword missing all but the very tip of Zorna's white beard. As Zorna jumped back, the tip immediately regrew.

Zili sneered disdainfully.

Wallace drew his sword. It glanced off Jax's blade. *Clang.* Dancing back from Wallace, Zili turned on his heel, peering down at Jax. Following his brother with his eyes, Wallace took a step forward. Having nothing more than a sense of foreboding, Zorna laid his hand on Wallace's wrist.

Spinning in one fluid movement, Zili hoisted his right arm, sliding his sword from its scabbard on his left hip. Wallace could hardly believe what was happening. Zili's action seemed to proceed in slow motion. The metal rang as the tip of the sword cleared the scabbard. Extending and arching his right arm, Zili lunged toward Wallace. In response, Wallace jumped back. He flung up his own sword. Their blades crossed—*clang*.

Left, right, back, and forward they swung. Wallace lunged; Zili parried and remised, continuing short attacks without cease. Wallace retreated again and again. Zili missed his mark. Forward, forward, Wallace swung and lunged his sword. *Whoosh*—Wallace sliced off part of the hanging sleeve of Zili's tunic. Angered, Zili slipped a dagger from his belt. Holding it in his left hand, he swiped back and forth in short, quick movements. Straight as a fleche, Zili attacked so quickly that he caused Wallace to nearly lose his footing on the rain-soaked ground. Getting out of Zili's path, Wallace stumbled forward, head down.

"Has the baby not yet learned to toddle, little brother?" Zili quipped. Taking advantage, Zili smacked Wallace behind the head with his elbow. Nearly on one knee, Wallace struggled to stay up. Finding his footing, he staggered up. Zili swiped the dagger across Wallace's chest, opening a superficial gash.

Jax ran in to help his master, but Zili shoved him back. "No. You shall not touch him," Zili snarled. "Only a royal should take the life of a royal." Zili glarred at Jax.

The men circled one another, their eyes locked. Glimpsing the red on the tip of his dagger, Zili snickered. "First blood. Oh, you're not hurt … yet." He laughed. "That was just a sample." Catching sight of Zorna and General Raptozk, Zili continued circling Wallace. "You should go back to your wife, Princess Marinna. Have babies and leave politics to those who know how." Zili huffed, "Unlike you."

With his sword, Zili jeeringly slapped the broad side of Wallace's blade as he held it out in defense—*clang*. Defiant, Wallace swatted Zili's blade away. "By the way," Zili said, "tell Marinna that horse-slaying brother of hers will not be coming home … ever." Zili saw puzzlement on Wallace's face. "Oh, come now, don't look so surprised, dear Wallace. It was his own fault." He snickered. "You will lose, you know. You are soft. While you've gorged on fine wine and teacakes, I have honed my battle skills. Yes, little brother, I have far too many battles behind me."

"Battles behind you, perhaps," Wallace said, "but none left in front of you. I shall see to that." His blade forced Zili's down. "Please forgive my not giving up to your ... superior experience right away."

Suddenly cross, Zili glowered sardonically. With a great huff and surge, Zili rushed forward in a determined remise, continuing his attack without withdrawing. He slashed, left, right, forward, forward, up, down. He spun, as did Wallace in their deadly dance. Wallace parried and equally answered every blow. His broadsword swept wide, missing Zili's chest by the thickness of his clothing.

Dashing into the skirmish, Jax grabbed Wallace's ankle, causing Wallace to stumble. Wallace rolled to his feet.

"I was always the better swordsman," Zili snarled.

"So long as you have your sycophants," Wallace snapped, glimpsing the troll hiding behind Zili's left leg.

Wallace retreated from Zili's path. Stepping back, Zili tripped over Jax. He stumbled sideways to the dirt. Surging forward, Wallace spun and struck at Zili's back, missing. Zili rolled. Wallace's blade hit the ground. But Wallace pinned Zili's sleeve to the dirt. As Zili tried to run, his pinned sleeve caused him to roll onto his back. Zili stared up at Wallace from the ground.

"I think you are wrong," Wallace said, glimpsing Zorna some distance away, his foot on the chest of Jax, who was on the ground. "Father always said I was the better swordsman." Swinging, Zili sent the blade of his dagger glancing across Wallace's leg, drawing blood again. Wallace reached for his leg.

"Ah-ha—I shall kill you a piece at a time if I must." Zili snickered, tearing his sleeve as he jumped to his feet. "You and Alexander were better at everything according to that old man. Father was a fool." He fisted his ring finger.

A red glow began to engulf Prince Zili's ring finger. With his hand, Wallace protected his eyes from the continual brilliant flashing of the ring, while thrusting his sword forward toward Zili. His thrust failed, stopping within a hair's breadth of Zili. It seemed to hit an invisible shield surrounding his brother. Again, Wallace thrust forward; again, the blade failed to penetrate.

Having immobilized Jax with a wave of his finger, Zorna climbed upon his horse and charged forward to help Wallace. Zorna reached him as Zili stabbed Wallace in the arm and leg. It happened so fast that Zorna could only watch. Zili moved in a blur, as if he had four arms.

Wallace hobbled backward as fast as he could, but his sword made a poor cane, bowing under his weight. He fell to the ground on his chest. A shadow fell over him. Zili straddled Wallace's legs.

Zili grasped the hilt of his sword with both hands, sloping its point toward the center of Wallace's back. Slowly raising his arms, Zili prepared to plunge his sword.

"You are hard of heart, Zili," said Wallace. "I can only hope one day your heart will melt."

"Perhaps one day, but today is not that day." Zili shook his head. "As you plainly see, *I am* the better swordsman. Good-bye, brother," Zili sneered just as his Firestone ring suddenly beamed red.

Lunging from his horse, Zorna streaked toward Zili. Zorna shouted, "Stop!" His eyes were nearly blinded by the increasing brilliance of the Firestone's light. Zorna saw it change from red to deep purple.

Zili felt his body weaken. "What is this?" he muttered. "This cannot be. I wear the ring." His arms shook violently. Suddenly, the sword above Zili's head weighed more than seventy stones. Its heft crooked Zili backward until he fell to the ground, the sword's point sinking into the earth above his scalp.

"*What is this treachery?*" Zili shouted.

From his chest, Wallace spotted Zorna, who had transformed. Zorna's eyes were those of a snake. His skin wrinkled and leathered, an orange glow surrounded him. Zorna knelt beside Prince Wallace, rolling him to his back. He examined his wounds.

"Lie still, Sire. I will help you." Zorna waved a claw beside Wallace's head; a small metal bowl appeared, which he had previously stowed in a bag on his horse. In the center of the bowl, Zorna laid a small crystal, over which he poured water. Closing his reptilian eyes, he recited an incantation.

Dumbstruck, Wallace could only stare into Zorna's snakelike eyes.

Zorna held the solution to Wallace's lips. "Drink this, Your Highness. It will make you well."

Wallace drank. His wounds began to disappear. Wallace's eyes did not turn from Zorna's transformed face. Within a few moments, the prince regained his strength. Climbing to his feet, Wallace glanced to where Zili had fallen. He paced to the body. Two feet taller, and in a robe suddenly too tight, Zorna followed.

"What is this?" Wallace murmured. "Where has he gone?" Lifting his eyes, Wallace looked everywhere, including the heavily overcast sky.

"He is … gone, Your Highness," Zorna murmured, touching the fragile cast that lay in Zili's place. Where Zorna touched, the thin shell fragmented and collapsed inward. The cast was flat white but otherwise identical in form to Zili in every way, down to the sword stuck in the ground above his head. Where it had collapsed, Wallace could see it was hollow inside.

Zorna knelt beside what was left of Zili. "He left … a statue."

"The height of narcissism." Wallace huffed. Perplexed by this odd transmogrification, he touched the cast with the tip of his finger. The entire form collapsed. Dust billowed into the air.

"He's escaped. Where?" Zorna said. "More importantly, why? He had you, Sire. Nonetheless, we must find him."

"Where has he gone?" Wallace murmured.

Zorna peered to the horizon. Puzzled, Wallace peered at a lampblack shadow hastily skimming an outlying field. It receded toward the horizon.

What Just Happened?

The rain returned, dissolving even more of the cast. A rivulet of water and chalk ran through the grass. The rain became a storm. The sky flashed and cracked with thunder.

"We must go," said Wallace, studying the sky. His face was awash, his hair layered across his brow. He snuffled and wiped his face. The rain hid his tears. "Our attackers may return at any time." He watched as Zorna returned to his human dimensions, although his skin did not completely revert.

"They shall not return, Sire. I no longer feel their presence," said Zorna.

"Very well," replied Wallace. "Let us gather our wits and nourish our bodies—once we find the others."

Gathering the reins of his horse, Zorna rubbed his horse's neck and brown mane, calming it. He mounted. Pacing, the horse clopped several steps, circling Prince Wallace. Zorna extended his arm to the prince. He hoisted Wallace to his horse's back.

"We will gather your horse, Sire, and the others," said Zorna. He could see Wallace's concern despite his affected stoicism. Atop his own horse, Raptozk followed them. "I see it in your eyes, Sire. But it is not over. He has *not* escaped," Zorna explained, attempting to but not quite settling Wallace's puzzlement.

Wallace watched as Zorna's skin reformed: softening and smoothing. Gray tresses abruptly fell from his reformed human scalp. Zorna looked back. His eyes were rounded, returned to their original form and color.

"My friend, but what is it I saw in your eyes? You became something else," Wallace uttered. "Truth. Tell me the truth. You must explain what just happened to you."

"Yes, Your Highness. I shall, shortly, but first we must find Lexi and Joseph. I am certain by now their safety hangs in the balance."

Retracing their steps, they traveled down the path to where they had encountered their original attackers. There, they came across a cluster of trees on a downgrade in the terrain, where Joseph had hidden among the rocks. Still dangling from the trees were loops and whorls of thick, leafy vines.

"What is this?" Wallace looked up into the trees.

"Help! Help! Somebody get us down!" cried a voice.

Wallace spotted Joseph and Lexi dangling high in the tree.

"We'll get you down!" Wallace shouted. "We'll have you down before you know it! We will, right?" Wallace whispered, spinning to Zorna.

Unable to reach Joseph from the ground, Wallace stood upon the saddle of his horse. He pulled his sword and swung at the vines.

"With the utmost respect, Sire," Lexi squealed, hearing the whoosh of the blade as he dangled, "I desire to remain in one piece."

"Oh, shut up, Lexi," Joseph barked, dangling beside him. "Or they may leave us here permanently."

Wallace continued slicing at the vines with no effect. "Stop. Stop. Stop," Lexi groaned. "Please. It's getting tighter." He felt the life squeezed out of him, and was beginning to lose consciousness. "You have to stop. The trees don't like it. They're squeezing tighter … Hard … to … breathe." He felt the pressure build in his head and the air push from his chest.

Zorna stood upon his saddle and positioned himself beneath Joseph. "Can you not use a spell or chant to cause our release?" shouted Lexi to Zorna.

With a serious expression, Zorna clutched the end of his beard and shook his head. "I fear this—this is no ordinary tree," said Zorna, gently but hurriedly stroking the tree while quickly examining its bark. "This tree is …"

"Is what, pray tell?" shouted Lexi. "In need of a hug?"

"No. It is connected to the magic of our world. I think it has certain … resistances."

"Has resistances?" said Lexi, "Great King Cazmerick, man, what resistances?"

Lexi and Joseph began to kick. The tree branches rustled. "Come on—ohhhhh," Joseph hooted. The vine tightened the more he kicked.

Reaching up, Zorna clasped the vines with both hands and palpated their loops. As the men stopped struggling, the vines loosened but still held them high.

The rain slowed to a fine mist. A crack of thunder echoed at the horizon.

Breathing hard, both men hung helplessly, while Wallace and Zorna put their hands to their hips. "Maybe we should just leave them?" said Wallace.

"Not funny, Your Highness," Lexi said.

"My, my, Zorna, don't we have a quaint pair of ornaments before us." Wallace snickered.

"Excuse us up here," Joseph pleaded. "We're, ah, not laughing, Sire."

"With all due respect, we're really, really glad to see that you are amused, Your Highness," said Lexi, "but can you find a way to help us down?"

From their horses, Prince Wallace and Zorna climbed down to the base of the tree. They raised their heads. "Okay, we agree with you—we see no further value to your hanging there."

Zorna touched ten fingers to the trunk of the tree and pressed. He closed his eyes. He hesitated, repositioned his arms, and gave the tree a hug—first loose, then tight.

"Mother willow, feel our sincerity," Zorna said. "Thank you for keeping our friends from harm. But, would you mind releasing them?" Like the sound of a ship on the sea, Joseph and Lexi could hear the cracking and whining of bent, stiff, hard wood. Creak, crack, the loops of vine began to not only unwind but also relax. Slipping from the loops, the men fell to the ground—*thud*. They yipped.

"That was easy," said Prince Wallace to Lexi, who was writhing on the ground. "What do you think?

"Oh." Lexi coughed. "It was many things, Sire, but *easy* does not readily come to mind." He moaned, rolling to his side.

"I agree," Joseph said, lying flat on his back, "I shouldn't like to repeat that. Thank you." He put his hand over his throbbing forehead.

"Shall we make camp here?" Zorna asked. He pointed to the exact spot where they lay.

"I'll secure a perimeter." Lexi groaned.

"You, Joseph, set up the tents," Wallace ordered.

"I," Zorna muttered, "will make a new beverage, introduced to me from the Middle East."

"New?" Lexi asked.

"I've tasted his drink." Joseph smiled. "I told Zorna I like it so much, he should name it after me. 'But who would call a drink Jo?' he said."

"I think," said Zorna, shaking his head, "we shall continue calling it *tea*."

⁂

The last light of day slipped away as the four men sat around the fire for a meal. The air had turned cool. Joseph's arms were stretched out between his legs in order to warm his fingers. In the yellow flames, Lexi revolved a wooden spit spiked through the carcass of a small animal. The smell of cooking meat wafted among the men. Zorna drank from a leather bottle of water.

"You surprise me, Zorna," Wallace said, tearing a piece of meat from the carcass. Pushing the meat into his mouth, Wallace blew through his lips to cool it. "Explain to me what happened here today. I don't understand the change." He sat on a boulder, his wrist resting on his thigh.

Wallace casually pointed his index finger to the field where they had fought. "Specifically, what happened with the—" His index and middle fingers formed a *V*, pointing at his own eyes.

Clearing his throat, Zorna resituated himself against the stone he was resting on. "Oh, ah, the eyes thing and—and dragon stuff," Zorna stuttered. "You see, Your Highness, we live in a wondrous world where things are interlinked and often are not what they appear."

"Please, my friend. I'd appreciate it if you limit the double-speak," demanded Wallace.

"Oh yes, Your Highness," said Zorna. "The energy of all the things that make up our world combines to create a balance of good against bad." Wallace maintained an unsettling but intense glare into Zorna's eyes. Zorna cleared his throat. "Ah, your brother Zili ... your— Sire, why do you look at me so intensely?"

"I don't mean to interrupt your explanation," said Wallace, "but I was thinking how long I have known you. All my life. And I've known nothing about this—this dragon transformation. I feel as if I don't really know you in some ways."

"Along those lines: how much does *anyone* really know about another, Sire?"

"No double-speak. But you are right." Wallace nodded. "Please finish. I do want to hear."

Rubbing his injured leg, Lexi watched as Joseph's eyes shifted from Prince Wallace to Zorna. Wallace waved a finger for Zorna to continue.

"Well, as I was saying," continued Zorna. "Like your brother Zili, there are individuals who would use the negative energies of our world to gain power. For example, the red Firestone ring Prince Zili wears on his right hand allows him to command those energies, with some limitation."

As he spoke, Zorna mixed a healing potion and handed it to Lexi. "Drink this. It will heal your wounds."

Lexi reached past Joseph to take the vial. He drank the potion, then shook from head to toe. "Ooo," he hooted. "Ghastly." Lexi watched in disbelief as his wounds shrank and disappeared.

Zorna continued. "As with humans, there are good and bad in all oddlings. Their experiences and choices determine which they will be. Prince Zili is so desperate for power, he will resort to any means to achieve it." Zorna began to stow vials in his pouches.

"Zorna, your appearance changed before my eyes. As I previously remarked, I have never before seen you that way," Wallace said. "How do you explain it?"

"When I drew near the stone Zili wears on his finger, its magic reacted with mine, producing my transformation."

Chewing the last of his meat, Wallace tilted his head. "I am befuddled. You have never reacted to any magic that way before. Why now?"

"Because, Your Highness, it was not just any magic. I am a dragon."

"A *what*?"

"Impossible," Joseph and Lexi simultaneously interjected.

"No. You cannot be," Wallace insisted, starting to his feet. He stared down at Zorna. "Dragons are dangerous, beastly killers, the enemy of man. I have seen several in my lifetime. A dragon. You have no scales, no wings, no tail, and no slanting eyes." He paused. "Well, except for this afternoon. How has this thing happened? You look human enough to me."

"Sire, centuries ago, in my adolescence, I was ordered by my clan to take the life of a princess who was offered to me as a sacrifice to ensure a fruitful growing season. When I refused, our shaman was forced to put a spell on me. I was to take human form and live a human's tortured life until I no longer sympathized with them. I was exiled from the dragon clan. While in the human world, I was taken in by the wizard who served your great-great-grandfather. He made me his apprentice. I have outlived four wizards and several kings, and I have come into my own. Your father and your grandfather were fair-minded men of honor. I took an oath when I joined your father's service to protect your family to my death."

"Why have I not heard this before?"

"Because, Your Highness, it was safer for all those around me that I keep this knowledge to myself." Peering into the campfire, Zorna saw images of himself being shrunk down to human form. He lowered and shook his head. "Sadly, dragons, no matter what their form, still strike fear in the hearts of men—as evidenced by your shock, Your Highness. Therefore, dragons are scorned and hunted. We have fought because we want to live, like everything else in this world."

Circumspect, Lexi added wood to the fire. The men warmed their hands, leaned back, and listened.

Zorna looked around at them all. "I think I have said enough."

"There is much to this Firestone my brother Zili wears. But what effects has it?"

Zorna said, "The manner in which it was harvested determines the magic carried within a Firestone."

"What do you mean?" asked Wallace.

"This particular stone," Zorna said, "was removed with violence; therefore, it concentrates avarice in its bearer. Your brother Zili saw the ring in the marketplace and was drawn to it. The ruby-red color stood out to him from all other jewels. It called to him."

"I have not seen the ring up close," said General Raptozk.

"Nor have I," said Lexi.

"The stone sits on a silver band," Zorna told them. "That band rotates upon another, allowing the faceted stone to whirl when twisted."

"How does this stone work?" asked Joseph.

"It concentrates many great magical powers in its wearer," said Zorna. "One example, for instance, is to look into someone's eyes and rotate the stone once. The person cannot look away from you. Rotate the stone a second time, and that person hears your thoughts in his mind. Rotate the stone for a third time, and if your target is weak minded, you will control his mind. At the time, your brother was a very angry and jealous man. The ring poisoned his soul."

The intermittent rain had once again come and gone. They could smell the grass and cedar of the field wafting upon the rolling fog.

"Earlier, during the fight, when the clouds were at their height, there was very little light," Wallace said. "There should have been no shadows, but there were. How do you explain the stark shadows that crept along the ground?"

"Shadows?" asked Joseph.

"Yes," said Wallace. "Shadows, cast from trees having very little to no light. They crept over my brother before he turned into the chalk shell."

"The smidgens," Zorna said.

"Who?" Lexi asked.

"The smidgens are shadow people," said Zorna. "They responded to the darkness in your brother's soul. When you injured him, you made him angry. The Firestone on his hand concentrated the anger within him, and all the avarice he has ever felt toward you and Alexander. The weight of that anger became concentrated in the steel of his sword. It became too heavy for his body to physically bear."

"I thought the Firestone was at his beckoning and would do any evil he commanded?" asked Wallace.

"Aye," Zorna said. "The fight was unbalanced, and there is still a need for balance in the world. Zili was hurt, his will broken. His power is not complete. There is some intrinsic fairness in the magic he has yet to override, Your Highness. Zili beckoned the smidgen to protect him. They intervened, whisking him to his hidden encampment.

Furthermore, Zili could not vanquish you because you are of the same blood. Bound somewhere in the dungeon of his heart, there is still some love for you. You cannot truly hate someone if you have ever loved them."

"If Prince Zili still has some affection for Prince Wallace," asked Joseph curiously, "can that part of him be reached?"

"Perhaps, Joseph. Perhaps that is possible," said Zorna thoughtfully. Having patrolled the perimeter, General Raptozk strolled into the encampment. He responded to Zorna's statement. "You must be getting soft in your old age. How old are you—four hundred?"

"How dare you?" Zorna snapped. "Three hundred."

Raptozk huffed. "Come now, Zorna," he said. "You cannot believe that. The poison in Zili's heart runs too deep. Zili has no more regard for Prince Wallace than he has for you or Joseph or this prey we turn on the spit. I am sorry, but I think you are off the mark, old man." Glowering, General Raptozk searched for more meat on the carcass over the flames but found little.

"That may be true, General," said Wallace, "but with hope there is possibility. Don't you agree, Zorna?"

"Your Highness." Zorna dipped his chin in agreement.

The general sat beside Lexi. Lexi leaned into the general and whispered into his ear, pointing his finger to Zorna.

"He is *what*?" the general shouted, sitting up, eyes wide, his hand grazing the hilt of his sword. He settled as Lexi whispered further. Dubious, the general allowed into his mind the idea that Zorna was some kind of human-dragon hybrid.

The five men listened to the song of the wolves as they enjoyed the last embers of the fire. They allowed the aroma of the damp forest cedar to calm their souls.

Chapter 11

THE DRAGONS

"Lexi," called Prince Wallace, "up there." Wallace tugged back on the reins of his horse. The others stopped behind. He pointed to an outlying ridge upon which paced several wolves. "Over the last two days since our journey to the dragon people began, the wolves have shadowed us. If they watch, so may others. We must remain vigilant—keep your eyes open. We cannot be certain of who is friend or foe." The wolves wandered to the far side of the ridge and out of sight. "Even when they are out of sight, we shall hear them for some time, and they may smell us at all times. Their cries are audible for five or more miles."

"Yes, Your Highness," murmured Lexi. "But I thought we were going to the lizard people?"

Zorna smiled. "I understand your confusion. Dragons and lizard people live among one another, much as humans from other lands occasionally do." Zorna saw Joseph's eyes were wide and worried, still looking to the ridge for the wolves. "Do not fret, my son. They are friends. They merely watch over their territory and us. We shall reassess our alliances with the wolves if you are eaten, however." Zorna softly snickered.

"I think they're following us because Joseph keeps feeding his horse rotten eggs," quipped Prince Wallace.

"*No*. I swear, Sire. It is not my horse."

"Therefore, I must assume it is you," Wallace jibed.

They heard a fusion of sounds coming from the forest. The crash of waterfalls joined the call of birds hidden among the trees. Their clopping mounts loped lazily through the woods. Finally departing the forest, the five arrived in a clearing overlooking a sloping rock palisade.

"Through and down this path," Zorna said, leveling his arm to point out a sinuous and steep downgrade. "It will lead through a narrow mountainous pass." Zorna lifted his chin. "Hydra Falls is that way."

"Is there no other way?" asked Prince Wallace. Zorna shook his head.

"According to the map," Lexi said, "we must descend the scarp, Your Highness."

"The scarp is steep and quite eroded," Joseph said. "I do not think we can climb down without ... without dying. I just think—"

"Thank you Joseph," Wallace said, "for bolstering our confidence." Wallace peered down the steep grade. "It is more cliff than downgrade, Zorna. The path seems to have been created more by mountain elk than humans."

"And other creatures, whose form we do not know." Joseph nodded, fluttering his lids. He knew they had no option. Joseph felt slightly self-conscious of his need for caution but vindicated by Wallace's accord about the danger.

Zorna pointed upward, beyond the hills. "Fifteen hundred yards northwest, on that far ridge, you should find the entrance to Dragon Mire. It comprises a medicinal fire swamp. The mud will heal wounds of body but not of mind. If your wounds are of the mind only, you had better remain here."

"So, if one is mad ... Why, there is no one here that fits that description. I'm good, right?" Joseph said, trembling. "I'm good. Hey, why don't we just *fly* down to the valley?"

They all looked sidelong at Joseph.

Climbing from his horse, Zorna slowly stepped toward the downgrade and gazed over the scarp. Standing alongside his horse, Onyx, Zorna clasped her bridle in one hand and pieces of carrots and apples with the other. Rubbing her ears, stroking her back and mane, Zorna walked her before Prince Wallace and his men.

"Gentlemen, I must have your full attention," Zorna said. "You know my beautiful mount, Onyx. Watch closely. I will show you great magic. I shall change Onyx into a perigorn, after which you shall do the same."

"A perigorn?" General Raptozk scowled, his eyes darting among the other men. "Perigorn. Pray tell, what in the name of the Powers That Be is a perigorn? You've made that up. I have never heard of such a thing." Lexi and Joseph shrugged. Tilting his head, Wallace shrugged too.

"Pray tell us, Zorna. What is this 'perigorn'?" Wallace asked.

"I assure you, Sire," said Zorna, "I have not made up this thing." He brushed his horse with his fingers.

Onyx stood over twenty hands high. Her long, golden mane and tail flowed and fluttered in the breeze coming up over the cliff. Onyx rubbed her face upon his chest. Zorna waved his arms over the beautiful mare. Her skin shook in response to Zorna's affectionate strokes. "If you recall," Zorna said. They listened closely. "I have given each of you a piece of hardtack: one for your horse, one for you. When I instruct you, and only then, shall you feed it to your horse. When I instruct you, and only then, shall you eat your own hardtack."

Wallace and his men exchanged tentative glances.

"This is no usual hardtack," Zorna said. "It has been treated with a very strong potion. It will transform your horse into a perigorn. Born of Pegasus and a unicorn, your perigorn is a very powerful friend. Once the transformation is complete, we shall descend these palisades."

"So we will ride into the valley, correct?" Lexi asked, smiling. "Yes, ride. We will ride. Right, right," Joseph said. His heart pounded and his mouth became dry.

Zorna rolled his eyes and continued. "Your horse will become a perigorn, who shall spread its wings …"

"*Wings?*" shouted the General Raptozk.

"If I may continue," said Zorna. "Once the wings catch the wind, we will begin our descent. You will witness a knob growing out from the forehead of your perigorn. It will become a horn. Be very careful with this horn; if it breaks your skin, you will disintegrate."

Joseph, about to protest, said nothing as Zorna raised his finger. Zorna continued. "If, however, you are wounded, your perigorn will stroke you with the horn, and you will heal. If we are in battle, do not stand before the horn. It will discharge a bolt of lightning, with a power you have never seen. The thunder it produces can fell a castle wall, if necessary."

Zorna looked at each man, his face stoic and unsmiling. He needed their complete confidence. Each man knew his life depended on Zorna's strong understanding of the magic.

"Are you ready, Sire?" Zorna asked.

"I am."

"Lexi, are you ready?"

"I am, Zorna."

"Are you ready, Joseph?"

Joseph hesitated, "Yes, yes, I am ready."

"I'm ready too," said General Raptozk before Zorna could ask. Zorna held the hardtack high above his head so all could see. When he had their attention, he said, "Break it. A green mist will issue forth. Feed it to your horse. Wait until I say, then mount."

Joseph appeared worried. Zorna gave him a soothing look. Uncertain, Joseph nodded. Joseph broke the hardtack, and a red mist arose. "Zorna, a red mist came instead of green."

"Stop. Here, take another. If the red issues and is fed to your horse, it will instead become a leviathan. It would eat you."

"What's a levia—levia ...?" asked Joseph.

"A leviathan? A very hungry winged serpent, a nasty creature," Zorna said, flailing his hand to fan the question away.

"Heaven shield me. This is not a confidence builder," Joseph murmured. He broke the new hardtack. A green mist issued. Eyeing Zorna, Joseph fed it to his horse.

Zorna turned to the general. "Are you ready?" Zorna said. "Here. Break this. When the green mist arises, feed it to your horse. Wait until I say before you mount."

"Zorna, this is not dangerous?" the general asked.

"No. Descending the scarp is dangerous. This is necessary," said Zorna. He repeated his instructions to the others, until every horse had eaten the hardtack. "Now, you take a bite."

Each man did as instructed.

"Now we wait." Zorna looked over the cliff and pointed. "Beneath the palisade is the entrance to the land of the dragon people. We have some time and we may rest. But be certain you know the rules before you enter."

Climbing from their horses Wallace and his men rested on the grass, away from the edge of the plateau. Zorna watched over the group as some slept.

In slumber, Lexi's head fell back. His shoulders leaning into the trunk of a tree, a snore erupted from his throat.

"His rumbles are those of a bull with a bezoar," mumbled Zorna, reaching to Lexi's shoulder. He shook to wake him. The others had just awakened.

"Did you not sleep, wizard?" asked the general.

"No, General, and neither should you now. It is the hour," Zorna whispered. "We have waited sufficiently. Mount your steeds and take your places next to me. Because none of you has ever ridden a perigorn, I shall instruct."

"Very well," Wallace said.

"Listen and pay attention. If you do not, your death might result. Steady yourself and be prepared."

Riders astride, their horses sidled side by side. They did as Zorna showed them, the front hooves of each horse at the edge of the cliff. The path was unreasonably sloped and cut off before the last palisade.

"Long before we approach the last palisade," Zorna said, "there will be no footing for your horse. At that point, you will jump your horse from the cliffside path or … or we shall jump now but no matter. Jump we shall."

"I say we jump the cliff from where we stand. All in favor?" Wallace asked, polling his men. Everyone cautiously raised his hand. It took Joseph longer to raise his. "So it is settled, Zorna," Wallace said. "We shall jump now."

Zorna nodded. "We shall get a running start. When you begin to fall, you will feel a jerk, a snap of wings catching the air as your perigorn takes flight."

Each man peered over the drop-off with clear or hidden trepidation. They glanced at one another and licked their lips. The reins were tight in Lexi's white knuckles. Joseph had never tightened his legs so hard at a horse's flanks.

"Remain calm," Zorna said. "Remember, they will be similar to unicorns. They are extremely sensitive to emotion. A perigorn will throw a nervous rider. Your steed is a fierce warrior who will defend you to its death, but you must have the same confidence in it as you expect it to have in you.

"The spiral horn upon its head responds to the presence of magic. In the presence of good magic, it will match the glow of the aurora. In the presence of evil, it will turn a dark blue. When the horn is blue and it breaks your skin, you will immediately disintegrate. When you reach the Dragon's Mouth, the unicorn light will allow you to safely pass. The potion you took will protect you from the poisonous gas that surrounds the entrance to the den of the dragons. In addition—"

"In addition? Zorna, please." Wallace saw his nervous men, staring over the cliff. "I thought the fall would be deadly. Will you instruct us to death first? Now give the order."

"JUMP!" Zorna shouted.

Roaring, whinnying, the horses leaped from the cliff.

Over the cliff the men plunged, their eyes and mouths wide, their hair blown straight back.

Hydra Falls

Horses and riders hurtled downward. In free fall, their hearts pounded. Hooves beat helplessly against thin air. With only seconds to live, the men prayed for a quick and merciful death upon impact. But in an instant, massive, feathered, muscular wings shot out from both flanks of each horse. Catching the air like sails on a ship, the wings opened, stopping their falls with a sudden snap. They shot upward. Joseph and Lexi crossed themselves.

"Yesssss!" shouted Joseph.

"Wha'? Who?" shouted Lexi, his heart racing, his stomach falling from his throat.

The general breathed again. He gritted his teeth and banked toward the outlying ridge, behind Zorna. Wallace nodded as they gracefully straightened out and coursed ahead with each slow flap of the perigorns' powerful wings.

"We are up among the eagles!" Joseph shouted, swirling through a cloud. He saw below a distant, bird-shaped figure thrusting down its wings. Upon closer inspection, Joseph saw no feathers but a long, serpentine neck. As his perigorn dived, he tracked the figure as it glided into a cave. Shrinking into his saddle, Joseph pulled back and became quiet. It was no bird, he knew, but a dragon.

"Look." Lexi pointed below to a rock canyon wall beyond the cliff from which they had jumped. He could see four miniature shapes chasing along the ridge: wolves darting into brush surrounding the trunk of a tiny persimmon tree.

Within a quarter hour, they were flying over a sculptured landscape of clipped grass and topiaries. They had left the forest behind.

"There, beyond, is the valley." Zorna pointed down. The sleeves of his robe fluttered in the updraft.

The five perigorns descended into the valley of Hydra Falls. Gliding low, the perigorns did not land but skimmed the ground. The bowl-shaped valley held a translucent yellow fog, stirred by the gentle breeze flowing over the ground. But its beauty belied its menace. They dipped into the mist and the acrid odor of sulfur burned the nostrils of men and perigorns. The perigorns flew just head high above the mist. Following Wallace's lead, the men covered their noses by their sleeves.

A rising trail came into view, which led down the side of the mountain. The perigorns' hooves touched ground. They became horses once more. The earth immediately crumbled beneath their hooves, stones rolling. With no foothold, the horses whinnied with fear as they slid, careening sidewise.

"Up!" Zorna shouted. "Pull up on the reins."

Each man did. Each felt a sudden steadiness as the horses leaped skyward. Again they became perigorns, unfurling their wings. They took command of the wind. From the air, the perigorns gracefully covered one hundred yards along the bottom of the canyon. With each flap of their wings, the knobs at the centers of the perigorns' heads grew into spiral horns, three feet long.

Wings spread, their mounts descended. Gliding into the valley, the men kept their noses, mouths, and eyes covered. The acrid mist remained above them, thinning and clearing as they neared the ground. Their view of the falls sharpened.

Prince Wallace and his men marveled at the forested mountains rising around them. The valley into which they descended ended in a narrow canyon, its terminal wall comprising towering twin waterfalls. As they descended, they could see a wedge-shaped cave entrance between the falls. Over one hundred feet above them, the waterfalls overflowed twin gorges. Water crashed, thundered, and roiled into a two large plunge pools. The resurging water joined to form a seventy-foot-wide pool and moat that circled back around an elevated terrace, upon which an esplanade led through the wedge-shaped cave entrance.

"Never have I seen water so blue," said Lexi, his mouth agape. "None of us have," General Raptozk slowly said, glimpsing the dark entrance of the cave between the waterfalls.

"Magnificent," Prince Wallace uttered, peering up to the rugged hundred-foot escarpment falls. His eyes came to rest on the cave and the twisted, rocky esplanade leading among the rocks and boulders, caked thick with yellow dust. A thick yellow mist poured from the apex of the thirty-foot entrance.

"What is this place?" Wallace said, barely removing his sleeve from across his nose.

Sidling his horse beside Wallace, Zorna gazed into the cave. "This mist is called the Dragon's Breath; the sanctuary entrance, the Dragon's Mouth." Zorna could see their noses, red and irritated. "The yellow dust that waters the eyes is—"

"—brimstone," interjected General Raptozk, a cough rubbing his stinging throat. "It's the sulfurous smell that fires our noses." He sneezed.

"Your Highness," said Joseph, loping closer than the others to the water's edge. "Look." He mused at the yellow crystals glimmering in the light upon the esplanade. He tasted the grit on his tongue. "Wherever the mist from the cave touches—rocks, grass—yellow crystals burn. They not only glitter in the sun, but they remain pungent even in the most minute concentration." He spat to the side of his horse.

"Come," Wallace whispered, gesturing to General Raptozk. "Let us explore further." Curious, Wallace swayed the reins of his horse to his right. A glint caught his eye. He fixed his sight on the moat runoff, where the water turned downstream into a larger, wider river, the bank muddy and heavily wooded.

The two horses strode along the twisting course. The widening bank of the river jutted in and out among mud, puddles, and thin and thick brush. The horses clopped deliberately and lightly over the wet ground. Wallace's horse spearheaded a path for the general to follow. Hooves sucked—*swish*—into the soft mud between the grass and stone. Their ears high, the horses whinnied, tugging their ankles from the mud.

"Your Highness, we shall go into the cave, correct?" asked the general, looking back the way they had come. "Your Highness, if our mounts are injured, we shall need to abandon them; then we must abandon all hope."

"I realize that, General," Wallace said, "but I beg your indulgence." Studying the ground as they rode, Wallace said nothing more. He dismounted, and the general did likewise. Wallace's eyes searched each clump of grass, each stone, each sinkhole along the bank.

"I think we can double back now, General," Wallace said, one foot in the stirrup.

General Raptozk, about to climb upon his own horse, hesitated, then mounted. His brow curious, the general turned to Wallace, whose eyes were still turned to the ground. "For what does Your Highness search, might I inquire?" asked the general, more curious than ever.

"You may, General," Wallace murmured, lowering himself from the stirrup back to the mud. He took several steps toward the river. He searched along the alluvial plain, among the silt and clay, right up to the shallow water of a small pool swirling off the river. Stooping, heels up, Wallace peered closely. A glimmer caught his eye. He plunked his right fingers into a shimmering pool of clear water. Escaping minnows swam aside; frogs leaped to small patches of grass.

Slapping a mosquito aside his neck, General Raptozk mumbled. He slapped another on the back of his hand. "Do they not respect His Majesty's top general?"

Wallace smirked at his irascible general. "Surely you can't think they care for— Oh."

"What do you see, Sire?" the general asked, climbing down from his horse again. He ambled up behind the prince, stooped at the puddle. Wallace bobbed his hand to drain his fingers. He spread his fingers.

"These," Wallace muttered. "I was looking for these." Wallace bent his face closer to his hand and pointed. The general saw he held emeralds, irregularly shaped, the size of quail's eggs. Further scratching the silt, Wallace outlined hard, whitish objects covered by clay. "Hello. What have we here?"

"What is it, Sire?"

"Bones ... finger bones."

"He found the fortune of a lifetime," the general said.

"He did." Wallace picked the bones and jewels from the mud. "This poor devil was very rich, but alas, very dead."

"How did you know to search here, Sire?"

"I've heard stories all my life," said Wallace, "of men lost, never to return, while on personal quests for destiny and distinction ... in the dragons' lair. This cave is of volcanic origin. Water often washes precious stones to the surface. This poor soul also understood that. I've studied these—"

Cries and screams of a man and beast came from the direction of the cave. Wallace sprang to his feet. "This story may have to wait for another time, General."

The men hurried to their horses and mounted. Locating a firmer path, they galloped several yards. Then, astride their own mounts, Lexi, Joseph, and Zorna converged with General Raptozk and Wallace. Wallace raised his arm, signaling they should halt. Reaching the cave, they faced the moat-surround. The five equestrians peered across the moat to the cave entrance.

Jinking from side to side, the unsettled horses puffed. Petting the neck of his horse, Lexi pointed to the cave.

"Screaming!" shouted Joseph, his eyes darting to the eyes of the others.

"Such baleful cries, the poor soul. I hear it too," said Lexi. He turned his horse to face the cave entrance.

"It came from inside!" Joseph shouted, pointing.

"Someone is in dire need," Wallace muttered, eyeing the moat he pondered fording. "Wait here, my friends. I will search this cave."

Hurriedly lifting his arm, General Raptozk clasped Prince Wallace's shoulder. "Sire, please. Let me. If I should find anything, I will signal."

"I will go with him," said Lexi, sidling his horse beside the general. Reluctantly, General Raptozk accepted young Lexi's offer. "I pray your ears are better than your eyes."

Zorna was on his knees at the edge of the moat. His hands dipped into the water.

"What pray tell, are you doing?" asked Joseph.

Zorna looked up to the general astride his horse. Back to the water he turned, closing his eyes. "These waters are deep, wide, treacherous, and not fordable. Who knows what lives beneath the surface? Through this moat, you shall not tread."

"Then, wizard," the general said, "you shall resummon the perigorns, and we shall *soar* across."

"Rather than stress these beasts more than is necessary, I have a simpler solution," said Zorna.

With expressions of foreboding, the four men looked at one another. Zorna plunked his right index finger into the moat and stirred. The ever-widening ripples crossed to the other side. Zorna glanced up. "You shall walk across."

"Walk?" General Raptozk exclaimed. "Walk, you say." Zorna was serious and stoic.

Asked the general, "Is the water solid that I may tread upon its surface? Is it frozen that I might glide across? Shall I be so light as a feather that the water will never note my crossing? Alas, my wizard, I think not. This water is fluid, and the instant I step, it shall cleave beneath my feet. Both me and my ... captain shall drown." The general stroked the neck of his steed. "I cannot speak for my horse, but I do not desire to drown."

Ignoring his clever rebuke, Zorna tore a length of material from the inner hem of his robe, and that into two pieces. Zorna wrapped one around the face of the general's horse to cover its eyes. "This will make him more comfortable. A horse is much like a human. If he cannot see it, it cannot hurt him." Zorna did the same for Lexi's horse. "Now, ride. The water will support you," Zorna urged. "*Now*. Ride your horse *across*, General."

Lightly tapping his horse's flanks with his heels, the general cautiously nudged the apprehensive animal forward. "Okay, boy. Slowly. It's okay." The horse advanced. The water rippled over its hooves as it stepped onto the surface: his first hoof, his second, his third, and his fourth. The water bore up the massive animal and his rider. The general turned and nodded to Lexi, who cautiously followed. Across the water they trod, step after step.

General Raptozk and Lexi could see the fish swimming beneath the horses. They appeared oblivious to the threat looming above their heads. The horses continued without incident until they and their riders were on the solid ground of the terrace. They turned to look back at

Wallace, Zorna, and Joseph on the other side. Then they were striding along the esplanade to the mouth of the cave. Their wary eyes looked high at the cavernous opening, the roar of the waterfalls buffeting their ears.

Prince Wallace, Zorna, and Joseph watched from the other side as the two men vanished into the mouth of the cave. They would wait for the men to return.

"Lexi," whispered the general, "I shall be vigilant, my sword prepared to react at an instant's notice."

He scanned every crevice and shadow. He knew most caves to be damp and humid; this cave was drier than any he had ever seen, and he had seen many. It smelled of brimstone. It gave the general pause. The cave was the home of bloodthirsty dragons.

"Do nothing," he said, "unless I tell you."

Again, they could hear the screaming of a man, and his harangues and harsh, punitive denouncements. Quietly the general pointed in the direction they would go. They cautiously went toward the loud condemnations. Lexi's fists tightened on the reins; his heart raced. The general seemed calm, in tune with his thoughts.

At a gesture from the general, Lexi dismounted. With quick hand signals, the general instructed Lexi to remove the rags from their horses' eyes. "Tear them," whispered General Raptozk, "and tie them around their feet to quiet the clop of their hooves." Lexi did as he was instructed.

"Through there," the general whispered, pointing with a lift of his chin to a tunnel leading off the side of the larger cavern. It in turn tapered to a smaller tunnel that continued along a ten-foot passageway, the ceiling of which opened into another large cavern.

They stopped.

There they peered from behind a wall of confluent limestone columns, conjoined stalagmites, and stalactites. Here was the source of the shouts and screams: a solitary, frazzled, and weary man dressed in armor. He swung a sword at four large, very engaged dragons.

Three large dragons stood upon their hind legs, their wings fully extended. They roared, fire issuing from their mouths. Clanking in his loose, disheveled armor, sniveling, shouting, the wiry, wild-haired man darted and parried, dodging billowing balls of flame and smoke. Behind the three large dragons, a smaller fourth dragon stood on all fours, protecting a female and her clutch of eggs.

Shielded from the fight, the female dragon quickly and gingerly lifted her eggs, secreting them in another room, out of harm's way. Violently swinging his tail, one large male barred the human from the female.

Determined to stay hidden, Lexi and Raptozk said nothing. They slowly backed from their cover into the small conduit tunnel, where the horses waited. Mounting their horses, they sneaked from the cave complex, across the esplanade, and across the moat to rejoin Wallace, Zorna, and Joseph.

"A single man dressed in dismal armor swung a sword at four large dragons," said Lexi breathlessly. "The three largest stood upon their hind legs, wings fully extended, roaring, breathing fire. Sire, they advanced toward him, yet he did not run. What courage he must have."

"Courage?" General Raptozk shook his head. "Or he is a depraved fool, Your Highness."

"And I would wager the latter," said Prince Wallace, tightening the cinch beneath the belly of his horse. It had loosened when the wings dissolved. Thoughtfully, Wallace bit his underlip. He turned toward Lexi. "You said he wore armor. What kind? Could you recognize his crests or flags?"

Breathless, sweating, Lexi glanced at the general and said, "No, Sire. He was poorly marked. I think … I think he was a lone dragon slayer—there to collect a bounty. The female, Your Highness—"

"A lone fool," whispered General Raptozk.

"What of the female?" Zorna anxiously asked.

Lexi caught his breath. "Well, she, ah, was dressed, Your Highness."

"Dressed, you say?" asked Wallace, surprised. "Yes, Sire. In royal attire of silk, purple and gold."

"Was she was involved in the fight with the armored man?" asked Wallace.

"No," said General Raptozk

Joseph muttered, "I wager the battling fool in armor will be dead within the hour. But I think-k-k—" Joseph choked in midsentence, his eyes on Zorna. "H-h-heaven shield me. Look." He backed away, pointing, his eyes never turning from Zorna.

"Upon my father's grave," Lexi muttered. General Raptozk shot Lexi a fleeting look.

Zorna had begun to transform. His skin scaled. Above his eyes, the orbital ridge thickened and grew prominent. The roundness of his eyes flattened. His sclera reddening, his pupils elongated to become slits.

General Raptozk reached for the pommel of his sword. With a quick, light touch, Prince Wallace stopped the general from pulling it. General Raptozk saw Wallace's reassuring smile.

His robe tightened at his waist. Zorna grew to sixteen feet. Talons growing over his sandals dug into the earth. Massive reptilian thighs supported his changing body. Prodigious, leathery wings protruded from his back, arching high above his head. Between wing spines, webbing fluttered in the wind. Atop his shoulders sat a graceful serpentine neck, upon which sat a crocodilian head. Atop Zorna's head sat a crest of three horns. Within moments, Zorna's transformation to dragon was complete.

Wallace strode toward his friend. "What may I do? Are you in pain?" he asked, his expression one of concern. This was the second time Wallace had witnessed Zorna's transformation. Speechless, Joseph, Lexi, and General Raptozk stood back. Having never seen Zorna's transformation, they were decidedly nonplussed.

Saying nothing, Zorna fumbled with his swollen fingers to unknot his sash, and loosened the cloak that had grown with him. Stretching out his arm, Zorna examined what were formerly his fingers. They had reformed into knurled, sharpened talons. Wallace saw the wings had torn through the cloth across Zorna's back. They caught the wind like full tree branches in a storm. He flapped slowly, moving a cyclone of air over his friends. At river's edge, hard ripples occurred with every flap.

Wallace circled Zorna. From beneath the hem of the tattered robe, he saw a muscular tail whipping. As thick as a man's wrist, the tapered end of Zorna's tail had four deadly five-inch spikes.

"Prince Wallace. I hear you, my friend," Zorna said, peering down at Wallace. His words ended with an unpleasant hiss. "Sadly, there is nothing you may do to mitigate my condition. This is something I must manage on my own. I am not in much pain." Directing his energies, he used his powerful mind to search the pouches tied to his saddle. Mentally manipulating the ties and straps, he removed and levitated a heavy pewter cauldron. It floated to his open, clawed digits. The lid of the cauldron separated from the body. Zorna held one clawed palm facing up.

With his piercing slit eyes, Zorna looked at Joseph, the apothecary. "Get to the tools in your saddle pouches," said Zorna, "and provide me the following."

Joseph went to his tools as instructed. He waited for Zorna to recite his list.

Zorna continued, "Bring me alum, valerianate, anise, arsenic, molasses, Dover's powder, ginger, and cod liver oil."

Joseph provided him with each ingredient. Zorna directed Joseph to place them in the cauldron.

Spreading his massive webbed wings, Zorna rose on his hind legs, now even taller than his original sixteen feet. His crocodilian rostrum high in the air, he huffed streams of blue fire from his nostrils. Tilting his head like a curious animal, Zorna scrutinized his discomfited cohorts while they cautiously backed to a safe distance.

In a language foreign to Wallace and his men, Zorna softly recited an incantation over the cauldron: "*Volvo et concitabitur, et quis commovebit. Facere id quod fieri mutatio.*"

The contents of the caldron burst into fire. Covering the container, Joseph suffocated the flames. In moments, he lifted the top, pouring a thick, goopy material into his hand. He molded it like clay into a model of a tiny soldier with a drawn sword.

"It is an *anthromorph*—man form," Joseph said. "The traditional enemy of the dragon people. Its destruction by a dragon signifies complete victory over a dragon's enemy. If the dragon is hurt, the victory will allow healing." The men looked at Joseph. "Zorna taught me that ... what?"

From about his neck, Joseph removed the mirror found on Prince Hezia. With it he focused light from the sun onto the model of the man.

Zorna's eyes turned bloodred as he recited the same incantation over the small figure. The figure began to duck and parry, yelling in a tiny voice as it fought an invisible adversary.

Prince Wallace and the other men watched with astonishment as Zorna shed his tattered clothing. With one mighty swat, he took the model between his front talons. Zorna shot high into the clouds. Rolling in the sky, he banked in a wide circle, dived, and swooped into the cave.

Confused, Wallace and his men looked at one another. The horses reared, whinnied, and tugged at their reins. Within a breath, Wallace, Lexi, Joseph, and the general heard no further yelling from the cave, only silence.

∽

Among the stalagmites, Zorna landed on the cave floor and drew in his massive wings. He stood silently over the armored man, peering down his snout at the would-be dragon slayer. The armored man lay dead on his back upon the cavern floor.

Hearing the moans of a young dragon, Zorna turned to see an adolescent had retreated to a corner of the cavern, where he licked beneath his arm to sooth his pierced, swollen flank. Looking down a tunnel leading to a back cavern, Zorna recognized the female. She was his sister, Princess Salamonica. Other dragons gathered before her to form a front. Standing high on their hind legs, spreading their wings, they stared down Zorna. The princess looked between the strange dragon and her protectors. Slowly blinking, she gestured to them to stand down.

"It is you, brother," she said, dipping her chin. She extended the tips of her upturned digits. Zorna carefully laid his digits upon hers, an affectionate gesture they had not performed in one hundred years.

"Princess Salamonica," said Zorna, "if you will permit me, I can help your son. I can stop his pain."

She saw the young dragon licking his flank. Cautiously, she gestured approval, speaking softly to her consort, who was easing up behind her. "Geldon, you may not know my estranged brother. We were unmated during his time." Geldon merely nodded.

Zorna placed the model soldier on the cave floor. Quickening, it immediately charged the ailing adolescent, who ate it. The young dragon changed colors from dark green and yellow to light green and dark red. Then he turned blue, and finally changed to his original green and yellow. Rolling along the cave floor, he moaned balefully.

"Ameryl … is … my son!" roared Geldon, his webbed wings hoisted high and wide. Hints of fire flicked from his lips in place of saliva. "You have poisoned him? He was hurt, and now you have—"

"No, brother-in-law," said Zorna. "I have given him a medicine, an anthromorph. It will allow him to pass the stone that is tearing his insides, and heal his wounds. It shall not take long."

Ameryl stopped rolling. Coughing, straining, a lump rose through his neck, visible from the outside. The adolescent dragon regurgitated into his mouth. A great lump issued from it, smelling of foul fluid. He fell into a deep sleep. Swimming within the effluvium lay a gray, metallic ball the size of an orange.

The princess nodded.

"He will awaken," said Zorna, "in about ten minutes. He will no longer be in pain."

Chapter 12

RECONCILIATION

Watching as their son slept on the cave floor, Princess Salamonica and Prince Geldon took a long stare at Zorna before speaking. "My wife's brother, you have been gone for some time, nearly one hundred years."

"I realize it has not been very long," Zorna said, "but it was time to return, brother-in-law."

"What made you?" Geldon asked.

"Alas, the turmoil roiling through our world; I am not alone. My friends King Alexander Dobromil and Prince Wallace would like to help to bring peace back to the two worlds."

"Is it not their brother Zili causing these troubles?"

"It is true, sister Salamonica," said Zorna. "He is the source of the ill breeze blowing through this world. But there is more than you know to the story."

"What do you mean?"

"Zili seeks the Dragon Stone."

"The same for which our father was murdered," said Salamonica. "Sadly, the same," Zorna said, looking at the gray stone. "Zili is a sad and angry man, a bitter man. The lust for the stone has poisoned his soul and his judgment. I know that acquiring the stone will do nothing to cleanse his heart. His brothers will fight to prevent his acquisition.

Prince Wallace, General Raptozk, Captain Lexi, and my apprentice Joseph are at the mouth of the waters just beyond the moat. They await my return. "I beseech you, sister. They want to talk."

"Humans never want to talk. Look at this one." She gestured to the corpse on the cave floor. "We do not want to kill humans. They make us. We have merely tried to defend ourselves."

Zorna stepped closer to his sister. He bowed his head. "Please, Your Highness, listen to their words. Your *gift* will allow you to decipher whether they bear the truth."

Ameryl awoke from his sleep. Dazed, he immediately staggered away, looking for his mother's clutch of eggs, which were no longer there. He swung around, his wings raised, fire rolling from his lips like saliva. Prepared to fight, he stalked closer to the strange dragon. His mother swung around, slapping the tips of her wings on the floor. A cloud of dust billowed to the ceiling. Ameryl bowed, retreated, and lay prostrate on the cold, sulfurous stone floor. He showed his submission and lay so low that his mother could see none of his shadow.

"Ameryl, this is your uncle Zorna, long lost from our people," said Princess Salamonica. "He has returned to us. He and his friends have come to help us and other peoples to regain peace in the realms and with the humans."

Pensive, Ameryl rose but stood some distance away, his back to his mother and her brother Zorna. His distance troubled Princess Salamonica.

"How say you and Prince Geldon? Do we listen?" asked Ameryl. "I shall think on it," Geldon said. Geldon thought of the discomfort he might engender within the other dragons if he voluntarily invited humans into his home.

"Before you answer …" said Princess Salamonica. She turned her eyes to her son. "How do you feel?"

"I am fine, Mother," Ameryl curtly said.

"Your uncle Zorna gave you a potion to remove the stone hurting you."

"And for that I should like him?"

Princess Salamonica looked at Zorna, who looked away. He didn't envy her having to reason with an adolescent.

Ameryl sat on the floor. He rested his chin upon a small stalagmite and rolled his eyes up. "I have no pain, and I feel ... stronger." He sighed thoughtfully. "To you, Uncle, I am grateful."

"Rise, my son. Then what say you?"

"I say to your brother, he has spent much time in sorrow; I believe he would return not without good cause. I pray thee, Father, listen. After hearing, decide."

"Well spoken, son. If your mother agrees, so be it." Prince Geldon looked around at his wife and the other dragon. Agreeing, all nodded.

"Go. Tell your compatriots we shall listen and decide," said Geldon. "And one more thing. You understand our usual conditions."

Zorna nodded.

"Your way out is secure," murmured Zorna's sister.

"Thank you, and I do understand. Thank you, Your Highness, my sister," said Zorna, bowing his head.

Satisfied, Zorna flew from the cave and landed before Prince Wallace. "Happily, they are willing to meet with you."

With some trepidation and tentative smiles, the four men glanced at one another.

"Sire, I am a soldier." The general frowned. "Do you trust these ... animals?"

"*Animals?*" Zorna shouted, spreading his wings. His nose high in the air, Zorna wagged his head from side to side. Dipping into the moat, his massive tail lifted a torrent of water. Snorting, he streamed blue flames, which tumbled into yellow balls of fire.

"I think you have irritated our friend, General," Wallace whispered. "I would watch my language if I were you."

Feeling the flash of heat upon their skin, the four men leaned away. Perplexed, the general stood with his mouth wide. Shrinking quickly, Zorna transformed into the form with which his friends were familiar.

"Animals, you say." Zorna sighed sorrowfully. He was troubled he had not altered his friends' perceptions of dragons. "Now, I ask. Who is the animal? We want to live like anyone else. It is humans who would take my people to the brink of extinction, and for what? Profit, destiny, and distinction? It is not we who destroy this land," Zorna said. He rubbed his weary eyes. "It is not we who run down the innocent, slaying them for what they possess."

Stoic, the general adjusted his posture and stood erect, his eyes cutting from Wallace to Zorna. "I am sorry," said General Raptozk.

"Forgive my general," Prince Wallace said, stepping up to Zorna. "He is a great general, but he is still a man. He is my friend and loyal subject. You are my oldest friend." Wallace gazed into Zorna's face. "Together we will learn, and quite soon I think. Since we will soon meet with the dragons."

"This way, Sire," Zorna said.

They mounted their horses and stepped upon the water, which bore them up. Over the moat and esplanade, they rode into the Dragon's Mouth and deeper into the caverns, which seemed to take forever. The echoed clopping of the horses' hooves kept the monotony of dead silence from driving them mad. They tried not to think of their natural fear of dragons.

Wallace marveled at the high black ceilings. Huge stalactites hung down, seemingly attached only to darkness. At certain points, the pendulous stones appeared as teeth, which the cave could use to consume them. They managed, sometimes poorly, to keep their imaginations in check. The men dragged their fingers along the rounded bottoms of low-hanging stalactites.

Lexi peered around the cavern as he rode. He sang a silly child's song, just to hear the echo of his voice. In the darkness overhead, sometimes he glimpsed flashes of light and movement. "Does anyone feel what I feel?" Lexi muttered, nudging his horse to trot up to Joseph's.

"I do. I think it's the saddle," said Joseph, "I tell you, my ass pinches right about here and—"

"No, you nincompoop," Lexi said. "I am not referring to your rear. I'm trying to say I feel as if I am being ... watched."

"Oh, Oh aye. I felt that too," said Joseph.

Lexi sighed, unaware he was correct in his feelings. The instant they passed a tight collection of stalactites, the rounded tips opened like eyes to watch them.

"Take care where you place your fingers, gentlemen," Zorna cautioned. "These ceilings are populated by the stone people. You may have already poked them in their eyes."

Quickly, Wallace's men drew in their arms. Joseph crossed his over his chest.

Zorna continued to lead. "Do you remember the way?" Wallace asked Lexi and the general.

"I am ashamed to say," Lexi muttered, taking time to view the expanse of the cave, "but one way looks just like the other."

"You, General. Do you remember?" Wallace asked.

"I took little note gong in or out." The general shook his head, his face both embarrassed and befuddled.

"So your horse must have remembered the way out." Zorna snickered. The general was not amused. "I make light not at your expense, General," Zorna explained. "It is not your leadership at which I muse. This is no ordinary cave. This is the Dragon's Nest—royalty. It is magical. These paths, in and out, change. They are never the same the second, and certainly not the third time."

"What do you mean, changes?" asked Lexi.

"The walls reshuffle; entrances close or open. Even the floor on which we ride changes its inclination, declination, or direction. New entrances form and established ones end."

"You speak of this cave is as if it were alive," Wallace said. "In a sense, it is, Your Highness."

"The stone people?" Wallace said.

"In part," Zorna said. "This path is the throat to the belly of my world. This way." Zorna waved his arm, directing them over a viable path. "Be full of care. There are steep ledges beneath you. It is a long way down."

"I am not scared," Joseph said.

"Perhaps you should be," Zorna said, not turning.

"I should?" asked Joseph.

"Most who enter these caves have never returned," Zorna said.

"Because the dragons killed them?" asked Lexi. General Raptozk said nothing.

Zorna slowed to stop. They stopped behind, hooves along the ledge of a dry gallery. Small pebbles broke away from Zorna's horse's rear right toe, knocking the wall as they scattered, tumbling down the steep ledge. "No. They became lost, caught within this labyrinth of caverns."

"Like the dragon slayer we saw, struggling to fight the dragon," said Lexi. Even the ones who got out did not get far, he thought, remembering the human bones he and Prince Wallace had found near the river.

"You never said anything to me about such a maze when I volunteered to scout the cave," said the general.

"You were safe. You would go in and come out." Zorna held out two fingers, "Twice, not a third." The general huffed as Zorna resumed leading the horses to a plateau, and then into a small, twisted tunnel.

"This is a third time," Wallace said.

"For them, Sire, but only once for you. The way will not change before we seek the way out." Zorna held up two fingers. "Ahead we shall arrive at the dragon pillars."

Joseph mused, "What of a fourth time?"

Taken aback by his question, Wallace's eyes cut to Joseph.

"What of a fourth?" Joseph repeated. "If you've re-entered the third time, and it has changed, you will just remember the way back, right? right?" Joseph smiled as if he had become the smartest man in the group. They all looked to Zorna.

"The journey out is impossible," Zorna said. "The way becomes a deadly maze from which one cannot emerge. Young Joseph, hubris has gotten many dragon hunters killed. Let us not be overconfident. Now to the task at hand. We must get to the pillars."

"Pillars?" Wallace asked.

"The pillars are where we shall meet an escort who will take you to Prince Geldon—my brother-in-law. Among his conditions to meet with him is that you must treat him with respect, and the same he will return to you."

At the pillars, the escort led them through a tunnel that opened up into a large, ornate gallery comprised of natural limestone formations. Layered limestone bases rose to conical columns; columns rose to the ceiling. Pools of clear mineral water intersected with flat stone plazas, the room defined by walls of natural phosphorescence. Stalactite and stalagmite posts studding the floor and ceiling acted as additional support. The men sighed with awe. The scope of their vista was astounding.

Sweeping before them from left to right, a grand staircase of over one hundred shallow limestone stairs descended to a shallow rectangular pit, within which rose a small, rectangular stage. Along the top of the wall demarcating the perimeter of the pit, Geldon, King of the Dragons sat, his wings proudly splayed. Wallace and his men saw Geldon's crowned head upon his serpentine neck, nearly scraping the ceiling. Other dragons sat on either side of him.

Seventy-five feet on the other side of the gallery, Wallace and his men dismounted. They could hear the hissing of subterranean lava doused with water, and the gurgling flow of more water through natural gutters.

"I am Prince Geldon!" the great dragon bellowed, his bass voice rattling in their chests.

"This is your brother-in-law?" whispered the general, leaning to Zorna's side.

Zorna nodded slowly. "Shhhh," Zorna cautioned. As he did, the horns of the perigorns commenced glowing, emitting the aurora light. A lizard-man escort waited at the top of the of the arena stairs.

"Welcome, friends of Zorna," Geldon said.

They descended the stairs to the rectangular arena. "Please watch your step, and follow me," said their escort. Their horses remained in the grand room near where they had dismounted.

As they went down, they passed piles of bones littering the stairs, both human and oddling. Some corpses of the recent dead were charred.

Their dried and leathered faces were forever etched with the fear and horror they had experienced before death.

"Apparently they did not fare so well," Joseph whispered to Lexi, gazing into the dead faces.

"I wager they died knowing they would never see their way out of the caves," said Lexi, "their paths having been forever obliterated."

"Be not afraid," Prince Geldon said. "No dragon harmed the souls here. Either they fell victim to the poison of the volcano in which we dwell, or they fell victim to the shape-shifting caves, our protection from intrusion. We brought them here for ritual ceremony and cremation. This is hallowed ground."

Along the descent, at a landing, they saw an archway into a large, hot, and humid chamber.

At the bottom of the stairs, upon the stage, there were several boulders arranged in a circle. "Gentlemen, please be seated," said Zorna.

"There are others who will be joining us shortly," said Prince Geldon from above. "I shall freshen and return."

Misperceptions Put Aside

Left alone, the men stood silent. Peering around the room, their eyes converged on the elevated floor upon which Geldon and his council sat. The air was foul; their throats burned or tickled. Joseph cleared his throat. Prince Wallace coughed.

"Smells like sulfur," Joseph said.

Lexi nodded.

Stopping before each of Wallace's men, Zorna gestured for them to open their palms. He pressed a finger-size glass vial upon each.

"What is this?" asked General Raptozk. They held the vials up to the light. Joseph's chest began to tighten from the noxious fumes.

"Drink this," Zorna said. "It will nullify the noxious fumes poisoning your systems."

Wallace sauntered to the wall of the arena and lightly brushed the slick limestone with his fingers. He wandered on through a short archway on the landing. The twenty-foot tunnel seemed to join the pit area with another room. He walked in. The room was larger. It seemed formal. "Some kind of ... religious edifice," he murmured.

The other men followed him, each man brushing his fingers over the few green crystalline stones embedded in the wall of the arch. They could see similar crystals all the way up to and lining the ceiling. The crystals sparkled among the stalactites dipping from the black ceiling. Except for an occasional yellow stone, Wallace could see they were the same as the stones he had discovered among the finger bones downriver.

Following Prince Wallace, they returned to the arena and positioned themselves on the boulders, where they could see one another, the stairs, the upper level where Geldon had appeared, and all the exits. Although smoothed and polished, the massive marble boulders were hard and cold. No sooner were they seated then they saw the body of the man who had fought with Ameryl. He lay motionless on the cold stone floor.

"Sire," Joseph said, calling to Wallace, already on his way to the body. Zorna followed closely behind.

"I thought him dead," Wallace said, turning the man to his back. "He barely breathes," Zorna said. "Joseph, quickly. Strophanthus tincture."

Wallace sat on the floor, his legs crossed. He cradled the man's head in his lap. He tilted the man's head back.

"Your Highness, please open his mouth," Zorna asked. "I must give him this." Zorna poured five drops of tincture into the man's mouth and massaged the man's throat, forcing the liquid down to his stomach. Joseph vigorously rubbed the man's chest.

"Sit him up," Zorna ordered. Prince Wallace and Joseph propped the man up.

Zorna called his horse. "Onyx!"

"But they are on the far side of the gallery, master," Joseph muttered. In seconds, the air began to ripple and twist. "Onyx, come *now*," Zorna called again, closing his eyes, his lips moving in an incantation. Beside him, the distorted air became opaque. A smoky image sauntered from the ring—a perigorn. The animal stepped before Zorna, its horn a foot long, a third of its length. Bobbing its head, it whinnied. Upon

Zorna's order, it lowered its head to the man.

"Rub your horn against his face," Zorna commanded.

Onyx stroked the man several times with the side of her horn. The man's condition did not change.

"I don't understand," growled General Raptozk.

"Should not something happen now?" asked Lexi, impatiently shifting from one foot to the other. They were baffled and confused, but no more than Zorna, who lowered his head thoughtfully. With his hand, he closed the man's dead eyes.

"By your explanation," Wallace asked, "should he not live again?" Zorna raised his eyes and stood. "Your Highness..." Zorna murmured. His voice quivered. "I cannot help him. He was too long exposed to the gases of the volcano." Turning away, Zorna sighed with frustration, placing his hand against the wall. He shook his head slowly. Several emeralds, freshly scratched from the wall, lay at his feet, while many large crystals fell from the fingers of the dead man's relaxed fist. "Like the ones we found in the bones of the fool near the riverbed," noted the general cynically.

Without sound, the great dragon reentered the cavern and was about to take his place. Taking notice of the fallen man, Geldon approached the group, his face mournful and resolved. "Men give their valuable lives for the most trivial of things." Geldon huffed; smoke rose around his head. "We use these stones to grind our bread. Men use them as an excuse to grind one another."

With great care, Geldon cradled the man in his wings. Scooping him up, he draped the corpse across the back of Onyx. Zorna summoned the other perigorns. Prince Wallace and the rest took their places upon the semicircle of stones before the arena, facing the back wall.

Stone stools, arranged in concentric semicircles, spanned from the left to right wall on the upper level. Wallace watched as Geldon, uttering no sound, turned to join the other dragons there. Many other dragon and lizard-men sat on either side of Geldon, facing Wallace and his men. Prince Wallace knew they were beings of importance, as indicated by the formal-looking robes they wore. Robes of ornate silk and gold, patterned with black calligraphic markings, designated the official rank of each dragon.

With their horns, the perigorns spotlighted the dim chamber, providing better visibility. To Geldon's right, Princess Salamonica appeared in the archway. She stepped to a purple carpet coursing down the shallow steps to the arena where Wallace and his men sat. They watched as she sauntered center stage.

"Brethren," said Princess Salamonica. "Today we have in our presence Prince Wallace of Waters. With him are General Raptozk, his subordinate Captain Lexi, apprenticing wizard Joseph the Apothecary, and his master Zorna, royal wizard of the first order."

Wallace and his men braced as the stage slowly rotated from left to right. Princess Salamonica acknowledged the assembly. "Master Zorna," she said, "has come with his men to ask for our assistance."

With stoic faces, the assemblage of dragons peered down at Wallace and his men. Slowly leaning toward one another, they grumbled among themselves.

Feeling the reserve in the dragons' behavior, Zorna bent his head to Prince Wallace. "This may not be as easy as we anticipated," he mumbled, watching the faces of the dragons.

"We?" intoned General Raptozk, overhearing Zorna's words. "It was your idea to come here, wizard."

Wallace's eyes widened.

"Tomorrow, if it works, it will suddenly be *our* idea, Your Highness," Zorna observed.

Princess Salamonica looked askance at the chattering men. They quieted.

She turned to the council. "They wish us to stand with them against Prince Zili of Illuminae." A wave of roaring voices crested at the sound of Zili's name. "Courtiers!" Princess Salamonica shouted over the surge of voices. "Please, please, Council, come to order. All beings, please." Suddenly, there boomed a ground-shaking roar. The squabbling among the council quieted as the echo died. Heads turning, the council saw Zorna shrinking from dragon back to his human form.

"I must have your undivided attention if we are to proceed," said the princess, raising her talon to quiet the court.

"Why?" lifted a higher-pitched voice among the gruff. A hush suffused the assembly.

"Who asked that? Whomever he is, he is out of order!" bellowed Geldon. The dragons searched among one another. They saw movement beyond the archway through which Princess Salamonica had entered.

"No. *They* are out of order," the voice shouted. A lumbering winged figure moved forward.

"Ameryl," someone murmured.

"Joseph, he is the dragon Zorna healed," whispered Lexi, leaning in. "The one who fought with the dead man."

The general nodded. "One and the same."

"I have much trepidation regarding these human beings," said the young dragon, shaking his head upon his massive neck. He peered at the humans with ambivalence. "Just today I had to defend our clan from a *man*," he said, distaste on his lips. "They hunt and kill us. Men are the scourges of the earth. For them I would shed no tear, even if they were wiped from the face of our land." Squinting his crocodilian eyes, he added, "I would breathe and burn every one of them if—"

"SILENCE!" Geldon shouted. "Whatever your prejudices, these men are our guest all the same, and—"

"But Sire, we have done *nothing* to deserve such despair and death at their hands."

Defiantly, Wallace stood. Glaring at the young dragon, he addressed the rest of the council. "Prejudices—I have old prejudices. Relatives of my royal family, princes, and future kings have been burned alive by dragons. I've seen ladies, princesses, and future queens taken hostage. I have seen villages burned to cinders, and I have sent men to their doom to fight your kind."

"*Our* kind!" shouted Ameryl.

"YES. I should hate every last one of you ... but, but alas," said Wallace, catching his breath. "I do not."

"Then that is your weakness," said Ameryl.

"It is my strength," Wallace retorted.

"Why should we listen to anyone of nonlizard blood?" said Ameryl. "Why should I believe you? It was men who caused my grandfather's death, and caused my mother's brother to be exiled from our clan for over one hundred years."

"You should believe because of one I call friend," Wallace said.

"Who do you call friend?" asked the young dragon, moving more into the light of the council chambers.

Prince Geldon climbed down from his stool along the back wall to join his wife, Princess Salamonica. He watched Wallace and his men as he descended the stairs. "One among these *men* is also one of us. He is brother to Princess Salamonica."

A confusion of voices rose loudly in the chamber.

"Master Zorna," Geldon said.

"Zorna?" asked Ameryl.

Geldon pointed to Zorna. "He is the true brother to my wife. Both are the progeny of Hessereth, our great leader, for whom we mourn."

"No. How can this be true?" asked the young dragon. "He bears no resemblance to dragons or lizard people. I met my uncle this very day, before me, here in this gallery. He is a massive dragon with great power. Pardon my boldness, but the puny human you show me neither bears resemblance to nor favors me or my mother."

Taking her husband's hand, Princess Salamonica continued with her address to the assemblage. "My brother," she uttered, "has borne a curse for many generations. A punishment for granting a kindness to a human princess offered to a dragon as sacrifice. For his refusal, he was forced to wear the mantel of man. This has been his predominant face. Although able to temporarily revert, he is compelled to bear human form until he helps the survival of his own kind or is complicit with punishing a deserving human."

Ameryl stood with his crocodilian mouth agape, puzzled.

"Yes, it is true," said Princess Salamonica. "He has been gone over hundred years. For nearly a century he has lived as a man. He serves Prince Wallace of Waters, as did his father and grandfather before him, but as a man. He has learned much in their service. Upon his remarkable arrival today, Master Zorna used his prodigious knowledge to remove the stone that caused pain to his nephew, Prince Ameryl."

Ameryl shrank back, his eyes locked to his mother's. Princess Salamonica saw that Ameryl's hubris had begun to diminish. "My dear son Ameryl is a proud young dragon, but his vitriol is misguided," she said. "He knows next to nothing of his uncle's travails."

Prince Geldon squeezed his wife's digits tightly, gesturing for her to sit. "As reward for healing my son the prince," Geldon said, "I have offered Zorna a release from the curse. However, he has chosen to maintain human form. Therefore …"

The gallery went silent. Geldon looked down at Zorna with green, smiling, crocodilian eyes. "Therefore … I have granted him the ability to transform at will, not just in contact with certain magical objects. He may freely pass between worlds." Applause erupted but was quickly silenced by Prince Geldon.

"We have a common enemy," he said, turning upon the platform. "So too, we share a common ally. Prince Zili's offenses are notorious to all the peoples of the auroras. I surrender the floor to Prince Wallace of Illuminae, that he may make his case for our assistance."

Chapter 13

CHILD OF TWO WORLDS REVEALED

Head down and eyes closed, Wallace clasped his hands prayerfully. He ambled to the center of the stage. With small sideways steps, he bowed respectfully to the assembly and his men. Brow drawn down, he took a deep breath and cleared his throat.

"By now you know who I am, the Prince of Waters. Others may know me as the Duke of the Duchy of Waters, or the son of the late King Richard Dobromil the First, defender of our faith and ruler of our kingdom. Today, I now add friend to the dragon people." He heard polite applause.

"As you may know, my kingdom shares borders with many, as it does with yours. With fairness and an open heart, I rule the land bounding the Sea of Lady Hydra. A bit more of my history: I am also the third and youngest brother of fraternal twins, King Alexander Dobromil of Illuminae, and Prince Zili Dobromil, Sheriff of Illuminae."

Wallace briefly heard awkward whispering and mumbles.

"Sadly, our brother Zili is attempting to take control of both kingdoms, Illuminae and Waters. Once an honorable man until his twenties, my beloved brother fell under the influence of the trolls' Firestone." Wallace heard his words softly echoing among the assembly members. "He wears it on his hand. Although I fear the truth is that the ring wears him. It has taken possession of every fiber of his being."

Zorna joined Prince Wallace center stage. "Your Highness," Zorna said, "if I may continue?"

"Please do," Wallace said, making way.

Zorna stepped into Wallace's place. "I am home, and old before you. But I feel I am home again, although my visit shall be brief for now. There are faces here I have not seen in a lifetime, and they give me pause. Many elders know me. But I do not want to ramble." Smirking he nodded. "We have spoken enough about me. I will become what is more pleasing to the eye of my countrymen."

His transformation to dragon commenced, with no break in his cadence. "Behold my true self, so all will know who I am. I must show my respect to your intelligence and culture, so you will know my words are true." His voice deepened. "King Alexander and Prince Wallace are allies with the Child from Two Worlds, as foretold by the prophecy of Hydra: Nicholas Northland, the son of Christopher and Margaret. We know him as Nicholas Claus, the adopted child of Thomas Claus, master carpenter to the kingdoms of Illuminae and Waters. His mother is Mary Claus."

A wizened dragon shook, the sleeve of his gold-and-purple robe unfurling as he struggled to raise his clawed hand. "Centuries we have been relentlessly set upon by humans. You are telling me it will be a human being who will end our sufferings?" he asked in a quavering voice.

"It is foretold," Zorna assured him. "We must work, all, with him in this common cause, or his efforts will fail. We must all look into—"

"Brother, thank you for your ... pretty words, but how do we know the words you speak are truth?" asked another, younger, more energetic dragon.

Zorna slipped a small cauldron from his pocket. It contained a bit of hay. He removed the lid and added a few drops of glycerin. He breathed a gentle fire upon it and set it on the floor. Zorna spread his wizard's robe between both talons like a curtain before the smoldering cauldron. Arching over it, capturing the smoke, the robe billowed, lifting from the floor. Zorna snapped the robe away, creating a sphere of thick black smoke. Twisting and roiling, it hovered in the center of the assembly. "Watch. Judge for yourselves whether what I say is lie or truth."

Zorna raised his arms above his head. Rotating his massive arm at his shoulder, he used his talon to inscribe a circle in the air, the diameter of which spanned eight feet. The inky black smoke took the form of a sphere. "This sphere of smoke," he bellowed, "shall serve as a kind of crystal ball, a divination device, into which all shall see the present as it exists far from here. Sister: speak aloud, ask what you wish to see, and you will see it in the smoke. Again, it will only show you what is happening presently—nothing past, nothing future."

Princess Salamonica and Prince Geldon stepped forward. Sitting quietly, the general stroked his chin. Lexi shifted on his stone stool. Prince Wallace watched the smoke billow and whirl as it took on various colorful patterns. A soft gasp suffused the assembly when a three-dimensional picture clearly formed from every angle of the smoky sphere. Joseph, filled with awe, stared ahead. "It is like a window connected to some other place."

Geldon softly ordered, "Show us the actions of Nicholas Claus." The smoke darkened and thickened at its center; colors whirled and mixed, before layering. The scene came into view. He could clearly see it, as if he were there.

Prince Wallace leaned toward General Raptozk. "The interior of the church is Elfin." General Raptozk nodded. They watched.

> Father Mark, Nicholas Claus, and Father Bruno lay prostrate on the church floor. Their heads pointed toward the altar. Their arms stretched out from their sides. They formed the shape of the cross. At their heads, Father Bernard stood over them. He shook an aspergillum, sprinkling them with holy water. Father Bernard swung a brass censer of smoking incense to bless the three men.

"You have completed your studies," echoed voices from the incense smoke. "Stand before me and state your vows."

Father Bernard moved before Nicholas.

"Nicholas Claus, stand before me and the Creator of all beings, past, present, and future. What do thou ask of the Creator?"

Nicholas stood. "I ask the Creator of all to accept my pledge of loyalty, obedience, and love. I ask that the Creator sanction service to all beings, human and oddling alike. If he accepts my pledge, I promise to fulfill it with all my heart, even if my pledge leads to my death."

His arm swinging before Nicholas, Father Bernard blessed him with the sign of the cross and sprinkled him with more holy water. Circling, he swung the censer of frankincense and myrrh.

"Your pledge to the Creator of beings has been accepted," said Father Bernard. "Your service and guardianship shall be to the Aurora Kingdoms."

The color from the smoke faded, and the picture unwound into thin threads of dissipating smoke.
Prince Geldon stepped forward again. "Show us Zili of Illuminae." Instantly the smoke darkened, involuting at its center. But the color of the smoke turned red, the color of blood.
At the center of the scrying smoke, the assembly saw the workshop of Thomas Claus. Tables, chairs, and workbenches were overturned; injured humans and oddlings lay on the floor.

Gasping, the assembly remained otherwise silent. Recognizing the home of Tom Claus, Wallace sat forward on the stone, his right elbow on his knee, his fist clasped beneath his chin.

A red-headed soldier held Thomas Claus down by his neck, his cheek mashed into a tabletop.

"I know you are hiding Sarah here." Zili growled, restless, pacing beside his red-headed enforcer. Jax strolled around the table, thwacking Thomas about his upper body with a riding crop. Mary bent over Thomas, crying and pushing at Jax. Another soldier pulled her back.

"The girl is nothing to you. She won't care if you live or die." Zili lowered his face to within an inch of Thomas's. "Consider your family, your wife. Tell me where she is, and I will let you go." He lifted an apple from the table and cut out a wedge with his knife. "If you do not, I shall slit this old wench's throat." Zili snickered, leveling the tip of his knife at Mary's neck. Jerking Mary from the soldier, Zili yanked her head back by her hair, her back extended over his raised knee. Her red headscarf came off in Zili's hand. He slapped the flat of his cold blade to her throat.

"Please?" asked Zili. "You have to the count of three, old man, to tell me where she is. One. Two …" He turned the edge of his blade to Mary's skin.

"No!" shouted Sarah, bursting through a trap door in the floor. She screamed to the limit of her breath. "Please, stop!"

Zili gazed at Sarah. He laughed. "There you are, you naughty girl, in the turnip cellar. Very clever. Oh, yes—three."

"NOOOO!" Sarah cried, rushing toward Mary.

Glaring, Zili drew the cold steel across Mary's throat. Thick, rich blood poured over Zili's right hand. Clutching her throat, Mary gurgled. Blood spewed through her wrinkled white fingers, her eyes fixed and wide. Zili tossed Mary's limp body to the floor. A pool of red grew slowly around her body, then stopped.

"Trash," he muttered, sneering. Tom broke from the soldier and Jax. He grasped futilely at Zili. Grinning in Tom's face, Zili, with as much force and hate as he could muster, thrust a dagger into Tom's abdomen. Reeling backward, Tom's face turned pale with an expression of dying horror. He turned from Zili. Reaching for Mary, Tom took one step toward her before his legs collapsed beneath him, the knife poking from his heart.

Up from his chair Wallace shot, reaching for the smoke, General Raptozk at his side, both rushed toward the vision. General Raptozk deflected Wallace's wrist while shaking his own head. "Sire, no. There may be more," he said.

Nonplussed, Wallace felt a mixture of rage and sorrow. The dragons gazed upon the humans with pity and empathy as the vision continued.

Zili took Sarah by the hair. She stiffened, resisting his advances. He pushed his face to hers. She turned her face.

He gritted his teeth. "You spoiled brat. You will ride in the carriage or I shall bundle you like a common parcel and tie you to the rear. It is your choice, princess."

Not awaiting her answer, he forced her into his carriage. There, all she could do was cry.

"Jax, take your soldiers and ride hard, ahead to my camp, and prepare a place for the princess. She shall make a fine consort, do you not think so?" Zili said, grinning. "Denied the older sister, I shall have the younger."

Thinning into the air, the vision was no more. Stunned, his stomach sinking, Prince Wallace started for his seat. Astonished, the assembly of dragons sat in silence.

Seeing Is Believing

Infuriated, turning, Wallace suddenly rushed from his seat back to the smoke, the general at his heels. "Princess Sarah!" Wallace shouted.

"Treason," the general muttered at Wallace's back, clasping the hilt of his sword. "I shall have his head and—" Wallace raised his finger to his shoulder, gesturing for the general to quiet.

No one wanted to believe what he or she had witnessed. The room quiet, they heard only the crackling and snapping of the cauldron's burning contents. Stepping forward, Zorna broke the hush.

"The magic remains fresh," said Zorna. "Prince Wallace is as invested in Zili's defeat as anyone here." Zorna respectfully bowed to the assembly. "Does anyone else wish to see anything?"

Prince Wallace's expression remained one of shock, dismay, and determination. Wallace hesitantly turned. The general stood aside. "Please," Wallace asked, his heart ambivalent. He was shaken. "May I see the castles of King Alexander Dobromil and Hydra?"

The smoke whirled and streamed together in a large cloud. It flashed over. Wallace and his men felt the heat. Again, the smoke turned from black to brown to red, bloodred. The center of the cloud thinned. Becoming colorful, it organized to form blurred images, a panoramic of the two kingdoms, side by side, separated by a column of smoke.

"Hydra harbor," Wallace murmured, pointing. "Those are soldiers under the command of Zili's generals."

"They are burning the grain ships, Sire," muttered the general.

"While the merchants are preparing to offload food," Lexi said.

"Why, it is for the people, Sire. The grain."

Wallace ached with pain and anger. He felt he needed to do something that very moment.

At first small, the fires grew, spreading beyond the initial ignition point. Sailors jumped into the water. Rats shot down mooring ropes to the dock. Black, billowing smoke and flame towered skyward, engulfing the masts and sails.

The assembly watched the visions of the ships burning. Then through the seeing smoke, the castle of King Dobromil waxed into view. Wallace saw Alexander.

"Sire, your brother, I mean, His Highness King Alexander," Joseph said, sitting forward on his stool. Wallace nodded.

In the magical screen of smoke, they saw the king and several of the castle guard were in the heat of a fierce battle outside the queen's chambers: swords crossing, men charging, and knives impaling. Wallace leaped to his feet as an arrow impaled Alexander's shoulder. Wallace lunged toward the smoke. Zorna gently blocked him with his left arm. Restless, Wallace watched Zili's men lifted the gravely injured king. They dragged him to the dungeons.

"Treason," muttered Wallace, his hand on the hilt of his sword. He watched helplessly as several of Zili's soldiers seized the queen and princess as well.

"Have you seen enough?" Zorna asked, turning to eye the assembly. The room was still.

"Do you now believe what we say?" asked Zorna.

Feeling his heart crushed, Wallace lowered his eyes. But he also felt righteous indignation. He lifted his head, looking up to the dragon council. "Will you help me stand against my brother?" he asked. "In return, I will help to repair your reputation. I will explain to all that you have not killed offensively but only in defense of yourselves and your homes. I shall explain that the deaths of the many who came here were due to their own folly. The air you breathe in this mountain is noxious, poisonous, to all but a dragon. Uninvited intruders starved for air. Some were lost in the changing structure of this mountain. I will also assure you that none of you or your children will ever go hungry again. Among other things, I will share part of the royal grain stores with you."

Geldon stood. Turning to face the assembly, he said, "Dragons and ye of lizard blood." His voice boomed, reverberating from the walls.

"You have seen for yourself the actions of Sheriff Zili of Illuminae. Give me your decision. Do we stand with Prince Wallace or let him stand alone?"

A deep, guttural rumble rose to a deafening level. Zorna closed the lid of the cauldron to extinguish the fire and contain the scrying smoke. Geldon turned to Prince Wallace and bowed.

"Prince Wallace. I, Prince Geldon of the Dragon Kingdom, have heard my people and speak for them. We will become your ally."

Wallace looked at his men. They smiled.

Chapter 14

HOPE

Prince Geldon and Princess Salamonica nodded. She watched with optimism as Prince Geldon and Prince Wallace shook, claw to hand. Geldon's mighty claw covered Wallace's hand and part of his forearm as they sealed their alliance. The skin of Geldon's claws was cool, yet the gesture warmed Wallace's heart. He knew they would put aside their negative notions of one another and work together.

At that moment, the floor began to tremble. Confusion rushed through the room as the rock floor quaked.

"Zorna, what is this? What wrath of the Powers That Be have you brought down on us?" Ameryl shouted, backing away from the chamber. Maintaining his balance, Zorna said nothing as he shrank back to his human form.

Amid the tremor, a starburst of brilliant light swirled at the center of the room. Scintillating flashes danced like raindrops on the shuddering floor. The assembly saw the aurora borealis take shape, rising from the stone floor, forming a cylinder wider than a man. The air sweetened with the smell of freshly cut flowers. Spiraling towards the ceiling, the cylinder of light widened and the light brightened. Joseph could feel the heat from the light upon his face. Princess Salamonica held her forearm high, her floating sleeve protecting her crocodilian eyes from the glare. Everyone did likewise.

As abruptly as it began, the light ceased.

Where the light had shone sat King Stanislaus, clad in a long blue robe and cowl. He sat upon a simple wooden throne, a crystal-knobbed staff over seven feet tall in his right hand. Measuring less than four feet high, his four elf attendants, clad in gold-and-white robes, stood, their backs to him, their arms to their sides. They faced the four corners of the earth.

The assembly bowed at his presence and maintained a humble posture, their eyes down.

King Stanislaus looked around the room. "Raise your eyes. It is I, Stanislaus, king of all that is. I am pleased to be with you. I have the honor of being in the presence of the courageous." He nodded. "It has been many generations since I visited the Dragon Kingdom. None of you were born during my last visit."

Ameryl stepped forward. "You are in the heart of our home, the Dragons Mons," said Ameryl. Princess Salamonica fluttered her wings. Huffing just a hint of flame through his nostrils, Ameryl instantly hushed and turned away.

"This is where the Crystal Chronaria is forged," said King Stanislaus. "It contains the magic one needs to defeat Zili. Give me the stone you extracted from Ameryl." One of the elf attendants slipped up beside Zorna to take the stone. He handed it to King Stanislaus.

Looking over the orange-size stone, King Stanislaus handed it to another of his attendants. The elves gestured for all to stand back from King Stanislaus. As they backed away, King Stanislaus closed his eyes. The attendant rotated the stone, stopping at each of the four corners of the earth. King Stanislaus grasped the seven-foot staff at its center with both hands. He presented it before him. Hoisting it over his head, he struck the staff point down to the ground. The ground shattered. The crack in the stone floor ran like threads in all directions. Wider and broader the crack rumbled and snapped. Shattering, stones crumbled into the abyss. The open crevasse revealed an underlying pool of seething red lava. King Stanislaus tossed the ridged, bile-stained stone into the lava.

Zorna gasped.

"Zorna," King Stanislaus ordered, leveling his index finger, "raise your mirror above your head, then tilt it toward the lava." Zorna did.

The light of the aurora borealis, filtering through the staff's crystal, shot light into the mirror, which reflected it onto the lava. The smell of burning sulfur and metal seeped along the floor in thin strings of white smoke. The general covered his nose with the crook of his arm. Muting his cough, Wallace covered his nose with the fingers of his glove. Covering their noses likewise, Lexi and Joseph stood back from the larger cracks.

The dragon assembly muttered to one another as they watched. From the center of the lava pool rose the Dragon Stone, now a pewter-gray crystal, flawless and purer than any crystal any of them had ever seen.

Stanislaus struck the ground with the end of his staff. He raised the staff above his head. With a puff of his breath, King Stanislaus spun the crystal knob atop his staff. It spiraled from the end of his staff, arcing into a ceiling-high circle. The Dragon Stone entered and hovered in the inscribed arc. "Jack Frost," King Stanislaus incanted, "appear before me now."

The assembly heard the distant whistle of a winnowing wind. Hesitating, Joseph looked at Lexi, an eyebrow raised. "I recall this Jack Frost."

"From the meeting at Tom Claus's farm?"

"No. I have experience with him prior to that," Joseph said. "He is the bringer of death."

"No. No. You're wrong. You're mistaken. He brings the winter, is all."

"And winter brings death," uttered Joseph, feeling the temperature drop. "I am weary of this Jack Frost."

"What is it?" Lexi asked, himself feeling a cold stream of air filtering through the cracks in the rock near his feet. He rubbed his arms. "It has become chilly despite the lava just below this floor. Joseph, what has gotten into you?"

Joseph rubbed his fingers together. "When I was a child," he said, his eyes down, "my family endured a particularly harsh winter, and very poorly I might add. Sadly, my infant sister died."

An ice-cold wind descended the mouth of the vents of Dragons Mons. Above the mirror that Zorna held above his head hovered an ethereal image of a three-foot-tall being. The figure formed from layered ice, a slab at a time, drawn from the water in the air.

A small man developed, appearing frozen and inanimate. When his head appeared, his eyes alone shifted, moving with the crackle of breaking ice as he peered around the room. From crystal-clear, the ice forming his body became colored. Frost's circulatory system appeared first, his heart pumping red blood through his crystalline body. The icy surface took on the appearance of blue skin. Scintillating with the colors, his clothing formed—red breeches, blue shoes, green waistcoat, and purple frock. As his form completed, his purple lips heaved in a gulp of air. He began to move, his blue skin pinking up. When he was dressed, his body became flesh.

He spun, his eyes searching the room in which he found himself. "I am Jack Frost," he intoned in a high register. "I have answered your call, Stanislaus, king of all that be."

"I remember this one," General Raptozk said, sitting back on his stool. "He has an appetite for the dramatic."

"Pardon my surprise that I find myself here," said Jack Frost. "I was in the middle of frosting a farmer's orchard when he failed to bring the harvest in on time." Jack's eyes cut to Joseph, somehow knowing Joseph's previous words. Taken aback by his stare, Joseph took a defensive stance.

"Death is a part of life," said Jack. "I advise thee not to take the natural vicissitudes of life as a personal vendetta against thee ... Joseph. It is nature's will." His eyes cut back to King Stanislaus. "How may I serve thee, dear King Stanislaus?"

"I have a task for you," said King Stanislaus, leveling his staff at the imp.

"As I have said, I am at your service, Your Highness." Jack doffed his hat.

"Call the power of the four winds," King Stanislaus said, whirling, his hands outstretched. "Send the winds into the Dragon Stone. Command their power be released by the light of the full moon when cast upon the heart of the Dragon Stone. It shall have the power to give life or take it away. The morality of that power is dependent on the heart of the bearer of the stone."

"Sire," Jack Frost lilted, "you ask much." He hesitated. "And I shall deliver much, Your Highness. Your desires have been delivered to my mind." His eyes locked on to the Dragon Stone. Reaching beneath his purple frock, he unfixed the lower buttons of his green waistcoat. Frost inhaled deeply. He pursed his lips, aiming his breath at the Dragon Stone. With a mighty exhalation, he blew. From his mouth he issued a typhoon wind. Jack's breath ensconced the Dragon Stone within a diamond encasement in the shape of a snowflake.

The assembly hushed in amazement. Lexi and Joseph shifted on their stools. Wallace and the general leaned forward. Satisfied, Jack Frost stood erect, arms akimbo, gleaming.

Stepping forward, King Stanislaus stared at the Dragon Stone. With the tip of his staff, he traced a circle in the air around the levitating stone. He raised the shaft above his head, its narrow point down. He plunged the staff to the stone floor three times in rapid succession. At each impact, the tip of the shaft issued a piercing crack and sparks. Again, the brilliance of the aurora borealis filled the chamber, floating gently like a curtain of light spanning from floor to ceiling. Lifting his open palm toward the Dragon Stone, he watched as it slumped into his hand like a feather.

"Behold the Crystal Chronaria," King Stanislaus said, slowly turning so all could see.

"What's he going to do now?" Joseph whispered to Lexi.

Lexi shrugged. "Did I get here before you? How would I know?" He huffed, rolling his eyes. "Be quiet and watch. I can't just tell you everything." Zorna shot the two young men a stern glance. His index finger to his lips gestured for them to quiet.

"I summon before me our champion, Nicholas Claus," declared King Stanislaus. The air before him blurred and shimmered as it took the shape of a man. The shimmer became opaque, then solid. The blanched, featureless solid formed a head, shoulders, arms, torso, and legs. In seconds, it commenced to take on features.

"He is a great conjurer," General Raptozk said, leaning forward. "Conjurers use tricks, dear General," Wallace muttered. "As yet, I have seen no tricks. He is a worker of wonders."

"Nicholas," Lexi murmured. All looked.

Astounded, confused, seeing the dragons along the wall, Nicholas spun. Startling, he backed away. Taken by his initial fright and curious behavior, the dragons shifted in their seats, several exhaling blue fire.

"Fear not, my son. You are among friends," King Stanislaus said in a soothing voice.

"What?" Nicholas asked. Knitting his eyebrows, he swallowed.

"Friends?" He had not settled in his strange surroundings.

Prince Wallace strode up behind him and put his hands on his shoulders. Nicholas jumped but calmed when he saw Wallace over his shoulder. Wallace brushed Nicholas's shoulder and returned to his stool. Nicholas stood before the assembly amid the dissipating brilliance of his arrival. His gaze cut to King Stanislaus.

"Nicholas, I brought you here because you consented to be our champion. I intend to now place in your possession the Crystal Chronaria. With this and only this crystal, you may counteract the enchantment of the Firestone."

Tentatively dipping a time or two in his stride, Nicholas took several steps toward King Stanislaus.

"Hold the crystal to the light of the full moon on the night of the winter solstice," said King Stanislaus. "When the moon reaches its apex, the light must fall upon the heart of the crystal." Nicholas saw a sparkle projecting from the heart of the crystal. "If you do this, the spell of the Firestone shall be broken."

Bobbing respectfully, Nicholas extended both hands to receive the crystal. Stepping backward, Nicholas knelt. "Thank you, Your Majesty," Nicholas said. "I shall do my best to fulfill this challenge."

"I will now return you from whence you came," said King Stanislaus. Stirring the air with his staff, he struck the ground three times. Again, the light of the aurora filled the room. Dissipating with a brilliant flash, the light winked out. Nicholas had vanished.

Chapter 15

DOUBT

Three days later, Nicholas adjusted the cap on his head to shade his eyes from the noon sun. Nearing home, he could smell the familiar aroma of the countryside. It had been a long ride from the church. His new commitment to service satisfied his heart. He looked forward to the good works he could do.

His mind drifted to the Dragon Mons. He remained astounded by his instant transport there. He had seen many wonders in his young life, but he knew many more would come.

Gratified by the gift bestowed upon him by King Stanislaus, Nicholas pondered his fortune, his home, his friends, his wonderful parents Tom and Mary, and his old friends Philly and Henry. Plodding along, the horses lazily pulled the wagon, clopping upon the loose rocks comprising the road. The gentle loping and the slow gyrations of the wagon lulled Nicholas into a state of delight. He felt the crunch of the rusty springs beneath the bench. He listened to the forest sounds, his nostrils constantly replenished with the aroma of the forest flora.

"Beautiful, isn't it?" Nicholas murmured, scanning the beautiful green scenery of the countryside, sure the horses were in accord. The long leather reins lay loose in his hands. Philly always pulled to the left. Nicholas occasionally had to pull the right rein to draw her in.

Nicholas paid little attention when he saw birds circling above, mere dots in the sky against the hills behind his home. For some time, the horses continued at their leisurely pace. Pots and pan clattered on the side of the varda as it traversed the uneven ground.

Only one hundred feet from the gate of the split-rail fence, Nicholas saw no movement nor activity. The farm seemed quiet and still. It did not feel right. He tried to ignore his feelings by suggesting he was just being silly.

"There it is," Nicholas said. He was home. That night he was sure to get home cooking and a sound night's sleep in his own bed. He drove the varda up to the great wooden gate and climbed down.

Striding past Philly, he stroked her neck. Reaching across, he stroked Henry across his face. Leaning down, he disengaged the long metal bolt latching the gate. It was usually unlocked; Nicholas found it odd that it was locked. He pulled the rusty crossbar through the cleats to release the latch. Walking the gate along a wide arc, he lowered an attached shank into the ground to hold the gate open.

"Philly, Henry," Nicholas said. "Come, so I may close the gate." Unsteady and irritable, the horses refused.

"What's wrong, girl? What's wrong, boy?" Nicholas asked, gathering a short section of their reins. The horses flattened their ears. Their eyes widened and their nostrils flared. They raised their heads as he tugged on the reins. They refused to allow him to walk them past the threshold.

Eventually responding to his coaxing, the horses moved up just far enough to clear the gate and no farther. Nicholas climbed up to the bench seat and lifted the reins. He snapped. As they rolled, Nicholas looked back at the conduit pipe beneath the gate. He saw a leather coin purse turned inside out near the head of the drainpipe. Several gold coins were scattered through the fosse, weeds, and mud. It belonged to the troll, Mr. Musker. He would not have left his treasure for anyone to get.

Nicholas rose in his seat and scanned the surrounding area. The horses advanced slowly. Nicholas felt odd, hearing no birds chirp. Yes, the country was serene, but it was never this quiet. He was less than a quarter mile from his parent's farmhouse, yet he felt a thousand miles away. Nothing felt right. The closer he came, the more uncomfortable he felt.

When the varda rolled up, he was only twenty-five feet from the farmhouse door. The birds that had been dots circling in the sky were revealed as scavengers, and they were directly overhead. Stunned, he felt a twisting in his gut.

Nicholas shouted, "Father! Mother!" Jingles had not met him at the gate.

"What's happened here? Where's Jingles?" He leaped from the bench and hit the dirt running. Replacing the aroma of the forest flora, he smelled the pungent odor of death filtering into his nostrils. He searched the grounds, but found only scores of small animal carcasses impaled by large arrows, as if used for target practice. Their farmyard was littered with dead chickens and piglets—some mangled, others beheaded.

"Wh-where is everyone?" he shouted. "So quiet. Here, boy! Come on, boy!" The dog did not answer, and he did not come. Henry and Philly were more skittish. The horses' ears went flat; they bucked, sidled, and whinnied. The varda shimmied, clanked, and jangled, the cart jinked back and forth by the action of the agitated horses.

"Whoa, my friends. Easy," soothed Nicholas. The horses did not settle. They wanted to proceed no farther. Where were the squirrels and cats? Where were the birds? The only birds Nicholas saw were scavengers and raptors circling high above. Talons fixed, a hawk swooped from the sky, just missing Nicholas's shoulder.

"No! Get away!" he shouted sternly, flailing his arms. Scooping a handful of pebbles, he hurled them at the hawk. Screeching, the scavenger shot into the air, quickly becoming just another circling dot in the sky.

As Nicholas approached the bunkhouse, the wind blew a red piece of cloth across his feet. It rolled in the wind, finally snagging on a spar of the varda wagon wheel. In his confusion, Nicholas paid little attention not realizing it was Mary's headscarf. The wash line, heavy with clothing, lay upon the ground. The smell, that too-familiar smell, carried on the breeze through the farmyard turned Nicholas's stomach.

The slaughtered animals alone could not account for the substantial stench. Nicholas counted every step as he drew near the house. He grew steadily ill and ill at ease.

He stood at the doorsill of the bunkhouse. The door was ajar by several inches. He felt trepidation. He knew he needed to go in, but his feet would not move. He could feel and smell air blowing from the house. "No," he whispered, shuddering. He recognized the smell assaulting his nostrils. It was the same as he remembered from two years ago, when he and Beast had towed a dead reindeer from a pond. The carcass had spoiled the water. His heart raced and his palms sweated. He wanted to flee, but he had to go forward, through the open door.

"Mother! Father!" Nicholas shouted, hoping they would answer. The bunkhouse was gloomy and eerily silent. He heard nothing. Reaching to his head, he clasped and crumpled his cap in his fist.

"Sarah? Sarah! Beast!" he yelled. "Is *anyone* here?" He tried to swallow, but his mouth was dry. His eyes darted over every corner of the house.

In the last room, he found the source of the rot—his father's prize hog, a mother of many piglets. The sow was dead.

He searched every structure: barn, smokehouse, shed. His mind became crowded with the images of mayhem. Everywhere were broken doors, slaughtered animals, and the bodies of elves, trolls, and even Ogre—all lying in the dirt, broken and battered. Nicholas checked every being but found no life. "Who has done this evil?" he murmured as he ran from place to place.

His anger and frustration grew, as did his fear of what else he might find. His fear grew beyond his ability to control. Feeling helpless, hopeless, Nicholas kicked at the dirt. He dropped to his knees. On his knees he spun, confused, not knowing which direction to go. As he turned toward the farmhouse, he saw a jumble of rust-and-gold fur protruding from beneath the front steps. Nicholas squinted and slowly rose to his feet. He crept closer. He saw.

"Jingles and Bowes," he cried. He ran to them and recoiled at their gory mess. They lay broken and bloodied in the dirt, half under the front stairs.

Lifting his eyes to the main house, he saw that door was open. Filled with trepidation, Nicholas paused at the doorsill. His sweaty fingers brushed the doorknob. He peered through the cracked door. He saw the curtains were drawn shut, which kept out the late-afternoon sun. Clearly, the front room was dark. Concentrating, he attempted to bring his heart rate down. He shook his hands to steady his nerves. Suddenly it seemed his feet would not work. He tried to walk inside, but he stumbled. His chest hurt. His oxygen sucked away, he could not breathe.

"Come on, feet. Move," he muttered. "Mother and Father are in there." But he hoped they were not.

Nicholas inched farther into the room. The floor was a mess. Sliding, he nearly fell. He peered into the turnip cellar. Oil lamps were broken on the floor; oil had run everywhere.

Near the table, he saw a leg, then another, then the hem of a skirt. He saw Mary.

"Mother!" He dropped to his knees. His hands up before him, he could not touch her. He would not touch her. Touching would make it real.

Her throat was cut. She lay on the floor before the hearth. Over her, a rocker was turned. Beneath her, a swath of blood trailed. Just feet from her, Tom lay on his back, his dead hand grazing hers. A dagger stuck out from his chest.

No longer able to contain himself, Nicholas dashed from the house to the yard. He fell to his knees, vomiting and crying.

"Who did this?" he cried. "Who? Who did this?"

Oblivious to his small concerns, the stars twinkled in the deepening dusk. Polaris shone directly overhead.

Nicholas wanted escape. He stared at the North Star and wished to go to a place so far away that he and those he loved could live and never be found.

He remained on the ground, unable to move or think, until dusk became night.

Crawling onto his knees, Nicholas lifted his arms to the sky.

"Master of All That Be. I accepted your charge to be my peoples' champion, but my load is greater than I can bear. Help me!" he cried, closing his eyes. "Lend me your strength that I may keep my heart and mind from breaking. Please tell me—how can I survive this? And who did this? Help me know what to do. So many decisions. I-I am only one being. One human."

Crystal

After sunset on that cloudless night, the temperature dropped. Chilled, Nicholas cared about nothing. Mother would have admonished him for being out without proper clothing, but Mother was no longer alive. He lay on his back on the grass. His paralyzing grief unwilling to relent, he stared up at the Milky Way. Motionless, he wished to become as small as he could. He tried to lock his thoughts away so he would not feel. He raked his fingers through the grass, clutching, hoping to become part of the earth. He did nothing to clear the grime on his lips or the dirt clogged in his hair or the tears swelling his eyes. If he thought enough, he could think his heart stone, and if he thought even harder, he could become stone. He envied the rocks. Rocks were not alive. Rocks had no feelings.

"Nicholas," a woman's voice called. Her euphonious intonation, delicate, light, and pleasing to the ear, contrasted with the feelings he battled. Was he dreaming?

Nicholas pushed up on his hands. Searching, his eyes turned in the darkness but were useless. Starlight did little to illuminate his surroundings. He perched on his heels, eyes still searching the inky blackness.

"Nicholas."

He thought he wanted to die when he heard his name. "Who is there?" he asked. "Where are you?" He lay back on the ground and stared at the stars.

"Nicholas, child of two worlds. Despair not. You are not alone. Everything happens for a reason."

"Reason?" Nicholas said, tightening his jaw. "Whoever you are, my parents are dead. Do you hear me? And you ... you spew out philosophical platitudes. Show yourself." Although Nicholas would not stand, he looked, but he managed to find no one. "Who is there? Where are you? Please, show yourself to me. Do I know you?"

He waited but heard nothing further. He thought it might have been his imagination.

Then, just topping the grass, he saw a glowing sapphire mist rolling toward him. It abruptly stopped before him, where it whirled and stacked up. Nicholas heard the voice emanate from the mist. "We have not met, but you do know me. I am part of you."

"What are you talking about?" Nicholas said, "Everyone I love has been taken from me."

"Not everyone," whispered the mist. It lifted and thickened. The floating face of a woman began to form at the level of Nicholas's eyes.

"Who are you? And what do you want?" he muttered, turning his face away. "You said 'not everyone.' Do not trifle with me. I warn you. I am unwell ..."

"Hello, *Unwell*. I am Crystal, your grandmother," whispered the voice. "I can help you, Nicholas."

"Grandmother? I don't understand," he said glumly. "Both my grandparents and my birth parents are long dead—since I was an infant. And now so are my adoptive parents," he added dolefully, glancing at the cold, dark farmhouse. "How can I believe you? How can I believe anyone anymore?"

"Use your gift, Nicholas. Your heart will tell you if I speak the truth." The mist wafted around Nicholas, reaching his face. Materializing against his cheek, her hand affectionately wiped tears from his eyes. Formed from the most delicate iridescent ice crystals, the sapphire mist assumed the features of the most beautiful woman Nicholas had ever seen. Throughout her body, the colors of the aurora sparkled individually with increasing intensity as Crystal stroked Nicholas to comfort him. "You do not know how special you really are," she said kindheartedly.

"I suppose I'm important enough," he grumbled.

"I mean to say you, Nicholas, are here because of love."

"My parents loved each other and me, I suppose. Is that what you mean?"

Nodding, she continued, "In life, I was the daughter of Lady Hydra."

"She is a powerful being," Nicholas murmured. "I fell in love with a mortal," Crystal said.

"As did my mother," he replied.

"We were married, and I had a daughter—Margaret, your mother. Although you are not immortal, Nicholas, you do possess all the magic of the Linkage."

"I know little of the Linkage or any magic I possess. My father said it is what relates and drives all living things. He knew those things. But what I know is that I never knew you."

"But I know you," she said, smiling. "My mother, the great Lady Hydra, foretold your destiny. She told it to your mother in a vision, for she knew your mother would never see you grow up."

"Father Time showed me that," Nicholas said.

Crystal nodded. "Of that I am aware." She pushed her ethereal face within inches of Nicholas's. "With the help of the Powers That Be, you were given all the tools and support you need to restore the balance of the Aurora Kingdoms. Rise." Crystal placed her hands on Nicholas and helped him to stand. The dulcet tones of her voice seemed to reassure and comfort him.

There was movement in his peripheral vision: upon the dark grass, darker shadows came to him. Nicholas turned his head. A throng of oddlings approached.

"Accept the help and strength of all your friends. All are part of you. We are here to guide and support you."

Nicholas recognized many familiar faces, and some new ones. Beast, Ursa, and Ursara stood beside Nicholas, accompanied by several more: elves, trolls, gnomes, centaurs, sprites, pixies, fairies, and many other oddlings. They seemed to come out of nowhere. Each oddling bowed before Crystal, after which they began working together to clean up the area.

Chapter 16

SOMETHING YOU SHOULD KNOW

"My mother loved me very much," Crystal gently said. "My mother knew how much I was giving up when I chose to become mortal." Clasping her hands like a clamshell, she slowly opened them. Whorls of mist spun between. There hovered a floating vision of a heart-shaped locket attached to a leather lanyard. She brought her arched hands up to Nicholas's eyes so he could clearly see. The vaporous locket slowly rotated, sparkling with internal brilliance. "She gave me this locket spun from moonlight. Inside, crystals from starlight hold the elixir of my immortality." The back of the locket magically opened as it rotated into view. "I call it the Elixir Illuminae. As it was given to me, in turn, it was passed to my daughter Margaret just before she married. Margaret tied the locket around your neck to protect you. One drop of the Elixir Illuminae will reverse the effect of death."

"It did her little good," scolded Nicholas.

"She would have had a long life, were that her destiny," said Crystal. "Sadly, it was not. Her life force was meant to continue in another—you, Nicholas. You."

"Certainly not I," he mumbled. His shoulders slumped.

"What's wrong?"

"I'm afraid to say ... I—ah—I no longer have ... the locket." Nicholas hesitated. He wondered whether he had done the right thing. "I didn't know of its magic. I was never told. I-I gave it to Sarah ... as a gift."

"Do you love her?" Crystal asked.

"Yes, very much so." Tucking his lips, he peered into her face for a second or two. "I have asked King Alexander for permission to court and wed her, but I foresee some difficulty. I am a commoner, and I have much to learn."

"Happily, I say unto you: you are more than commoner. As for protecting Sarah, even if she is unaware of the magic of the locket, it will protect her, dear grandson."

Beast and two yetis transported corpses to the storage area at the rear of the workshop. They gently laid them beside others, previously set side by side.

"The distress of this night is evident on your face," Crystal said. "Washed by the tears from your eyes, the lines on your face reflect the pain etched into your heart. But life given by the Creator can never be extinguished."

Distracted by the activity around him, Nicholas turned to watch Beast and the two yetis bear more bodies to the storage area. With a gentle hand, Crystal turned Nicholas's face to her. "Concern yourself not with them. You cannot walk forward with your face turned backward. They shall neatly arrange things before daybreak."

Still, Nicholas's eyes drifted. "Pay attention young Nicholas," she pleaded, "for my time is short. You have much to learn."

"Yes, ma'am."

Floating atop a roiling haze, Crystal spirited him to the house. Several tall and thin elves with delicate, elongated, chiseled features, dressed in long white gowns, busily straightened the homestead. Pixies, color sprites, and fairies flitted about, using tiny wands to erect furniture to its proper position. Men of sand, as if gusted by the wind, trundled across the floor upon great shifting mounds of granules instead of feet.

The wood-slat floor was not only cleaned and dried spotless but also polished.

"Look around you. You will have certain powers and more at your command when you truly need them, Nicholas, but only when you truly need them. To use them, simply ask the Linkage to help with a specific need. You do not have to speak the words aloud. But you must ask permission. If the Linkage judges the need is true, it will help. If, however, there is something you must learn, the Linkage shall stand down.

"I know—I know what you are thinking." Crystal sighed. "As it was for me, it was for your mother, and it was for Tom and Mary. They may not return to you. It is too late for them; their destiny is complete." Crystal's density began dissipating. "And my time is nearly done. Come. Let us discover what you have learned."

Surfing the rolling mist, she floated beside Nicholas as he strode to the storage area where the dead rested. By her thoughts, Crystal called to the oddlings, who came from the fields, the grass, the trees, and the storage structures. They came individually and in groups. They walked, flew, crawled, and gathered behind Nicholas and her.

"Friends, please join Nicholas and me. It is time for saying good-bye." Silently, everyone turned in solemn procession. Providing illumination, a light sprite hovered above and before each living being. In moments, Nicholas and Crystal stopped. They positioned themselves before the fallen beings. The procession of oddlings formed a semicircle several steps behind. Crystal turned to Nicholas and looked him in the eyes. She released his hand. "The time has come for you to use your magic," she said.

"But I don't know how to," he murmured.

Holding up one finger, Crystal whispered softly, "Close your eyes and say a prayer."

Nicholas closed his eyes, folded his hands, and said a silent prayer. Turning, he faced those behind him.

"My friends, together with those who have fallen, we have shared love, faith, and loss. I do not know the details of your traditions for the fallen. But if you hold the thoughts of each loved one in your mind, I will ask the Linkage to recognize your traditions and fulfill the needs of your grief. Please close your eyes in a moment of silence for the fallen." Nicholas looked into the faces of the throng standing before him.

"Please call your traditions to you now."

Nicholas felt the ground tremble beneath his feet. Strata of loose, clattering rock along the path rattled together in small handfuls, then rolled apart. The shudder spread through the ground from an epicenter in a stone-laden field thirty yards away.

"The stones are gathering themselves," someone whispered in a wee voice.

"They seem to be alive," said another.

The throng lifted their heads. Nicholas glanced into the dark field. He saw sparks with the sound of each clattering stone. By the light of the sprites, they could detect shadowy objects moving. Stones in the field, the small, and the great, as if magnetized, gathered themselves into a circle, eight stones high. Into the circle, leaf litter and large dried logs stacked and bound themselves to one another.

"Nicholas!" shouted Beast, walking among the rows of dead. The bodies vanished from where they lay in the storage area. Stepping back, he pointed. "Where have they gone?"

"Where?" asked a troll. "Over there." He pointed the stubby finger of his stubby arm toward the field of rocks. The bodies rematerialized within the circle made by the stones.

Extending her closed hand, Crystal held it before Nicholas's face. She opened the fingers. "Take this, Nicholas," she commanded. In her ethereal palm lay a mirror the size of a large coin, tied to a lanyard. Nicholas took the mirror. "Use this to communicate with the dragon."

"But why—"

"I shall instruct you," she said.

He stood closer. Her light faded again. "Hold your needs in your mind, and look into the mirror. If they are able, they will come to your aid." Nicholas did as instructed. No sooner had he completed his thought than he heard the sweep of wings, like the whoosh and pop of wind caught in a massive canvas canopy. Nicholas looked up. A dragon descended from the sky. His heart racing, he rushed back, slicing through Crystal's body of mist. He heard a soft gasp in the crowd.

"*Do not fear!*" Crystal shouted. "Remain still and watch."

The dragon landed beside the circle and bowed to those gathered.

Over sixteen feet high, the dragon focused his golden eyes on them.

Golden rays of the sun glimmered over the mountains, painting the dawn above the eastern horizon. The dragon reared his head, then lowered it to the circle of stone where the bodies were now stacked. The dragon sent a blast of flame to ignite the funeral pyre. The conflagration burned for hours, consuming everything.

Everyone watched until the last ember died. By then, the heat of the sun had burned away the morning dew.

Climbing to the roof of the varda, Nicholas scanned over the heads of all. He looked into as many eyes as he could. "Thank you for honoring all who have fallen. Thank you," he said, his voice breaking, "for honoring my parents." Swallowing, he composed himself. Nicholas took a deep breath and sighed. "Help me honor their lives by joining me tomorrow. Together, after proper mourning, we will put a plan in action to end the treachery of Zili."

Only a faint glimmer of what she had been, the mist of Crystal was barely present. She lay what was left of her hand on Nicholas's cheek. "You have learned quickly and well, grandson. Know this: I dwell within your heart always," she whispered.

Nicholas had no time to reply. Crystal dissolved into scintillating light. Her image mixed with the morning rays and she was gone.

That night, for the first time in many moons, the aurora borealis fleetingly displayed the colors of peace.

Chapter 17

TIMING IS OF UTMOST IMPORTANCE

As a child, Nicholas had always enjoyed his trips to Elfin to visit his uncles. In the past it had meant pleasure or business, but this time his heart was empty. There was no joy. He would come with a heavy heart.

Now they were his only family, the last of his family. Nicholas was uncertain as to whether his uncles knew of their sister's and her husband's deaths. He had not talked with them since his submission to the church and his mission four months ago. The towns and villages were small, however, and bad news often traveled fast. He did not know how to tell them about Tom and Mary.

Outside the rectory, in the rain, Nicholas paced for some time before he decided to knock on the door. As he faced the wooden door, his uncle Mark by chance opened it to find him standing at the doorsill. Nicholas stood quiet, his head down, a bag at his feet. He was sopping from his shoes up.

"*Nicholas!*" Mark shouted, bounding back. "I was, uh, I was just about to leave when ... Well, there you are." He checked up and down the walk for anyone else. The rain continued to pour. "Are you alone?"

Mark asked, poking his head from the door, searching behind Nicholas.

Mark saw no one else.

"Nicholas is here. Alone," he shouted back into the rectory. His fingers behind Nicholas's neck, Mark ushered him into the front room. From another room, Nicholas could hear his other uncle.

"What do you mean, alone?" asked Bruno.

Father Mark quickly drew Nicholas near the fireplace. Nicholas saw Father Bernard standing at a table, holding a slicing paddle beneath a loaf of bread he had browned on a rack in the hearth. The smell of food caused Nicholas's stomach to growl.

"What brings you here?" Father Mark asked. "I mean, we are glad to see you. But Tom and Mary did not come with you?"

Having finished cooking, Bernard plated dinner.

"Join us, Nicholas," Mark invited, puzzled that Nicholas had not answered his question. Nicholas's other two uncles likewise gestured toward the table, begging Nicholas to sit, and sit he did.

Following prayers, they began the evening meal. From the start, his uncles knew something was wrong. Nicholas barely ate. They could see he was not himself. At their insistence, he told them his tragic tale, weeping continually. Eventually no one finished his meal.

They fell into grief.

Nicholas's reddened eyes searched their faces for solace, while his ears listened for some word of comfort. He told his uncles of Crystal and the things she had conveyed to him. "You know, uncles," he slowly said, sliding the remainder of his food around on his plate, "before I took vows with you, I never—I never thought I would have a role of importance in life. I worried. My dreams haunted me. I have had few silent nights. But for the lessons you've taught me, I would have been lost. They have suddenly become so essential. They have made me stronger. But my temper ... my temper, as of late, is still an issue." Nicholas exhaled, sad faced.

"Well, my son," said Bernard, "the more you practice patience, the better you'll become. Give it time.

"Mark and Bruno have just returned from the Kingdom of Waters," he continued. "Zili's people are still pillaging the villages, taking everything they can find."

"He continues sowing the seeds of not only discontent but also misery," said Mark.

"Tragedy and death," said Bruno. "If I were younger and not a man of God, I would …" Curling his fingers, Bruno slammed his fist to the table. Mark left.

"The people of the kingdoms are at the end of their rope," said Bernard.

"We've supplied the people; Zili has gladly supplied the rope," muttered Nicholas.

"The people are grateful for the things you have smuggled to them. Especially toys for the children. Your actions have allowed them to see that *good* is still in the world. You are good, Nicholas."

Returning, Mark passed a pewter pitcher around the table. "Beer?" he asked. Nicholas put his head down and peered over his forearm, his eyes searching the room. "Just milk from me," he muttered. "I want the children to grow up straight and strong, busy and happy."

"The parents cope much better when the children are busy and happy," Bernard agreed. He drank beer from a cup. He sighed, licking his lips. "The ships from Prussia are due to arrive Monday. It will do the people good."

"That won't be much help," interrupted Bruno. "Zili's men are already there to take the cargo. He is determined to starve the people." Bernard jutted and tightened his jaw as he turned diagonally in his chair. He stared into the flames of the hearth across the room. "Uncles, our plan of action appears to be right on time."

"Plans?" remarked Bernard.

Nicholas nodded. "As I've explained, he has Princess Sarah Morning-Light of Illuminae."

"He will force her into matrimony with him," Mark said.

"He'll try." Bruno raised an eyebrow.

"Exactly," said Nicholas. "He will be preoccupied with his plans for this sham, and will not discern the assets we will have put in place to defeat him—or our arrival the day after tomorrow."

Nicholas tapped the table. "Uncles. What do you know of the specific arrangements for this so-called wedding at Illuminae?"

"Already, there are many strangers in and around the castle," said Bernard. "There shall be more: caravans of troubadours, cooks, servants, dignitaries, soldiers, translators, and many others, all arriving for the celebration. They've been setting up their stations for the past thirty days."

"Thirty days," said Nicholas, tucking his underlip.

"Yes," said Bernard. "The wedding tent will be set up next to the chapel. I will officiate."

"Perfect," said Nicholas.

"Mark and Bruno will assist me during the Mass," said Bernard.

"Excellent," Nicholas said, his right hand gently grasping his chin. "Do you personally know any of the entertainers who will be setting up?"

"Why?" Mark asked.

"Because I'm looking for someone to guide me to the area where Sarah and the royals are being kept," Nicholas said.

They heard the creak and click of the front door as it opened and shut. Before Nicholas could complete his thought, a stoop-shouldered man hobbled up to the table. "I hope I have not disturbed you," he said.

"Who are you?" asked Mark.

"Yes. Who are you?" asked Nicholas. "I don't remember your knocking. Do you know it is impolite to enter someone's abode with no specific invitation?"

The man said nothing. From inside his dark blue vestment, he withdrew a leather parchment case. He untied the binding, unrolled it, and tossed it on the table. Although the three priests rarely locked their door, they startled by the old man's sudden, brazen, unannounced appearance, seemingly out of nowhere. They just watched.

"Start with this," said the stranger. "It will tell you where to begin."

"Who are you? And where did you get this? What is this?"

"Oh, please pardon me, sirs. My name is Gregory Hayman." He tipped his head. "I am a farrier of the elves' stables."

"Hayman? And you're a farrier. Why is a man who tends to horses on a mission of espionage?" asked Nicholas. He winked his eye and tapped his finger three times against the side of his nose. The truth came to his mind. He looked into the old man's eyes. "Huh, farrier indeed. Now, sir, that's not quite the whole truth, is it?"

The room went still. No one moved or spoke.

Nicholas's uncles and Mr. Hayman laughed and poked one another with elbows.

"I'm confused. What's going on?" asked Nicholas, breathing shallowly.

"So, Nicholas, your gift does work," said Mr. Hayman.

"Are you testing me?" asked Nicholas.

"A lie shall not escape your detection," said Hayman, untying his robe and laying it over the map. "Your uncles mentored you well. Oh yes, the maps are real. It is my name that is the deception."

"Then sir, pray reveal your name," Nicholas demanded, still befuddled, feeling like the victim of a charade.

The man took a bite of something hidden in his hand. His face contorted and his skin tightened. The hardtack in his hand transformed his appearance, one familiar to Nicholas. "I am Prince Wallace of Waters."

Nicholas's eyes widened. He bowed and smiled. "Pardon my brashness, Your Highness. I didn't know—"

"Forgiven." Prince Wallace clipped.

"Your Highness's disguise is much improved," Nicholas said. "You resembled nothing of the man who once stayed at my home. I had no idea that you were—"

"Your reaction pleases me. As I said, forgiven."

Nicholas cleared the dinner dishes from the table and poured steins of tea for everyone. Prince Wallace arranged the map of the castle in a way that all around the table could see.

"I have fifty men and women posing among the crowds at the castle. They have been positioning themselves throughout the grounds. Each identifies the others by a tricolored braided bracelet worn on the wrist: red, green, and gold silk. Here is the layout." He pointed to the map, which illustrated the land, moats, exterior, and interior walls of the castle. He had *X* marks indicating the likely places any captive might be held, and other marks for the positions of guards, watch towers, and key entrances to the castle, both well-known and hidden.

"This is good," Nicholas said. "My uncles have already had delivered very special presents to the castle. Terrariums." His uncles glanced at one another and seemed self-satisfied.

"Very special," Bernard said. "Tom built them for Queen Isadora. Now sitting in the castle are two large terrariums created with the assistance of our friends from the Orphic Forest. In Princess Angelica's room are thirty-six clockwork soldiers fully capable of fighting if needed. There are four steam-operated animals in the jousting arena: a lion, an elephant, a crocodile, and a hippopotamus. These can be used to hold back some of Zili's men. The royal guard whose loyalties lie with Alexander know how to operate all of our special presents."

Wallace looked long at Nicholas and his uncles. "I need only ask," he said, "and Zorna will gladly help us get the toys in motion. He has sent some of his dried meat with his surprise ingredient. And I know some secrets. Rodents and birds can help us get through the castle. All we need now is to know where my family is being held."

Chapter 18

THE RESCUE

Prince Wallace, Zorna, Joseph, General Raptozk, Lexi, and Nicholas reached the ridge above the clearing, which overlooked Castle Illuminae. Scarce foliage dotting the ground before the ridge gave them minimal cover. As the sun set behind the horizon, the delineating rays darkened the vermillion sky. Between the ridge and the forest, the castle sat. It cast long shadows upon the flat, cropped grassland in the valley surrounding the castle. From the mountain ridge, Wallace's men could easily observe the winding, yellow, dirt road coursing through the grassland to the castle. They knew the grassland was a potential killing field where they might confront Zili. No matter whether there or in the castle, there would be a fight.

Wallace and General Raptozk lay on their bellies, peering over. The escarpment leading to the ridge was high, rugged, and not readily breached. It could serve as a comfortable and safe locale for their opposing force's observation and encampment. Tied close by, the horses behaved restlessly, whinnying and sidling. A mile away, birds soared one hundred feet over the castle's highest tower, level with the height of the mountain ridge.

Leaning from his horse, pursing his lips, Lexi spat over the ledge. "A hundred-foot drop," he muttered, wiping his lips. "Up here I can see the whole field. I thought the castle would be built on the high ground."

"It is," replied General Raptozk, scanning the area. "This is just higher. But if you look …" He gestured, his arm arcing horizontally one hundred and eighty degrees, outlining the land from the horizon behind the castle to the ridge. "From here to there."

"Where we stand upon this ridge," Wallace said, "was heaved up by a quake in the years following the castle's construction." He paused, remembering. "I told my brother Alexander he should have begun new construction, but he didn't want to burden the people with more taxes for a new build." Wallace sighed, "Here is a good observation point for me, if I should ever need one."

General Raptozk looked to his right. "Nicholas," he said, "we have nearly six hours remaining before nightfall. I suggest we rest the horses and wait here until then. Move cautiously until night. It will be easier to conceal our presence in the dark."

From their vantage, Wallace and his men could see a small contingent of equestrians riding up the sinuous path through the grassland toward the castle. Wallace expected at least fifty of his men in common attire to arrive. But at the height of the mountain ridge, he could not discern whether these arrivals were friend or foe.

Lexi, Zorna, Nicholas, and Joseph backed from the ridge and dismounted. Gathering the leather reins, Joseph tied the horses to sapling trees and set feed and water for them.

"Please, my forest friends," Joseph asked, "would you keep our horses safely hidden until it is time for us to depart?" Nicholas observed with interest that Joseph was the one to appeal to the forest. No sooner had Joseph finished his question than a thin wall of foliage rose from the ground, thickened, and encircled the horses as a shelter. The sapling willows gently bent their graceful branches over the horses to form a lattice ceiling and wall. The branches cloaked them in a green blind.

Having spent some minutes and effort on his knees applying friction to wood with a stone, Lexi blew gently into the kindling lodged in the crease of the stone. When he finally encouraged the smoldering kindling to ignite, he broadly smiled. He was pleased with himself. Marching up behind, General Raptozk bent down and whispered over Lexi's shoulder, into his ear. "No fires," said General Raptozk, motioning to the castle below the ridge. "They will see the smoke from the watchtower. If they know we are here, it will endanger the princess's life." Lifting the sole of his boot, General Raptozk quickly crushed the infant fire.

Stars dotted the inky-black sky like diamonds faceting the blue, purple, and white Milky Way. All shone brilliantly in the cloudless sky. There was little wind, and the air was cool. Hidden among the small trees, the men huddled separately in their blankets, unsatisfied by the little heat they got from shivering. They often looked to the center of the camp, where the warmth and light of a fire should have been.

"I'm hungry," moaned a voice from the darkness. Lexi deeply kneaded his stomach like a knot of bread dough.

Joseph gave him a quick side glance. "For a man so thin, you are a hungry swine—a thin, hungry swine. Where is that fruit I gave you?"

"You mean this?" Lexi said. From a pouch he carried within his tunic, he withdrew a squashed, brown, and greasy mess of what was left of a banana.

"Wasteful. I don't know why I keep giving you those," Joseph snapped.

Amid groans, Lexi tossed the mangled fruit to the ground in the center of their circle. "I never get a chance to eat it," Lexi grumbled. "It hasn't much staying power."

"Neither do either one of you. Now, enough of this childish bickering," snapped Zorna. "Save your feistiness for the enemy. You'll need every last ounce."

Prince Wallace nodded. "Nicholas …"

"He has said nothing since our arrival," Joseph muttered. "Be like Nicholas. He does not complain." Joseph glanced at Lexi. "Look at him. He is planning. A man who thinks," Joseph said. Nicholas pulled his blanket over his face and turned on his side.

"He is a man with grief," said General Raptozk. "Mind your words, and leave him alone. He has a lot on his mind. We all do."

"And nothing in our stomachs," moaned Lexi. "Our bodies need sustenance."

Sitting up, Joseph rolled his eyes and lay back on the ground, his head resting on flat, smooth stone.

"I'm twenty. Unlike the rest of you, I'm still growing. Growing smarter." Lexi laughed, pointing at Joseph.

"Nicholas there is just eighteen. Sure, you're growing, Lexi," Joseph muttered, pointing toward his buttocks, "Like fungus on the skin of my a—"

"*What* did I say?" admonished Zorna, irritated by the childish banter. "We *shall* eat. I have prepared a method of heating our food with neither yellow, red, nor blue fire but a fire that is clear."

"A fire one cannot see or feel?" Wallace asked.

Zorna snickered. "Oh, you would feel it, all right. Now, gentlemen, lay your food out before you." Gesturing, he borrowed the flat stone upon which Joseph rested his head. Withdrawing a vial from his large pocket, he poured its contents onto the stone. The liquid soaked completely into the rock. The rock sizzled. With a wave of his hand, Zorna caused the food each man had laid out to gather and be suspended in the air just above the rock. The food began to heat and cook.

On impulse, Lexi reached for food. "Ouch!" he cried, hurriedly withdrawing his burned fingers, sticking his right forefinger and thumb into his mouth.

Zorna breathed deeply. "The fire is so hot, so all-consuming, that not only is it invisible, it will burn without light." Zorna smiled, using an arrow to skewer a piece of the hovering food. "The fire shall not likely give our position away, and we shall heat our food and stay warm. And it will burn if you are foolish enough to put your fingers within it."

Lexi studied his index finger and thumb.

"They are stung," Zorna said, "but they are not damaged." Dining on cured sausage and hardtack, their fingertips greasy from the meat, the men's bellies were satisfied. The horses cloistered in the blind remained quiet.

"When the sun breaks the horizon," Zorna said, "I will give us the potion. It tastes bad but works quickly."

"This night we sleep," Prince Wallace said. "Tomorrow we fight." As the night wore on, each man took turns keeping watch while the others slept.

※

The last to stand guard, General Raptozk lay on his stomach on a bare piece of ground twenty feet from where the others slept. As the sun broke on the horizon at his right shoulder, Zorna found the general peering left, northwest over the ridge to the castle and the surrounding grounds.

Briefly looking over his right shoulder, General Raptozk turned his eyes back to the castle. "Morning, wizard. Huh." Pointing to the castle, the general nodded. "I've been monitoring any goings on, movement in and out."

"Reconnaissance. Very good, General."

"I wouldn't be much of a general if I didn't, would I?"

"What have you seen?" Zorna asked, situating himself closer. "Much activity. It has picked up since just before sunrise." General Raptozk sighed. "It's easier when one's allies are in uniform," he muttered. General Raptozk felt exasperated that he was not out front, atop his horse, leading a charge, but he was more exasperated now that he could not tell friend from foe.

"You seem frustrated," Zorna said. "You have a daunting task, General."

"*We* have a daunting task, my wise friend," the general said, raising an eyebrow. "I've seen several foreign dignitaries arrive early this morning, some with their carriages marked by banners familiar to me, others not so marked." Rolling to his left side, General Raptozk peered up at Zorna kneeling beside him. "How is our champion?" He saw Nicholas sleeping, his mouth wide open. "He reminds me of a fledgling bird wanting to feed."

"Asleep, as you see." Zorna shrugged, looking over General Raptozk's shoulder, past the ledge. "Have you seen anything of Alexander?"

"No. Surely he is inside," General Raptozk muttered. "Zili is likely holding him in a very secure place, maybe those towers. There." The general gestured, pointing to the rear of the castle. "He wouldn't want to disturb his guests. He probably wants everyone to think Alexander is on a diplomatic mission. He's in the towers or the dungeon below, I wager. I feel it. I'm sure Zili realizes his brother Wallace will not allow his treachery to succeed."

"It is morning," Zorna said flatly, groaning, raising to his feet. "I must wake each man. Come with me, General." He marched to where the others slept. He passed from man to man. Starting with Joseph, he reached down. From half a dozen silken braids of red, green, and gold silk in his hand, he pressed one into the palm of each man.

"Tie these around your wrists," Zorna said. "We have friends inside; they also wear these."

"What are these adornments, my wizard?" asked Prince Wallace. "Are you now trying to pretty us?"

"With all respect, Your Highness, nothing will accomplish that," Zorna cracked.

Laughing, Wallace held the braid high for his men to see. "Anyone loyal to Alexander who wears a braid will feel a small vibration," said Zorna, "as will you. You can trust they will aid you in any way you need." When they tied their braids, the men felt the small vibration. Each mused at the magical charm passed to them by Zorna.

Wallace watched movement from the corner of his eye. Arising from the underbrush at Prince Wallace's feet, freshly fallen leaves danced in the wind but in an unusually ordered way. They crushed down to powder. The leaf powder took the form of a tiny man, no taller than a mouse. He spoke, startling Joseph.

"As per your command, Sire," he said, looking to Wallace, "beyond the forest, the outlying bridges to the Kingdom of Waters have been destroyed, but your return trails have been marked. We have thwarted Zili's plans. Two grain ships remain unharmed in the harbor. They are being unloaded and the cargo distributed to the people now."

Prince Wallace nodded in recognition. As the man deconstructed, the leaf powder forming him gently blew into the underbrush.

◈

"General, much longer?" Lexi asked, checking the position of the sun to his far right at the eastern horizon. "It is still just after dawn."

"Not long, Lexi," said General Raptozk. "About three hours. All our assets should be in place by then."

Joseph's eyes darted nervously as he tried to occupy himself. With a tall stick, he drew pictures in the dirt. He felt uncomfortable. "Does anyone else have the feeling we're being watched?"

Before anyone could answer, a large black raven dropped from the trees, landing before Prince Wallace. Its right wing outstretched, its left tucked at its black breast, it bowed.

"Sire. My name is Tapfer Krahe," said the bird.

Clearing his throat, Wallace glanced at Zorna and Nicholas. "I know something of you," said Wallace. "I have been told somewhat of your strange tale. I have not had the pleasure. So, tell me, who are you exactly?"

"I am more than I seem, Your Highness. Alas, my tale is a sad one. It is one of a life forced on me by my own actions and by Prince Zili."

"Please explain," said Wallace.

With small black eyes of pitch, the bird looked into those of each man. "For many years, I was compelled to serve your brother—His Highness Prince Zili—in his cause. Parenthetically, *His Highness* is an unworthy soubriquet." He sighed. The bird stood as straight and tall as it could. "I humbly beg your forgiveness. I ask that you accept my service to help defeat your brother." He knelt, his wings outspread.

Sneering, Lexi took a step toward the bird. "Lies. He is as big as a skunk and smells the same. Does he think us fools?"

"Sir, I speak the truth."

Lexi spun to address everyone. "Lies spew from his scrawny carcass as scat would from a goose." Lexi reached for the hilt of his sword. "For our next meal, perhaps I might fashion a blackbird-meat pie. T'would make a fine breakfast, would it not, Sire? Shall I—"

"*No*," Wallace commanded. "Rise, Raven." Wallace lowered to one knee. "Raven. Look me in the eye."

The raven did as he was ordered. Hanging from his neck, all could see a braid of red, green, and gold silk with a small amber stone tied at its apex. Their wrists vibrated.

"Stolen!" Lexi shouted. "I beg you to reconsider, Sire."

"Anyone connected with Zili cannot be trusted," entreated the general. "This—this thing is little more than a flying rat. He would lay our hearts on a silver platter."

"I'll have him on a silver platter, with a stein of beer on the side," Lexi muttered.

"Stop. Please, Sire." Nicholas raised his hand to settle the general. "I can tell without fail whether he speaks the truth." Nicholas drew near. "And he did speak true."

Wallace glanced at the other men. "So, let it be," Wallace said. "Raven, if you will help, there are things you may do for us."

The Raven's Tale

"And for you I will do anything you command, Prince Wallace," Tapfer Krahe said. "But I need you to know everything about me and my situation."

Leaping from the ground, the bird spread its wings and flew to the shoulder of Nicholas, where it perched. "Nicholas will alert you of any lies." The bird surveyed the dubious faces of everyone. "Many years ago, Sire, while King Richard's sons were still children, the king was in peace talks with the neighboring kingdom. His Highness's father, at the suggestion of his advisers, negotiated the marriage of one of his three sons to Princess Isadora of the Kingdom of the Four Winds. Alas, which son would marry her was left to be determined later. The sovereign of the Four Winds needed to ascertain which of Richard's sons would be the best husband for his daughter. So both kings decided to wait. Their written agreement included what was termed *the uncertainty Clause*."

The bird looked at Prince Wallace, who nodded for him to proceed. "The marriage would financially bind the two kingdoms," said the raven. "It would assure peace between the two nations. I, Sire, was a *man*, young, newly married, and learning my father's trade. My father was the falcon master for King Richard and had arranged for me to help the wizard clean his shop. To stack the decision in his own favor, young Prince Zili ordered a wizard—"

He hushed as Zorna shot him a disapproving glare, eyes flashing their dragon form. Tapfer Krahe continued. "In their late teens and twenties, the young princes met Princess Isadora on many social occasions. One prince took a fancy to her. That prince was young Zili. When he found out about the uncertainty Clause in the contract, he decided to stack the odds in his favor. He contacted a wizard for whom I worked. He commanded the wizard to put a potion in the princess's food to make her fall in love with him. Although Alexander was the firstborn, through deceit, Zili hoped to assure his ascent to the throne. He was determined to have Isadora betrothed to him. He, however, lost any chance of her love on the day your father died.

"Zili did not count on the wizard refusing to put a spell on a royal. This angered young Prince Zili. This is when he forced me to make the potion. I warned him of my incompetence. I was not a wizard's apprentice. I cleaned the shop. But Zili threatened my wife. Under duress, I took the bottles from the wizard's shelf and put the ingredients together according to his book of spells. Or so I thought. I said the incantation as written beneath the ingredients. But I must have said or done something incorrectly, because it did not work. Her love for him did greatly increase, but it was an unromantic, sisterly love. She married another—his brother Alexander, the rightful heir to the throne."

Prince Wallace glanced at Nicholas, who nodded to confirm the truth of the raven's story. "How did he force you to do this?"

Tapfer Krahe gazed into Wallace's eyes. "I should've gotten away. I should not have done his bidding. But my mother was also ill, and we could not afford the medicine. My father was a proud man, unable to accept the wizard's help without paying for it. I offered my service to the wizard as payment for her medicine. This is how I came to work for the wizard in the first place. I was glad to do it. I loved my mother. Zili threatened to kill my parents and my wife if I did not make the potion."

General Raptozk interrupted, "Why do you choose now to change your loyalties?"

"My loyalties have always been with Prince Alexander. Since my parents died, Prince Zili has continued to threaten my wife. He has someone shadow her always. His threats never end. I'm enslaved, and I must shed this burden."

The five men and the raven looked to Nicholas. Again, Nicholas nodded to confirm the truth of the raven's story.

"I understand. Pray continue," said Wallace.

"Yes, Sire. The wizard offered Prince Zili a compromise to spare my life. If Zili let me live, the wizard promised he would not tell King Richard of the prince's treachery. Agreeing, Prince Zili added the stipulation that only he would decide when I could revert to human form. I am grateful to the wizard for helping to spare my life. I was wrong, but I have been wronged. This was more than twenty years ago."

"Yet you are still cursed," said Joseph.

"Prince Zili often promises to change me back, only to renege." The raven sighed. "My wife has kept her loyalty to me, never lusting, never wandering. She still loves me despite my appearance and my inability to speak to her—alas another 'minor stipulation' of this curse. I may speak to others but not to the one I love," the raven muttered in despondent tone. "No matter the weather," he added, his voice quickening brightly, "she leaves a window open for me to spend the dark hours of the day."

Throwing up his hands, the general turned to walk away. Pivoting back on his heel, he faced the bird. "What does that mush have to do with—" He glowered.

With a stern glance, Prince Wallace raised his hand to silence the general. "What do you propose, Mr. Krahe?"

"Allow me and the insects, mice and rats—those you refer to as pests—to be your eyes and ears in and around the castle. We can go where no other can," he said proudly. His chest swelled. "No one guards his speech or actions in our presence. We can hear much."

Clasping his hands, Wallace paced before his men who nodded.

Lexi blinked tentatively.

"A fine offer," Wallace uttered. "What do you ask in return?"

"Yes, bird. What?" Lexi blurted. Wallace cast Lexi a cautionary glance.

Affrighted, the bird fluttered its wings as if to take flight. "*Wait*," commanded Wallace. "I *will* hear your terms."

The bird swallowed. "Allow your wizard," he said, seeing Zorna nodding behind Wallace. "Allow your wizard to return me to my human form. In return, I and my wife will serve out our days as your humble and loyal servants."

His hand on his chin, Prince Wallace raked his underlip with his top teeth. Holding the hilt of his sword with his left hand, he pointed with his other at the general and Zorna. He curled his finger for them to follow him. Together the trio walked a few feet. They huddled and spoke so softly that even the insects could not hear.

After speaking for several minutes, the trio returned to the bird, who was hovering. It landed back on Nicholas's shoulder.

"Nicholas."

"Yes, Sire."

"Does he speak truth or falsehood?"

"Truth, Sire."

"Then we begin our descent to the castle in an hour or two," said Wallace. "Mr. Krahe will go at once, find the location of the royals, and bring that information to me as soon as possible."

From Nicholas's shoulder the bird leaped to the ground and bowed before Prince Wallace. "Your Highness," said the raven, lifting his eyes to the sky. He jumped, folding his legs to his body. Outswept wings gulping air, he flapped gracefully, launching himself up and over the ridge, then down into the sparse mist rising in drafts over the grassland and castle below. Nicholas watched him disappear.

Beside him, Joseph stood peering into the valley. The bird was no more than a dot circling the castle towers. Within minutes, he entered through a narrow murder hole and vanished.

◈

Away from the ledge, Zorna handed out a pea-size portion of hardtack to Wallace, General Raptozk, and Lexi. Prince Wallace gestured for Joseph and Nicholas to come from the crest of the ridge and collect their portions. Hesitantly, each man swallowed the hardtack. Lexi placed the pea speck in his mouth. His tongue tingled with an acrid tang. He shook from his head to his feet.

"It's easier if you just swallow," Zorna said. "The transition won't be so painful."

"Painful? Ooo. But it is the *taste*," Lexi hooted, scraping his tongue behind his top teeth.

"The taste of my mother-in-law's soiled leggings," the general quipped, pursing his lips.

"How would you know such a thing?" Wallace cracked. The general tightened his cheeks. Prince Wallace closed his eyes, breathed deeply, and swallowed, contemplating his next move to stop Zili. He realized the general was right. Tensing, Nicholas and Joseph blew from their lips and sucked in their cheeks.

Wallace, Joseph, the general, Nicholas, and Lexi gazed pensively at one another. Not reacting to the flavor, Zorna swallowed his portion as if swallowing a cherry. He smacked his lips and slapped his stomach as if he had consumed a hearty meal.

"Ah, now friends," Zorna said, standing before and speaking to oak and willow saplings. "Please, would you kindly conceal our transformation?"

The ground holding the trees liquefied, releasing the trees from their moorings. Forming a circle around the men, the branches laced themselves together until the men could see no portion of sky. Their transformation completed, the trees returned to their original positions.

Prince Wallace bowed respectfully to the willows. "Thank you, my friends."

Chapter 19

THE CASTLE

Leaving the ridge, over the next hour Wallace and his men descended the escarpment via a rugged, brush-choked trail. Sometimes the trees closed in, crowding the narrow path even more; other times the path vanished entirely. At still other times, the path broadened, leveling into terraces comprising smaller ledges ending at drop-offs. Some were stark cliffs. Sometimes the trail ended abruptly, leaving the men to hack out alternate routes. They often dismounted, leading by the reins, their nervous and less than sure-footed horses down treacherous paths.

"Sometimes it is no more than a foot trail, Your Highness," said the general, hacking the stray branches not hacked first by Lexi.

"It is a treacherous way," muttered Lexi, out in front, taking care to place his feet surely. "There is much rubble and—"

"What would you have us do, Lexi?" Wallace asked. "Take care. Watch your step. This trail is dangerous, wet in places; there are roots arching across our path. It would be easy to catch your foot, fall, and break your neck."

"A fall might spoil your pretty face," Joseph said.

At that instant, Joseph's foot caught on a root bowed up from the path. Forward he flipped, hurling past Lexi. He fell. Bouncing on a short, steep path, he flipped over a low ledge. "HELP!" he screamed.

Lexi gave chase. The thud of Joseph's body hitting the path caused every man's eyes to turn to his direction.

"*Joseph!*" Lexi screamed, following after, keeping his balance. "*General!*"

General Raptozk turned sidewise to chase down the path after Lexi. Prince Wallace was behind him. Higher up on the hill, sliding through the brush, Zorna quickly looped the reins of his mount loosely around a thin root. He controlled his slide, sidewinding down the slick path.

"JOSEPH!" Lexi screamed. He leaped and skipped down the rocky decline. He came to the narrow ledge over which Joseph had flown. As he neared, he peeked over to the tops of trees far below. He feared Joseph had plummeted to the ground beneath the ledge.

As Lexi descended, the ground on which he tromped came up at such an angle that he was able to stabilize his descent by grasping roots looping from the ground near his shoulders. Above him, the general looked down upon Lexi, while holding on to an overhanging branch, his foot on a stone jutting from the ground, now a wall behind.

Lexi's foot rested at the edge of a foot-wide terrace. He braced himself by grasping roots poking from the dirt wall behind him. Carefully, slowly, over the ledge upon which he stood, he peered down at an increasing angle. He neither saw nor heard Joseph.

His sorrowful brow lifting, he glanced up to the general five feet above him, and Wallace behind him. Zorna peered over Wallace's back.

"He has fallen. Sire, I think ... I think he is dead."

"Give me your hand!" shouted the general, stretching his arm down, his fingers wagging. "Come on!" Lexi was reaching for General Raptozk's hand when he heard Joseph's voice.

"I am not dead ... yet. Help me!" cried a distant, quavering voice. Leaning at a greater angle to see over, Lexi felt the edge of the ledge crumble beneath his toes. He heard the rubble hit.

"Watch it. Those rocks hurt," Joseph shouted, sweeping the fallen rubble from his face. Lexi felt a blast of air hit him as he peeked over the ledge.

Suddenly, he saw Joseph rise above the ledge, clutched in the talons of the young dragon Ameryl. Nicholas was on the dragon's back. They hovered an instant and swooped to the ground seventy feet below.

"How did you?" Lexi muttered. His eyes fixed on Nicholas. Ameryl set Joseph back on the trail near Lexi. From a safe height, Ameryl observed them until they descended to a safe path. Slowly they made their way until they reached the forest floor intervening between them and the castle. It was midmorning by the time they reached the base of the escarpment.

At the bottom, they hitched their horses to trees in a thick part of the forest, to ensure they remained hidden from view of the watchtowers a thousand yards away. There the raven swooped to a branch to meet them. He watched for a moment or two as Joseph approached Lexi, tying his horse.

"You came for me," Joseph said softly, his left hand on Lexi's shoulder.

"Of course I came. We're like brothers," Lexi said. "We fight like brothers."

"No ... No," said Joseph, his face stern and distant. Lexi tensed, glimpsing his eyes. "Not *like*—we *are* brothers." They shook hands. The caw of the raven drew their eyes to a branch above.

"We must go," the raven said loudly, peering down. He flew to the ground. "I will lead you through the forest to the castle wall. There, I have comrades in arms waiting to meet us."

Soon they were at the castle wall. There the raven introduced them to the mice, rats, and ants that would be their guides.

"The southwest curtain wall, which runs beneath the stables, holds a secret passage that connects the upper towers and the chambers of the royals. It was constructed to allow them to escape in an overwhelming attack," said a mouse. "We can get in this way." The mouse scampered inside.

Lexi peered behind an overgrowth of thorny hedges up against the granite wall. "Behind this row of thorn hedges are great iron bars set into the stone into which this mouse ran," Lexi said. "We are much bigger than a mouse. How will we get inside? We cannot just walk through."

"It's big enough for the rodent. We shall make it big enough for us," said Zorna. He recited an incantation, and the black iron bars began to vibrate, singing softly like a tuning fork.

"Nicholas," said the raven, "this is where you enter. Just follow the signs to those you seek."

"What signs, Mr. Krahe?"

"You will see. But do not yet enter. The bars are not yet pliable," said the raven.

Zorna nodded.

"Please observe my friends as they position themselves on the soil before you," Mr. Krahe said, aiming his wingtip at the scampering varmints. Nicholas gazed as the mice, rats, and ants scurried about to demonstrate their acrobatics. Upon the damp stone rock before the bars leading into the tunnel, they formed arrows of several different shapes—straight and curved. "With these signals as navigational aids, they will make the way clear," said the bird confidently.

"Indeed, they shall be effective guides," Nicholas said, observing with amazement their synchrony and speed. Amused and astonished, Wallace and his men quietly chuckled.

"The signs will be quite clear," said Mr. Krahe. "Are you ready to begin?" Mr. Krahe beckoned Lexi and Joseph to come closer and stoop beside him.

They stooped.

"It is vital," said Mr. Krahe, "that you remember this passage, for there are many like it." The bird gazed into their eyes. "There is a maze of tunnels through the castle, most long forgotten; many appear the same. Some of them are dangerous and may lead to traps from which you might not return. I caution you: watch your landmarks."

Joseph began to titter.

"Do you find something amusing, boy?" the general snapped, scowling down to Joseph, who was stooped before the bird.

"I'm sorry. As he tells us what to do, he is like—like a *little* general." He snickered. "Like you, sir." Joseph grinned, pointing at Mr. Krahe.

Joseph looked up into General Raptozk's stern face. "Not that you are little, sir. You are not, but …" General Raptozk was not amused. Joseph stopped grinning.

"There is a time for levity, Joseph," said Lexi. "This is not that time."

"We have a battle to wage," General Raptozk said, glaring at Joseph.

"Once you were nearly killed by your own bungling. Try not to succeed where you failed before. *Listen*."

"Thank you, General." The raven was pleased to have elicited a modicum of faith from such skeptics as the general and Lexi. "If we must divide our efforts, or if we lose contact with one another for a great length of time, return. We shall meet here."

Nicholas said a silent prayer. Turning to Joseph and Lexi, he blessed them with the sign of the cross. Nicholas used the mirror from his pocket to show their exact location to General Raptozk and Prince Wallace. Nicholas spoke to the mirror. "Sire, we have begun." Approving, Prince Wallace nodded.

Closing his eyes, Nicholas brushed the thorny hedges with his fingertips. Wallace and his men watched. Zorna stood behind Nicholas, his hand on his shoulder.

"My hedgerow friend," said Nicholas, "will you please allow us to pass?"

Nothing changed. Nicholas peered curiously at Zorna.

"What? Is something supposed to happen?" asked Joseph impatiently. "I know. We could tie one end of a rope around the hedges, another onto the saddle of the horse and—"

"Let Nicholas," Wallace said, cutting in.

Nicholas repeated his words. "My hedgerow friend, will you please allow us to pass?"

The hedges parted, exposing the drainage port with the vibrating bars. Nicholas placed his hand upon the stones binding the iron bars. The stone began to crack, and rubble poured like sand to the bottom frame and soil behind the hedge base. Clanking, the loosened bars fell from the shattered stone. The three men passed through the gap in the remaining bars.

"Move as silently as possible and follow the rats," said Nicholas.

An army of large black ants, roaches of all sizes, and several dozen mice and rats surrounded the men as they coursed among the passages through the belly of the castle. They eventually ascended near the dungeons where they suspected Zili had imprisoned the royals. They spiraled up dark, humid stairs until they reached the level of the main bailey. There, the stairway ended at the wall of the tower of dungeons. From some distance, they could see the guarded entrance. Perhaps one or two at a time but certainly not as a group would they be able to just stroll in and break the royals out. Their numbers would arouse suspicion. Climbing still higher, they went passed the armory walls and proceeded to the chambers of the royals. There, they would perhaps find some clue of Sarah—not likely, in their estimation, held in the dungeon.

Five mice formed an arrow at the wall. Nicholas placed a finger to his lips, gesturing for Joseph and Lexi, on either side of him, to maintain their silence. By their necks, Nicholas tugged them to him. "You will go to the towers. I will continue up the stairwell to the chambers of the royals to free Sarah," Nicholas whispered.

"How do you know she is there? Lexi asked.

"I feel it. Zili wants to marry her and gain her sympathies. And locking her in the dungeon would only further alienate her."

Nicholas noticed something in the masonry. "See that?" He pointed to the wall a foot or two away from them. "See? That lever hidden between the masonry, on that curved granite wall."

Lexi and Joseph looked but they could not see. Not much light reached that area, and it was nearly dark. Squinting, they could make it out, a narrow, hand-sized channel in the wall. They nodded.

"What is it?" asked Joseph. Lexi peered quizzically at Nicholas.

Nicholas supported his upper body with one hand on the wall. Leaning forward, he reached into an alcove with the other hand and pulled the lever. A narrow wall passage opened before them. Lexi and Joseph stepped from the stairwell onto the new landing and into an area of shadows. The musty corridor was dim and narrow, lit only by wall-mounted, oil-filled lamps flickering in the cold draft. Doors positioned every fifteen feet on the interior wall offered access to the castle interiors.

"Maybe we are between the inner and outer walls," Joseph muttered.

Nodding, Lexi said nothing.

On the outer walls, shuttered murder holes and small barred and shuttered windows offered no light to guide their passage. They came to a dead end. Lexi pushed on the two-foot-wide wall. It moved. Harder he pushed, and the hinged wall opened a wider but dim main corridor. No sooner had they entered the open corridor than Lexi and Joseph heard the faint jangle of keys. They could see the shadow of a guardsman cast on the floor from down the hall of an intersecting corridor. The shadow grew as he approached.

Their hearts raced.

Each slowed his breathing, while wishing Zorna had given them invisibility instead of just new faces. Pressed against the cold stone wall, they remained quiet. Next to Lexi and behind, Joseph clasped his arm.

"What are we going to do?" Joseph whispered.

Their true identities magically concealed by Zorna's hardtack, their corporeal bodies were still as vulnerable as any man's to any weapon. If caught, they still could not account for their presence in a restricted area. They really hoped they would not have to.

Tilting his head, Lexi, signaled to Joseph to follow him. They slid along the wall, remaining in the shadows until they ducked into an archers' station, a small room opening midcorridor. They heard the footsteps turn the corner and the jangle of keys approach them. The sounds were getting louder.

Cautiously peering around the corner, Joseph began making out the man's shape. "I sure hope, whoever you are, that you are loyal to Alexander," Joseph muttered, his sword clasped tightly in his hand.

Lexi, stooping beneath Joseph, also peered around the corner. He could feel Joseph's breath at the back of his head. Closest to the floor at the archway, Lexi stole stealthy glimpses of the corridor. The footsteps grew louder, closing in on the archers' station. Quiet, they remained crouched.

"If thee are an evil smidgen," Lexi whispered in the shadows, "one of us shall die today." He slowly drew his sword. "I shall pray for your soul or your good fortune that our wit and magic have kept us hidden."

When he stopped his prayer, the footsteps stopped at the archway. The braid bound around Lexi's wrist vibrated, calming his fear.

"Whoever you are," said the man, "I feel your vibration. So, if you don't foolishly kill me, we shall get started on freeing the king and his family," He was a bulky castle guard, rubbing the braided band on his wrist. Observing the keys on his belt, Lexi and Joseph looked at each other and grinned.

"Zili's rebels have continued moving the royals," said the guard. "Sadly, it will be a game of chess to find them."

They're Here

Amid the muck of the dank, low tunnels, a division of ants, mice, rats, and roaches scurried far ahead of Wallace's men. Through the walls, rafters, and floors, scattered varmints diffused throughout the castle like water. Out from the crevices of the stone walls, along the floors, and among the ceilings; into various corridors, castle keeps, closets, and living quarters, the army of critters slipped unnoticed. Like minute military batteries, they fanned out along the restricted recesses of the castle, searching for any recent signs of the king and his family.

At a rear castle tower, Lexi and Joseph stealthily tipped up stone steps in a spiral staircase, their backs close to the cold stone. Lexi trailed Joseph by a stair or two. Lexi remained vigilant, peering below for anyone who might enter the staircase, guards especially. Joseph watched for anyone coming down. Both listened for any footsteps around the cylindrical wall where they could not see. The last thing either of them wanted was to become trapped and have to fight hand-to-hand in the restrictive staircase.

Clutching the keys handed to him by the friendly guard at the archers' station, Lexi held them tightly in his sweaty fist to prevent their jangling. Step-by-step, Joseph crept up the staircase, both men careful to dodge the half-foot square windows and arrow slits at various points along the inner aspect of the circular outer tower. Neither man wanted to chance being seen by anyone on the ground who might happen to glimpse up at the right time.

They crept higher.

Joseph could see that within a few steps, the stairs ended at an open, unfenced terrace facing the blue sky. Both could feel the breeze blowing onto the wooden terrace. Both could hear the screech of the birds in the outlying forest.

"What will we do when we find the king and his family?" asked Joseph, his voice echoing in the tower stairwell, looking down at Lexi on the steps below.

"First," Lexi quietly admonished, "keep your voice down." He gestured by pinching his lips. "It carries in this stairwell." His eyes darted up and down. "I *would* like to come out of this with my throat intact."

"Well?" Joseph whispered, nodding, his eyes likewise darting up and down the stairwell.

"Well, what, you nuisance?"

"What shall we do if we find the king and his family?" said Joseph. "We shall do as we were instructed, of course," Lexi whispered. "If we need to fight to free them, we shall. We will crush any opposition, fight our way out, secrete King Alexander and his family from the castle, and get them to the shire ridge."

"Then what?"

"What do you think, Joseph?" said Lexi. "We'll deliver them to his brother, Prince Wallace, and with a little faith—" Lexi hesitated. "The general and Zorna will transform and fly them to where they'll be safe." Tilting his head, he extended his arm and one finger, gesturing for Joseph to hush.

"If any one of them is hurt," Lexi whispered, "oddlings will tend to their needs." A finger to his lips, Lexi crouched and gestured for Joseph to do the same.

"Listen. Up the stairs," Lexi whispered. They curved their bodies along the rounded inner stone wall of the stairwell. "I hear—"

"Nothing. It stopped," Joseph said, grinning, "We can go up. It's clear." Joseph bounded up three to five stairs.

"*Wait*," Lexi shouted at his heels, reaching for him.

Thud. Kicked backward in the stomach, down the steps Joseph fell, groaning. He had slammed into a beefy tower guard, clad in a chain mail coif, standing at the top of the stairs. Surprising the intruders, the guard had kicked Joseph in the torso and was raising his ax. Caught in Lexi's arms, Joseph defensively threw up his arms. At the instant before the guard could bring down his ax, a massive, hissing cockroach sprang from a crevice in the wall and onto the guard's face.

Startled, the guard screamed like a child. With a head butt, Joseph rammed the man in the gut. Trundling him along the wall, he forced the confused guard back up the three or four stairs to the landing. Still spinning, the guard frantically slapped at the cockroach on his face. His eyes shut tightly, he twisted in a disordered, frantic rush backward, the bug still stuck to the center of his face. Whirling, he hurled himself off the terrace and plunged fifty feet below into the brush behind the castle.

Lexi rushed up to the terrace platform. Joseph followed, massaging his stomach.

Peering around the open terrace and the plank floor, Lexi spun. "What do you think this is for?" he asked, peering out from the unfenced porch to the forest behind the tower.

His back to the open terrace, Joseph leaned forward, his hands on his knees to support his upper body. Joseph did not much care to guess its use. He was in pain. He thought his rib might have been cracked or bruised, and he had a headache starting.

"What's that?" Lexi whispered, tilting his head. He heard sounds. He hoisted his finger to his lips. "Joseph. Quit your moaning. Listen."

Joseph turned to face the terrace outlook.

"Hear that?" Lexi asked.

"Aye, voices," Joseph said.

"Voices. Moaning voices," Lexi said, sucking his cheeks. Lexi stood erect.

Joseph took a deep, painful breath and pointed with his chin to a corridor to their right. "Through there."

As they took their first steps, they both heard muted screams and people moaning.

"Heaven help them," Lexi whispered as they crept toward the poorly lit corridor. They stopped by a short wooden stool stationed by the archway leading into the corridor.

"Likely the seat of your dance buddy, the guard," quipped Lexi.

Joseph rubbed his chest.

A burning oil lamp was set low on a wall sconce above the stool, while subsequent lamps leading into the corridor were set high.

"He sat here," Lexi said, peering down at the well-worn stool.

"I see his fat cheek marks in the seat." Joseph snickered.

With the tip of his shoe, Lexi tipped up a lead platter upon which rested a large roasted hock of swine and a chunk of hard bread. With his foot, Lexi fanned away the flies. "This must have been his lunch, and this upturned chalice, his drink."

Joseph held his nose. "The smell ..." He coughed. "I would not feed that to my little snaggle-tusked water strider."

"When did you have one of those disgusting Outland creatures?" Lexi asked, watching Joseph retch.

"It is not his lunch that smells," said Joseph. "It's the odor from this corridor—wet hay, dirt, smoke, and ..." Joseph flexed the crook of his right arm to his nose and coughed.

"Blood," Lexi muttered. "I smell blood wafting on the drafts. And it comes from there as well. Not only that, but I smell excrement." Lexi stepped into the corridor.

"Wait. Before we go too far," Joseph said. From the sack suspended from his shoulder, Joseph removed a tin of camphor salve and smeared it under his nose. "Here." Bobbing the tin toward Lexi, Joseph gestured for him to do the same.

"This is the smell of death and mayhem," Lexi said. "I have to think. We are in the towers of torture. We are on a terrace useful for watching the rear approach of this castle."

"Or throwing your enemies over," said Joseph. "Like our fat friend, the guard."

"But this structure goes down as well as up," said Lexi, his ear to the wall. "Below must be the dungeons."

"This is Alexander's castle. Would he even have such a place as this?" Joseph asked, incredulous of the implication a torture chamber would have on the reputation of benevolent King Alexander Dobromil.

Lexi stared into Joseph's face. "I believe, over the years, much was hidden from the king," he said. "I am certain this has less to do with what Alexander might have permitted, and more to do with what Zili has engineered." Joseph nodded. "He was the sheriff and his methods have always been suspect," said Lexi. "I would wager Alexander has never even been to this part of the castle. I have seen this type of place before. The more punishment you are deemed to deserve, the deeper in this edifice they place you." Lexi peered to the stairs. "We need to go down to the dungeon."

"We have keys," Joseph said. "We must release all those imprisoned here."

Through the archway they dashed.

Soon, Lexi and Joseph stood in a narrow hall. Rows of thick, heavy oak doors with tiny, shuttered vents lined the walls. Having second thoughts, the two men paced furiously. Lexi struck the wall.

"Damn. Whom should we release?" Lexi shouted. "Who is friend?"

"More importantly," Joseph muttered, peering at the rows of prison doors, "who is foe?"

On the floor, they saw an assembly of critters: mice and rats. Several mice lined up in the formation of arrows at some doors, and at others the rats formed *X*s.

Once Lexi and Joseph released those loyal to the king, they continued down to the dungeon.

"There, we may find Alexander," Lexi said.

In the bowels of the castle Lexi and Joseph stood in an octagonal anteroom. Reinforced with steel straps holding oak slats together, eight heavy black doors on each wall led to the prison halls, along which were dark prison cells.

"Which way? Which way?" Joseph ruminated, spinning from one door to the next. "Which way?"

"Any of these doors may lead to the king and his family," Lexi said quietly.

"I could just yell."

"And bring the castle guard down on our heads," Lexi said. "Did you lose your mind when you head butted that hulk on the stairs? The whole of the castle guard would be down on us like a pack of wild yetis. Think, Joseph."

Stifled by the complexity of the stockade, Joseph and Lexi made several false starts before they saw four mice form an arrow to indicate the door to the corridor that might lead to the king.

"The third door to the left," Lexi said.

Joseph lifted an ax above his head to strike the oak door. His hand quickly upon Joseph's shoulder, Lexi dangled the keys beside his face and grinned.

"Sure, but which one? Joseph asked. "Is it even on that ring?" They crept through the hall until it opened into a circular cell block, encircled by a plank walkway. The cells were set back from the walkway. A down staircase led to the sunken center of the cell block, a torture chamber at its center. All cells had a view of the torture chamber from above.

Posted at the entrance of the cell block sat a five-foot-tall, five-foot-wide armed guard on a short wooden stool. Sleeping, the guard had angled his stool back against the wall, saliva soaking his long black beard.

From several yards away, Lexi and Joseph watched as a carpet of red and black army ants gathered from all directions. The moving carpet of ants surrounded the guard. They furtively crept closer. No matter where they stepped, the floor around Lexi's and Joseph's feet remained clear of ants. They seemed to purposefully leave islands of floor so Lexi and Joseph could walk. From their place of safety, Lexi and Joseph were astonished as the ants linked themselves together before the guard. The black ants twisted and climbed until they rose to a solid mass, an exact replica of Prince Zili's seven-foot-tall, armored Black Knight. The black ants became his armored body, the red ants his hair and eyes.

"I shouldn't enjoy this." Lexi snickered. "But this should be good." Completely raised and completely formed from the hoard of ants, the sham knight shouted to the slumbering guard. "FOOL!"

Startled by the booming voice, the guard flailed, his angled stool shooting from beneath his buttocks.

"How dare you sleep on duty?" shouted the knight.

Back sliding down the wall, the sleep-drunk guard landed sharply on his buttocks.

"I should have you tied to your own rack," sneered the Black Knight, its red eyes going to the rack at the center of the torture room.

"Milord, I-I-I," the guard stuttered, scrambling to his feet. "I thought you were on quest in the Outland, milord." The short, round man stared up into the red eyes of the Black Knight.

"Prince Zili demands a report on his brother," said the Black Knight. "You will open this door and stand your post. Or shall I let Prince Zili know how you *do not* carry out your duty?"

Turning clumsily, the guard fumbled for the key among many on his ring. The guard's voice quavered. "Sir. Right now, milord." He separated out the proper key.

From behind the knight, a troll wearing a wrist braid appeared from the shadow. The fat guard leaned forward, staring down at the troll.

"A toll to pass you did not ask; now you become a man of brass." Hearing another voice, the guard spun. "What is this? Who—" Laughing and dancing, the troll reached out and touched the

inattentive guard on the knee. From the knee up, the man slowly stiffened into a brass statue. From the knee down, his leg remained flesh and flexing. Lexi snatched the keys from the guard's hand an instant before it stiffened into a permanent brass fist.

"This one," Lexi said, holding out the key. Both men watched the replica of the black knight deconstruct and the red and black army ants scatter away.

Chapter 20

SARAH FOUND

In another part of the castle, several flights up, Nicholas found the humid staircase had grown warmer. At the top, he could ascend no higher. Climbing the last steps, he reached a small landing. The steps led to left and right archways. Both archways led to long corridors: one corridor to the king and queen's chamber, the other to their chamber staff and guards.

"Which way? Which way?" Nicholas muttered, tapping his finger against his nose. He turned on his heel from one archway to the other. "Which way?" He raked his fingers back through his hair. Hearing chattering, he looked to the stone floor before him. He was delighted to see ten mice make a right-angled arrow leading to the royal chamber in the left corridor. Into the corridor he dashed.

His delight was short-lived.

The corridor was long and there were many doors. Immediately, his frustration compounded. There was no doubt in his mind that Sarah was held captive here. Somehow, he could feel it. But which room? He remained cautious, knowing that dashing into a room full of armed captors was a choice that would net him poor results.

Removing the mirror from his pocket, Nicholas held it tightly in his hand. "Show me the queen's chamber," he whispered, staring into the tiny mirror. If by chance they peered into Hezia's mirror, Prince Wallace and the general would see what Nicholas saw.

"The black door," Nicholas uttered. He charged the black door but stopped within inches of his nose. His heart pounded. He wanted to knock on the door; he wanted to scream "Are you all right?" but he also wanted to remain stealthy.

Instead, he smoothed his palms over the wood as if to feel for weaknesses. The door was eight feet tall and five feet wide. Having made a few for the castle with his father, he knew them to be at least three inches thick. Clasping the curved handle, he carefully squeezed the trigger lock so it would not click. He leaned into the door. Locked.

The cast-iron slide bolt on the inside was likely engaged, but crosswise at the end of the bolt, a slug prevented it from sliding through the loop shackle. Nicholas carefully put his ear to the door. He could hear the clanking armor of at least two guards just behind and on either side of the door. He could hear them talking.

Unaware on the other side of the door, Sarah sat unbound at a small table positioned in front of the fireplace beside the bed. A hog-faced guard bearing tusks chatted about her with a human guard as if she were not present. He watched as a handmaiden combed Sarah's hair, while another poured a glass of tea for her.

"Royals. Huh." The hog-faced guard huffed, his speech muddled by tusks curling from his upper and lower jaws. "Look at her in her crown and jewels, her supple nose and mouth, her soft features, green eyes, and yellow hair. She is no pig. I can hardly stand to look at her. She's just a woman, and a skinny one at that."

"What are you snorting about, Hog?" chided the human guard, "She is a beautiful human girl. Zili has much interest in her. In his realm, she will be our queen. I should watch my tongue if I were you."

"Huh," the hoggish guard snorted, lifting his snout. "There's not meat enough on her bones to provide a substantial meal."

Sarah glanced coyly at the hoggish beast, smiled, and nodded to her handmaiden.

"Will there be anything else, Your Highness?" asked the handmaiden.

"Later," Princess Sarah said, folding her hands in her lap. "When this is over, perhaps you will provide me with some … sustenance. Perhaps more drink, a slice of bread, and …" She paused. "A slice of ham."

Peevishly wrinkling his snout, the swine jutted his head forward and growled. She could smell his fetid breath from across the room.

Simpering yet poised, Sarah casually looked away. Nervously snickering up her sleeve, the handmaiden curtsied while backing to her stool near a full-length mirror.

The mirror stood next to the head of the queen's canopy bed. Adjacent, an archway led to Princess Angelica's sleeping area. Silk curtains drawn back from the archway divided her chamber from the queen's room. It remained open. Angelis, the doll Nicholas had made for Angelica, lay where the princess should have been sleeping. The three terrariums made by oddlings of the Orphic Forest stood against a far wall near the window, their high tops just below the ceiling.

Scattered about the chamber lay the princess's clockwork toys: a dozen mechanical soldiers, four feet high, poised to fight. They stood beside miniature polar and grizzly bears, a lion, and an elephant, all no smaller than a large breed dog. Keeping them company, mynah birds nested within the terrarium.

Nicholas knew he needed to get into that room. He had heard Sarah's voice, and he needed to get her out. Into his pocket he slipped his hand and again withdrew the mirror. Desperately, he hoped for something that would help him get her out.

"Mirror. Show me something that can help me."

The minute reflection of himself in the mirror vanished, replaced by a visual of the room. He could see Sarah, her handmaidens, and Zili's two guards. He saw nothing in Sarah's room that could help him, but in Angelica's he did. He saw the toys.

"Good," Nicholas murmured. "I see some old friends who can lend a hand ... or at least a tooth."

He prayed, "Grandmother Crystal, you told me I have all the powers of the Linkage. You said I should think about what is needed and ask for help. If truly needed, the Linkage will help."

Completing their chores for the morning, one of Sarah's handmaidens sashayed before the human guarding Princess Sarah. She curtsied and spun slowly before him. Her hands perched on the hips of her brown bodice, she looked him over, up and down, smiling coyly. He grinned, his heavy beard and moustache hiding the few teeth remaining in his salivating mouth. She glanced at her mistress, Sarah.

"We would like to leave now so we might attend to our ... other royal duties," the first handmaiden said. The second handmaiden stood behind her.

"*No.* You will stay here and out of trouble," the human guard said.

"Your master Zili has instructed you to watch the princess. Has he not?" asked the first handmaiden. "As you see, we are not she." The untidy guards looked at each other.

"Did your master not say to treat the princess with all the respect of your future sovereign?" said the second handmaiden.

"Well, I guess," said the human guard. The hoggish guard only sneered, while picking his hoof-like nails with the tip of one curled maxillary tusk.

"If that is so," she said, "why do you guard her like a prisoner? Because you were told?" the second handmaiden asked.

"No ... Yes," The human guard snapped, easily becoming befuddled.

"Do you always do what you are told?" asked the first handmaiden. She glared at the hoggish guard.

"*No.* I mean, *yes,*" snapped the hoggish guard.

"Yes ... I think?" The human guard said. Each turned to the other.

"Huh, you are—you are trying to make fools of us," snarled the hoggish guard, baffled.

"Oh no. I do not have to *try*." The first handmaiden smirked. "You may leave—I guess," grumbled the human guard. "Then you must leave with us," said the first handmaiden. "You are trying to trick us," both guards said simultaneously. "No tricks. That would be taking advantage of you." She smiled. "But you do have to leave," said the second handmaiden. "For your staying alone with Her Royal Highness would be improper. You cannot stay with your future queen without a lady chaperone."

"No, no," said the first handmaiden. "It is unheard of."

Stoic, Sarah watched the attack of the handmaidens with interest. The guards unlatched the door. Hesitating, they strolled out behind the women.

After everyone had gone, Sarah dashed to the door and relocked it. The guards marched through the hall and watched as the two handmaidens sauntered down the corridor to the landing, then down the stairs. The maidens furtively soothed the vibrating bands on their wrists.

Distracted by the maids, the human guard—first through the door—never noticed Nicholas ducking behind a buttress at the next door. Nicholas held his breath. At his left, at the buttress, was a second door. Reaching, he tried the lever. It did not work.

"Crystal," he thought, "there's no time like now."

Nicholas placed his hand on the wall; he felt it soften. It dissolved into a cloud. Through it, he stepped into Sarah's lit fireplace. The wall immediately resolidified.

Sarah gasped as Nicholas stepped into the lit fireplace. Not singed, he slapped soot from his torso. As Nicholas looked up to Sarah, the hoggish guard knocked at the door.

"I hear talking. Who is in there? I hear talking." Key in the lock, his shoulder against the door, the hoggish guard pushed the door open. His eyes met Nicholas's as Nicholas hugged Sarah.

"Halt. Who are you? *How did you get in here?*" demanded the guard. "INTRUDER! INTRUDER!" he bellowed into the corridor, his voice echoing. "In the queen's chamber!" He ran for reinforcements.

Taking Sarah by the hand, Nicholas stepped backward into the fireplace, Sarah still on the floor. She tried to tug him out of the fire. He laid his hand upon the wall, but this time it did not open. "Sarah, you have to believe for this to work," Nicholas whispered, his eye entreating.

"He is crazy," said one guard. "Look at him. He walks in fire."

"And is unburned," whispered another, cowering as he inched forward. He clasped Sarah's wrist, but she twisted from the guard's hand. The guard fell into the flames, screaming as he burned. Rolling from the fire, the guard slapped ash and smoldering cinders from his clothing.

More castle guards loyal to Prince Zili hurried down the hall from both directions. Leaping from the fireplace, Nicholas drew his skinning knife from the holster on his leg. He shoved Sarah behind him with his other arm. Perplexed by his inability to open the passage, Nicholas was angry. His thoughts raced.

Suddenly he heard Tom's words repeating in his mind: "An angry man will never accomplish what he sets out to do. Think before you act. Do not only react."

Calm yourself, thought Nicholas. Remember what you've been taught. You've sparred with these men.

The room crowded with guards, Nicholas looked around for an escape route. His mind reeled with so many thoughts. He heard Father Bernard's voice in his mind. Father Bernard always said, "Keep your faith strong. Keep yourself and the innocent safe from harm."

Nicholas thought, breathe. Calm yourself. Think.

The guards gathered at the door. Assembled, they hesitantly strode toward Nicholas and Sarah. Time seemed to move in slow motion.

Nicholas heard his grandmother Crystal's voice: "Nicholas when you truly need them; but only when you need it. You will have all these powers at your command."

The guards stepped closer, attempting to circle him as a pride of lions might an antelope.

Nicholas heard Crystal's voice again in his mind: "To use the Linkage, you need not speak the words aloud. You must merely ask permission."

Nicholas took a deep breath. Exhaling slowly, he said to himself, "Beings of the Linkage, if you agree with my actions, please give me strength. Assist me in the task before me."

Spreading out, suspicious of witchcraft, the guards stayed back, forming a semicircle around Sarah and Nicholas before the fireplace.

"Why is everyone frightened of a boy with a small knife?" asked one human guard.

"He is bewitched," said another. "We've heard of him. This one is renowned for having … great magic at his call. We have seen it, my leader. He was in fire but not of the fire."

"He walked in fire and was unburned!" shouted another.

Their backs to the fireplace, Nicholas and Sarah began sidestepping their way toward the door. The guards advanced on them.

"Nonsense!" shouted the leader. "He is just a boy. You will prevent them from leaving."

"Halt. Stay where you are. You are both coming with us," said several others, some crouching, their arms forward in a cautious posture. Others brandished swords.

"I am prepared to defend Princess Sarah at all cost," snarled Nicholas. Tightly, he held his knife waist high. His elbow close to his side, he took short steps while watching the guard closely. Hidden behind Nicholas, Princess Sarah reached behind to the fireplace. Within one hand she grabbed a poker from the fire, and with the other a shovel.

"Sarah, stay behind me," Nicholas cautioned, gritting his teeth. Several more guards pushed their way into the queen's quarters. "You need the whole army for little old me?" quipped Nicholas in a falsetto voice.

As they reached to grab Nicholas, he parried their thrust, blocking their reach with the flat of his knife. From beneath his cloak, Nicholas yanked a hammer from his tool belt. With the hammer, he blocked a sword that neared his shoulder. Four guards moved in to surround the pair, each swinging swords.

"You will surrender!" shouted the leader, lunging forward.

"Take that!" Sarah shouted, stabbing one guard, too near, with the poker. She pulled back quickly.

"Stay behind me," Nicholas repeated sternly.

Brandishing their swords, the guards continued to advance. Nicholas blocked a hammer with his knife. His elbow took a glancing blow from the blade of a sword. Cut, bleeding, he crouched. Pivoting on the ball of his left foot, he whirled. His foot extended, he quickly swept the guard off his feet. The guard toppled to his back, his feet up in the air. Darting forward, Sarah stabbed the guard in the calf with the poker.

From the other room, Nicholas could hear the grinding of gears. Nicholas and Sarah saw the clockwork toys enter. Teeth of the mechanical animals gnashing, they clasped on to the clothing and flesh of several guards, while the swords of the toy soldiers thrashed, inflicting leg wounds on others.

"Sarah!" shouted Nicholas, his ear ringing with the clang of a sword hitting near his ear.

"*What?*" she snapped, smashing—*clang*—the head of a guard with the shovel.

"Stay back. Please," insisted Nicholas, blocking and parrying sword hits and lunges. *Clang. Clang.* "You're going to get hurt."

"I can—" Sarah swung the shovel, "—take care—" she uppercut a guard with the shovel, "—of myself." She hit a guard across the jaw with her fist. "Let me." Hoisting up the hem of her gown, she kicked a guard in the groin. He slowly sank to his knees. "You need ... help," Sarah intoned.

A fist hit her chin. She was dazed. Nicholas spun. He stabbed in the hand the hoggish guard who had hit Sarah. Wounded, the guard staggered back, squealing like a stuck man.

Nicholas shouted to the guard, "Weren't ... you ever ... taught not ... to hit a lady?"

"I suppose I *will* get that meal," Sarah quipped, seeing the hoggish guard lying on the floor. Nicholas gave her a quick, quizzical glance.

More guards entered the room. They backed Nicholas and Sarah against the wall beside the fireplace. A smug guard, leveling the tip of his sword, nicked Nicholas's arm, causing it to bleed. Nicholas withdrew, pressing Sarah behind him. Many of the menacing fighting toys had been smashed or fallen to their sides. A surviving few mindlessly flailed, toppled onto their backs.

Nicholas kept his eyes on her and the threatening guard.

"We have you now," growled the guard. "Tell His Highness, Prince Zili, we have caught the carpenter's son."

Nicholas peered at the guards, who were laughing and grinning. He thought of his grandmother. Nicholas prayed, "Help me. Tell me what to do? Please, help Sarah."

Suddenly, seen only by Nicholas and Sarah, a flash of light sliced the air as a knife would cheese. The room divided in two. A longitudinal wedge of gray, a dimensional tear in space, separated the halves. The no–man's–land led through the guards and across the room.

"What has happened?" asked Sarah.

"My grandmother," Nicholas murmured. He snatched Sarah close.

Everyone in the room appeared to be still, with the exception of Nicholas and Sarah. Nicholas grabbed Sarah by the hand. Both stepped into the nothingness. Slowly they strode into the grayness. Their feet trod upon nothingness. The guards on either side of them remained stationary, a snapshot of confusion. Cloaked in the alternate dimension, Sarah and Nicholas were invisible to them. As they walked, they examined the zoo that was Zili's guard. The guards were not statues, but they moved so slowly that they seemed so. One man's eyeblink took the same time as Nicholas and Sarah's trip from one side of the room to the other.

Nicholas touched the wall. This time it dissolved. They entered the secret passage and moved toward Joseph and Lexi.

The Dungeon

His eyes opened. Layers of rope weighed him down. Tied, his flesh returned from brass. The fat man struggled within the turns of rope. The dungeon guard who'd been intimidated by the sham Black Knight found himself looking up from within a three-foot-wide, six-foot-long wooden box. Standing over the box, Lexi peered down on him. Lexi shook his head. Joseph ran up beside Lexi.

"I'm going to start looking for Alexander," Joseph said. He held out his hands, looking into the box. "What are we going to do with him, Lexi?"

"Close the box," said Lexi flatly. "Here. Make yourself useful." Lexi tossed the ring of keys into Joseph's waiting hands.

Joseph pointed to the cell block. "I'm going to start looking at the end of the cell block first."

"Please take notice of the braid you wear on your wrist," said Lexi. "Free only the royals and those loyal to them."

Lexi peered at the guard he had bound in the box. "He's going to make a lot of noise," Lexi murmured. With that, he drew a short knife from his belt. The man in the box began to squirm, his eyes enlarging. The man squirmed furiously when Joseph reached into the box. Beneath the guard's chain mail, Joseph clutched the tail of his shirt. Lexi used his knife to slice off a generous length of the guard's shirttail. Wadding it in one hand, Lexi stuffed it into the guard's mouth, then slammed shut the lid of the box with his other hand.

"There. That should keep him quiet … for now. That was easier than I thought," Lexi said. He was about to dash off to find Joseph when he heard Joseph call.

"Think again, Lexi!" Joseph shouted loudly from across the large room. Lexi saw Joseph standing at the door leading into the cell block. But he had not entered.

"You're supposed to be looking. Why haven't you gone in? Is there a problem? You have the keys."

"I can't go in there."

"Of course you can, Joseph; one foot after the other." Lexi jogged up to his side. "Give me the keys," Lexi demanded. He jerked the keys out of Joseph's hand. Joseph tilted his head to a small, slatted window in the center top of the cell block door.

"What?" Lexi asked. Glaring into Joseph's face, Lexi moved toward the window.

"Take a look, go on. There are more guards," said Joseph, his chest deflating. He paced in a tight circle before the large oak door. "They look asleep or drunk."

"Let's hope drunk," Lexi muttered, stepping back from the window. He peered once again through the slats. "It looks like there are two or three in there. One is definitely sober, and he looks serious. Heaven help us." Lexi groaned. "I'll wager Alexander is there."

"I wager double or nothing," Joseph answered. "You're the soldier, Lexi. What are we to do?"

Lexi dashed away, leaving Joseph standing at the cell block door.

"Hey, come back!" Joseph shouted, his heart racing.

In a moment, Lexi returned with the sword and shield of the fat guard he had bound up in the box. "These were near the stool where he was sitting," said Lexi. "I'm ready. Now, use the keys. Open the lock. Go on."

Joseph eased the heavy key into the lock and turned it. It slowly clicked. Joseph leaned into the door carefully, jarring it open.

"Watch this." Lexi grinned.

"Oh—you're not going to do what I think. Are you?" Joseph asked dubiously, his voice quavering.

"I don't know what you're thinking, brother," Lexi replied sternly, putting on his war scowl. Sword drawn, Lexi flung open the door, burst into the cell block yelling, and repeatedly pounded his sword against his shield as he would a drum.

"You people are a disgrace. Wait until His Highness Prince Zili finds out you are drunk. He will place you on the stake and burn you." The men stood erect for a moment while Lexi pretended to represent Zili. Joseph stood behind Lexi.

From his stool rose the serious guard. He rose and rose, to seven feet in height. He stared down at Lexi. "I do not know you, little man," he said.

Into Lexi's ear, Joseph whispered, "We should go."

"I am the second captain of the prison guard, assigned by Prince Zili's first captain of the vanguard," Lexi declared.

The tall guard reached down behind an abutment at the open cell where he was seated, and clasped a mace in his fist. It was a three-foot-long, handled weapon with a heavy winged striking end of iron. "I do not think so. I think you are a liar."

A drunken guard turned toward Lexi and Joseph and postured. "I am captain of Prince Zili's dungeon guard. What do you say now, little man?"

"I say ... I say ... I might have the wrong cell block."

"There is no other. Men! Take them!" shouted the captain of the dungeon guard.

When the captain lifted his chin toward Lexi, the guard of the watch stood from his stool. He drew his sword and swung relentlessly at Lexi, using his stool as a shield. The ring of metal on metal and metal on wood echoed throughout the dungeon. Prisoners jeered and cheered as the two men fought.

Through a vent window, Mr. Krahe flew into the dungeon. From above, Mr. Krahe dropped from his beak a vial of liquid given him by Zorna. The guards fell unconscious to the floor.

"This way, Joseph!" the bird shouted. "The king is in a bad way." Joseph ran behind the raven as it quickly flew to a cell at the back of the dungeon. Lexi followed. "Help is coming," said the raven. "Prince Wallace has told the archer Amoretti to bring her elf archers to assist us in the battle."

Kneeling beside Alexander on a pallet of hay, Lexi heard the thunderous steps. "The palace guard. They are coming," Lexi said. Joseph nodded.

Queen Isadora sat on a stool above the king. Lexi looked up from the injured Alexander, who lay still. "We'd better get moving," said Lexi. He could see that Joseph had heard the approaching horde. "Here comes Joseph, the apothecary. See what you can do for the king."

Joseph attended to several of Alexander's more ugly wounds. He used various powders from his pouches. Joseph took a deep breath. "I hear them, very near. They either look for us or for Nicholas and Sarah," Joseph said. "In any event, not being a warrior— Please, Your Highness, turn your arm a bit. Thank you." He tightened a rag around Alexander's left arm to tamp oozing blood. "It won't be pleasant if we are caught here—if they get here and we are still here."

"We will go, Joseph, as soon as you stabilize the king."

Joseph worked hurriedly. "I don't like this fighting. I'm an apothecary ... an alchemist ... I just—" Joseph gestured to several freed prisoners beginning to gather. He instructed them to get something upon which to lay the king. A half dozen hurried out to search about the cell block. Some scrounged the guard station for weapons, while others tied together heavy spears and loose clothing to make a litter on which to lay the injured king.

Joseph had begun to sweat. "I know," Lexi said, seeing the perspiration on Joseph's forehead. Joseph peered up. "I never really noticed. But the cells of this dungeon spiral through several levels ..."

Having secured the king, the loyalists hoisted him upon the litter. With Queen Isadora and Angelica inches behind, they rushed from the cell to the cell block entrance. Lexi, far behind, checked the unconscious guards to be certain they were still out.

Stopped at the entrance of the block, the king motioned for Isadora's ear. She leaned down to him. He whispered.

She peered up to Joseph and the loyalists. "The king expects you will come," the queen said.

"There are other loyalists we must release, Your Highness," said Joseph. "The king would want us to release them. We will find you when we have finished. Your brother Wallace—"

"Wallace is here?"

"Somewhere, my queen," Lexi said. "He is prepared to evacuate Your Highnesses' family to the shire ridge above the castle."

"Where shall we find him?" whispered the king.

"Sire," Lexi said, "he will find you. Now you must go. We must secrete you to safety."

As soon as the king and loyalists entered the cell block, the air filled with an odor.

"What is that I smell?" Lexi asked.

Joseph sniffed. "It is like a swamp stirred on a rainy day," he muttered. He peered from the corridor of the cell block to the anteroom and the torture pit below the stairs. The area was lit by yellow fire on rows of three-foot-long torches projecting from the wall.

Lexi followed a wisp of smoke. He crept cautiously from the corridor into the anteroom, passed the box where he had laid the guard, and went down the steps into the torture pit. Joseph remained in the cell block, fingering through the key ring, finding keys, and opening cells. He released each loyalist as he found the correct key.

"What is this?" Lexi muttered to himself, inching through the torture pit toward the stage of the rack. The table sat before him. It was encrusted with dried black blood. He saw it as an odious device. It symbolized Zili's desire to force his will.

Lexi inched closer. The wisp of smoke had become an acrid cloud, blackening and thickening. Lexi could see the source in the shadows beneath the stage of the torture rack. The musty odor intensified. Collecting on the bed of the rack, the smoke swirled, taking the form of a troll.

"What is that horrid smell?" Lexi said holding his nose. He watched a small humanoid form materialize. "*You.*"

"Yes. I am Jax, standing on the rack." Sneering at Lexi, it drew a small sword. "Alexander from here you will not free. Home for you also this is to be. Truly, by order of king, our sovereign Zili." He lunged with his small sword. Lexi dodged. With no words, Lexi punched the troll in the face. From the bed of the rack, it tumbled to the stone floor. The troll lay motionless and unconscious.

"The king is already gone. Stupid troll," Lexi sneered, rubbing his fist in his other hand. "What a cow patty."

Sarah and Nicholas made their way among the castle wall passages. They came to a stone at a dead end. The damp, moldy smell at the backside of the stone took Sarah's breath. The wet soil heaped along the edges of hers and Nicholas's shoes. Sarah crouched in the darkness.

"I hear something on the other side." Nicholas pressed his ear to the stone. "This is the dungeon, I wager."

Breathless, Sarah sighed. "I have lived here all my life, Nicholas, and I have never known of this tunnel. How did you—"

"Shhhh," Nicholas whispered, crouching beneath the low ceiling. Taking a deep breath, Nicholas listened with his ear to the stone. Suddenly, he heaved his weight into the seam of the granite wall and pushed. The stone block remained unmoved.

Sarah positioned her left shoulder against the stone, her right leg angled out along with his.

"Whoa. Sarah. What are you doing?" Nicholas asked, his brown eyes level with hers, her face inches away.

"I'm helping you ... please," she said. Nicholas opened his mouth but decided it was better not to protest. She raised her eyebrows. "I'm *helping*."

Nicholas prayed. "Friends of the Orphic Forest, if you agree with my actions, please assist me—*us*—in the rescue of our king and his family."

Shoulders to the stone, they both shoved.

Having bound Jax in heavy rope, Lexi trundled the imp into the box with the guard. He slammed shut the lid and sat on the box, brushing his hands. He heard scraping in a remote corner of the dungeon: the faint timbre of stone scuffing over stone.

Leaping up, Lexi darted to the wall. Grasping a torch, he followed the noise. Unseen by him, thorn bushes sprouted rapidly. Branches began snaking and creeping down the dark dungeon walls. Twisting through crevices, cracks, windows, and vents, the branches bifurcated repeatedly, thorns sprouting continuously. The branches swelled larger than a man's thigh; the thorns stretched as long as swords.

Lexi tightened his fist when he saw two heads pop out from behind the stone angling away from the wall.

"Nicholas. Sarah," he said, helping them through.

They heard footfalls. Three guards marched before them. "They are here," sneered the one out in front.

Nicholas and Lexi rushed them before they could draw their swords.

Lexi immediately punching the third unconscious.

Sarah grabbed the sword of the fallen guard and ran to assist Nicholas. She hammered the back of his opponent's head with the hilt of the sword as they fought.

Out of the darkness, hundreds of branches arched forward like serpents. Thrashing and slithering, they isolated and surrounded the guards with three-foot thorns and looping around their bodies. The branches held the guards so they could no longer fight.

Sarah recognized the thorn bush from the two large terrariums kept in a sewing room, gifts delivered from the Orphic Forest. They had been birthday presents to the queen from the king. She did not recall them being this large and certainly never able to move like animals.

Cursing, guards streamed into the chamber, but they stopped short upon seeing the massive, serpentine thorn branches. The branches whipped through the air, whooshing, dragging heavy tables, chairs, armor, men, and weaponry along the floor. The vines wove a barricade of thorns across the dungeon doors. The trapped men and beasts hacked at the vines, but each time their swords broke a branch or thorn, five more took its place. The bush stretched like long, ominous fingers to help the royal family's egress. The family was far along but not out of the castle.

A smidgen wearing a wrist braid slipped between and beneath the woven thorn barricade. Out from the dungeon it slipped to catch up with the king on the litter. Some freed loyalists remained in the dungeon. There, they lay in wait, trapping and imprisoning more of Zili's guards and others loyal to Zili.

Nicholas, Lexi, Joseph, and Sarah reached the royal family as they were on their way to Wallace, Zorna, and the general. They learned Zorna, in his dragon form, would fly them all to the shire ridge.

Up on the shire ridge, Alexander rested in a tent constructed large enough for him and his family. Several oddlings attended to his wounds and soiled clothing. "Brother," said Wallace, kneeling at the head of his recumbent brother,. "I am relieved now that you are safe. Whatever it takes, we will stop our brother Zili."

Coughing, lids half open, Alexander nodded. He gently placed his right hand on Wallace's shoulder and patted. "He is not the brother we knew," Alexander softly said, pulling the edge of the blanket covering him to his lips. "They chained me to a stone wall," moaned Alexander. "I was near dead when someone released me. My dear wife and the princess were in the adjoining cells—no light, no windows."

"Our only comfort," said Isadora, "was a bale of hay on which to lie." Several smidgens watched over the shire ridge, while others gently encircled the royals as protection. Others disappeared, leaving the ridge by magic to reenter the battle.

"I will give you something that will heal your wounds, Sire," Zorna said. "Allow me." The queen moved aside as Zorna positioned himself to slip his left arm beneath the king's neck and support his head. He held a vial of liquid to his lips. "Drink this, Sire," Zorna said.

Chapter 21

WALLACE TAKES CONTROL

From the dungeon to the keep, the battle raged. More of Zili's men converged on the confrontation. Having escaped his bonds, Jax the troll kept watch for Lexi. He was angry about his abrupt treatment and defeat at Lexi's hands. Acting as Zili's quasi surrogate, Jax directed the fighting castle guard while his eyes scanned the confusion for Lexi.

Mr. Krahe flew up to Prince Wallace on the shire ridge. There, he was pleased to find the polar bears Ursa and Ursara, and Chlora, the elf prince, in conference with Wallace. Princess Faunett, the sister of Chlora, and Beast tended to the king and his family. Calming Alexander's momentary hesitancy, Wallace approved when Zorna offered King Alexander the healing potion he had administered to Wallace and General Raptozk.

"Master wizard," Wallace said, his voice breaking. He hesitated to regain his composure, while Zorna scrutinized Alexander's wrists. They were raw and suppurating from iron shackles.

"Master wizard," Wallace repeated, "I trust this potion will work quickly enough to relieve my brother's pain?"

Alexander laid his limp fingers across his belly and atop Wallace's resting hand, ironically to comfort *him*.

"My hurt is here," Alexander murmured, dragging his hand over the center of his chest to his heart. "Our brother is my greatest hurt, and nothing … nothing I know will heal that." Alexander closed his eyes and coughed. "We can only defeat him before more souls are lost, human or oddling."

Zorna glanced Wallace at his shoulder. "It *will* take longer for the potion to work," Zorna said. "For swiftness, it is past the time it should have been given. Asking the Powers That Be to help would also be of assistance." Scanning the room, Zorna spotted Queen Isadora. She sat on the tent floor, to the right of Alexander and at the head of his cot. Her soiled blue dress served as cover. Princess Angelica slept, her head resting in her mother's lap.

"The king will need to rest without stress," Zorna murmured, "or certainly the potion will not be effective."

Although they seemed safe for now, Queen Isadora's face could not hide the distress in her heart. She found it hard to be stoic. Her eyes were red, and Zorna could tell she was crying.

"Calm yourself, Your Highness. You are well protected on the shire ridge." It was still bright outside, and Zorna could see very well through the tent flap. Several armed smidgens, humans, and others stood guard outside.

"Within the shire are several hundred elves and dwarfs; all of us are loyal to your loving husband," Zorna said. She raked her fingers through her sleeping daughter's hair.

Two elves sauntered close to the queen and Zorna. They spoke in unison. "You will stay with us," said Faunett and Chlora, intoning in soft, calming whispers.

"We will see to all your needs," said Faunett. "The white bears Ursa and Ursara will be near, guarding this, your temporary home, while the Wolf Shadow Spirit and her pack guard the perimeter."

Tugging a leather lanyard from his pocket, Zorna dangled a small mirror from his fingertips. A glint of its light flashed in Alexander's eyes.

"This is called a Dragon's Eye, Your Highness," Zorna said. "It provides a kind of remote vision that will permit you to safely watch as we take back your kingdom." Zorna curled the king's fingers around the small mirror. "I have placed a reflective shield of aurora light around the shire ridge. It will protect you and your family."

Standing, Wallace peered down at his brother and caught the eyes of Isadora. Hesitating, he inhaled slowly while straightening his tunic. "Now that Alexander and his family are safe, it's time to deal with my brother Zili," Wallace said. Leaning, he gently wiped Alexander's forehead. "Raptozk, Zorna, Beast, and I will return to the castle. Nicholas and Lexi and Joseph need our help."

"I'm going too."

Wallace turned to the woman's voice. Sarah approached from the entrance of the tent.

"I'm going as well, Wallace," she repeated.

"Don't be ridiculous. Of course you are not going. You are staying here. All you can do is make the situation more complicated."

"Your Highness, I am going."

"I am the prince, and I say no."

"I am the princess, and I say so."

"*Stop*. I am queen," said Isadora. "You shall save your fight for the enemy of our realm. Stop acting like children. What kind of examples are you to Angelica? Wallace, you were once young—and in love."

"But I am not so old now, and I love," said Wallace.

"Sarah," said the queen, lifting her nose, "you must follow your heart."

"Then you shall not stop me. My heart is with Nicholas, and I will be as well. I shall go, with or without you."

"Sire," interjected the general, "that is not acceptable. Sarah is a—" Wallace lifted his hand, gesturing to silence the general. "General, she will follow," said Wallace. "I'd rather she be in my sight than not. At least I may keep your sister safe." He looked at Isadora.

"And perhaps I shall keep you safe," Sarah quipped, lifting her eyebrows. Wallace grimaced.

Beast and Zorna glanced at each other as they left to rig the horses. Guffawing, Beast slapped the general on the shoulder. "You were outnumbered before you began, my friend," Beast said in his chest-rattling voice. "Sarah is in love. Nothing will stop her."

Mounting his horse, Zorna raised his right hand. The reins in his other, Zorna turned his horse from the tent. He briskly wagged his fingers before his face, and another Dragon's Eye appeared, the lanyard looped around his fingers. He slipped it into his pocket. "We must go now," he said, coaxing his horse. "Nicholas needs reinforcements."

Setting the Stage

Queen Isadora stood at the door of the tent, gazing toward the shire ridge. Sauntering thirty feet to the very edge, she stood. She looked down; pebbles crumbled and trundled beneath her feet. She mused at the falling grit. She even gently kicked some stones and earth to watch them tumble to the rocks below.

Through the mild haze, she peered at the outlying castle, her home, and the forest behind. She gasped at smoke pouring from some castle windows, from rooms she knew very well. To her side, she heard footsteps and glimpsed a shadow. A short being with the torso of a boy and waist and legs of a goat stood on hooves within mere inches of her flank. Silently, he offered a crystalline chalice of fruit juice, which he presented on a wooden tray. In no mood for food or drink, she waved him away. She clasped her hands prayerfully. It occurred to her that a fall from this height could easily kill a man—or queen. Alexander would live; therefore, she managed to dismiss such contemplations.

Her heart still full of sorrow, she wept. Not only for the senseless loss of life but for the senseless loss of innocence. Her daughter might never know the kingdom as Isadora had. Her memories were of a kingdom of joy, free of war and strife. Isadora recalled the years of constant peace she and Alexander had enjoyed. Now all of that might be gone.

Shaking her head, she watched the smoke and whimpered. Again, she was about to wave the boy away when she felt the delicate hand of a child slip into her hand. It was Angelica. They both gazed at great black pillows of smoke rising from scattered areas around the castle.

⁂

At the castle, the former prisoners stood back, while one man dashed forward to the stairs with a jug of lamp oil. The stairs led up into a back tower of the castle. Over the base of the stairs, he spread the oil. Beside him, a man eagerly touched the oil with a burning three-foot torch. Flames rushed up the stairs.

"Let's see Zili's men get through that," said the man with the lamp oil.

Charging throughout the castle interior well ahead of Zili's outlaws, many other freed prisoners loyal to King Alexander caused distractions. Some burned wooden staircases, while others barred doors and barricaded corridors, preventing access by Zili's men.

If poor visibility in the smoky corridor were not enough, confronted by a small contingent of Zili's men, Wallace, Lexi, and Joseph fought for their very lives. Not only did they swing swords and fist, they also lobbed any broken masonry they could lift. They heaved furniture, hall statues, and anything they could get their hands on to fend off the onslaught of Zili's advancing men. Those men continued to force Wallace and his men backward down the corridor. Fully armed, Zili's men were clad in chain mail shirts and coifs. They blocked with shields on one arm and struck with swords in the other.

Lexi parried strikes, catching blades on the shaft of his pike. After four quick strikes, the pike cleaved in two. Blocking the next with his sword, he breathlessly shouted to Wallace beside him, "We ... have got to get ... out of here!"

The guard struck again, knocking one half of the pike from Lexi's hand. Hoisting a vase from a teetering pedestal, Joseph heaved it toward a guard, who immediately ducked. The vase hit and splayed out the guard behind him. The man lay unconscious on the floor as the contingent retreated down the corridor.

"Look!" shouted Lexi. "Down the hall." Behind the men they fought, the three briefly saw someone enter the hallway. That instant, two of them jumped high to parry the sweep of a sword when a guard lunged for their legs.

Lexi shouted, "That's ... him!" Lexi coughed, wiping his forearm across his burning eyes.

"It is. I see the knave. Zili." Wallace snarled. Beaten back, they continued to retreat.

"*Zili?*" Joseph muttered, surprised. "Here?"

Coughing from the smoke, Joseph threw a punch into the face of a guard rushing him. The three men fought while continuing to back down the smoky hall.

A stairwell appeared at their right flank.

"Let's go!" Joseph shouted.

Smoke billowed from the stairwell to the ceiling. The three men ducked into the stairwell and charged down several flights of stairs.

"They are headed for the throne room," Zili growled, catching up to his men at the entrance of the stairwell. "The one who catches my brother, I shall reward with nobility. Well. Why are you standing here listening to me? After them, you milk-livered sons of curs." Four eager guards dashed into the stairwell.

Zili dashed into the smoke behind them. He heard screams and wailing from deep within the stairwell. He peered up to see a hole in the tower wall left by broken timbers. Channeling up the stairwell through the hole, the smoke cleared. His hand braced against the charred wall, Zili looked down into the chasm where the stairs had been. The burned wooden stairs had collapsed. He saw his men had fallen twenty feet down. They lay atop rubble, two writhing in pain, another either unconscious or dead. He did not see the fourth.

Somewhat higher along the wall, he saw Lexi and Joseph resting on what appeared to be a giant human hand formed from bricks of the wall, the bricks somehow alive. At eye level, Wallace stood on the remnant of the landing, beyond jumping distance of Zili.

"My, my, it would be like shooting fish in a barrel," Zili said. "If I only had my bow. But it is not only a long way up, brother—it is a long way down." Zili smirked, peering at his men lying further down upon the jagged stone and charred rubble. "It looks as if you and your ... pets could use a rope. Alas, the only one I can offer you is one around your necks."

Zili shouted down to his injured, moaning men, "There is nothing I can do for you. You have killed yourselves."

Abandoning his own men at the bottom of the burned-out stairwell, Zili backed from the shattered landing and left the stairwell the same way he had entered.

Slipping about the castle unnoticed, Nicholas avoided a flurry of activity. Zili continually searched for him and for Wallace's men. Zili's soldiers had put out most of the fires and contained the chaos created by Alexander's loyalists.

Zili's army had all but smashed the counter revolt. So far as Zili knew, only a few loyalists like Nicholas and Wallace's men were still at large in the castle.

With a bit of persistent skulking and luck, Nicholas planned to get close to Zili. Nicholas watched through a pinhole in a hollow wall behind the throne. There he patiently waited for Zili. He'd heard Zili would arrive to meet and dine with his top commanders.

It was hard getting in a comfortable spot. Nicholas pulled back from the pinhole when he saw Zili enter the throne room. He scraped his shoulder on a nail, on which hung a sash. Nicholas brushed it with his fingers. He huffed. The cloth was embroidered with Zili's crest. This must have been where he spied on his brother Alexander.

The inner confine of the wall was musty. It was all Nicholas could do to keep from sneezing. In the corners of the rectangular space lay refuse, comprising animal bones, a broken ceramic plate, and a wine-stained chalice tipped on its side. Nicholas could easily see that someone had spent a great deal of time spying from this blind. Feeling around inside the wall, he detected a latch to a narrow door panel, no more than two feet wide. Through it, he could exit into the throne room—if necessary.

His hands sweated. He could hardly believe he was this close. The chance everyone waited for, Nicholas thought. He dreamed he could shut down Zili's coup with one strategic blow. But he was certain he should not try it alone. Besides, Wallace had made it clear that the blow should be left to him.

Nicholas waited and watched, hoping Wallace, Lexi, and Joseph were well and not far behind. He was sure they were safe. He thought of Sarah and hoped she remained safe on the ridge with Alexander.

In the smoldering stairwell, Wallace balanced himself on a narrow timber and against the wall. He hoped he had not gotten himself and his men killed. Since Sarah insisted on coming, he hoped she had found Nicholas.

Wallace surveyed his men's predicament. He was perilously perched on an unstable timber protruding from a weakened stairwell wall. His men, Lexi and Joseph, were ensconced in some odd handlike projection of the wall just beneath him. Wallace blew; indeed, Zili was correct, he thought as he scanned the stairwell. It *was* a long way up to the shattered landing, and certainly a long way down to the sharp rocks and shattered timbers below.

The stairwell was a death trap. The marble walls, slick and oily with smoke, were without adequate handholds. Wallace could see Zili's injured men below, dying on the smoldering rubble. He saw Joseph and Lexi teetering, clasped by a hand-shaped outgrowth from the marble wall, embraced in fingers of stone. Seemingly unsteady, the fingers of stone writhed unceasingly.

"Can you move?" Wallace asked.

"We can. The stone hand holds us snugly but unsteadily. Should we move?" Joseph asked, his arms out to his sides to assist his balance.

"We don't know whether it is the magic of friend or foe," Lexi said. "The stone people," Wallace murmured to himself. "Try taking a step up to the protruding timber where I stand. Together we may scale to the landing above," he shouted.

"How, Sire? There is nothing upon which to perch our feet."

"The stone will provide the step. Your task is doing what I command and lifting your legs," Wallace said firmly.

As Lexi and Joseph began to step, the stone fingers reached out beneath their feet. A stone finger rotated beneath each foot to support each higher step. The men gleefully stepped, the living stone creating a stairway upon which they ascended, reaching Wallace and beyond.

Through the pinhole in the blind, Nicholas watched.

"Are all of my commanders present?" Zili asked. He sat at the head of a long table, his attending subordinates at his side. "Where is that wench with my food?" Zili groaned, "and where is the captain of the guard?"

"Here, Your Highness," said the captain.

"Are the castle grounds secured?"

"Yes, Your Highness. We have extinguished all fires and recaptured a majority of Alexander's loyalists."

"Not all." Zili huffed. "Where is my malodorous sycophant, Jax? I do not see him." Zili's eyes searched the room.

"He was here—we thought," the captain of the guard said, spinning around.

Behind the castle and several yards into the forest, a small tent sat in a clearing. The thin material forming its walls transmitted a dim, reddish light from the source inside. Within the shelter, on the leaf litter upon the soil, Jax sat, staring into glowing embers. His arms widely spread, his stubby fingers waving over the embers. He recited an incantation: "*Hostis procul hinc* remove."

He knew by this spell, he would remove the enemy far from the castle.

⁂

Relieved to have climbed to safety, Wallace, Joseph, and Lexi stood on the landing. Lexi casually looked over the edge of the shattered landing to the rubble below. He wanted to take a last look at the place where they nearly died. He began to stare.

Wallace peered into Lexi's face. "You appear as if you have seen a spirit."

"Sire, at this point, I would be pleased if I had."

"What do you mean?" Wallace asked.

"Look down there, Sire. I was certain Zili's men lay dead at the bottom."

"They are," Joseph said. "I saw them for myself." He and Wallace peered to the bottom of the crumbled stairwell.

"There is no one there," Lexi said.

"Could they have escaped?" asked Joseph.

"No. I heard the last man when he took his last breath," said Wallace. "Sire, the fire ... There is none, and no more smoke," said Lexi. "The walls are no longer scorched."

"Smell." Joseph sniffed. "And the air is clear." He was baffled. "Come, let us go to the meeting place," Wallace commanded. They left the stairwell, gazing as they strode. The corridors were deserted. "Nicholas and Sarah will be waiting there for us."

As they approached the meeting place, they saw Nicholas from a distance. He approached them running. He appeared confused. Shrub leaves brushing them as he passed, seemingly made of canvas and paint. The blue sky resembled a painted ceiling. Birds hung like black dots in a mock sky. Even the sun looked like a disk of white-hot steel.

"Prince Wallace, Lexi, Joseph—I'm so glad to see you," Nicholas said. His eyes appeared tentative and searching. "I-I found Zili. He is— he was in the throne room. I was behind the wall watching. He is—he was looking for us. But something … something strange is happening, something beyond my ability to articulate."

"Then, Nicholas, you are truly here and not a dream," Joseph said, his eyes darting around his odd, stilted surroundings.

"We all are here," Lexi said. "The castle is deserted: no people, no horses, nothing is real. It is some kind of artificial creation, an imitation of what we know. Nothing appears alive but—but us, Sire. I don't understand."

"And the smell," Nicholas said.

"I know. There is no smell. Even the fires of torches have no heat. What is this place?" Wallace slowly asked. "We are in some sort of unreality." Wallace scowled. "Hello! Listen. There are no echoes."

"It looks like the castle, but that's about all," Lexi said. "I think we are in a dream." He pinched himself, and winced at the pain. "*Ouch.*"

"This is no dream—a nightmare perhaps. Somehow, the life of this world is drained away. Are—are we still alive?" Joseph asked. "Are we … dead?"

"Of course we are alive. Are you mad?" Lexi asked. He spotted a sliver of burning wood. Clasping the unburned end, he lifted it to his face. "I feel nothing. This is someone's idea of purgatory."

"May I see the fire, Lexi?" Joseph asked. He took the end of the stick and whipped it through the air. The yellow flame did not extinguish. He thought that was abnormal. He plunged the flaming end into Lexi's flank. Startled, Lexi lurched backward, holding his side, but a curious expression came to his face.

"I am not burned. The fire has no heat." He clutched the burning end of the torch. Fire flowed around his hand.

"None of this is real: this castle, the sky, this fire." Wallace knelt and scooped water from a puddle. He drank. "There is no taste. The water is not wet. Truly, this is black magic. We are captives of an illusion."

"Where is Sarah?" Nicholas asked.

The other men looked at one another. "We thought she was with you."

"Why would she be with me?" Nicholas asked. "She is on shire ridge, safe ... with King Alexander, yes?"

"No. She insisted on coming with us," Joseph said. "She wanted to find you. Are you saying she did not?"

"I have not seen her." Nicholas's voice became high. "We must find her and—"

"Sadly," Wallace interrupted, "we are captives in this strange world."

⁓∞⁓

The head and tusks of the hoggish guard came through the breach of the tent. He watched as Jax extinguished the embers. Jax smiled coyly as he peered up.

"Jax. Your master Zili demands your presence in the castle, at once." Jax bowed his head as he entered the throne room.

"Where is the girl, the Princess Sarah?" asked Zili, spitting, peering down from his seat at the long table.

Jax bowed again. "I'm afraid I do not know. They went where the wind doth blow."

"*What*? Jax, you tottering, boil-brained codpiece, you were supposed to ensure she was guarded." Rising from his seat, Zili backed the troll into a corner. Jax cowered as Zili sneered. Zili walked away. Jax stood straight. Zili spun and put his sword to Jax's gnarled chest. Zili shouted, "Did you find my enemy, Wallace, and that carpenter's son, Nicholas? She was with them, and that warlock, Zorna."

Jax shrugged. "Sire ..." he said, backing away. "I have banished them with a spell. They are ... over the horizon, far away in hell, wrapped in an illusion, a dream that they cannot break."

Zili's jaw jutted. He cracked his knuckles at his sides. He stared into Jax's face.

"They are at the Borderlands, near the Outland. That's where they'll die," said Jax, quickly lapping his lips. He grinned tentatively, bowing submissively while wringing his hands.

Zili sat at the long table.

"Borderlands? Well, bring them back with another spell," Zili commanded.

Jax hesitated, his eyes darting along the floor. "I'm—I'm afraid I—I cannot, Sire," he muttered timidly. "I have cursed them and damned their lot."

Zili shot to his feet, his chair falling back, slamming to the floor. A hush came over the meeting room. "If I were you, I should be afraid *not* to bring them back, knave. To the Borderlands, you fool—I should send you there," snarled Zili. "She is with them? Why do this?"

Jax shrugged. "When we could not capture them, Sire, I knew we had failed. I created a spell that fashioned a mock castle, and I put them in hell—one devoid of any hint of Your Highness and his loyal subjects. They are trapped in another world where they can do Your Highness no harm, beyond the forest, beyond the farm. They wander in a castle that looks much like this one. They are far from here … Sire. Yes, they are gone."

Zili started at the troll. His eyes burned. Zili smacked his moist lips. "I can release them, Sire," said Jax, "by reversing the curse, but—"

"But *what*, defective troll?" Zili said.

"But they must return by their own devices. I've done them the worst," said Jax.

"For your sake, you should pray they do," Zili snapped. "I want that girl. You trifle with me far too much, little demon. Do not disappoint me again—your life may depend on it."

Jax closed his eyes and began reciting the incantation.

Far away, the mock castle vanished from around its captives. Free of the illusion but baffled, Wallace, Nicholas, Lexi, and Joseph stood in the middle of a strange and foreign forest. They heard their horses yards away. They glimpsed Zorna near the horses. He seemed perturbed. "I—I strode toward the meeting place … and now I am here."

"We must find our way back from this strange land to the Kingdom of Illuminae," Wallace said. "We must get into the castle undetected."

"Is there such a way, Sire?" asked Joseph.

"There is," Wallace said with determination. "And when we get there, secret passages used by Nicholas are likely still undiscovered. They offer easy access for us. I know every inch of this castle. A passage known to me connects with thirteen more. If we are discovered, we shall claim to be Gypsies entertaining King Zili's men."

"Yes, Sire. I shall produce a protective enchantment for all who ride with us," Zorna said. "All here will remain unseen until you, Sire, command us to become visible."

"You have plenty of surprises, my friend," said Wallace, nodding. "Let it be done."

Zorna dipped his chin respectfully. Slipping his Dragon's Eye from his robe, he held it high above his head. It sparkled, the reflective surface bursting into a brilliant beacon, a cone of white light projecting outward. The wind began to whip, lofting leaves and twigs from the forest duff. While reciting an incantation, Zorna closed his eyes. Wallace and his men turned their heads, shielding their eyes. A shelter of multispectral aurora light twisted, enveloping each rider. The shield shone as reflective as the mirror in Zorna's hand.

"Any light striking our front will be sent behind; any light striking our behind will be sent front. The same is true of our flanks, Sire. We will, in effect, become invisible. The spell shall reverse at your command. We shall appear to those with true hearts—those who would join our cause."

Prince Wallace mounted his horse. He pointed his gauntleted finger in the direction of their ride. Wallace smirked. "Zili is mine."

Out in front, Wallace snapped the reins of his horse, bringing her to a full gallop. Lungs heaving, the horses blew, their manes flagging leeward. Relentlessly, hooves pounded the soil, dug deep, and lofted clods of dirt into the air. They galloped through the hills and valleys of the countryside. Through dense, dark forest, shielded by the aurora field, Wallace and his men rode, seeing as clearly as if riding on a sunny day. Yet no one perceived their approach or passage.

After hours, they were in the Kingdom of Illuminae. The pace slowed. The horses loped along steadily. Soon they would need to watch their moves. Lexi glanced at the western horizon. They were within an hour of dusk.

Behind, Lexi saw Joseph glowering. Zorna looked back and stopped. Nudging his horse with his heels, Joseph sidled up to Lexi. "Who are they?"

"Who are who?" Lexi asked. "No one can see us."

"They do," Joseph said. He tilted his head rearward, persuading Lexi to turn on his horse to see.

"Heavens to ..." Lexi said. He nudged his horse to trot up to Wallace's. "Sire. Behind us," he pleaded.

Wallace turned.

Less than fifty feet to the rear marched more than twenty men and women: clowns, jugglers, animals, and trainers. With more than ten additional horses in tow, they followed Prince Wallace.

Wallace pursed his lips and nodded. "My men," Wallace said, "we are a circus of Gypsies."

At the bottom of the shire road, four varda joined the prince. One varda held eight elf archers; two more contained sixteen of Prince Wallace's highest-trained warriors; the fourth carried fifteen oddlings capable of changing their shapes and sizes.

It was evening when the riders drew near the castle. The braids of those loyal to Alexander vibrated, allowing them to know their compatriots were near. Wallace's men and the mock troubadours followed their plan: to use circuses and brawling in the outdoor venue to confuse and stifle the reaction of Zili's men. Their targets would include the area around the north curtain wall, near the tents of the visitors and dignitaries.

As the plan unfolded, several men pretending to be drunk began harassing many of Zili's guardsmen. Sifting through the crowd, a handful of trolls and ogres mingled among the gathering crowd, picking the pockets of people who watched and teased the drunkards. In scattered areas, several moles working for Wallace started fights. Villagers loyal to Alexander lit small, surreptitious fires and performed juggling, acrobatics, and dancing shows; while still others, gambling and carousing, instigated arguments among the guests.

Wallace's finest female elf archers were undercover as fortune-tellers in five tents set up near the east curtain wall. Near the south curtain wall, two large tents filled with oddlings of all kinds staged animal acts and freak shows. Everyone in place, they awaited Prince Wallace's signal to proceed with their plan of attack.

Everything seemed to be coming together.

At the southwest curtain wall, Prince Wallace, General Raptozk, and Zorna were set back from the crowd in a quiet area near the passage they would enter. There they were free to watch the crowd while remaining out of the general line of traffic.

Uncinching his horse, Joseph contemplated what he needed to do. He glanced Lexi. "I haven't seen Nicholas for the last quarter hour," he commented as he prepared his equipment before changing his clothing.

"Missing again?" Lexi asked, exasperated, looking into the crowd. "Why can he not stay in one place?" he muttered angrily, counting several gold coins he slipped from his pocket. "Now we have two missing, including Princess Sarah. How long will we have to babysit this—this princess?" The gold coins, sliding upon one another, fell from his fingers to the dirt. Groaning as he bent, Lexi reached to the ground. A small hand snatched the coins from his grasp.

"HEY!" Lexi shouted, looking up to see a boy. "Those coins belong to me!"

"Sir," whispered the boy. "Your coins." The boy released the coins into Lexi's palm. "I wasn't stealing them. I was returning them."

"I am not an old woman," snapped Lexi. "Who asked you?"

Clad in rags, the boy appeared to be about fourteen years old. He dropped his eyes and lowered his chin.

"I have business to which I must attend," growled Lexi. "Find some else's coins to toy with. Go away, boy."

"Must you be so rude?" asked the boy.

Irritated, Lexi said nothing further.

Wallace turned to the commotion. "What is going on? Who is this boy?"

Lexi interjected, "Someone who will get a thrashing if he does not move away from me." Spinning, Lexi angrily flared. Startled, the boy flinched.

Wallace laid his hand on Lexi's shoulder. Joseph sauntered up behind. From afar, Wallace examined the boy's beautiful eyes. Wallace nodded in recognition.

"Lexi," Wallace whispered. Lexi looked up to the prince. "You would thrash my sister-in-law."

"Where?" Lexi asked. He stared at the boy and lifted his eyebrows. "Sire, this is a boy, no more. He should be thankful I do not whip him for thievery." He hesitated. "I am no one's fool … and …"

Before Lexi finished, the boy removed his hat and caressed Wallace at his flank. Lexi saw.

"Princess Sarah!" Lexi exclaimed.

"Princess Sarah. The one you babysit," she said, pirouetting to show off her disguise. "I am ready, dear brother–in-law."

"What a fool I am, Your Highness," Lexi murmured, huffing. Joseph patted Lexi on his shoulder as he turned to finish his preparations.

"Princess Sarah?" Wallace said.

"Yes, Your Highness?" replied Princess Sarah.

"You were supposed to be with us—to stay within my sight," Wallace admonished. "Where have you been?"

"On the contrary." Her eyes were downcast. "I humbly submit, it was you who was missing—endless hours, Your Highness. I—I thought I had lost you."

"It is true," Wallace said, glimpsing Zorna, Lexi, and Joseph. "We were bewitched by a curse that whisked us very far from here—I think to the Borderlands near the Outland. We are lucky to have returned."

"No, not the Outland?" She shivered, shaking her head. She turned to view Wallace's men. "Zili searches for me, Your Highness. I have gotten wind of that. I am worried. Nicholas and I …"

"Nicholas was with us, but at the moment he has made himself scarce." Prince Wallace peered into her eyes. "How did you find us?"

"I saw him. We spoke," Sarah said, pointing into the crowd. "Somehow he found me. After briefly speaking with me, he ran into the crowd. He said something about Zili and the throne room. He was going to watch him. He might go there, but he sent me here to your meeting place." She looked away.

"You seemed troubled," said Wallace, placing his fingers on her shoulders.

"He is changing, Your Highness," Sarah said resignedly. "In some ways it scares me, but in other ways it fascinates me. He is very curious, and he can be serious, yet fanciful."

"Did our ... *champion* say when he would return?" asked Joseph.

"Aye, did he say?" asked Prince Wallace.

"No, Sire. He said to me, 'I will be there when you need me.'"

Exasperated, Wallace breathed deeply. Silent, he turned and bent down to the castle drainage port where they would once again enter.

"To the throne room is where we were headed before we were inexplicably banished to the western horizon. We hope to have no more unexpected trips," Wallace muttered, his eyes examining the entrance. Zorna opened the secret passage.

Mr. Krahe landed on Wallace's shoulder as they entered. Once again Mr. Krahe, and his pestilent friends led the group beneath the castle. After several moments, they emerged, one after the other, through a trap door that opened into a royal privy. It was a small room, barely large enough for two people, usually the king and the groom of the stool. The first to emerge saw the outline of velvet-lined wooden chair with a large hole in the seat. The air in the darkened room was musty and humid, despite the small window venting high near the ceiling.

"I'm afraid this is the royal privy," said Joseph, climbing out before Lexi. Lexi came before Zorna, Zorna before Sarah, she before the general, and he before Prince Wallace. All bunched in the small room, shoulder to shoulder. Lexi peeked through the door, which was ajar. From there, they prepared to merge into the bustling corridors of dignitaries, guest, and entertainers, all there in preparation for Zili's wedding and coronation.

Zorna's magic disguised Prince Wallace's contingent one by one as they exited the cloister. They slipped into the crowd, blending in well with the castle servants. They were astonished. Even amid ongoing conflict, they sensed an air of forced celebration. Moving down the halls, they espied carpenters and stonemasons attempting castle repairs. Servants dressed some open rooms in celebratory regalia, while others cordoned off areas too damaged for quick repairs. Flower petals strewn about the halls masked the odor of smoke.

"Zorna, General, are you ready?" asked Wallace. Both men nodded.

Zorna wiped his hand before his face and Wallace's. He did the same for Joseph, Lexi, and Sarah. Their faces tightened or loosened, browned or blackened. Hair grew or cropped, darkened or lightened. Each appeared Gypsy. For a moment, each was speechless, astonished by the new appearance of the other. Sarah looked more boyish than ever.

Feeling his new face, Joseph smiled. "How do I look, huh?" he asked. "What do you think?" He grinned broadly. He threaded his long, blackened rings of hair through his fingers. Biting his tongue, Lexi shook his head.

Zorna breathed deeply. "I think … we need to mingle."

"I agree. We should mingle in the crowd. Remain undetected," Prince Wallace said. "And Sarah?" Wallace looked into her eyes. "Stay close." His eyes widened. Sarah nodded.

All felt a gentle vibration of their wrist braids as some servants, secret loyalists, carried food and drinks for Prince Zili's combined coronation and wedding dinner. Prince Wallace, his men, and Sarah merged into the parade of servants.

While he merged with the throng, Wallace mouthed a silent pledge to his brother, King Alexander: "This war is mine to win, brother. You and father taught me well. Watch as I return you to your throne."

Through the Dragon's Eye mirror, King Alexander watched unfolding events within the castle. Knowing his brother Wallace's resolve gave Alexander the inner peace he needed to rest and heal.

Beneath the stick of an oil torch in a sconce on the wall, Wallace's dark shadow was cast long across the marble floor. Cohorts waiting, Wallace was the first to peer around a corner and down a dim castle corridor. He saw no one in the crosswalk.

On the wall behind him grew an amorphous, enigmatic spot. Slowly forming a deep black shadow, it grew into the shape of a man, attached to nothing. The ominous silhouette inched closer to Wallace. In slow, menacing undertones, it spoke to Prince Wallace's mind.

As if a feather had brushed him, Wallace scratched the auricle of his ear. Refocusing his attention, Wallace waited. He watched the dinner guests as they entered a room not twenty feet from the corner around which he spied.

"Wallace," spoke the airy voice. Turning his head, he saw no one. The voice continued. "Although it is of little seriousness, Nicholas is injured. He waits as instructed in the passage behind the throne." Wallace brushed his ear. "Beware of the evil troll Jax. Beware …" Like water, the shadow soaked into the mortar between the granite wall and limestone floor.

Prince Wallace gestured for his men and Sarah to close in behind him. "I will go first."

"Sire," whispered General Raptozk.

"No, General," Wallace said, holding up his finger. He pointed to the throne room. "I will go first. You will watch me from here. When it is clear, catch up. Follow my lead into the throne room."

Unseen, Wallace entered the great hall and slipped behind a wall curtain. There he softly stomped his foot twice. From cracks in the base of every wall, a carpet of mice and insects streamed across the floor. At the long dining table, women and men alike leaped to their feet and screamed as they felt creatures running across their insteps and toes.

Screeching, shouting, men and women bolted from the throne room as roaches, mice, and rats dashed up and across the tables. The innocents chased from the room, Prince Wallace stomped his foot three times. Zorna nodded his head and disappeared, reappearing within the room.

In a flash, one hundred dragons simultaneously descended to the castle towers. They bathed the sky in fire to light up the dusk. Zili's tower guards were helpless to defend. As they drew much fire, the dragons' hides were too thick for simple arrows to penetrate. Their rise signaled Wallace's menagerie of human and oddling warriors to attack. Pushing in against the stragglers running from the throne room, a guard screamed to Zili, "It has begun! They have attacked!"

The carpet of pests gone, Zili rose within his self-induced zone of protection. "Very clever, brother. I know you are here. Come out, come out, wherever you are." Zili stood on the first of two steps up to the throne.

Flummoxed, Wallace knew not what to say. His men came out of hiding, glimpsing one another and their new faces. Wallace stepped from behind the wall curtain.

Zili recognized him immediately. "Oh, please, Wallace. You're pathetic," Zili quipped. "Don't look so surprised. I see through that weak magic. I see every face, all of you. I see your warlock behind you—forgive me—your *wizard*. Brother, he is not surprised." They looked at Zorna's face, and his expression was flat.

"A diversion by confusion." Zili smirked. "What better way to draw my men and guests away from me. Sadly, it will not work. You can crawl back into your holes with your rats and mice." Zili sighed. "The prosaic days of Alexander are ... over." Zili cracked his fingers while tightening them into a fist, "And, sadly, it's over for you too."

Chapter 22

DISTRACTIONS

The room empty of guests, each of Wallace's men and Sarah furtively fanned out along the floor, forming a triangular pattern, Wallace on point before Zili. His fingers writhing, his eyes burned into Zili's. Sneering, Zili turned his back and sauntered away toward the long dinner table. Lifting the cloth, he quickly peeked underneath.

"No mechanical toys or dwarfs beneath my table to fight for you, to keep you safe," Zili quipped sarcastically. Keeping his head slightly turned, one eye tracking Wallace, he ambled a short distance back to the two platform steps leading up to the throne. Circling the broad stage upon which the throne rested, he stopped. There he leaned upon the gold-trimmed side of the tall velvet chair and sneered. Lifting his foot, he planted his boot in the center of the seat cushion. Wallace marched forward a step or two.

"I wouldn't," Zili growled, seeing his brother approach. "I see it in your eyes. You want to kill me."

"You're wrong, Zili. Lately you've been wrong a lot. I don't know you anymore. And apparently you don't know me."

Exploding into laughter, Zili laid his head along the vertical back of the throne. "I know you better than you think. We are very much alike."

"As always, you are far off the mark, brother. We are nothing alike."

"Alexander always thought you were better than me," Zili said.

"It's not true."

"Oh, yes, it is true, Wallace. Do not be naive. Father made you think that way," Zili said, "and you believed all the lies."

"Father never did that. He loved you," said Wallace. "You were always cruel and willful even as a child, Zili."

"Alexander and I may not be identical, but we are twins!" Zili shouted.

"Yes," Wallace intoned, "but you two were as different as any men born of separate mothers."

"And Father made sure I knew it every day," said Zili, slowly sliding his sword from his scabbard. He gradually lifted the tip toward Wallace. "On and on, every day. It never stopped." He wagged the tip of the sword in Wallace's face.

Ready to defend Wallace, his men stepped forward, their eyes on Zili. Zili cautioned them with a threatening scowl.

"It was always in your head, Zili. You magnified minor differences in your mind. If Alexander got it, you wanted it. If he succeeded, you thought it should have been you. He never showed such envy toward you. Alexander was good to you."

"Good to me," Zili intoned. "Is that why he made me his serf, his lackey?" Zili laughed, laterally shuffling along the edge of the platform. He peered into the eyes of each man. Taunting, he lunged the tip of his sword toward Wallace. Wallace parried.

"Zili!" shouted a woman's voice.

"Hello?" Zili said, searching around the throne room.

"Stop this!" the voice cried.

First fixing his eyes, Zili rotated his head to the voice.

Sarah shuddered.

Zili saw her in the rear of the room. He saw through her boyish disguise and altered face. He stepped forward on the platform. "I wondered where you'd gone," said Zili. "Come here."

"No. Stay back!" shouted Wallace, glimpsing Sarah at his periphery.

"Lexi, Joseph, Zorna, leave. Take her with you. Find General Raptozk.

Rally our people." He paced forward to meet Zili descending the steps.

"You are not leaving my party now. The festivities have yet to begin," Zili told them.

Lexi, Joseph, Zorna, and Sarah stood fast. "We will stay and help you, Your Highness," Lexi shouted, the others nodding. Lexi dashed toward the steps leading to Zili.

"No," Wallace snapped, cutting his eyes to Lexi. "You will do as I command. You will take Sarah and leave."

Behind the wall of the throne room, Nicholas felt at his belt for a tool with which to pry open the trap door in the wall. He tried to insert his small multitool between the doorjamb and the door, but he could not pry open the door. He had a hammer, but any pounding would give away his position. He would lose his element of surprise. His heart about to jump from his chest, he nervously watched through the peephole, raking his sweat-damp hair from his eyes.

"Be gone with her, little brother. Have no woman behind whom you may hide. I do not care," Zili snarled. "But who will protect you now? Take her. Go. There is nowhere you can go where I do not have eyes. I will find her."

Enraged, Lexi made a step to charge Zili. "I challenge you to a—"

"No!" Joseph shouted. Clasping Lexi by his left arm, Joseph strained to tug him back and out of the room to join Zorna and Sarah. "We must find General Raptozk." Lexi twisted from Joseph's grip.

Wallace motioned toward the door. He marched toward Zili. "Go. Zili's fate is in my hands now."

Zili approached Wallace. "On the contrary, runt of the litter." The two men stood nose to nose. "*Yours* is in mine."

"That is what this is all about. We shall see," snarled Wallace. The men circled each other like sharks, but slowly.

"Wallace, where is Nicholas, your so-called Child of Two Worlds? Hiding somewhere, I wager," Zili said. "Why don't you let me have him and the girl?"

"You *are* mad. Why should I?" Wallace asked.

"Oh, Wallace, Wallace, Wallace. You know exactly why I want the boy. You know he is the key to my succession."

"Or failure," Wallace snapped.

Turning his back, Zili paced away from Wallace. He drew a three-inch knife from up his left sleeve. He picked under his fingernails with the tip while admiring the Firestone ring on his hand. "Think me not a fool, Wallace. We know the story. Twenty years ago, it was foretold this boy child would be my downfall." He leveled the blade at Wallace. "For the life of me, I could not figure out what he was to bring me down from." Zili sucked his bottom lip. "That is, until I decided I would be a better king than our brother Alexander …"

"You decided!" Wallace said.

"Oh, please, Wallace," Zili intoned. "Then I had an epiphany." He spun to face Wallace. Marching, he closed the ten-foot gap between them. With no further word, Zili stuck the short knife into Wallace's left flank. Wallace felt it as a punch. Groaning, he clutched his left side. Zili stepped back. Beneath his threadbare disguise, Wallace felt the knife when it slid from his chain mail into a soft, unprotected area. He staggered back. He tugged his sword from beneath his overlapping garb.

"Oooo," Wallace hooted. "Why have you done this? We could have settled this as brothers." Wallace's face morphed back to normal. He coughed blood.

"Ah, there you are little brother," Zili snarled, peering into Wallace's true face. "As good as old." Zili assumed an offensive stance. His right flank and foot forward. Zili leveled a flat blade horizontally at his brother. Zili thrust forward. Wallace tilted and whirled backward. *Whoosh*—up flew Wallace's blade, catching Zili's forward thrust. Zili's arm arched upward by its momentum.

Wallace steadied. Turning, he caught his balance. He assumed an erect stance despite the acute pain in his left flank. Blood ran to his waist. Wallace's right foot and right arm came forward as he whirled the sword, its tip cutting the air into a wide figure eight. He leveled the sword at Zili, the broad of the blade out stretched vertically.

"We don't have to do this," Wallace said.

"Sure we do," Zili said. He struck a blow that glanced off Wallace's blade.

Wallace lunged. Their swords crossed near the hilt. Each man vibrated as one tried to force the other back. Cheek to cheek, they groaned.

"You knew it would come down to this, Wallace," said Zili, tilting his chin back. "Even your cryptic friend behind the wall of my throne knew this would happen."

Wallace looked surprised.

"You didn't know? Oh, yes, brother. I knew. I've felt his eyes behind the peephole."

Silent, Nicholas reeled back from the peephole and fell against the inner wall, a thin shaft of light beaming upon his chest.

"Who is he, Wallace?" asked Zili. "Another of your toads? Does he have a bolt aimed at my backside, old boy? Perhaps a poison pin aimed at my neck, huh?"

In the pigeonhole Nicholas scrambled to release the latch to escape but could not.

Trapped.

Wallace pushed off from Zili. Bounding backward, Wallace regained his footing. Wallace flèched forward: his right foot slapping the floor, his right arm lunging, and the tip of his sword thrusting dead ahead. Zili parried his blade, which rang as it plunged into the oak floor. He lost his grip. The sword sprang from side to side.

Yanking it from the floor with some effort, Wallace faced away from Zili. Not seeing, he swung his blade behind, horizontally, diagonally, and down. He spun to face Zili, who vanished before his eyes. He reappeared at Wallace's rear. His hand on Wallace's shoulder, he spun Wallace to face him. Zili advanced to punch Wallace in his injured flank.

Wallace folded like a broken twig and fell to the floor. He struggled to stand erect. "Let's stop this, Zili. There is room enough in my kingdom for you. You may share my rule with me."

"Rule by committee, and you my superior." Zili snickered. "Very generous of my little brother. But I shall not take crumbs when I may have it all."

"This realm belongs to our brother Alexander," snapped Wallace, "and you shall not steal it from him."

Wallace riposted hit after hit: left, right, left, right, left, up, down, around. He whirled, lunge, lunge. Wallace wielded his sword relentlessly. With a large clang, Zili's sword fell to the floor. Wallace grasped it with his other hand.

Zili saw that Wallace now had two swords. Zili ran across the room and grasped a sword mounted on the throne room wall. Whirling both his own swords, Wallace dashed toward Zili. Two-handed, he struck up, down, around, one hit after another. Wallace pounded Zili's sword. Zili blocked left and right. He ducked and jumped. Zili threw his blade up crosswise to protect his head. Down Wallace brought his sword. With six successive hits, he pounded on Zili's sword.

On his back, Zili peered up at Wallace's sword coming down on him. Stretched over the dinner table, Zili held his sword over his face, resisting Wallace's attack. His sword broke in half. At that instant, Zili rolled and reached back to grasp a candelabrum. Groaning, Zili struck Wallace at the root of his neck with the candleholder. Dazed, Wallace dipped.

Zili slid off the table. Darting to the center of the room, weaponless, Zili spun on the floor. Wallace saw Zili's body blur. His onyx robe drew in, cloaking him like skin. He exploded into a cloud of fine black smoke and flame, and vanished.

Befuddled, Wallace struggled to regain his wits. His eyes fixed on the wall behind the throne, Wallace hobbled up the platform and past the throne. He shuffled to the wall behind. Looking closely, feeling the wall, he repeatedly knocked on the wood. He could detect the change in pitch. The wall was hollow. He heard muffled screaming.

"Sire, I am in here, behind the wall!" Nicholas shouted.

Wallace looked for something with which he could break through the wall. He noted the throne but it was more than a mere chair with which to bang on a wall.

"No, Sire," Nicholas said, peeking at Wallace through the peephole. "Get back," Wallace ordered. He aimed the tip of his sword into the seam between the trap door and the wall. Drawing the hilt of the sword to his chest, Wallace thrust forward into the seam up to the cross guard of the sword. Twisting, working it, he forced the thick panel open.

Nicholas tumbled out, back first, to the floor. Sweating, holding his head, he peered up at Wallace. Brushing himself off, Nicholas said, "I don't know if I'll ever get used to small enclosed spaces. Zili wants war, doesn't he? We'll tell him—"

But before Nicholas could finish, a brilliant light drew his attention away from Prince Wallace. He heard Wallace gasp. Up at the ceiling, he saw a whirling ball, spinning and emitting lightning.

The snapping, fulgurating sphere softened, slowed, and organized into the colors of flesh. The room filled with the smell of ozone. Emerging from the snapping ball of electricity was the ethereal image of Zili's face and upper torso. Wallace turned to look and stepped back, his sword at his side, his right hand beneath his clothing as he tried to sooth the wound between his ribs.

"Look what rolled from my wall. As I suspected—vermin," Zili derided, his ethereal eyes burning into Nicholas's. "I thought it might be you, Child of Two Worlds. You and your family are a mischief of rats, the chuckhole in my adult life. But you and your kind have irked me for the last time.

"You are a lost soul, Nicholas Claus. You will one day be forgotten." Zili guffawed. "You look at me as if you have no idea, boy. You poor, sick puppy, everyone who loves you has abandoned you. No one believes in you, and no one ever will. No—one—ever—will. Your mother, your father, those serfs you called your parents—gone because of you."

"Liar!" Nicholas shouted. "I have family."

"Liar? You don't know. You haven't heard."

"Heard what? *What have I not heard*?"

"Your uncles, boy. I'd invited them to officiate at my ... wedding. Yes. But just two days ago, they were all in pieces about your parents." Nicholas stared up to the image of Zili. He thought. His eyes began to dart.

Swallowing, Nicholas felt heaviness within his stomach at hearing the suggestive derision.

Zili laughed wildly. The image fulgurated. Bolts of electricity struck the floor near where Nicholas and Wallace stood. Thunder rumbled through the room. They held their ground.

Zili stared down from the air. "Which one was the little one? Oh yes, Mark. What kind of man of God was he—squealing for deliverance?" Zili's face drew closer, just feet from their faces. Bolts of lightning twisted before Nicholas's face. Zili's eyes burned like fire. "What of you, Nicholas?" Zili's sonorous voice rumbled. "Are you a squealer?"

Prince Wallace observed the contracted expression on Nicholas's face. Wallace stepped behind, firmly grasping Nicholas's arm to help him center his thoughts.

"Where is Alexander?" shouted Zili, "Where will I find the girl? You will tell me, boy, or join your uncles."

"What have you done to them?" Nicholas shouted. "If you have hurt them, I ... I ..."

"Are you trying to *scare* me?" The room vibrated with Zili's voice. "With regard to your uncles, let us say that I asked them questions and they fell apart at the answers. They let the cat get their tongues. So I took their pieces, and the cats will get their tongues. What do you say to that, boy?"

"I'm going to—" said Nicholas.

"Going to what? Cry all over me?" Zili snarled. "Remonstrate with cruel criticism? Rebuke me with abrasive language? Hurt my feelings? I think I can withstand that."

Zili turned his wrath to his brother Wallace. "You want war. You will have it." A clap of thunder rocked the room and Zili vanished.

"He thinks himself God, despite his limited powers," Wallace muttered.

"Until he gets the Dragon Stone," Nicholas despondently whispered. "Then he will be impervious."

"If he wants full war, then he shall have it. Let it begin," Wallace sorrowfully said. "On the backs of griffins ride my most skilled knights.

From the air they will release boulders and trunks of trees. I depend on their accurate destruction of Zili's trebuchet, cannon, and oil cauldrons. I trust they will successfully clear his assets. This will allow our invasion forces, including the allies, free access to the castle."

Armed with farm implements and instruments of trade, angry villagers and oddlings from all corners of the Aurora Kingdoms converged on the castle to defend King Alexander and Prince Wallace. In desperate simultaneous battles raging from the edge of the Orphic Forest to the walls of the castle, men, women, yetis, ogres, trolls, elves, fairies and sprites of many types, centaurs, minotaurs, fauns, and gnomes riding tortoises engaged in hand-to-hand combat with Zili's rebels, both human and oddling alike. Many combatants, Alexander's loyalists and Zili's rebels, were either injured or killed.

Chapter 23

THE BROTHERS

On the shire ridge overlooking the castle, King Alexander groaned as he struggled to sit. Queen Isadora pulled him to her. Cradled within her arms, he relaxed as she stroked his head. She knew she had always loved him and would endure any struggle to the end, so long as it was with him. Within her arms, he watched the battle through the Dragon's Eye.

His face contracted in pain.

"How could I have been so blind, my love, my queen? Why did I not see coming the mayhem issued by Zili? I never ordered any of which he accuses me. His treachery and this war are by his own design."

King Alexanderwatched the elf, Prince Chlora, in the tent, directing servants to care for him. "This is my battle, and it should not be fought by proxy. My dear brother Wallace is outnumbered."

"No, Your Highness," said Chlora. "Their numbers are great, for they are supported by all the Linkage." With a wave of his hand, Chlora dismissed the servants from the tent. He waited for the last to leave. His eyes locking to Alexander's, he approached. "Your Highness," Chlora said, his face intense and serious. "Your brother Zili used dark sorcery to accomplish his greed. You, Sire, you ... have the support of all that is good. Trust and rest, that you may heal."

Alexander saw the sincerity in his eyes.

"Trust that you may reclaim your rightful place on the throne," said Chlora.

※

"Sire, perhaps we've won. He vanished," Nicholas said excitedly, spinning about the empty throne room.

"No, Nicholas. He left too easily. Do not be overconfident. This is the beginning," Wallace muttered, jutting his jaw. His eyes scanned the high ceilings and walls, and the slivers of smoke still dispersing. "This is a trick to lull us into false self-assurance. I feel his presence," he added, clasping Nicholas's arm. "We must be gone with great haste. Zili is bound to return, and he will bring others with him."

Wallace started toward the throne room door. Nicholas followed. "He'll take us down if he has the chance," Wallace said with confidence. "He's my brother. He'll not give up so easily."

Wallace flung open the throne room's double doors and dashed over the doorsill. The doors swung out. The handles scarcely out of his fingers, Wallace felt pressure within his midchest, like a hammer blow. He lost his breath as he flew back. Zili had centered his foot and kicked his brother back.

Wallace's upper back slammed into the door, shutting it—BANG— before Nicholas could enter the corridor. Guards fell upon the doors, keeping them closed with Wallace stranded in the corridor, Nicholas within the throne room.

Thrusting toward Wallace, Zili threw punch after punch. He smirked. "I need no magic—for the kind of beating—I give a naughty child, little brother," Zili said between his punches.

Spinning away, Wallace wove and ducked, easily blocking every lunge and strike his brother issued. Zili looked wildly about the hall, pleased his armed guards had gathered around. The hall had become a virtual pugilistic ring, with Zili and Wallace the combatants. Determined to beat his brother as he had when they were children, Zili waved the guards back.

"No!" Zili shouted. "I can handle this thankless pup. I shall make an example of him." He grasped a saber from the scabbard of the nearest guard. Although Zili was an accomplished swordsman, he acted with little thought.

"You were often wild and undisciplined," Wallace said, watching his brother's uncoordinated movements. "What has happened to you?" The rest of Zili's guards arrived in large numbers, clad in full armor. Having flailed wildly, Zili was out of breath. He panted. He slumped against the doorjamb, peering up at Wallace from beneath his brow. Wallace puzzled over his brother's expression, one filled with vitriol and confusion. Zili looked not only evil but also ill.

"Take him," Zili slurred, limply waving his left arm. "Kill them both ..."

Puzzled, his guards hesitated.

"There is another." Sneering, Zili pointed to the throne room that entrapped Nicholas. "In there, you nincompoops. None of you will stop me. Tonight I take my crown." A guard helped Zili to his feet. Zili twisted from his grip.

Bowing, the chief guard moved to carry out his orders, throwing the doors open as he shoved Wallace into the arms of subordinates.

Zili's guards watched with intense expressions as Nicholas backed from the doorsill deeper into the throne room, his hands forward, gesturing for them to stop.

"No. Please. Listen to me. You have to let us go. I—I do not know what—" he began to stammer, "w-what Zili told you ab-about the royal family but ... but Zili is a liar and—and a usurper ..." Nicholas's words echoed among the gathering crowd.

"King Alexander Dobromil *lives*. The royal family lives!" Nicholas cried.

Instantly the mood of the room changed. Onetime guests stood poised to fight, to resist Zili. The distant thundering of footfalls closed in on the corridor. With each passing second, the word spread through the great hall that the royal family lived. Men and creatures following Zili found no leadership from him, only intimidation and disdain.

The crowd within the great hall parted as General Raptozk and Lexi pushed through.

"No one touch Zili. He is mine," the general said. "Nicholas, keep to our plan."

Nicholas wrung his wrists loose from the befuddled guards. They began to reassess their allegiances.

Kicking a guard to the floor, Zili pushed away to run. Prince Wallace clasped him at the back of his shoulders and turned him. Zili swung his fist. Wallace ducked.

"What? A punch? No magic?" Wallace chided. "No clever vanishing act?

To invoke his magic, Zili reached to turn the ring on his finger. Wallace jerked his hand away. "Hold him!" Wallace shouted. "Keep his hands apart; away from that Firestone ring."

Sarah, still disguised, watched from behind the throng gathering within the corridor. Alarmed, the crowd turned when the clang of distant swords sounded, mixed with screams, grunts, and cries.

Humans, boar-men, trolls, and elves fought their way through a cross hall leading to the great hall of the throne room. They poured in from the corridors of the main castle. The corridor filled with warriors of all types but no one noticed tiny warriors joining the fray until they began to fight. Warriors as small as a priest's chalice, wearing tiny wrist braids, chopped away at the fingers of those holding swords.

Twisting, Zili tore loose from the confused guards. Wallace gave chase.

"Grrrrrr! No! It is mine! It's mine!" Zili cried out like a distressed animal. He rushed toward the throne.

Jumping on his back, Wallace clasped Zili under his arm. Threading his arms beneath Zili's armpits, Wallace constrained Zili in a half nelson so Zili could not spin the ring to call up the dark magic.

Thrashing to throw Wallace from his back, Zili was a madman. He struggled to sit on the throne.

"This ... you will never do," Wallace groaned, preventing his brother from sitting upon the throne. Wallace stretched out Zili's right arm so he could not reach the ring on his right forefinger.

Before the throne, the brothers continued battling. Throwing his head back, Zili head butted Wallace. Still dazed, Wallace lunged forward. Striking his forehead against Zili's skull, Wallace returned the favor. Turning, Zili bashed his face into the back of the throne. Blood ran from Zili's nose like a fountain. Each man drew much blood. Away from the throne, they spilled to the floor, rolling over on each other. Down the two steps of the throne platform they rolled. Back on their feet, both men fought.

A circle of guards and onlookers watched. At Zili's captain's gesture, they gave the brothers a wide area in which to fight. Wallace backed Zili into a corner, where Zili grabbed an oil lamp. He smashed it against a table. Scattering oil over the floor and walls, Zili attempted to douse Wallace with lamp oil while shoving him toward the open flame of a wall torch.

Grasping a sword hidden behind the throne, Sarah rushed up behind Zili. Catching Wallace's eye, Sarah lunged forward.

"Watch out!" she shouted. With the flat of the blade, she slapped the lamp from Zili's hand.

Hurled from across the room, a chain bolo whirled around her sword, flinging it from her hand to the floor. A guard with the head and eyes of an eagle and the arms of an ape stood at the doorway, relaxing his posture after hurling the bolo. Sarah ran toward him.

Others of Zili's new contingent entered the throne room. Unaware their beloved Alexander lived, they attacked the boy who was Sarah. Charging them, Sarah scooped up another sword in one hand, a dagger in the other. She matched the guard's strikes blow for blow. Avoiding the lunge of a sword, Sarah sprinted away toward the wall. Vaulting from the wall, she latched high on a wall curtain. They gave chase. Entwining her fingers in the fabric, she flexed at the knees and sprang off the wall. In a wide aerial arc, she swung out of their reach. While crossing a lit torch, the curtain ignited. Jumping down, she landed near Nicholas.

"Nicholas, get her out. Leave this place," ordered Wallace, glimpsing her. Nicholas dashed toward Sarah but not before the fist of a boar-man connected with Sarah's jaw. Her face instantly morphed back to normal.

Furious, thinking of nothing else, Nicholas shouted for the Linkage to remove Sarah and him from the fight.

The magic failed.

Larger and wider the fire grew, chasing up the wall curtains, consuming them one after the other. Timbers comprising the ceiling rafters became alight. Great tentacles of yellow flame and smoke raced into wall tapestries, brightening the room with fire. The serpentine fingers of flame belched black smoke, which crawled like a massive spider along the ceiling. People and creatures separated from the clutches of those with whom they were locked in battle, flames at their backs. The hardwood floor, a battleground, was coated and slick with lamp oil and blood. Varnish bubbled off and slowly blackened to carbon as the fire advanced. The room was an oven. Those too close to the fire suffered as their clothing bursting into flame.

Ripping, tearing, chomping, the flames ate floor, wall, human, and oddling alike. Roaring, it was a crazed eater with an insatiable appetite. The floor succumbed to the flames, groaning with the cries of the dying. The ceiling began to fall, adding to the meal as the floor dropped away and fighters with it. They battled on—blow after blow, strike after strike. Arms tumbled while legs kicked. Mouths screamed as flame, floor, and flesh became one.

The room darkened with choking smoke. Throngs of combatants screamed, some balancing on burned timbers, others falling fifteen feet to the castle underbelly. Thick black smoke overflowed into the corridors, forcing many through a crumbling wall and into the bailey.

Nicholas raced to the corner of the room where Zili's guard lifted Sarah by her waist. "Sarah!" Nicholas yelled, coughing from the smoke. "*Put her down!*" His hand grasping the man's chain mail shirt, Nicholas spun him around. Back he shoved the man, causing him to fall over a bruised and bloody man crawling along the floor toward the light filtering through the pillows of smoke.

"Come on." Nicholas clasped Sarah's hand hard, and they were on the move, his eyes fixed on slivers of light coming through the smoke. Swiftly they charged, dodging, stooping, and jumping combatants.

He towed her through the smoke to the light glimmering through the broken wall.

Slipping away from Wallace's grip, Zili dashed through the smoke, Wallace just behind. Wallace leaped on Zili's back.

"Don't ... you ... have ... a horse, Wallace? Get off my back," Zili snarled, reaching for the Firestone. Wallace flung Zili's ringed right hand in the air, out of reach of his left. Wallace was determined not to allow Zili to spin the ring three times. They fought. Wallace took a blow to his right cheek. Recovering, Wallace landed his knee in Zili's groin. Zili fell forward.

Behind Wallace, Jax the troll clasped Wallace's leg. A swift kick forward, and Wallace launched the troll across the room. Impacting a wall, Jax slid down. Wallace never let go of Zili's right hand.

They fell into the corridor, onto several men fighting on the staircase. The wooden staircase, now uneven, spiraled down through the interior of the keep. Having spread through the floor and walls, the conflagration had weakened the staircase. Sections of the steps gave way, causing combatants to fall atop Wallace.

Upon the shire ridge, Alexander remotely observed the clash through the magic of the Dragon's Eye. His arm falling limp, Alexander dropped the mirror to his chest.

"Chlora. Come to me," entreated King Alexander, the scenes of destruction flying through his head. "Please send help to Illuminae. Our home is in flames." Against the queen's physical resistance, Alexander struggled to his feet.

"Help me!" she cried, looking to Chlora. "The king is delirious. Help me."

"I am not delirious, my love. I am determined to go. I must ... must help. I cannot ... I cannot leave my brother Wallace to die at the hands of ... Oooo," Alexander hooted. He moaned, wincing with pain. His body glistened with sweat. His chest heaved.

Bursting through the tent, Chlora ran to Alexander's side. "Sire," Chlora whispered. "Remember what Zorna said. You must rest to regain your strength."

Chlora helped Alexander lie back upon the cot. As Alexander sighed, Chlora covered him with a quilt. He slipped the Dragon's Eye from Alexander's flaccid grip.

⁂

At Castle Illuminae, the combatants fought on. They rode on a bloody wave of writhing humanity and creatures. The brawl carried them from the corridors through the walls and into the open air. Smoke rose high into the dusky sky. The castle bailey now filled with the roiling melee. Nicholas and Sarah raced about, searching for any glimpse of Wallace. Prince Wallace, his men, and other loyalists continued to fight amid the confusion.

Locked in close combat with Wallace, Zili whispered into Wallace's ear as they rolled in the dirt and blood. "Alexander ... will ... not ... survive ... his wounds," Zili said on his back, struggling for breath.

"You are wrong, Zili," snarled Wallace. "Zorna's potion ... cures him."

"No, brother," said Zili, Wallace's forearm pressing at his throat. "The ... sword that struck him ... was ... poisoned."

Fire

"Rest, Your Highness. Look no more," urged Prince Chlora. "Help is already there. You must rest to heal. Your wife and daughter are resting. So should you."

Isadora quietly watched her husband. She was relieved that Chlora was about to settle her husband down for now. But the queen knew. She knew he would not rest so long as Wallace was in peril. She knew she could not rest; neither could she show foreboding. She put on a brave facade to be strong for her daughter. As queen, she had to be the backbone upon which the ailing king could rely.

Wallace caught and turned Zili in the courtyard. One, two, three punches Wallace delivered to Zili's jaw. Zili fell as Wallace threw the last. Zili dropped to his knees and forward on his face. Up over his head, his black cape fluttered in the breeze.

Wallace peered around at the waning fight. His heart sank. He could clearly see his men were exhausted and seriously outnumbered. Humans and oddlings of every type engaged in hand-to-hand combat, but for every one who fought for Alexander, five fought for Zili.

Racing to Wallace, Joseph, Lexi, and General Raptozk scooped Zili from the ground, each man lifting a limb. He was facedown. Wallace's men left the thick of the fight, going to an outlying corner of the castle. Releasing Zili's ankles and wrists, Joseph, Lexi, and the general laid Zili facedown in the dirt. The men stood around Zili, peering down at his motionless body.

Wallace knelt at his brother's torso, his hands beneath Zili's shoulder and chest. He slowly trundled Zili over onto his back. Up shot Zili's right hand. He slipped a short dagger beneath Wallace's chain mail hauberk, piercing his side as he had done before. Wallace's eyes widened, surprised as he felt a familiar pressure.

"Fool you twice, shame on you. Do you never learn, little brother?" Zili smirked.

"Stop!" shouted Lexi. Rushing forward, he dropped to one knee and drove his left fist into Zili's smirking face.

Joseph jumped to catch Wallace, who slumped over, the dagger in his side.

General Raptozk darted toward Zili. Trampling on Zili's ankle, General Raptozk felt the joint pop as he dropped. Zili grimaced with pain as the general rammed his knee into Zili's chest.

Wincing, Zili still managed to grin. "If at first you don't succeed ..." Zili coughed and laughed, his face contracting into an intense sneer. Zili yanked the dagger out of Wallace as General Raptozk clasped Zili's wrist. With one great heave, Zili rolled the general from his chest and lunged upward. He shoved Lexi aside.

The raven, Mr. Krahe, dropped from the sky, his talons out and forward. He attempted to block Zili's escape, but he was too late and too small. In the course of his pass, the raven only managed to scratch Zili's cheek.

Zili spun the ring and instantly burst into a cloud of black smoke. He vanished.

With a few flaps of his wings Mr. Krahe shot high into the air above the castle. A dot in the sky, he banked and looped circles in the blue, where he awaited his call.

Wide-eyed, his mouth agape, Wallace, speechless, wavered on one knee. Clasping his chest, he glanced his fingers stained with his own blood. Lids fluttering, he toppled to the dirt.

In a secluded stable, Zili roared with pain as he rematerialized. His ankle was broken. And open fracture, the bone protruded through the skin. His left cheek bubbled and steamed from the single slash Mr. Krahe had inflicted. The Firestone's red glowed and deepened as Zili began to heal himself.

Peering into his Dragon's Eye, Zorna closed his lids and whispered words. From the castle grounds, Prince Wallace's fallen body vanished in a glint of light. Instantly he lay on the dirt before Zorna on the shire ridge. Zorna commanded oddlings to take the fallen Wallace upon their backs and walk him to Zorna's tent. There he laid Wallace out upon a cot. After great preparation and mixing his chemicals, Zorna treated Wallace's wounds.

Left behind at the Castle Illuminae, General Raptozk took charge of Prince Wallace's allies. He sent orders via Mr. Krahe to the loyal sprites, trolls, and fairies, and told the dragons and griffins to evacuate injured civilians and soldiers to the shire ridge. Within the hour, Wallace's allies managed to overpower the cannonades and archers stationed atop the curtain walls.

⁂

In the meanwhile, Nicholas and Sarah slipped beneath the collapsed stairwell of the castle keep. Sliding and moving past hot debris, they trod carefully, placing their feet among the scorched stone and charred timbers. A glowing ember glanced off Sarah's arm.

"Ouch," Sarah murmured, jerking her arm away from the glowing tip of a thigh-high timber. Climbing through the fallen and charred tunnel, Nicholas and Sarah trod further.

"Careful," Nicholas muttered, his eyes seeing little. Pushing around debris with their feet, they tromped through groundwater, smoldering embers, and floating wood. Shoving shards of stone, broken weapons, and body parts aside, they continued slowly working their way to the stables.

"What is this place we're going to, Nicholas?" asked Sarah. "Stockmen store feed for the big cats. Aged meat. I smell it already," said Nicholas, sadly well aware of the smell of putrefaction.

"How do they eat this?" Sarah asked, her eyes darting around. "I have never been in this part of the castle."

"This is some of Zili's work," Nicholas muttered. Looking back at her. Nicholas tightened his jaw. He just wanted to get the princess through.

"What are we searching for?" Sarah asked. "Something I hope to never find."

"What does that mean?" she asked.

Nicholas did not answer that. "Just watch your head Sarah. These are heavy beams. You must be careful. I wouldn't want you to—" Looking back at her, he smacked his head on a wooden I-beam. He clutched the back of his head. Sarah raced forward to him. She looked longingly into his eyes but quickly stepped back.

"I think," she whispered, "we should go that way."

Nicholas lowered his head, embarrassed by the excitement he felt at her touch. She pointed to a darkened passage that led to an area that had some light.

"That's it. But I thought you'd never before been in this part of the castle," said Nicholas.

"I haven't, but ... it seems to open up into a small lighted area ahead. See? There is light through there. I see structures ... *Oh!*" she said, holding her nose. "The odor is awful."

"It may be spoiled meat. This is the undercroft, where meat for the special animals is prepared and stored. I was here with my ..." His voice broke. "My father, to do repairs once."

Nicholas looked back at her. "You remember the day we met."

"In the courtyard? How could I forget?" Sarah said. "You were a playful brat."

"I was no brat," said Nicholas.

"I know that now, but no one else did. You were like a big kid. I was certain that, had you been caught, Zili would have had you flogged," said Sarah.

Nicholas pointed forward through a tunnel made of fallen timbers. Through cracks in the castle masonry, the raging firelight flickered, issuing just enough illumination for them to navigate. They entered the claustrophobic space. They could see it was a room. On an opposite wall, they saw a door. They felt grit beneath their feet from sawdust strewn on the floor. Blood-crusted chopping blocks stood in the center of the room. A row of five four-foot-high barrels started near the door and lined two opposing walls.

Nicholas put his shoulder against one of the barrels. "Uh. These are ... pretty heavy." He pushed, but they seemed filled with liquid, and something else was knocking around. He could hear it slosh when he pushed against the barrels.

"Nicholas, you are being mysterious," said Sarah. "What could you possibly need from here? Maybe we should just go."

The black barrels resisted tipping when Nicholas tried shoving one. He frantically searched the small room.

"What are you looking for, Nick?"

He stopped. "You have never called me Nick before."

"Well, it is kind of your name. Right?" She hesitated.

He peered into her face. He nodded and pointed at a barrel. "I need something with which to uncap these barrels."

Her finger beneath her nose, Sarah resisted throwing up. "Like this?" she said, handing him a heavy, short iron lever.

"Yes, like that. Where did you—"

She pointed to a tool chest beneath the chopping table. Nicholas nodded. She shrugged.

Nicholas searched along the back wall. "I'll search the ones over here," whispered Sarah, not really understanding what they were looking for.

Nicholas uncapped two barrels. The search seemed to take hours, even though only minutes passed. He cracked open more barrel lids, quickly one, then the next. He saw three barrels segregated from the others. They looked relatively freshly made, cleaner than the others.

He felt a tremor run through his body, and he remembered his prayer. Nicholas asked of the Linkage: "If you agree with our cause, please help us. Protect those in battle. Protect the royal family. Please do *not* let me find my uncles." But his uncles Nicholas did want to find.

In a far corner, light sprites hovered about them like fireflies. They came from nowhere. Nicholas and Sarah cautiously cast their eyes to each other. Yet neither wanted to see what was contained inside the barrels. Nicholas was compelled to open another. He tried the lever, but the lid was too tight and the lever too short. He took a deep breath of the fouled air. Grabbing a hammer he kept on his belt, Nicholas hooked the claw under the lid and pried it open a little. The stench was overwhelming.

He exhaled and bit his underlip. The smell of rotting flesh choked them. The room overflowed with the unbearable stench.

The top creaked and cracked as he pried. He tried not to breathe.

Sarah turned her head and held her nose.

As Nicholas completely opened the barrel, the rancid liquid frothed. A head popped to the top. He froze and could move no further. The fleshy skull rolled over, the eyes staring into his eyes.

"What did you find?" Sarah whispered. She came up behind and shook him, but he felt nothing. "What is it, Nicholas? *What did you find?*"

The head rotated faceup as the air entered the barrel.

Sarah vomited.

With profound quiet, Nicholas dropped to the sawdust floor.

Stunned, he could not cry. Eyes downcast, he just stared into nowhere.

He tried to wake but he could not, for he was awake and not dreaming.

Yet it was a nightmare.

Sarah stood back and wept profusely. "Your uncles?" she asked, her hands to her mouth, her eyes on Nicholas.

Several of the sprites orbited around the locket, which hung safely beneath her jacket. At first she did not understand what they were trying to say. They orbited her locket like buzzing bees.

"Nicholas, Nicholas," she whispered. "Nicholas," she repeated, dropping to her knees on the sawdust beside him. Tentative hope flashed in her eyes. She was unsure whether or what to say, and Nicholas responded slowly.

"You gave me this, Nicholas, remember? This—this contains the Elixir Illuminae," she said, unlooping the locket from about her neck. "Listen and recall," she said, presenting it to Nicholas.

Nicholas slowly turned, remembering Tom's words.

"Place one drop in the mouth; death will no longer be one's keeper," Sarah said somberly.

"What?" Nicholas said, his eyes darting.

Sarah looked him in the eyes. "Place one drop in the mouth, in each mouth, Nicholas, and death will no longer be one's keeper," she said hopefully. "Death no longer their *keeper.*"

Sarah carefully laid the locket over Nicholas's fingers. Still despondent, tentative, Nicholas said a prayer to himself. He took the locket. It dangled on the leather lanyard as he blessed himself with the sign of the cross.

He stood. He shuffled to the barrel. Turning the head, he could barely peer into its face. Pulling up the head of each man from the barrel, Nicholas placed one drop of the liquid into each mouth. They gasped as the head in his hand began to chew. The room filled with bright aurora light. The eyes popped open. Nicholas and Sarah shaded their eyes with their hands. Nicholas peeked between his fingers. The face on each head began to pink.

The dismembered parts of his three uncles rolled over the edge of the barrel and fell to the floor with the thud of a cut melon. They rose from the floor to hover in the air above the barrels within which they had been stored.

The heads lined up single file, side by side. Limbs of each corpse jumped from the barrels like flying fish. Hands rose above the barrels and hovered beneath the head of Father Bernard. His head and hands sorted from the others, and the same for the body parts of Father Mark and Father Bruno. When the components of the men were properly aligned, the liquid within the barrels arose, spinning like a waterspout. The waterspout divided into three, each aligning with and engulfing the body segments. The surrounding light became even brighter, too bright through which to see. The room whirled with the sound of a powerful wind. The water, turning to blood, entered the body parts.

Nicholas and Sarah shut their eyes tightly. When they heard voices, they hesitantly opened their eyes. The light faded. His uncles stood before them. Crying, Nicholas dropped to his knees. Sarah followed. Their hands clasped, they whispered prayers.

Father Bernard rubbed his stiff wrist and turned his head, cracking his newly assembled neck, following it with a satisfied expression. "Yes," he said. He placed his hand on Nicholas's shoulder. Nicholas startled.

"Come, we have much to do," Father Bernard said.

"Yes, no, no." Nicholas was relieved but confused. "Uncle, wait. You, all of you were ... dead. Don't you need some time ... to ... feel better?" Rubbing his knee, Father Mark smiled. "This knee hurt me for years. It seems fine now."

"That's funny," Father Bruno murmured, a curious expression on his face, rubbing his knee. "Mine never hurt until now."

"Are you sure you are ready, Uncle?" Nicholas said to Bernard. Father Bruno chuckled. "That was then. This is now. We have work to do now."

Not far from the fore building where they stood, they could hear ear-piercing screams.

"It is from the garth and bailey, where the battle still rages," said Sarah. "It echoes throughout the castle. So many people are dying or hurt, Nicholas."

As they entered the area of the castle from whence came the screams, they saw Zili's guards removing their armor as fast as they could manage.

"Oooh. Look!" Sarah hooted. She flung several ants from the back of her hand as she looked up. "Look at them!" she shouted, now seeing the true source of screams. Up and down the halls, Zili's guards flailed wildly, flinging themselves to floors or walls. They were under attack. Red and black army ants filled and overflowed the interior of their clothing and armor. Every exposed area of skin or fur was covered with biting, stinging ants. Zili's army quickly dispersed into naked chaos.

To avoid the lurid sight, Sarah kept her eyes tightly shut—most of the time.

<hr />

Mr. Krahe flew from the castle walls to the terrariums within the royal bedroom, Queen Isadora's bower. He saw that the base of the thorny plant had spread from the two glass cases to cover her room. Vines burrowed through the floor and climbed over the windowsill. From ceiling to stone floor, across her empty bed and mirrors, the room was thick with foliage: curling shoots, broad leaves, and canes.

He perched on a branch of the thick vines. "The Child of Two Worlds requests your assistance," he said.

No sooner had he completed his request than the terrariums of the Orphic Forest responded. Disassembling and vanishing, Alexander's magical allies, creatures and plants, dispersed to many battlefields, where the vines grew and multiplied. Lending their magic to Alexander's loyalists, they choked the battlefield and Zili's rebels, including those outlying and within the castle. Throughout the lower bailey and garth, vines with thorns three feet in length completely enclosed the cannon, oil pots, and spear launchers, rendering them unusable. Springlike shoots slithered like snakes, twisting, winding, and binding Zili's soldiers to the ground, trees, horses, buildings, and anything else they could whirl about.

Above the moat, Mr. Krahe flew, shouting, "The Child of Two Worlds requests your assistance!" Immediately the water of the moat elevated, forming a wall thirty feet high and twenty feet deep, preventing Zili's mercenaries from entering the castle. Their charging horses stopped dead at the wall. Zili's generals feared the tide might turn to Wallace's favor.

Followed by Sarah and his three uncles, Nicholas made his way to the courtyard. They slowly strode around the carnage: Nicholas on point, his uncles behind, and Sarah in the rear. Nicholas shook his head at the sight. Was there nothing men would not do to one another?

A bloody shambles, the courtyard was as bad as any slaughterhouse Nicholas had ever seen. He saw loyalists and rebels locked together, poised forever in murderous repose. Men were impaled on pikes. Hacked to pieces, others lay with clotted, open wounds—most dead, others barely alive. Carts were upturned. Horses dragged dead riders by stirrups. Smoldering ash fluttered from the sky like black snow. Their minds raced, full of questions. Then, from behind, Sarah screeched.

The men whirled back. But they saw no Sarah, only a thick cloud of gray dust. Sarah was gone.

"Sarah!" Nicholas shouted. "SARAH!" Alarmed, Nicholas repeatedly called her name, his eyes searching the courtyard. He spun. Where there had been only flat ground, a lengthy cloud of dust settled above a freshly carved furrow in the yellow dirt, a trench as wide as a man's waist amid scattered patches of overturned grass.

Nicholas's uncles dashed alongside the deep furrow and followed it to its origin. As they followed, they saw it turn sharply into a hole surrounded by mounds of freshly dug dirt, heaped up like the rim of a crater. Clear, gelatinous slime oozed and bubbled from the hole.

Nicholas's uncles stopped and circled the hole. It was as round as the circumference of the waist of two men. Mark punched a five-foot-long stick down the hole all the way to his armpit. Mark shook his head. "It goes deep."

When Mark withdrew the stick, the hole collapsed. Crumbling, the hole filled in from the rim. Half in, half out the hole lay a tangled tube of crusted, shed skin.

"It appears to be of a snake but no ordinary snake," said Bruno. The texture of thin, translucent paper, it was as wide as the hole from which it protruded.

"A giant ground-serpent," Father Bernard uttered. "I've seen them but never in this part of the kingdom. Mean devils from the Outland."

"Outland?" Mark murmured, his eyes shooting up from the burrow. "From the Outland, here? Outlanders cannot be trusted, and they are dangerous. If they ever gain a foothold here … they'll never leave. They are likely under the control of Zili."

Nicholas gazed into the eyes of his uncles. "Will Zili stop at nothing to gain his ends? Has he no limits?"

Bruno growled. "No. He won't. Reason has its limits, my son. Ignorance does not."

Nicholas shook his head. "We must stop him and get Sarah before it is too late."

Closing his eyes, Nicholas called to the sprites and the insects. "Sarah has disappeared. Please help me find her."

Father Bernard took control. He pointed to Nicholas, Father Bruno, and Father Mark, and prayed. Father Bernard held his finger up to his lips. "Quiet. We cannot be detected. Not yet."

Father Bernard pointed to the direction they should search. Nicholas removed the Dragon's Eye from his pocket. He could see that Sarah was unhurt. But he saw her sitting, tied to a chair, her feet bound to the legs, her hands behind her. She was surrounded by guards, both human and boar-men. The ground-serpent wove slowly around her chair, its dark, dead eyes watching, its bifid tongue flicking the air.

"Zili," Nicholas muttered. "I cannot identify her location."

Unexpected Ally

Overcome by fatigue and emotion, Nicholas wandered to the courtyard colonnade. There, he leaned against one of the last of the standing columns. He needed to compose himself and think. The worst thing about resting was that his mourning, frustration, and anger had time to surface. He dried his eyes as the anger strengthened his resolve.

He could not believe how alone he felt. Where was Sarah? He had no inkling. He thought, "So stubborn is she—hardheaded and beautiful." He drove his fist into his hand. "But she will not listen!" His expression softened. He breathed. She was tied up but unhurt—for now. Nicholas thought of Alexander; he was safe with family. Wallace was safe with Zorna.

He calmed himself and remembered what his father had told him: things worked better when one was calm. He scrutinized the destruction. The broken castle walls were not secure. He peered throughout the bailey, garth, and courtyard. There were so many beings injured, others homeless. So many rumors had flown as had arrows, and many just as dangerous. Stories and more stories swirled in his head. Nicholas breathed audibly. There were lies at the heart of the conflict. They had caused this great downfall, yet the only thing not fallen were the lies.

Nicholas ambled over a crosswalk from the column to the shattered wall of a drum tower and the arch of a door therein that led to a small room. He watched the courtyard from the doorway. There, his three uncles stood, watching.

Almost not sure of the truth anymore, Nicholas aimlessly strode inside.

"All Zili's lies," Nicholas whispered. "What truths have these walls witnessed? If walls could talk."

They watched him go into the drum tower. "Poor Nicholas," Father Mark said. "I think he's losing his mind."

"Nooooo," Father Bernard lilted. "With a little faith, brother, you can go far."

"A little faith," said Father Mark, "and a sharp sword go farther."

Nicholas's energy was nearly sapped. He wandered to a broken wall just feet away on the other side of the small room. Both hands out front, he leaned forward against the wall, his feet back and legs spread. "Do you talk?" Shaking his head, he put his eyes down and was about to walk away.

"Yes."

"Whoa! Who said that?" shouted Nicholas. "*Who said that?*" For an instant the voice made him questioned his sanity. Perhaps these were the mystic stone people. Nicholas was acquainted with their legion, but he had never knowingly recognized them.

"We did."

"Who are *we*?" Nicholas glanced up to see the heel of his palm half over an eye peering out from the wall. Swiftly pushing off, he snatched his hand from the eyeball. Suddenly he saw fifty pairs of eyes staring at him, at least one pair per marble brick. "You *talk*?" Nicholas yelled.

"Yes. Do you? That is, without yelling. We have ears."

"You do? I mean, I am sorry. Where do you come from?"

"Everywhere Nicholas. We are the rocks in the castles, the cave floors, the chimneys, and even the bricks of hearths. You are not alone," whispered a chorus of voices as one from the wall. Clutching his chest, Nicholas glared at the wall. Out of his line of sight, a face came together among the crystal colorations of the cracked marble.

"You are not convinced, Nicholas. I see questions on your face."

"It is not that I doubt you talk, for you do; I hear you. Others, however, may doubt my sanity if they witnessed me talking back to you. I have doubted when I've seen others talk to walls, trees, air, or their pets—especially if they behaved as if those named talked back. But lately I have seen much to convince me that there are indescribable things beyond my meager understanding."

"We are your friends."

Guardedly, Nicholas turned, looking into all directions to see if others saw him talking to the wall, but he saw he was alone. "Who are you? Come out where I may see you."

"You still do not believe. Remember what you told Sarah?"

"Sarah. You know of her? It is she I seek," Nicholas muttered.

"From the fireplace, you told her she must believe," said the stone wall. "You do see us; you are looking right at us."

Nicholas lifted his eyes. He could now clearly see the face. It smiled. "Come closer ... stand before me. Talk with us," coaxed the deeply bass voice.

Digging around the serpent hole, Nicholas's uncles looked up to see him across the courtyard in the drum tower. They saw him search the room with his eyes and hands, apparently seeking someone or something that might be hiding amid the clutter.

"In this tower, this part of the castle tannery? Yes?" Nicholas asked, sauntering to the center of the room. He could make out the broken and smashed contents of the shop. His eyes searched for anyone alive who might be tricking him.

Stepping forward over the doorsill and back, he studied the wall near the door. He saw eyes on the inside and wall on the outside.

"I still don't see anyone. I suppose you are who you say," Nicholas said as he felt his head spin. He stood unsteadily. The wall watched as Nicholas held his head and his stomach, which ached.

"What is it, Nicholas?" murmured the voice.

Startled, Nicholas reeled. "I don't know. I don't know." He held his stomach. His eyes fluttering, he stumbled back.

"Food," Nicholas breathed. "I haven't eaten in ... in ..." Nicholas toppled forward. Two stone arms with delicately sculptured hands shot forward and caught him in midfall. They lifted Nicholas as if he were a child.

"Not only do we do talk, we listen and watch."

Recumbent in the cupped hands cradling him, Nicholas withdrew a piece of hardtack from his pouch and ate it. Nicholas became alert. He sat on the stone hand as on a chair.

"Thank you ... but why show yourself to me now?" Nicholas said.

"King Stanislaus commands it to be so."

"I don't understand," said Nicholas. "Please explain."

"Castle Illuminae is created of materials from the Orphic Forest. The castle is a living entity. You, Child of Two Worlds, have awakened Castle Illuminae."

"But the battles have been great, though Zili's reinforcements have been kept out," said Nicholas. "That cannot last. Zili still controls this castle. No one can get in, but no one can get out. And Sarah ... he has her."

A voice shouted from the courtyard. "Feeding time for the animals!" Loud voices, both man and troll, came from the interior of the fore building, all converging on the drum tower. "We must do something with these corpses," one said.

"Why?" asked another rough, laughing voice.

"Because Zili commands it. That is why," replied yet another.

Nicholas looked from the room in the drum tower to the courtyard. At the sound of the voices, he saw his uncles dash behind an upturned cart.

"To the lions you will feed a friend or foe; never more will you see them though," Nicholas heard the interior voices sing.

"Zili's trolls," Nicholas whispered. "They are coming this way," he said to the wall.

"We shall hide you," said the stone wall. It transformed the stone beside Nicholas to powder. Leaning, Nicholas sank into the dust, into the wall, which immediately solidified over his body, concealing his location. Nicholas could see through the solid wall as if it were made of glass, and the wall fed him air. From the outside, however, it was mere solid stone. His view of the room changed and became blurred.

Chapter 24

SOLSTICE

When the danger passed and he was safe, the stone wall released Nicholas. He popped from the wall.

"That was *amazing*!" Nicholas shouted. He quickly remembered to lower his voice. "That was amazing."

They had cared for him in the warm bosom of their interior. He hadn't suffered. No dust scratched his eyes. No dust plugged his ears. He felt the timelessness and immutability of stone flow through his body. When unfiltered sound returned to his ears and unfiltered light came back to his eyes, Nicholas carefully took inventory of his surroundings.

"I've just passed through solid rock." Nicholas grinned, imbued with a renewed energy and sense of promise.

"That is right, Child of Two Worlds."

"Where am I?"

"We are transporting you past the turret and up to the chapel, Nicholas," said the stone wall. "This is where the coronation and wedding are scheduled. Here—tonight." Becoming a kind of highway, the stone wall transported him to another part of the castle.

Standing erect, Nicholas stuck out his chest. "Then this is where I must be."

"Excellent. It's good that you know where you are," the stone wall slowly said.

Nicholas stood near a fountain of water. Peering in, he did not see his reflection. "Am I still within your stone?"

"No, Nicholas, but you are invisible to all at this moment. You have access to one of the powers of stone: the power of glass."

"I hear, but I do not see you, stone man. Where are you?" asked Nicholas, peering where the wall had been—and the stone floor, for that matter.

"That is of no importance at this time. Tell me, Child of Two Worlds, what is it that you see?"

"The power of stone has allowed me to see straight through the stone walls and floor to the grounds below," said Nicholas. "How is this possible?"

"As glass is made from stone, we've conferred on you the power of transparency, and at this time I have conferred on you the ability to see through any relative of ours—any stone. Again, what do you see?"

Nicholas gestured as he identified the strange scene before him. "There are many beings below us this day who still battle in isolation. They appear stopped in time, along with their weaponry. Thrown stones, launched arrows, and flying spears all hang in midair."

"Because I have intervened, Nicholas," said a voice from behind him. "I have stopped time."

Nicholas turned to see a tall, thin man wearing a woolen robe and cowl. He had a white beard and wizened face. His long, spindly fingers projected through his wide, loose sleeves. Within his right hand, he gripped a seven-foot, gnarled walking stick whose crystal end came to his chin.

"What else, Nicholas? What else do you see, Child of Two Worlds?" asked Father Time.

"The Aurora citizens I know to be neutral to the battle are also stuck within time. Dragons, yeti, centaurs, minotaurs, griffins, and elves lift them like chess pieces and carry them to safety into the forest."

"Excellent, Nicholas. We, the Powers That Be, have given you a gift. You may, if it benefits others, see all beings in both worlds. In addition, you may hear the inner fears, wishes, or needs of the innocent. When you need, you shall recall that information. And you shall be seen as you wish it."

Nicholas began to understand the weight of the responsibility and trust given him.

"I shall continue."

Nicholas heard a voice come from the other side of the deck. "Beside the chapel beneath us, stone men are constructing a stage. It will be fifteen feet long by ten feet deep and ten feet off the ground. Steps on either side will lead to the top. Atop the platform will be an altar with two thrones in the center and two chairs on either side. Beside the altar, a table shall hold two crowns and a scepter locked within a glass box. Centered on the altar will be a silver box with a glass top—also locked."

Suddenly, peoples in the courtyard, in the bailey, throughout the castle, and everywhere he could see began to move at ten times normal speed. Nicholas's knees trembled. All those in battle who were loyal to King Alexander and Prince Wallace moved with the speed of hummingbirds' wings.

Nicholas watched as oddlings from the terrariums set themselves as decoration around the stage and guest seating. Zili was going to have it his way. Nicholas's anger grew intense as his fingers rubbed against one another. He could not let this stand.

"My uncles,!" he abruptly remembered. "The last I saw them, they were in the courtyard. Where are they?"

"They are safe," said Father Time. "General Raptozk, Lexi, and Joseph took them to King Alexander."

"Father Time, will King Alexander and Prince Wallace be in attendance at the eclipse this evening? Will they be safe?"

"At the proper hour, they will be there. As for safety, all those in the audience have been selected by Prince Wallace."

Nicholas heard the whooshing of wings and a caw. Mr. Krahe perched on the turret beside Nicholas. The mynah birds arrived an instant later.

The larger of the mynah birds innocently tapped his beak on the stone that had enchanted Nicholas. "Father Time, your older brother Stanislaus pleads with you to hold the twilight no longer."

"I shall pray for the stone men and topiaries to heal Castle Illuminae."

Lifting to the air, the birds coursed in divergent directions, to areas broken or destroyed in battle.

"The birds shall help with the repairs. Wherever the breeze generated by their wings touches, all parts above and below shall be repaired," said Father Time. "Topiaries and wood nymphs shall grow new floors and stairways for the castle."

"Father Time," Nicholas beseeched, "will not Zili believe he has won? Will he not presume the repairs are an endorsement of his quest for the throne?"

Father Time stepped closer to Nicholas, peering down into his eyes. "A presumption that shall beget his downfall. I know your question before you ask, Nicholas. I know what you think. But I must let the fate of free will unfold. I cannot change with a wave of my hand the fate as it is written."

Nicholas sighed. As a carpenter, Nicholas watched in awe as the damage he estimated would take years to repair occurred in seconds. The water settled back into the moat and became still, as if no battle had ever occurred. Cracks in walls zipped closed; towers rose. Blood on the dirt soaked away. Scattered fires died and scorch marks faded, and it went on.

"Pardon me, Father Time. I mean no disrespect. I wish only to understand. How can events be changed? Have these events not already been written in time?"

Father Time smiled. "Now, Nicholas, you have asked the correct question. As Father Time, I am privy to ineffable knowledge: things beyond human power to tell or understand. Castle Illuminae is damaged, but it can be repaired because all those involved within the main time line would have that damage undone. The final course of a time line will be determined by the choices or actions taken by the beings, individual, or groups most affected by that time line. Time exists for only one main purpose, Nicholas. Implicit within that purpose is time's ability to allow us to have experiences and learn from them. Along the way, we learn to help others to make choices that will result in better outcomes. This is such a case."

Solstice Night

Each year on the longest night, citizens of the Aurora Kingdoms gathered to celebrate the return of the long season of light. Generally a joyous occasion, this night was bittersweet. This time, darkness could lengthen.

Tonight the reign of evil could begin.

The citizens of the Aurora Kingdoms occupied the rejuvenated castle, garths, and baileys of Illuminae. As part of his plans to seal his ascension to power, Zili decreed that there would be revelry and circuses or there would be death.

From the tourney field to the streets, from the baileys to the courtyards, the people watched the procession leading to the stage outside the chapel. Within the turret, trumpeters sounded. Criers raised their voices, roaring, "Hail to Zili!"

"All hail, Prince Zili of Illuminae!" voices echoed. The mention of his name seemed to electrify the chanting throng. "Zili, Zili, Zili," they called.

"Tonight," said a voice, "Prince Zili shall become the rightful ruler of the Kingdom of Illuminae." Echoes reverberated.

"Tonight," the crier continued, "Crown Prince Zili shall wed Princess Sarah Morning-Light of the Kingdom of the Four Winds."

Within the stone wall, Nicholas listened, biting his lip, controlling his contempt. He shook his head. Her name should not be said within the same sentence as his. That he might touch her was a knife in Nicholas's belly. His mind turned away and Zili's name faded, if just for a moment. Nicholas imagined his birth father and mother. He thought of his parents, Tom and Mary. Within his heart, they spoke to him. They brought him solace.

A procession of musicians, jugglers, live animals, and clockwork animals preceded Prince Zili's royal bodyguard. The mechanical animals clattered and whined as their gears ground autonomously, driving them forward. Installed by Zili, the bishop of the high church led the procession, followed by Prince Zili dressed in his finest, most flamboyant armor.

On the stage, Zili's wizard waited to begin the coronation ceremony. A tentative to resigned expression on her face, Sarah wore a floor-length blue satin gown. Torchlight accented her hood of Irish lace and gold, her auburn hair spilling forward over her low décolletage, framing her soft, white skin. Flanked by two guards, she stood nervously at the back of the stage, her green eyes pleading for help, seeking Nicholas.

On the dais, a stage only two steps up, Zili sat on the larger of the two thrones. Zili's wizard accompanied the bishop. Zili stepped to the altar. The bishop removed the crowns and scepter from an encasement. After shaking a censer over the crown, the bishop carefully passed his hands over the crown and whispered a prayer. After blessing the crown, he faced the crowd.

"Tonight when the moon reaches its highest point in the sky," said the bishop, "the aurora will send its light to bless your new king."

Again moving out of the stone wall, Nicholas hid among the crowd, allowing his face to remain eclipsed by the head of each guest as he moved through the audience. Furtively creeping toward the stage, he continued weaving among the crowd.

Zili's wizard moved to the altar and unlocked the box containing the Crystal Chronaria. He removed it from the box and held it up for all to see. A hush came over the crowd.

"This is the Crystal Chronaria." He grinned. "When the moon reaches its apex, the power of the Linkage is strongest."

He held the Crystal Chronaria high above his head. "When the moonlight passes through its center, it will grant immortality to me, Prince Zili Dobromil, and mark me as king of the Aurora Kingdoms ... for all time." He handed it to the bishop.

Just before the moon reached its highest point, the bishop handed the Crystal Chronaria to the wizard. After passing a wand above it, the wizard placed it in Prince Zili's open hands. Zili lifted it over his head. When clouds passed before the moon and the stage darkened some, Nicholas dashed onto the stairs leading to the stage.

"You, Zili, are not worthy to hold the Crystal Chronaria!" Nicholas shouted.

The audience gasped; a hush hastened through the mass. Zili's guards advanced toward Nicholas. Zili raised his hands to stop them.

"Wait," Zili cackled. "Let this fool's own words condemn him." Nicholas twisted his wrists from the guards' grasp.

"It is you who shall be condemned. Your soul is poisoned. There is only coal where a heart should be." Nicholas quickly advanced from the steps to the stage. He stretched out his right arm and open fingers. Dropping his chin, he closed his eyes and clenched his jaw. "Come." But the crystal did nothing.

Licking his lips, Nicholas again shouted, "Crystal Chronaria, come to me!" He threw his left arm out with his right. The sphere suddenly flew up from Zili's tight grip, spun in the air, and shot to Nicholas's hands. Zili staggered back as he glanced up. The moon was coming into position.

"Now he is condemned!" Zili roared. "Guards! To the dungeon with that—that ... boy!" He smirked, flinging his arm toward Nicholas. A brilliant flash from the crystal caused the guards to retreat, and they hesitated. They stayed back.

"To me! *Come!*" shouted the wizard, staring at the Crystal Chronaria.

But it would not leave Nicholas's hand.

The bishop advanced to the edge of the stage. "People of the Auroras, join me as I call for a sign from the Powers That Be. Send us a sign to let us know what is true." Instantly the cloud moved from before the moon.

Zili saw the moon was completely eclipsed.

"I ordered you to take him!" Zili roared.

Zili's guards advanced on Nicholas, prying the Crystal Chronaria from his fingers. Fumbling, the guards dropped the Crystal Chronaria onto the stage.

"Bishop!" Nicholas called out, glimpsing the eclipse as the clouds parted, "There is your sign."

Guffawing raucously, Zili marched across the stage. Flinging his arm down, Zili scooped into his hand the orange-size crystal. Huffing, he looked to the sky. "Sign? What sign, fool?" Prince Zili smirked. "It is a glorious night for a coronation … and marriage. The bright full moon shall shine upon this crystal, my reign will begin, and the destruction of you and your cohorts will be complete!" Zili shouted.

From the ambivalent crowd arose a cacophony of jeers and cheers. Zili's guard immediately combed through the crowd, plucking out the malcontents. Guards were about to drag Nicholas away from the stage, but Zili halted them.

"Stop. No. Before he dies, I want him to see this. I want him to witness the satisfaction in my eyes as I rightfully take what should be mine." He gestured to Sarah and the crown.

"We are a peaceful, freedom-loving people!" Nicholas shouted. "Here in this land are many wondrous things. When you take power, this kingdom will suffer. It shall become devoid of kindness and joy and goodwill toward men and oddlings."

"Suffer indeed. Goodwill indeed," Zili scoffed. "I love this country. I fully intend to fundamentally change this land from the ground up. I will give it a new hope and change."

"Why? Why? Mold it in your image? Into what you think it should be?" Nicholas shouted. "From the ground up? Why would you change something you truly love? You, the people, will in fact hope for change and get worse. You don't love this country. You love yourself. You love power."

Zili dipped his head and grinned. "There is something to be said for raw power, boy. Hmm?" He held the Crystal Chronaria above his head. "But I have this and you do not. It is mine, mine forever."

Nicholas broke from the guards.

"Get him, idiots!" shouted Zili.

Nicholas grabbed the king's scepter and dashed toward Zili. With one blow, Nicholas impacted the outer shell of the crystal, cracking it in Zili's hand. Zili pulled the broken crystal close to his chest. The massive hands of a guard caught both of Nicholas's shoulders and towed him back.

Eyes darting, again Zili cautiously elevated the Crystal Chronaria above his head.

Nicholas yelled emphatically. "*Please*! Beings of the auroras, choose! Choose now, before the moonlight hits the Crystal Chronaria. Good or evil!" He struggled in the guard's massive clutches. "The crystal will bring the king of your choosing. Choose Alexander, not Zili. You know what is right."

Zili turned the crystal over in his large hands.

"*Give up your crusade*!" Nicholas shouted, tugging at the guard who held him. "Do not do this, Zili. I warn you!"

"*Warn* me?" bellowed Zili. "It is you who should be warned, boy. By coming here, you have warranted your own death!"

"No! By doing this, Zili, it will be your own death you warrant!" Zili faced the throng and laughed wildly. "The eclipse shall not pass!" The moon was dark over his shoulder. He held the crystal high above his head.

In the shadows of the audience, cloaked in a disguise, Zorna peered at the sky. "Look. The eclipse is passing," he said.

"But this is not just any eclipse," said Joseph, hiding alongside Zorna. "The whiteness of the full moon does not peak behind the shadow. There is something else …"

The face of the moon surged blood red as its angry light grew and shot through the center of the Crystal Chronaria. From the crystal blared a piercing high pitch. The entire throng screamed. Facing his shuddering audience, Zili's smile soon turned to cries.

"What is this? What's going on?" Zili muttered.

Blasting from the ring on Zili's hand, scintillating light twisted into the colors of molten lava.

"No. Help," he murmured. "What's happening? Help. Help! *Stop this*!" Zili screamed. Dropping to his knees, his body flailed. Tugging, wrenching, flinging his hand from side to side, he tried frantically to loose the ring from his fingers.

"Take it off. No! I don't want this," Zili whimpered, tugging at the ring. "It won't come off. I can't get it off!" In fact, it tightened.

"It's tightening! Somebody *help* me! I command it! I am your new king—obey me! Please? Or die. I'm burning. Oooo," Zili hooted, crying with agony.

The air flooded with the odor of burning flesh. Zili's body smoked and contorted, twisted and shrank, his voice quieting. Gasping, the audience backed away from the edge of the stage. Offstage, Sarah looked away. Nicholas shut his eyes and turned away.

Aghast at the horrific transformation, Lexi tugged at Zorna's sleeve. "What is happening to him?"

Zorna looked to Lexi. "This form reflects the evil that has consumed his soul."

Dread left Zili's wizard nearly struck dumb. With trepidation, he reached for his master's trembling hand. Zili's dying hand bobbed from the mass. Reeling wildly, it blindly latched on to the wizard's wrist.

"Noooo!" the wizard cried, futilely resisting Zili's dying arm. But it towed him into the deadly pool. He became one with Zili. Both went to their oblivion. The odor of brimstone and decaying flesh intensified. On the steps of the stage, Jax popped out of existence.

Although frightened, the bishop rushed forward, repeating the sign of the cross.

"The moon," Zorna whispered, "has again turned silver white." The Bishop's voice quavered. "Choose now, before the moonlight hits the Crystal Chronoria. My ch-children, good or evil—release the princess!"

Released, Sarah ran to the guards holding Nicholas. Stunned by their master's obliteration, their fingers fell away from Nicholas. Sarah and Nicholas embraced. He glared into her eyes and she nodded. She knew what he had to do. He charged center stage. Upstage, he stopped, the thrones behind him. Warily, Sarah paced far to his left.

"The time," Nicholas said, peering into every eye and into every heart, "is NOW."

The moon cast its white light upon the stage. Zili, no more than a tarry soup, flashed over to black smoke. At Nicholas's feet, the Crystal Chronaria lifted from the stage and rose with each passing instant. Hovering, rotating, it blared a bright light, a white light so brilliant it made a sunny day seem cloudy.

The high-pitched tone returned, forcing everyone to cower and cover their ears.

Father Time strode from nothingness to center stage. Then suddenly, there was silence. Mr. Krahe lit upon the staff of Father Time.

Slowly fanning the right arm of his robe out like a curtain, Father Time quickly retracted. From behind, King Alexander, Prince Wallace, and the royal family stood together on the stage. Father Time sat. Beside him sat King Stanislaus and Zorna; behind sat attendants of the royal family, at their right.

A roar of applause rose like none ever heard before.

King Alexander, Prince Wallace, and the royal family turned to their right, and bowed in recognition of King Stanislaus and Father Time. Mr. Krahe landed on the floor before Zorna. His dark, round raven eyes peered up to Zorna. Shaking his tail feathers, he waited with anticipation.

Zorna leaned forward.

With the first two fingers of his right hand, Zorna touched the raven on his head. With Zili no longer holding magical sway over his fate, Mr. Krahe grew taller and broader, his bird features absorbing and shrinking. His black feathers becoming a black cape and clothing, his black talons became boots, and his hair turned white. Attaining his full height, Mr. Krahe writhed hands with human fingers. His bird eyes turned human. He turned his human face to the audience.

He was again human.

From the audience, a middle-aged woman rushed forward, placing her fingers on the edge of the stage. Staring into his human eyes, she laughed and cried with happiness as she stretched up her arms, whispering his first name for the first time in more than twenty years. He knelt to passionately kiss his wife from the stage.

The sky cleared.

The stars looked like diamonds spilled across a silken black cloth. The aurora borealis rippled across the sky as a blanket of breathtaking color.

King Stanislaus turned to face the royal family.

"The people have chosen peace," he said. A roar of cheering and applause swelled from the assembled crowd.

"King Dobromil of Illuminae," said King Stanislaus, "you have regained control of your kingdom. Remember all that has happened here. Rule wisely."

Chapter 25

COUNCIL OF ELDERS AND KINGS OF THE AURORAS

Early spring came, when all beings awakened from their winter slumber. The Council of Elders and Kings of the Auroras called a meeting in the valley at the base of Hydra Falls. Clad in their finest clothing, ablaze with the various colors of the rainbow, honored guest arrived in carriages of all kinds and sizes and states of adornment. Ambassadors arrived from remote kingdoms and duchies. Honored guest arrived on foot, by water, and on the wing. Leaders of every human and oddling community gathered in cheerful attendance.

When all had arrived and settled beneath the canopy of trees, King Stanislaus took his seat of prominence and charge upon a large green-and-gold chair at the end of a long table, the gathering abuzz with excitement. A cacophony of voices and accents blended in joyous chaos. Many who were not seated stood around the walls before murals and tapestries to commemorate the occasion.

With a large mallet, the sergeant at arms percussed a giant, sonorous cymbal—*bong.*

"His Majesty, King Stanislaus, commands this meeting come to order." Bowing to His Majesty, the official stood aside.

King Stanislaus lowered his arms.

The room hushed. He peered into the eyes of his audience.

"I have called this meeting to discuss Mr. Nicholas Claus and the service he rendered freely for the restoration of peace in the Aurora Kingdoms. His great service must be rewarded. Is there anyone present who would speak to his reward?"

"Aye," spoke a lively voice. The speaker stood, showing himself. "For those who do not know me, I am King Alexander Dobromil, ruler of the Kingdom of Illuminae. Four months have passed since solstice night." An assistant translated his words in sign for those who received spoken words differently. "Nicholas Claus has continued to serve the people of both human and oddling worlds. He has concentrated especially on the children, with concern for their happiness and well-being. I favor his reward."

"As is your nature, King Dobromil," said King Stanislaus, "you speak with humility and without presumptions."

King Alexander dipped his chin and sat.

Another stood. "I am Chlora, eldest prince of the elves of the forest. Nicholas continues to help provide the needs of daily living for those families whose members were permanently affected by the actions of Prince Zili."

From the rear of those assembled, someone shouted to Chlora. "He teaches right from wrong, faith, self-reliance, and self-worth to the children. He rewards them by fulfilling their wants or needs. He did so especially in these past winter months. When all were starving, Nicholas said prayers, asking that all the kingdoms of the aurora never go hungry. The grain ship in the harbor at the Kingdom of Waters still provides a continuous supply of manna, which feeds all in need."

A troll climbed atop a rock. "I am Eroll, King of Trolls. Nicholas gives to those who are in need, even if they do not seek, but for himself he has no greed."

Father Time stepped to the edge of the lagoon formed by Hydra Falls. "Brother, Nicholas gave all he cherished to restore peace to our worlds. His parents of blood were murdered to prevent his birth. His parents of Linkage were murdered as they protected the life of Princess Sarah Morning-Light. His uncles were murdered as they protected the Crystal Chronaria. We rejoice at his uncles' timely restoration to him. He has asked nothing for himself, only for others."

Voices from all directions confirmed the words of Father Time. In the warm spring breeze, Jack Frost sat above the water on an iceberg of his own creation. "Nicholas's heart longs to be joined with that of Princess Sarah Morning-Light. I recommend we let them join hearts, as they are in spirit already one heart. Princess Sarah Morning-Light also has continued to help those harmed by Prince Zili."

Upon the air, with his breath, he fashioned a gossamer depiction of their joined hands, which evaporated in a ray of sunshine.

"If all here agree, let them be joined and share the immortality that the Linkage can provide."

Prince Wallace stood, glimpsing King Alexander smiling and nodding in agreement.

"I, Prince Wallace Dobromil, speak for the Kingdoms of Illuminae and Waters. Princess Sarah Morning-Light is of our blood. Our kingdoms consider the proposal of Prince Frost a great honor. I request of this council that we accept this proposed honor."

King Stanislaus looked over the council. Seeing no sign of dissension, he asked, "Does anyone else wish to speak?"

Hydra Lagoon withdrew from its banks. A mountain of water gathering at its center took semihuman form. It began to fashion the face of a lady. The remaining lake became the hem of her gown. Fully formed from the waist up, Lady Hydra towered above all to speak to the council.

"I agree," she intoned. All were awed at the sight of small fish doing loop-the-loops in her body of water. "The gift of immortality should be granted with two conditions. First, there must be a marriage; together their love will make the magic of the Linkage stronger. Second, immortality should be granted *only* if Nicholas and Sarah agree to continue to serve those in need."

Father Time stepped forward. "All who are in agreement, indicate with sound or light on the strike of three."

He stamped his staff on the ground three times. Throughout the council sounds and flashes in clusters of three returned in response. "All those not in agreement, indicate with sound or light in strike of one." Silence: no response given.

"King Stanislaus."

Stretching her dragon's wings, Princess Salamonica peered over the table. The princess of the dragon people lowered her massive head to the height of the table.

"Yes, Princess Salamonica," said King Stanislaus.

"Please, Sire, allow this gift be witnessed here, before the council?"

Honor Bestowed

Staff in hand, King Stanislaus made his way several feet to a throne situated upon on a small, foot-high platform, a dais covered with red velvet. The lake behind him, he sat, his robe flowing over the step to the ground. He peered to the near and the far ends of the long table projecting away from him. Guest and dignitaries remained seated along either side the table.

Closing his eyes, King Stanislaus drew a circle in the air and stamped the end of his staff on the ground. Sparks flew up from the impact. By his magic, Nicholas and Sarah materialized before the council, apart from each other on either end of the long table.

Again King Stanislaus drew a circle in the air and stamped the end of his staff on the ground. This time, to the great surprise and pleasure of Nicholas, Father Bernard, Father Mark, and Father Bruno stood before the council. Excitement among the guests grew. They were rife with anticipation.

King Stanislaus stamped the end of his staff on the ground a third time. He peered into Nicholas's eyes. He gestured for Sarah to come forward from the far end of the table. They soon stood shoulder to shoulder.

"Please, face me."

Aligning in an arc before the throne of King Stanislaus, each bowed with respect.

"We, the Council of Elders and Kings of the Auroras, have brought you before us to recognize and honor your services in pursuit of peace in the Auroras," said King Stanislaus. He stood. His attendants lifted the edges of his robe, clearing the path of his steps.

"Nicholas and Sarah, I have heard that someday you would like to marry. Is this true?"

Without hesitation, Nicholas and Sarah answered simultaneously, "Yes, Your Highness." They smiled and looked at each other.

"If you are wed, will you continue to serve all who are in need?" Nicholas and Sarah without hesitation answered.

"Yes, Your Highness," Nicholas said, swallowing, his throat a bit dry.

"Oh yes, Your Highness," Sarah said, her voice quavering. Her face beaming, she blushed.

"This day," King Stanislaus said, "is that day." He laid his staff aside and lifted his scepter, pulling it from a sleeve at the arm of the throne. He touched his scepter to Sarah's shoulder. Instantly she was dressed in a sparkling gown spun of blue moonlight. The assembly politely applauded.

King Stanislaus touched his scepter to Nicholas's shoulder. Instantly he was dressed in a tailored red suit, trimmed with the cropped fur of the white and the red bear. Sarah gazed into his eyes longingly. His hands arched to hers as they stood side by side.

King Stanislaus lifted his eyes from the two and summoned his officials.

"Father Bernard," asked King Stanislaus, "will you perform the marriage ceremony, please?"

Father Bernard stepped beside King Stanislaus. Closing his arms together, he gestured to position Sarah and Nicholas before him.

Father Bernard peered into Sarah's face. "Sarah, may I please have the pendant that Nicholas gave you many months ago?"

Sarah handed the pendant to Father Bernard. He blessed it and handed it to King Stanislaus.

"Who speaks for this woman?" asked Father Bernard.

"I, Prince Wallace." He smiled, holding the hand of his wife, Princess Marinna. "I know Sarah Morning-Light to be a woman of excellent moral standing." Marinna nodded.

"Then let us begin," whispered Father Bernard. "Your Highness, Princess Sarah Morning-Light of Illuminae, do you willingly join your heart with that of Nicholas Claus, with the promise to lust for no other?"

Blushing, Sarah answered, "Yes, I do."

Father Bernard turned to Nicholas. "Nicholas Christopher Northland Claus, do you willingly join your heart with that of Sarah Morning-Light, with the promise to lust for no other?"

Standing erect, turning to face Sarah, Nicholas peered deeply into her eyes. "Yes ... I do." He loved her so much. He wanted to shout it loud enough for the whole world to hear.

Father Bernard turned to King Stanislaus. "Your Highness, it is time for the binding token. Do you wish to bind this couple?"

King Stanislaus exchanged places with Father Bernard.

"Child of Two Worlds, Nicholas Claus," said King Stanislaus, "and Sarah Morning-Light, you have proven yourselves uncommonly dedicated to the life force that is the strength of the Powers That Be. To honor this, you are to receive a unique and rare gift. We, the Council of Elders and Kings of the Auroras, grant both of you ..."—he looked to each of them—"immortality."

Nicholas and Sarah gazed into each other's eyes while tightly squeezing their interlocked fingers. Attempting to express their feelings, each was speechless.

Father Time stepped forward, raising his right hand above his head. "Crystal Chronaria, come to me."

As he commanded, so it appeared. He held the Crystal Chronaria over the pendant containing the Elixir Illuminae. Together, they caused the aurora borealis to appear in the elixir.

"Please, open your mouths," ordered Father Time. In each of their mouths, he placed two drops of the elixir.

The light of the aurora engulfed Nicholas and Sarah, and they rose into the air. The assembly hummed and hooted as they appeared to become transparent. Gently they fluttered to the ground, appearing different than before. They became mature, their abundant hair sparsely graced with a nearly undetectable smattering of gray.

"For the price of no less than five and no more than ten years of aging, you have received immortality and the additional wisdom of those paid years," said King Stanislaus. He placed the pendant around Sarah's neck.

"Nicholas and Sarah," said King Stanislaus, "from this day until the end of time, death will not touch either of you. You, Nicholas, will be known for all time as Santa Claus, guardian of those in need."

Seeing only each other, in their minds the audience vanished. Nose to nose they gazed into each other's eyes. He scanned her delicate face, the contour of her neck, and the bow of her blushing lips. In turn, she scanned the strong line of his jaw and the sincerity of his brow. They pulled closer to each other, her hands around his back, and his at the slope of her waist. Their lips drawn together, they kissed. Nicholas thought she tasted of candy apple and cinnamon.

A roar of applause went up, quickly reaching a crescendo.

King Stanislaus raised his hand to elicit silence.

King Stanislaus continued, "Use the love you have with Sarah to keep the Linkage alive in the hearts of all children of the world. Go. Let your adventures begin."

END

www.ingramcontent.com/pod-product-compliance
Lightning Source LLC
LaVergne TN
LVHW091700070526
838199LV00050B/2220